THE MARK OF FALLEN FLAME

A Weapon of Fire and Ash Novel

By Brittany Matsen

The Mark of the Fallen Flame
A Weapon of Fire and Ash Novel
© Copyright 2019 Brittany Matsen.
Published by IngramSpark

Cover by Dean Packwood

ISBN: 978-0-473-47145-3

For Noah

"Where a faint light shines alone,
Dwells a Demon I have known.
Most of you had better say
"The Dark House," and go your way.
Do not wonder if I stay.

For I know the Demon's eyes
And their lure that never dies.
Banish all your fond alarms,
For I know his foiling charms..."

-Edwin Arlington Robinson

TABLE OF CONTENTS

LAURA

Laura's heart pounded as she stared down at the illuminated screen of her phone, reading the message for the third time. **Stay inside, I've got my contact clearing the area. I'll let you know when it's safe. -S**

She had seen three similar messages just this month. When activity picked up like it had, it usually meant it was time to move on to a new location. Her shoulders slumped at the thought. She had begun to enjoy living in Seattle. So had Emma, it seemed.

Emma. Her seventeen-year-old daughter. The reason she refused to conform to the same way of life her family had. Emma always made a reasonable effort to go wherever Laura took them, pasting on a smile as she packed up her things, again and again, rarely asking questions. Laura only offered small lies to cover for the times they stole away in the dead of night, sneaking away like thieves. Bad boyfriend, a family member of a patient she couldn't save that was stalking her, and the list went on.

Though she didn't buy Emma's silent acceptance, she appreciated her daughter's ability to do what was necessary to survive. She would be eighteen in a month and would have to face the prospect of another change.

When Emma had asked to go out with a friend, Laura had only agreed when she knew it was safe. They were never truly safe, but Emma's existence would always be endangered. Now she would have to once again cancel Emma's plans. It made her ache to imagine her daughter's crestfallen face. She might get angry, and Laura didn't blame her.

She was angry too.

Angry that her parents had forced them to live like this. Angry at herself for letting her guard down for a moment at the flash of a smile that cut through her inhibitions better than any blade. The eyes of glittering emeralds that mocked her mistake. For letting him near her. Before the striking green had faded away, marking the cruel man for what he truly was. A monster.

Laura didn't share the details with Emma—of how she had been tricked into the arms of a man whose ethereal beauty was a mask for the horror that lay beneath. Her own thoughts didn't often delve into that bottomless well of misery. Like many mothers, Laura knew she wouldn't undo that horrible night for anything. It gave her the beauty that slept soundly in the room upstairs. And she had never met anyone more selfless and pure. Emma's heart was void of the darkness that was her father.

Laura rose, stretching her stiff muscles. There was nothing she could do until she got the all-clear, so she climbed the stairs to the upper level and cast a glance at the closed door that was Emma's with a sad smile.

In her own room, the apprehension that rose inside her every night surfaced. She eyed the bed with a deep, steadying breath. Though she did everything she could to keep her nightmares away, they plagued her, trapped her, forcing her memories into vivid light.

She pulled open the side table drawer, spotting the last vile of shimmering purple liquid that rolled to the front. Her hand shook as she pulled it out, making a mental note to get more first thing in the morning.

Her fingers pulled the cork stopper free before Laura threw her head back, draining the contents. She savored the comfort of its earthy taste. As her head laid back on the pillow, the lingering scent of cloves from the empty space beside her made her sigh.

The simple herbal calming solution worked instantly,

unwinding the tension in her body, allowing her lids to grow heavy.

Sleep wrapped its inky fingers around her and pulled her into her own personal hell.

Images surfaced, the memory from so many years ago as clear as the day it had happened.

Her mother's muffled sobs echoed from the back of the small cottage, the meager furnishings tattered and worn. The wooden chair Papa had broken was Mama's favorite, and it sat in a shattered heap. A splintered leg was clutched in his beefy hand at his side as his dark wild eyes locked on the shaking form pressed in the corner of the room.

Frozen, the small girl choked back a whimper. He stepped forward, a grin splitting his thick, ugly face.

"Why do you hide in the corner, daughter?" he taunted.

Her mother howled, most likely too injured to get to her. To put herself in the path of the drunken man who punished them for anything and everything. His gambling debts, his inability to hold a steady job, one of his many mistresses fleeing his abuse. The girl wished he would just go away, leave them to starve and freeze in the harsh winter. But always her mother begged him to stay. Laura didn't know why she wanted him to stay.

Her father stopped in front of her, the alcohol thick on his breath as he leaned down. "Come, give your father a hug." His voice was not warm. If anything, the biting wind that howled through the rafters grew colder at the sound.

When the small girl didn't move, his smile faded. He lashed out faster than she had time to prepare for, the jagged wooden post connecting solidly with her skull, knocking her back against the wall. Her teeth knocked together, and stars exploded in her vision.

She did cry then. He would coax her cries from her eventually, so she gave in, hoping this beating would be shorter.

Whatever had set him in a particularly nasty mood, was not eased by her screams as he brought his weapon down on her again and again. She cowered on the floor, shielding herself with her arms, trying to ignore the pain that made her breaths come quicker.

From above, she heard his menacing growl, "Just like your mother."

But besides their strawberry waves, they looked nothing alike. Above them all, there was one fundamental difference between the girl and her mother. She swore to herself she would never be seduced by a monster.

Laura gasped awake, her heart thundering in her ears. It was still dark outside, but she had no intention of falling back asleep.

She ripped off the duvet, feeling her clammy skin sting from the cool air. As her panting breaths returned to normal, she headed for the bathroom. She would wash away the ache of memory as she did every morning.

Steam curled above the shower as Laura stepped into its delicious heat. The water pounded against her sweat-slicked skin, but still, the phantom aches remained, inflicted by a man she had not seen in over eighteen years. Her father.

She rubbed the spot on her scalp that gave another throb with a wince. When the hot water was no longer a welcome sensation on her overly sensitive skin, she turned it off and stepped out, grabbing her towel.

When she was back in her room, she noticed the flashing light on her phone, indicating a new text message. A surge of eagerness bubbled up that she quickly shoved back down. Her eyes scanned the words that read: **My informant has the area secured. Come 'round at 5 for tea? I'm sure you're in need of more lilaseed.** Cautious relief filled her. She wouldn't have to keep Emma from having a much-needed night out with her friend.

Laura quickly replied with: **love to** before placing the phone back on the side table. A rare smile split her face as she dressed, and if not for Emma asleep on the other side of the landing, Laura might have skipped down the stairs.

Both girls were particularly chipper as they went about their day. A weight was lifted from Laura's shoulders. Before Emma was meant to leave, dressed in a black sheath skirt and a faded band t-shirt tucked into the top of the skirt, accentuating her slender waist, Laura felt an entirely new sensation of unease slip into her gut. The monsters she diligently shielded Emma from, were not the only threats. Emma was growing into a stunningly beautiful woman, tempting to the best and worst of mankind.

But before she could demand Emma go upstairs and change, her phone rang. Dread spread through her gut. Was there more danger? Had Seattle been compromised again? But when she picked it up and looked at the screen, her hammering heart slowed. It was the hospital.

"This is Laura," she answered.

"We need you," Alexander said. A capable surgeon—if he needed her help, it was serious.

"I'm on my way," Laura said, then hung up, rushing for the door. She turned with her hand on the doorknob. To Emma, she said, "You look beautiful." Emma smiled brightly. Laura scowled. "Now go change into something less revealing. Try a snowsuit." She heard her daughter chuckle as the door closed behind her.

At the hospital, she worked for long hours on a life-saving surgery that was thankfully successful, but when she, at last, slumped into the plush chair in her office, she noticed the light blinking on her phone.

With a heavy swallow, she checked the screen. Her breath left her in a ragged gasp, the words: **Activity everywhere, get home now** leaving her shaking. She rose from her chair, her fingers trembling violently as she searched for Emma's number. *Stay calm, she's probably at the concert, surrounded by hundreds of people.*

Her office door burst open, Derek, a surgery nurse looking wide-eyed.

"Your daughter is in the Emergency room with her friend."

EMMA

Two hours earlier

The final breath of summer's muggy heat wrapped around Emma like a thick blanket as she and Adrianna stepped out of the boisterous restaurant, chatting loudly. The scent of fresh rainfall cleared her head like nothing else could, and she found herself inhaling it deeply, a smile curving her lips.

The cars that drove by splashed water up onto the curb, their headlights reflected off the road.

"I can't help it," Adrianna said matter-of-factly, "drummers are my weakness."

Emma laughed. "Aaron plays the guitar, that's close. Besides, he's a good-looking guy, not to mention extremely smart. He couldn't keep his eyes off you at band practice."

"Yes, but he's a ginger."

"Ouch." Emma mock-winced. "My mother has red hair, you know."

Adrianna's snort was nearly drowned out by the clacking of her heels on the wet pavement. "She has strawberry-blond hair. That doesn't count," she countered.

"I think you're just scared to go outside your comfort zone. Give Aaron a chance. He might rock your world." Emma winked. Both girls burst into laughter.

As they rounded the corner, their laughter faded. The air became like ice, sending a shiver down Emma's spine. Clutching her arms around herself, she shared a look with Adrianna that said, *Why didn't either of us bring jackets?*

A whimper that stretched into a whine brought them to an abrupt halt.

"Did you hear that?" Emma asked.

Adrianna's thick brows creased. The whimper came again, followed by the unmistakable howl of an animal.

They approached a darkened alleyway on their right from where the sound seemed to emanate. The hairs on the back of Emma's neck stood on end, her skin clammy.

Emma started forward, but before she entered the side street, a slender hand gripped her arm, whipping her around.

"You can't go down there!" Adrianna hissed.

"There's an injured animal down there, A." Emma turned her head and squinted, trying to catch a glimpse of the creature. As if in answer, a light from above a shop door flickered on for a moment, illuminating a dumpster and a dark form on the ground beside it.

"And what are you going to do about it if there is?" Adrianna asked, panic growing in her voice. "Just call your mom and have her come take a look."

Emma shook her head. "She's in surgery until at least eleven tonight."

"Well, we can call a veterinary clinic on our way to the concert," Adrianna suggested, gripping Emma's arm with both hands as if anchoring her to the pavement. Adrianna was only about an inch taller than Emma, but unlike Emma, Adrianna's mother hadn't insisted she take self-defense classes on a regular basis. Emma glanced down at her friend's tightening grasp.

"Come on, Em, please," Adrianna whispered. "You know I don't like alleys. Or the dark. Combine the two, and you're just asking for a panic attack!"

Emma stared into Adrianna's dark, frightened eyes. With

a small, reassuring smile, Emma eased the fingers off her arm one-by-one.

"You stay right here; I'll just be a minute." Emma pulled out her phone and turned on the flashlight feature. The animal let out a low, pained moan, making Emma's chest ache. She stepped forward softly, crouching so as not to scare the creature. Each step pushed a dagger of ice further between her lungs, the weight heavy in her chest, making it hard to breathe, but she didn't stop.

The light from her phone showed the black, long-haired dog, lying on its side. Its breath came in quick, raspy pants. The fur on its heaving chest was matted with blood, which pooled beneath the creature. Emma didn't have to scan the dog long to find the injury; a large hole, about the size of her fist. Her stomach turned. *What on earth did this?*

"What is it?" Adrianna whispered loudly.

"A dog," Emma choked out. The sight of the blood didn't bother her. Her mother was a cardiothoracic surgeon, so Emma had seen gruesome photos from textbooks lying around when she was younger, but the sight of the injured animal shook her to her core. Her eyes filled with tears as she met the creature's wide-eyed gaze. The animal was going to die, and it knew it. Emma lowered herself even further, a hand outstretched as she crept closer.

"It's okay, fella," Emma said gently. The dog stared at her apprehensively as she made her way to its head.

Adrianna's heels clapped loudly, the sound echoing off the brick walls as she shuffled into the alley. The dog's eyes snapped to the approaching stranger, and it gave a low, half-hearted growl.

"Quiet!" Emma hissed, trying to make herself heard over her friend's thunderous footfalls. Adrianna paused, then continued with exaggerated slowness.

Emma stroked the wiry, unkempt fur of the dog's head.

"We won't hurt you," she murmured. It relaxed into her touch, an animal starved for affection. The aching in her heart grew at the resignation in the creature's face.

Adrianna hovered above them, arms crossed over her ample chest, her dark skin barely visible in the dim alley. "How did this happen? There aren't any bloody tracks," she said, looking around.

Emma looked around too, shining the light from her phone. There was a second large dumpster in the dead-end alley and some trash that had either been carried away by the wind or left by those too lazy to deposit it in the very obvious receptacles.

"I don't know."

The dog shifted, knocking her phone from her hand. It clattered to the ground, the light offering just enough illumination to see around them. Emma ignored the phone and used both hands to steady the creature, coaxing it to lie still, her voice gentle as she soothed it. Its breathing grew more ragged. It was almost over. Her hand trembled as she stroked its face, tears burning her eyes

"There's nothing I can do." A tear slid down her cheek, its warmth leeching into her skin.

"So much for seeing my favorite band play," Adrianna muttered. Emma shot her a glare, her mouth opening to reply when a chorus of hisses sounded from behind them. They whirled around.

The beast beneath her gave a final, rough exhalation before going still. A small sob escaped her as she looked back down at the dog's lifeless form. *What wretched timing.*

Emma rose to her feet. Neither girl was intimidating, each just a few inches over five-foot, but they were both fairly fit. Adrianna had a curvier shape, but she was all lean muscle from playing sports. Emma had a slimmer build but was just as strong.

"If you're the ones who did this to this poor, defenseless animal, you'd better run because this chick is a black belt in like... everything!" Adrianna shouted shakily.

Emma made a small noise in the back of her throat, her eyes wide as she glanced at her friend. In truth, she wasn't a black belt in anything, but Adrianna's scare tactic made sense. More hisses cut through the biting air, sounding suspiciously like laughter.

Three figures materialized from the shadows between the two dumpsters. Glowing yellow eyes locked onto them. The creatures hunched forward on two sets of bony, jutting limbs, like spiders. Their heads were elongated, with two bulges on the tops of their skulls, mouths split wide with eerie smiles.

Emma and Adrianna stood, frozen to the spot as the creatures walked toward them—*no, glided* toward them. They were too graceful, too fast. The girls took a step back in unison, and all three creatures hissed again.

"Run," Emma croaked.

They spun on their heels and ran. Adrianna was slower in her six-inch stilettos, and she slipped. Emma grabbed her hand and pulled her faster toward the mouth of the alley, thankful for her more practical footwear.

There was a crack like thunder then a wall shot out of the ground, raising up several stories high, blocking what little light they had. *What the—?*

Emma brought her arms up, shielding her face just before she hit the wall with an *oomph*. Adrianna screamed as she collided with it less than a second later. The rough, stone wall was as cold as the air outside, but it did little to soothe the sting in her forearms from the impact. Adrianna swore loudly. Their eyes were wide as they stared disbelievingly at each other. Emma's hands shook as she slapped her burning palms against the solid stone. It was real.

"What the hell?" Adrianna cried, scraping at the wall, unable to find purchase. They were blocked in.

Emma's throat was too thick with terror to respond. The creatures made high-pitched noises of glee behind them.

Slowly, Emma turned, pressing her back into the rough stone, hoping it would swallow her up. The three shadowy creatures with deadly, glowing eyes like wolves, scuttled gracefully closer. The darkness that clung to them dissipated, revealing tattered skin, and exposed bone and sinew.

Adrianna whimpered, then spun and began pounding her

fists against the wall, screaming for help, but Emma couldn't move. Her eyes were fixed on the three creatures. The light her phone emitted lit the one closest to it from the side. They were all at least seven feet tall with elongated heads with sharp chins, and two rounded bulges on the top of their skulls. But it wasn't that, or the way their dark skin hung off their bodies like tattered rags that made Emma gag. It was the smell of burnt, decaying flesh mixed with the sharp, metallic scent of blood. Beside her, Adrianna struggled to keep her dinner down.

"Sssso fun," the first voice said in a taunting, snake-like voice.

"Myyyy favorite part," the second chimed.

But the third, the one touched by the dim lighting, taller than the others, cocked its head to the side, its glowing eyes fixed on Emma. It stepped forward in one gigantic, smooth stride. Emma pressed herself harder into the wall, willing it to swallow them whole.

Adrianna sobbed, shifting the creature's gaze to her for a second, then as if dismissing her, looked back at Emma.

"Interesting," it rasped. This one's voice was different from the other two. It sounded more…human. A chill snaked down Emma's spine.

She thought of her mother and closed her eyes, waiting for death. She'd had to beg and plead with her mother to go out with her friend tonight.

Emma wondered how long it would take for her body to be found. People would undoubtedly notice a wall had enclosed the alley that held the back doors of several shops. But someone would have to break it down to find them. By the time she was discovered, her mother would have worked herself into a flurry of panic. Her mother's bright smile and shining eyes filled her mind. Tears slipped from under Emma's tightly shut eyelids.

The putrid smell was practically suffocating her now. A deep, throaty inhale made her eyes shoot open. A pair of large, sickly yellow eyes stared back at her.

"Very interesting," the creature repeated.

"P-please. Let us g-go," Adrianna begged through poorly-stifled sobs. Emma reached out and grabbed her hand, giving it a light squeeze. At least she would face her last moments with her friend. Neither would have to die alone. Emma tried to speak, but her mouth wouldn't open.

The three creatures gave another round of laughter.

"Ah," the middle one said after breathing deeply. "Tasssste that fear, brothersssss?"

"Enough of thisss, I'm ssstarving," the one furthest in the darkness hissed.

Emma saw the two creatures lunge for Adrianna. The one standing directly in front of her had her practically caged in against the wall, making it impossible to help her friend. Its mouth opened, stretching wide enough to fit an entire human head inside of it.

Emma's reaction was quick, her fist coming up in a right hook. It collided with the cold, papery flesh of its low-hanging jaw, snapping it shut. A jolt of something dark and powerful flooded her. Her blood burned like fire in her veins, and she cried out.

The creature's eyes widened in shock. *It felt it too.* The sensations of power and heat faded, but the creature remained stunned. A scream echoed deeper in the alley and Emma leaped around her attacker. One of the creatures had its long, spindly arms wrapped around Adrianna like an enormous insect grasping its prey. The other was trying to get its gaping mouth around her thrashing limbs.

Emma charged at the two creatures, but her movement startled her attacker from its stupor, and it grabbed for her with its hand-less stumps. It moved sluggishly, and she dodged its limbs, but not before its skin brushed against hers again. The creature screeched so fiercely that Emma spun back toward it. Another surge of what felt like pure adrenaline coursed through her.

More something inside her demanded. Her head spun as

she lunged for it, wrapping her arms and legs around its thin, spider-like arm. She ignored that smell that filled her nostrils and made her stomach roll. A rush of energy crashed into her, invading every cell with power. A laugh of pure ecstasy bubbled up out of her throat.

The creature's scream was more of a croak. It tried to shake Emma off, swatting at her with its other three uncoordinated arms. But everywhere its skin made contact with hers, the heady rush grew, and the creature stiffened. Emma watched with fascination and wicked delight that didn't feel like her own as the enormous figure began to wilt. Its dead eyes lost their glow and shrank back into its skull. After another moment, the energy stopped pumping into her, and a dry, brittle husk crackled into a fine powder in her arms.

Emma couldn't help but stare for another moment before her friend's agonizing screams made her whirl around. One of the creatures had gotten Adrianna's arm in its mouth and clamped down. It slurped noisily as blood dribbled from its mouth and onto the pavement. Emma sprinted toward it, her body light and fluid.

She moved so quickly that everything was a blur. She flung her body around the decaying flesh of the creature's leg. The creature shrieked and writhed, releasing Adrianna, who hit the ground with an audible snap and a strained sob. It stepped back with slow, jerky movements. Emma clung to it, needing to feel the incredible power that filled her. She could snap the entire thing in half with ease, but the thought of letting go for even a second made her cling tighter. She wanted it. No, she *needed* it. The remaining dregs of energy permeated her skin like a sweet, sticky sap. The second creature was a heap of dust before Emma got to her feet. It coated her clothing, her skin, and her hair. Head lowered, her eyes locked onto the remaining creature. *More.*

Emma stalked forward. She wanted to enjoy this next one. She wanted to drain it slowly. She wanted to watch the life leave its eyes. A grin split her face as she prowled forward.

I want you to look at what's left of your friends and know what's coming for you, Emma thought. It backed away, stumbling as if it heard her thoughts. The lanky stick-creature hit the side of the building and hissed threateningly.

"What are you?" it asked, each word a hiss. Its fear was like a drug that Emma craved, and her smile grew. All she cared about was getting close enough to touch it. Seeing it cornered like they had done to her, filled Emma with a glee that whispered: *death*. It was unlike anything she had ever felt before. She felt *alive*.

"Emma." The name made something inside her freeze. It sounded familiar. After a moment she realized it was hers. She turned slowly on the spot.

A girl cowered on the ground, bleeding from her arm. She gripped her ankle, staring at Emma. She blinked, as the heat inside her slowly dwindled. Details started to click back into place. Who she was, what she was doing here, and more importantly, that the injured girl was her best friend.

Emma took a step toward her and Adrianna made a sound akin to the pained whimper of the mutilated dog. Emma stopped dead as her heart lurched painfully. The remaining energy inside her left in a rush, and suddenly she was ice cold all the way to her bones. Her skin ached, her muscles strained and overworked. A bitter taste had filled her mouth, making her want to spit.

She whipped back around to drain the last creature, only to find that it was no longer there. She searched the alley, and her eyes landed on the open street, which was no longer blocked by a wall. That must have been what Adrianna was trying to tell her.

Emma spun back toward her friend and rushed forward, but the girl scooted away fearfully.

"A?" Emma said tentatively. "I'm not going to hurt you. I would never hurt you."

Adrianna's eyes were filled with uncertainty, her brows creased, but she let Emma close the distance between them without moving again, her eyes never leaving Emma's.

She bent down, observing Adrianna's bloodied arm first.

The teeth had only punctured around the elbow and could be explained away as cuts, but she didn't know how deep they were. She did a quick scan of the rest of Adrianna's body, her gaze landing on her ankle. It was at least twice its normal size, and she could make out a bone jutting to the side, stretching the skin. Definitely broken.

"Let's get you to a hospital," Emma said, offering her hands to help her up. Adrianna flinched, forcing Emma to meet her gaze. "What's your deal, A?" she demanded. Her chest swelled as emotion worked its way up her throat. She had just saved Adrianna's life, and now her friend was acting like she was a plague.

"Your eyes," Adrianna whispered. "They were glowing."

Emma shook her head. She had no idea what had just happened, but nothing made sense. She looked over her friend's shoulder to her phone, and her stomach dropped.

The dog that had died right before her eyes was no longer there. There was no blood on the pavement except for Adrianna's. No evidence of anything that had just happened. The dusty creature's remains were already being swept away by the brisk breeze. For a split second, she questioned her sanity.

"The dog isn't there anymore." Her voice was a whisper. She wasn't even sure if she was saying it to herself or her friend. Adrianna twisted slowly, wincing as she looked behind her. When she turned back to face Emma, her eyes were wide and filled with tears.

"What's going on?"

Emma shook her head again. "I don't know. We couldn't have *both* imagined the dog and the wall. We touched them. They were real. And I killed…" Her voice cracked. She had killed. They were horrible, inhuman *things*, but she had killed. Her head gave a mighty throb.

Tears spilled over Adrianna's cheeks. Her whole body shook, struggling to contain her wails. Their fear was bone-deep. But there was relief too. They were alive. Emma rubbed Adrianna's back until her tears slowed to a stop. Then her friend asked, "How *did* you kill those two things?"

"I don't know," Emma replied truthfully. "My touch sort of... dried them out from the inside?" Even as the words left Emma's mouth, she knew they sounded insane. *I drank their power*, she didn't say.

"This is too freaky." Adrianna tried to move to her feet but immediately collapsed again, unable to support her weight on her ankle.

"Let me help you," Emma offered. She placed her hands under Adrianna's arms and pulled her to her feet.

Adrianna leaned into Emma as they hobbled out of the darkness, stopping briefly so Emma could grab her cellphone, keeping the flashlight lit. Once they reached the light from the street lamps, they both let out a sigh of relief. Adrianna handed over her keys before Emma lowered her into a sitting position on the curb and told her to stay while she grabbed the car. She heard Adrianna give a small, humorless laugh before she sprinted to the next block where the car was parked.

Emma helped lift her friend into the passenger seat, her arms and legs quivering with the effort.

"The hospital is only a few miles away," Emma said as she fastened her seatbelt. Adrianna nodded stiffly, her eyes closed.

They drove in silence, Emma pushing the speed limit just enough to get them there faster, her mind still racing. She pulled up to the emergency entrance, then shifted to face Adrianna.

"You fell, cut up your arm and broke your ankle. Don't mention monsters or anything else, okay?" Emma said. Adrianna nodded. "You tripped and fell on the way back to the car. Glass cut up your arm." The words didn't seem terribly unbelievable given their footwear, but the lie seemed to glare back at her.

Adrianna unfastened her seat belt with a shaky breath before Emma went to grab a wheelchair from inside the sliding doors. Within a few moments, several staff members came out to help load her friend into the wheelchair while asking them both a slew of questions.

Emma paused outside the automatic sliding doors, as a tingling sensation crept up Emma's neck, sending goosebumps down her limbs. She turned, squinting out past the area lit by the parking lot lights, into the darkness beyond. A cold lump dropped into her chest as her heart picked up speed again. *You're safe*, she told herself. *No more monsters.* But she couldn't shake the sensation that somewhere within the shadows, she was being watched.

LEVAROTH

S creams rang out through the house, announcing that the prisoner was awake. A slow smile danced on Levaroth's lips before he pushed up from the musty, threadbare armchair. The floorboards creaked as he stalked from one end of the derelict house to the other, where a set of stairs led to the basement.

Ragged sobs grew louder with each step he descended. The smell of mildew, the prisoner's fear, and agony mixed in the air with his blood, making Levaroth's stomach clench hungrily. He drew in a deep, greedy breath through his nostrils.

His gaze drilled into the thin man dangling by his wrists in only his boxer shorts. Dried blood caked on almost every bit of exposed flesh. One leg was bent at an impossible angle, and the swelling in his chest indicated a broken rib, possibly a punctured lung. His eyes were blackened, and one was swollen completely shut. A purposeful move.

Levaroth enjoyed seeing their palpable fear, particularly in their eyes. Fear registered on the man's face as he began thrashing against his restraints. New screams reverberated around them and fresh blood trickled down his wrists from where the metal ripped the scabbing skin raw. Levaroth watched with rapt fascination as one bead wended its way through the maze of blond hairs on the outside of his forearm before disappearing around his thin bicep.

"Please, I told you everything I know," the man wheezed in broken English.

Levaroth smiled. "I know you did."

"So, you vill let me go?" he replied hopefully. Levaroth chuckled.

"Why would I do that? I still have use for you, Robert." The man started at the use of his name, and hope seeped from his pores. Killers rarely used names; they bred a humanization that left guilt in its wake—but Levaroth was incapable of such emotions. His lip drew up in disgust.

To clear away the annoyingly bitter taste that had left an unpleasant burn in the back of his throat, Levaroth stepped forward. He wrapped invisible tendrils of power around the man's neck. A grin spread on Levaroth's face as he squeezed. The man's eye bulged as he choked and sputtered. His mouth worked like a fish as he tried to take air into his lungs. Before any irreversible damage could be done, Levaroth released his hold. The atmosphere was thick with fear again, making his mouth water. His blood hummed with anticipation.

He crossed the room to the sleek, metal table where various tools and instruments were laid out. They all winked with the promise of death. His fingers hovered over a twisted tri-claw tool that looked more suited to gardening before selecting the gleaming scalping knife. His gaze inspected the rectangular blade for dullness. Then he turned on his heel to find the prisoner sagging in his manacles. The fool was unconscious again. Levaroth gave an exaggerated huff of irritation.

He smacked the man's bruised and bloodied face. Nothing. This time harder. Still nothing. The anger that always burned just beneath the surface began to boil under his skin. He turned his empty hand palm up. A single flame danced and twirled within it. With a small smirk, he pressed his hand to the man's chest.

Robert's eye-lid flew open, a blood-curdling scream forced from his scorched vocal cords. Between his ribs, the skin was blackened. Beneath the torched flesh, his heart thundered loudly

19

enough for Levaroth to hear.

"That's better. It's rude to pass out while I'm torturing you, Robert," Levaroth said.

"Please, just let me go. I have a sick mother and two sons who need me," the man begged, slipping into Russian, his voice hoarse.

"Not going to happen, Bob. Do people call you Bob?" The man was speaking again, but Levaroth continued chatting, more to himself than to the prisoner, "That's not a very Russian name."

The man's eyelids shuttered. He was slipping again. Rage erupted, and the blade in Levaroth's hand glowed red as it sliced into the man's chest. Once. Twice. Three times. The gleaming edge cut through bone and tissue like warm butter.

"Sssssir!"

Levaroth's triumphant roar silenced and he turned slowly. Warm, thick blood coated his face, filled his mouth and dripped onto his crisp, pressed suit. He wiped it from his eyes with his sleeve and then grimaced. He'd have to have his favorite suit cleaned yet again.

"What, Berak?" Levaroth snapped. The tall, thin creature looked past Levaroth to the suspended man who was now dead. A rumbling, animalistic growl sounded in the back of Levaroth's throat as his already thin patience threatened to snap.

"There was an incident in Seattle this evening—"

"Well I should hope so, that is your job." The dark, disfigured creature dipped its head in a show of mock respect, though its eyes were filled with loathing.

"Three of ussss wassss lookin' for a bite when we sssspied two wee hum'n girlssss—"

"Get to the point Berak," Levaroth sighed as he pulled bits of flesh and gore from his front.

The creature hissed angrily. "One of the girlssss turned Reck and Abad into dusssst."

Levaroth stilled. Slowly, his head lifted as he stared at his subordinate. "Into dust," he repeated. "How did you get away? The short version if you please; you take entirely too long to string a sentence together."

The creature let out another hiss at the insult, but it spoke before its leader could react, "The other girl dissssstracted her whilsssst I hid."

Levaroth gave the creature a skeptical look. The loss of Reck and Abad brought forth no emotion in Levaroth. Curiosity, yes, but remorse was as unreachable as the furthest star. "Did you see where she went after?" The thrill of another potential kill made his blood simmer with excitement.

"I followed her to a hosssspital," the creature hissed, seemingly proud of its forethought. As if recalling its experience with the girl, it shuddered, dropping its rotting, stinking flesh to the concrete floor with a splat.

"I see," Levaroth said eyeing the floor with disdain. "And using as few syllables as possible, how exactly did she turn them to dust?"

The creature pondered for a moment, opening its large mouth and then shutting it again. The corners of Levaroth's lips twitched as he suppressed a smirk. "I haven't got all night, Berak."

"Touched them," it replied at last, its words harsh and clipped to appease its master. Levaroth's eyes widened. *A human girl with supernatural powers? Things are getting more and more interesting,* he thought to himself.

He stalked across the room and carefully laid his sticky tool among the clean ones. "And did you get a name for this girl?"

The creature straightened up, pride lighting its eerie eyes.

"Emma Duvall."

EMMA

The bone in Adrianna's ankle was reset, and her arm, which hadn't needed stitches, was bandaged. After a few hours, she left with her mother, grumbling about crutches and her neon pink cast, shooting Emma a sympathetic look over her shoulder before the double doors slid shut.

Emma's mother drove her home in silence. She slouched down in her seat as if trying to become a part of it. Her mother shot occasional glances toward Emma, and she wondered if the truth was somehow visible on her body, even though she had scrubbed off what she could in the bathroom.

The night replaying itself in her mind. She could still smell the putrid stench of the creatures' skin lingered on her. Her skin crawled, and it was a constant battle to fight the urge to scratch it.

At last the car came to a stop and Emma risked a look next to her. Her mother's intense, expectant stare made her stomach clench. Had she been speaking?

"Sorry, did you say something?" Emma rasped. Her throat was dry and scratchy. She tried to swallow, but her tongue was pasted to the roof of her mouth.

Her mother's expression softened. "I asked what you had left to get tomorrow, for Monday."

Oh, right. School. Emma loved school; she was the type that got giddier during back-to-school shopping than when stores went into Christmas mode. School seemed like such a mundane thing after what had happened earlier that evening. To even think about carrying on with life as if everything were normal—as if she were normal—seemed wrong. Impossible.

"Just some binders and small stuff," Emma replied wearily.

"Okay, well, I'll go with you. We can make a day of it… Get lunch."

Emma attempted a smile, but her lips wouldn't cooperate. "Sounds like fun."

Her mother reached out and tucked a stray curl behind Emma's ear. "Get some sleep," she said. Emma nodded and pushed the door open. Her limbs were heavier than they had been an hour ago. She turned to look back at her mother, wanting to beg her to come in but she didn't want to worry her.

Her mother opened her mouth to say something, then closed it. Then opened it again. "Lock all the doors and windows," she said with a strange strain in her voice. Emma gave a stiff nod, finding it hard to draw a breath. *She knows*. Emma closed the door and practically sprinted up the paved walkway, which was visible in the glow of the street lamps and the solar-lights that lined the path.

The car idled in the street while Emma grabbed the hide-a-key from under a large stone by the weed-filled flower bed near the front porch and opened the door. She cast a final look toward her mother as the car began to pull away.

Once inside, she bolted the door and checked every window to be sure they were latched. She flicked on every light in the house as she went, ending with her bedroom upstairs. She still felt spooked and couldn't shake the heavy feeling of eyes watching her. The clock on her side table said it was just after one in the morning. Both mentally and physically exhausted, she dropped like a stone into the chair at her desk and opened her laptop. Sleep would have to wait. She needed answers.

Her fingers hovered over the keys as she stared at the empty search bar. What was she even looking for? She typed: *life-suction powers*. She gave a dry laugh at the results. Superheroes, fanfiction, comics. There was nothing about real life. Not even from the wacky conspiracy theory nut-jobs. In her frustration, she typed: *four-armed death stick creatures.* Her head dropped into her hands as she gave a long sigh. The images didn't even come close to matching what she had seen.

Defeat, and a growing inability to hold her eyes open any longer won out. She shut her laptop and changed for bed. She wanted to wash her face and take a shower, but she couldn't bring herself to leave her room again. Her throat was raw, her eyes prickling with tears as she struggled to come to terms with tonight's events. It could have been worse. They could have died. Adrianna was injured and would need crutches for several weeks. She shoved away the pang of guilt and shame that rose up like a cobra ready to strike. They were alive. That was all that mattered.

She plugged in her phone, which had died at some point while at the hospital. She picked up the book she had been reading, planning to stay awake until her mother got home. But her eyelids were too heavy, and by the second sentence, sleep had pulled her under.

At some point during the night, she became vaguely aware of a comforting and gentle presence moving something from her lap and draping a blanket over her; a few whispered words and a soft kiss on her head.

The dull roar of a lawnmower made Emma jerk awake. Bright morning sun poured into her room from around the edges of her thin curtains. Her neck was stiff and sore from resting against her shoulder all night. She rubbed it gingerly as she scooted to the side of her bed and tried to stretch. A hot shower was definitely in order.

Her door cracked open as she rose to her feet, her mother's face peering in. Dark circles lined her bloodshot eyes.

"How are you feeling?" she asked with a tired smile.

"Great," Emma replied with forced enthusiasm.

Her mother opened the door further and leaned in the doorway wearing dark denim jeans and a navy-blue cardigan that hugged her tall, trim frame. As a medical professional, she rarely had time to don regular clothing. When she did, Emma always thought she looked like an entirely different person. One she could laugh with, and see the creases that lined her face from concentration and a stressful job, soften.

"You look tired," Emma said.

"Long night," she sighed. "I made breakfast."

The faint scent of buttery biscuits and sausage gravy wafted into her bedroom, making Emma's mouth water.

Grinning she said, "Be right there." Her mother gave a smile and turned to go back downstairs. The shower could wait until after breakfast, she decided.

Emma sent a text to Adrianna asking how she was feeling. In less than a minute, she got a response that made her lift a brow in question. **1m soar theez drgs r Uhm@zng**

After studying it for several moments, Emma managed to glean that she was sore, but the pain meds she had were amazing. Emma laughed, shooting back a quick reply: **Get some rest. I'll see you tomorrow.**

She padded into the bathroom to splash water on her face. As her head lifted and her vibrant emerald-colored eyes met those of her reflection, she paused. Her eyes shone brighter. *Your eyes, they were glowing.* Emma's breath caught in her throat.

She felt like a walking hazard to everyone around her. Ripping her gaze away, she dried her face, then tossed the cloth back onto the edge of the sink. With a deep, cleansing breath, Emma schooled her features as she exited the bathroom and descended the stairs.

The aroma in the kitchen was heavenly. Classical music played softly in the living room as Emma, and her mother piled their plates with freshly cut fruit and warm, flaky biscuits that they drenched in sausage gravy.

They ate in satisfied silence for several minutes before her mother spoke, "Well, you can take a shower," her eyes flicked to Emma's hair, and Emma had to force herself not to recoil, "while I do some cleaning up around the house, and then we'll go shopping. Sound good?"

Emma nodded. Her appetite had vanished. She pushed herself up from the table and cleared her plate. Without a backward glance, she trudged up the stairs, eager to shower.

She hadn't realized how dirty she had been. The water running off her, swirling at her feet was a murky gray. She scrubbed her body more forcefully than was necessary, her nails scraping her skin. The steaming water pelted against her back long after the water went clear. When she stepped out, her skin was an angry red.

She made quick work of drying and straightening her wild, auburn waves, then brushed some mascara over her long lashes. After assessing her reflection for a moment, she stalked out of the bathroom.

A faint garbled sound drifted up to Emma as she reached the top of the stairs, and it took her a moment to realize it was the TV. Emma frowned. Her mother rarely watched television. As she neared the bottom, she began to make out snippets:

"—global bombings—"

"—thousands dead—"

"—no known person or group—"

Emma hurried into the living room to find her mother leaning against the armrest of the cream-colored loveseat, her shoulders hunched, a shaking hand covering her mouth.

"Mom?" Her mother's head swiveled in Emma's direction, her eyes wide and cheeks wet with tears. "What happened?" she asked.

Her mother's hand slowly fell to her side, brows drawn. "All over the world, bombs have been going off," her mother replied in a crackly voice. "So many people…dead."

Emma's gaze flicked to the TV screen as she came to stand beside her mother. Bile rose up in her throat, her eyes stinging. It seemed like only a handful of countries were left untouched. Los Angeles, London, Paris, Moscow, New York, Tokyo, Hong Kong,

Beijing, and many others all targeted. Major landmarks and buildings with a significant number of people inside were blown up. Footage of injured people being loaded into ambulances, tearful children wrapped in their family's arms as they wept, played over and over. Devastation everywhere.

Emma let out a choked sob. Her mother wrapped an arm around her and squeezed. "Who would do something like this?" Emma asked when her mother switched the TV off.

Her mother gave a shaky breath then shook her head. "I think we should stay home. It's not safe out there."

"It's not safe here either," Emma challenged, "Washington hasn't been hit yet. It doesn't really matter where we are if we're targeted. I doubt they are going to cancel school tomorrow, and they sure as heck won't cancel work for you."

Her mother looked as though she wanted to argue but seemed to ponder her words.

"Perhaps you're right," she replied at last. "It'll be a good distraction, so we aren't sitting around here feeling twitchy."

Emma nodded, wiping the streaks of wetness away.

The sun hid behind dark, ominous clouds and by the time they parked, a torrential downpour had begun. Steeling themselves, they ran through the icy rain. Once inside the dry safety of the building, they grabbed two hot lattes to warm themselves back up.

It was quiet, somber, as Emma and her mother grabbed far more than just school supplies. In the clothing section, her mother pointed out the necessity for a new outfit.

Her mother had frequently voiced her opinion about Emma's wardrobe choices and stressed the importance of dressing up. Emma preferred the comfort of jeans and a t-shirt to skirts and dresses, though she agreed to wear something new on her first day of senior year.

Her mother held up a pin-striped pencil skirt and a lacey,

black, short-sleeve shirt that Emma turned her nose up at. They bickered loudly outside the dressing rooms until Emma agreed on the top but convinced her mother to compromise with a pair of black skinny jeans with no holes. The finished look was very chic. Emma couldn't suppress her smile when she saw her reflection, but it vanished when a sudden chill snaked up her spine, and a punch of cold hit her chest.

She mentally shook herself, reasoning that it was just a lingering effect from her terrifying ordeal in the alley, coupled with her damp hair brushing against the back of her neck.

As she placed the items into the overflowing cart, her gaze pulled away, toward movement behind a clothing rack. It was a man with eyes of swirling molten gold—beautiful and unnerving. She glanced at her mother to see if she had noticed the onlooker, but she was busy contemplating aloud if they *really* needed four types of peanut butter. Emma spun back to where the man had been, but he was gone. Emma dashed to the center aisle, claiming to need the restroom as her mother called after her. She scanned the aisle, but other than a slender, black-haired woman who was chasing after her babbling toddler, it was empty.

Emma walked to the front of the store where the restrooms were, scanning for the unnatural golden eyes. Her brow furrowed as she looked around. Several of the workers had begun to look at her suspiciously. She gave one a tight smile, before heading for the restroom, hoping she could simply look lost.

Her eyes caught on her reflection and she let out a gasp. Her irises were like vibrant, glowing emeralds. The light emanating from them didn't seem real—as if they were somehow lit from within. She shook her head. *It's just the lighting.*

Stumbling out of the bathroom, her heart hammered. She gulped in a steadying breath, spying her mother at a checkout, loading up the belt. A bored-looking female cashier listened as her mother made excuses for the four different flavors of peanut butter.

"Are you hungry?" her mother asked while Emma composed

herself and began loading full bags back into the shopping cart. Her stomach churned, but Emma nodded anyway. Tacos were the Saturday tradition. Despite Emma's mother being a cardiac surgeon, they ate out at least once a week, mostly due to their busy schedules.

The restaurant was unusually empty. Emma exchanged a look of understanding with her mother. People were shaken up by the recent events. Suddenly their boldness to venture out and enjoy themselves felt disrespectful. They sat at their usual table in silence, waiting for the waiter to take their order. Ice shot through her abdomen, wrapping cold fingers around her lungs and squeezing, halting her breath.

A man in a black suit entered the restaurant, his golden eyes drawing Emma's stare away from her menu. His face was seductively handsome for what looked like a man in his mid-to-late thirties. Dark stubble decorated his chin, but his eyes—living, swirling molten gold—were the same ones she had seen in the store. He was too masculine, too otherworldly. A powerful air radiated from him. He stared at her a moment, his expression one of curiosity, punctuated by the way he cocked his head to the side, as if trying to figure her out. Then he turned and exited again as if deciding he had gotten what he came for. The menu fell from Emma's shaking hands and clattered noisily to the tabletop.

It's not the same guy, Emma told herself. He was probably just some businessman who had come to the wrong restaurant... with the same eyes as the ones she had seen hiding among the clothing racks. Besides, why would he have followed them there?

Her mother raised a brow at her when a muffled vibration sounded against the leather booth. Emma instinctively reached into her pocket for her phone at the same time her mother went for hers. No new notifications. Emma looked up at her mother's face just in time to see the color drain from it. She hastily shoved it back inside her purse.

"Come on, we'll get our food to go," she ordered, sliding from the booth.

"Why?" Emma's heart began to race.

"It's nothing to worry you with, but we need to go right now." Her tone brooked no room for argument.

Emma slid out from behind her side of the booth while her mother tried to wave over the waiter who appeared to be deep in conversation with a tall, beautiful, olive-skinned waitress.

"It's okay if you just want to go, I'm not that hungry." Emma looked over her shoulder at the door, half expecting the man to walk back through it.

"Don't be silly, we still have to eat. It's just best if we head straight home." Her mother attempted a reassuring smile that was more of a grimace.

They had their meals boxed up and were back in the car racing home within fifteen minutes. The worry in her mother's eyes and the way they kept flicking left to right as if trying to spot some potential threat kept Emma on edge.

"What's going on?" Emma tried again after her mother practically ran a red light.

"Nothing is going on, Emma; you saw that restaurant. Everyone but us had the sense to stay home in case Seattle was targeted," her mother said defensively, shifting in her seat—a dead giveaway to the lie.

"If Seattle were to be bombed, we'd likely be dead no matter where we were. What's really going on mom?"

"Nothing, Emma. Drop it!" Her voice carried a fearful edge that made Emma's breath hitch in her throat.

She looked out the window again as they pulled onto their street. Everything seemed quiet. Too quiet. Like everyone was afraid to go outside for fear of being blown to pieces.

They carried in every single shopping bag, along with the warm tacos, in one trip but the thick tension in the air kept Emma from cracking a joke about it. After they got everything put away and sat down to eat their moderately squished lunch, they both visibly relaxed.

As the evening went on, her mother smiled at a sarcastic remark Emma made, and they were both almost able to forget about the weird events of the day. They ate junk food for dinner while watching *The Phantom of the Opera*. They argued about whether Christine should have chosen the Phantom like they always did, which usually resulted in her mother tossing popcorn at her and telling her she was naive.

Exhaustion made Emma's eyelids heavy during the final scene, but she was determined to stay awake. Her mother glanced down at her phone as the end credits appeared, accompanied by the melancholy tune that Emma hated. Peering over at the screen that read eight minutes after nine, Emma readied herself for her mother's speech about getting plenty of sleep for the first day of school.

Instead, her mother stood, offering her hand to pull Emma to her feet, then wrapped her in an uncharacteristically long hug. The tension of the past two days melted in her embrace. Tears pricked behind Emma's eyelids. A hug from her mother was exactly what she needed. She wanted to confess what had really happened to Adrianna. To both of them. But sense held her back. Whether it was because she didn't want to sound crazy or because even she didn't fully understand what had happened, she didn't know. And Emma didn't allow herself to explore her reasons.

When they broke apart, Emma turned the TV off and her mother started up the stairs, Emma following closely behind. They parted on the landing to go to their rooms. Her mother shouted a promise over her shoulder to get Emma a coffee in the morning before taking her to school. Emma smiled despite the anxiety that rose unbidden through her.

Inside her room, she set herself to rechecking that her bookbag was ready for tomorrow. She double-checked her books, notebooks, binders, folders, and writing utensils, and had everything in order. Almost everything. Her class schedule was nowhere to be found. She rifled through all her supplies and checked by her bed, but she couldn't find it anywhere. Not that she needed it. She'd had her schedule memorized two hours after she had received it in the mail.

A yawn escaped her, drawing her attention back to her nightstand. Ten o'clock. She unlocked her door, rushing to brush her teeth. Paranoia caused her to practically sprint through the dark hall back into her room. She locked her door then sent a text message to Adrianna telling her where to meet her in the morning. Then she climbed into bed, scooting herself under the thick duvet.

She drifted off to sleep, pushing all thoughts of golden-eyed men far from her mind.

EMMA

E mma was up before her alarm, showered and dressed in the outfit she had picked out the day before. Her hair was kept in its natural wavy state, tamed with the help of anti-frizzing oil. She went the extra mile with her makeup, applying liquid liner and light shimmering eyeshadow.

She stared at her reflection for several minutes, tilting her head at different angles. Her eyes were bright with excitement, but they didn't glow. The sliver of normalcy helped to unknot the twisted mess inside her stomach.

A knock startled her from her jumbled thoughts. Her spine straightened as she smoothed her hands over her shirt. Opening the door, she stalked out of the bathroom, avoiding her mother's amused gaze.

"I'll be ready to leave in ten minutes," she heard her mother call before Emma closed her bedroom door. She decided to check for her class schedule again, rationalizing that in her nervousness she wanted to be sure she had every detail memorized. Not because she thought her missing class schedule was odd, she told herself.

She searched through everything, scouring her room in case it had fallen somewhere, but to no avail. Several minutes later, her mother called up to her from the main floor. With a frustrated huff, she slung her backpack strap over her shoulder and headed downstairs.

"Have you seen my class schedule?" Emma asked once they were in the car, shivering from the cold morning air that blasted through the vents.

"No, sorry, honey." She glanced sidelong at Emma. "You can get a new one printed at the main office if you're worried."

"Yeah." The pesky thing would probably turn up sometime next week once she was settled in all her classes.

"So, what's your first class?" her mother asked. Emma knew her mother's interest was partly meant to fuel her excitement. It worked.

"Organic Chemistry," she sighed as if those two words were a romantic date and not a high school class. Senior year meant she got first pick of classes and teachers. She had meticulously studied the options, weighing the value of each one based on what her college schedule was going to look like next year. She wasn't entirely set on a particular major yet, but she knew it was going to be science-oriented. She went back and forth between marine biology and hydrology despite her mother's more than suggestive hints that she would make an excellent surgeon.

Stuffy hospitals weren't Emma's idea of an exciting and fulfilling career. Whatever she chose, she wanted to be physically out in the field, touching and observing things for herself. She loved all living things, especially those that resided in the dark, watery depths.

Her fascination with the collectible children's books on creatures and plants of the deep kept her awake late at night when she was little. Beneath the covers, she read about every scaly and finned creature by flashlight. When she would gush random facts that she had learned the next morning, the expression her mother wore was conflicted. Once Emma got a bit older, she realized it was because her mother hadn't wanted to dampen her enthusiasm by putting an end to her late-night reading sessions.

"What's your next class?" her mother asked, the corners of her lips twitching.

"Calculus." Emma's voice went flat. She didn't hate math;

math was required in chemistry, but without the scientific application, the subject was as dry as a desert in her mind.

"You'll do wonderfully," her mother assured her as the car pulled into the coffee shack's drive-thru.

Emma didn't respond, her mind had already switched gears.

"Large, triple-shot, Irish cream latte," she said after a quick glance at the board.

Her mother snorted. "When you're old enough I'll get you a real Irish cream latte and see if you still like it."

Emma suppressed a smile. She didn't dare tell her mother she had already tried alcohol once in the sixth grade when a girl she had befriended had snuck a small bottle of liquor in her backpack. They both had taken one swig before spraying it into the bushes with revolted gags.

Her mother passed her the steaming hot cup. The heat thawed her fingers as she sipped with a contented sigh. Her mother followed suit. Emma smiled against the plastic lid. This was what happy memories were made of. It was a tradition for the two of them to get drive-thru coffees on the first day of school.

The remainder of the short drive to the high school was filled with more chatter about Emma's classes.

"So, I'll try to be here to pick you up at three, but I'll send a text if I can't get away," her mother said as Emma swung the door open and hopped down from the SUV.

She shouldered her backpack and nodded.

"I love you," her mother added softly, her eyes misty.

"I love you too, Mom."

With that, Emma shut the door and turned to face the familiar brick building with a deep breath in through her nose. She smiled as a surge of nervous excitement washed through her.

They had moved to Seattle at the end of the previous school year. Adrianna had spotted Emma sitting at a lunch table by herself, trying to hide from the stares that came with being "the new kid" by burying her nose in a book. She had dropped into the seat across from Emma, staring at the cover of the book she was reading until Emma's emerald green eyes peered over the top.

"I just didn't want you to have to eat alone," Adrianna had explained, but her tone held no remorse. Emma said nothing as she closed the book. They introduced themselves, Adrianna extending a rich, mocha-colored hand. Emma had laughed.

"Is that a Washington thing?"

"No, that's a my-dad-is-a-lawyer thing," she replied with a wink.

Emma laughed again.

"What were you reading?"

"It's a sci-fi romance," Emma said.

Adrianna wrinkled her dainty nose. "I don't do sci-fi."

Emma shrugged, still smiling. "It's not for everyone, but the spaceships are actually fashion runways." Adrianna's eyes lit up. "You're welcome to borrow it when I'm done."

It was the start of a wonderful friendship, but like all the friends she'd had in her life, she knew to not get too attached. Every so often, with little-to-no warning, her mother would announce they were moving. Even when they'd stayed in the same city for two whole years, they had switched houses three times. Like her mother, Emma had learned to live with half her belongings packed in cardboard boxes stashed in her closet, because they lived life with one foot out the door.

"Dang girl, you look smokin'!" The sound of Adrianna's voice snapped Emma out of her reverie. Adrianna propelled herself toward Emma on her crutches. Emma closed the distance, carefully wrapping her arms around her friend.

Emma lifted a single brow at Adrianna's outfit. Her daringly short black skirt was paired with a bright pink peplum top that matched her cast. Emma's eyes lingered on it then shifted to the bandage on her arm. Her chest tightened painfully before she forced a smile.

"That skirt is way too short for dress code," Emma said.

Adrianna waved a hand at the crutches. "I'm disabled. They can't send me home for wearing the only thing I could get over my cast."

Emma snorted. "And I'd have thought you would have ditched the crutches."

"No way! Maybe this way some hot guy will offer to carry my books." Adrianna's eyebrows waggled suggestively.

"How romantic," Emma replied. Her lips were pressed tightly together to keep from laughing, as Adrianna struggled to weave through the sea of teenagers who were utterly oblivious to them.

"C'mon people, move it, cripple coming through!" Adrianna bellowed. After a few more shouts and waving her crutches in people's faces, the masses parted, giving a clear path to the glass double doors. The hundred or so pairs of eyes that swept over them, some with irritation, others with amusement, had Emma's face hot with embarrassment by the time they got inside.

"Was that necessary?" Emma asked.

Adrianna shrugged. "Got them to move, didn't it?"

Emma didn't answer. She helped Adrianna open her locker, shoving the books for her later classes inside before they stopped at her own.

"So, I'll see you in third period?" Adrianna asked, eyeing a group of guys, laughing as they passed by. A basketball was being flung from person to person. One of the guys who noticed her blatant stare, gave her a wink before disappearing behind the corner.

"Looks like Sean might be willing to carry your books," Emma teased, nudging her gently. Adrianna gave a dreamy smile in return.

"Right, well I'll see you in history." Adrianna waved, setting off for the elevator. Emma trudged up the stairs, wishing she had her class schedule to confirm the room number. Her fingers twitched, and she wound the strap from her backpack around her fingers to steady them.

Organic chemistry was in the science wing at the far end of the school. The walking space had become limited now that all the students were bustling around to their first classes. Now that she was a senior, she had figured out how to avoid getting jostled by the guys who, it seemed, had shot up at least six inches over the summer break.

"Completely unfair," Emma grumbled under her breath, narrowly dodging a particularly heavy-set boy who was staring down at his phone.

Etched on the glass panel above the door at the end of the hall read 32B. A tang of sulfur lingered in the hallway but dissipated as soon as she stepped into the room. The classroom was smaller than most, and the long black table-tops were bare of the usual equipment. The front row was taken, much to Emma's disappointment. She found a seat in the second row, dropping her backpack onto the newly repainted surface. All of the previous years of students carving their names or their current crush's initials were still vaguely visible, as if the effort was half-hearted, given that the tables would be marked again by the end of the year.

She unzipped her bag and began pulling supplies out when a tingle danced from her fingertips, up her arms.

Her head whipped up just in time to lock onto a pair of stunning espresso-brown eyes. For a moment she forgot to breathe. Her blood pumped so loudly in her ears that she could hardly hear the gasps and whispers from everyone else in the room. The boy was gorgeous in a dangerous way.

He stared back at her as he sauntered in. His chestnut-colored hair styled in a fade, looked artfully windswept. His Metallica t-shirt clung to his toned frame, and peeking beneath his sleeve, snaking around a firm bicep, was a tattoo, though she couldn't make out what it was of.

His mesmerizing gaze remained entangled with hers as he passed her. The space between them was charged with electricity, and goosebumps broke out of her skin.

The girls in the front row all craned around to stare at him, and she felt the desire to do the same. He chose a seat in the back row, diagonal from her. In her peripheral vision, two golden brown eyes were fixed on her. Yet something deep within her chest could sense his attention without seeing it.

Her body was both hot and cold, invisible threads pushing and pulling at her. She wanted nothing more than to climb over the table that separated them, and equally to run out the door, down to the registrar's office and have her classes reassigned. Better still, to beg her mother to move anywhere else as long as it was far away.

She shook her head, trying to clear it as a few more students filed in and took their seats. A boy by the name of Jared settled into the seat next to her. She groaned internally.

His boyish, pimple-covered face turned to smile at her. He pushed his glasses further up the bridge of his skin-flecked nose, practically cramming the frame into his eye sockets. The indentations of the nose rests were proof that it was a nervous habit. The pungent scent of body odor turned her stomach.

"Looks like we're both taking Ms. Fararr's class again this year," Jared said breathlessly, leaning toward her.

"Sure does appear to be that way, Jared," Emma replied, trying to keep as much space between them as possible.

A low chuckle came from behind them. Heat bloomed in Emma's cheeks as she swiveled in her chair. Cruel amusement lit the boy's features.

"What?" Emma snapped.

He shrugged, his eyes boring into her. Her heart kicked up into a frenzy. She glared, hoping to make him uncomfortable, but his grin only grew. When at last she thought her face might burst into flames, she spun back around.

The bell sounded just as a tall, gray-streaked woman with bird-like features walked in. Her gaze was as sharp as a hawk's as she assessed those seated before her. Emma noticed, with no small amount of annoyance, that her eyes lingered on where the new guy sat in the back. The severe woman's back straightened as she set her briefcase down, flicked the latches open and began removing stacks of papers. The room was silent, awaiting instruction.

"This is Organic Chemistry. I am Ms. Farrars. If this is not where you are supposed to be, I suggest you leave." An awkward silence stretched on for what felt like ages. When no one moved, her eyes flicked up, looking past Emma and then back down as she closed her case and set it under her desk.

Emma glanced out of the corner of her eye to see the new guy's intense stare still trained on her. If he had noticed the teacher's attention, he didn't let on. The heat returned to her cheeks. She drew in a quiet breath and tried to focus on what the teacher was now writing on the chalkboard.

The words reached her ears, but she didn't hear a single one. Her heart pounded in her chest as she tried to keep up with the lecture. Why did he have to look at her as if assessing an opponent? What was it about him that seemed to pull at her, as if she were magnetized to him while simultaneously pushing away?

When the bell rang, she started. She hastily grabbed her materials, stuffing them into her bag before she headed for the door. Unable to resist, she risked a glance over her shoulder. The boy lounged in his seat. The girl who sat beside him chattered away, but he didn't seem to notice. His eyes swept up to meet Emma's as if sensing her gaze.

She pushed her way into the crowded corridor before he had risen from his seat. It looked almost as if he had wanted to give her a head start. Like he knew he made her uncomfortable and hoped to put her at ease.

It did just the opposite.

As Emma checked over her shoulder again for him, she collided with something—or rather, someone. They tumbled to the floor, books, and papers scattering around them.

"I'm so sorry," Emma gasped as she untangled herself from a pale, frightened-looking girl. Emma offered a hand to help the girl to her feet, which she accepted with pink-splotched cheeks.

"It's okay," the small girl replied. Her frizzy blond hair stood out of her ponytail in lumped tufts. They made quick grabs to pull their belongings away from the flow of traffic. Emma handed a paper she didn't recognize to the girl, who smiled her thanks.

"Do you need help?" Emma offered as the girl stared back down at a wrinkled page in her hands. Relief flooded her face.

"Yeah, I was looking for physical science?"

"Down the hall to the right." Emma pointed in the direction she had just come from.

"Thanks." The girl gave a grateful smile before shoving her things back into her tattered denim cross-body bag that was covered in pins. Emma's eyes caught on a silver one that looked like a pentagram.

"Sorry again for running you over," Emma said.

"No worries," she mumbled before giving another small smile and turned to head back into the mass of students. Being several inches shorter than Emma, she was lost to the sea of passing students within a second.

Emma walked the rest of the way to calculus, careful to not knock over any more unsuspecting freshman. Before she even stepped over the threshold, a punch of electricity jolted through her chest. Heat and ice mixed, numbing her hands and feet. Her tongue felt heavy and swollen.

The boy with amber eyes and mussed hair looked up to where she stood, frozen and transfixed. It wasn't the fact that he was in the classroom that made her stop. It was the fact that the only other seat available in the room was the spot next to him. He pulled out the chair for her with a tug of his lips.

"Take your seat please, Miss," an elderly, nasally voice said behind her. She jumped, recognizing Mr. Cummings as he strode past her. The numbness in her extremities was replaced with an uncomfortable pins-and-needles sensation that made her teeth grind together.

She followed him in as the tardy bell rang, forcing herself to walk to the open seat. One foot in front of the other. Her eyes roamed the room—anywhere but at her tablemate as she sank into the cold plastic chair. His gaze was hot on her skin, daring her to look at him.

Mr. Cummings was a squat, balding man with a thick, red, bristly mustache, that looked like it could be used to scrub pots and pans. His lips were barely visible beneath it, and he spoke with a gravelly monotone. Emma was too concerned with keeping her breathing even to register what he was saying. Currents of heat shot through her, while her skin prickled with cold. The desire to lean a few inches closer to the enigma beside her was almost unbearable.

Blood was rushing in her ears, blocking out voices and sounds. There were too many eyes on her. Why was everyone looking at her? The boy beside her jabbed her in the arm with his elbow.

The shock of their physical contact was stronger than any common static shock. It zapped Emma's blood, heating it. White flashed across her vision, and she thought she heard someone gasp. Was it her?

Strength.

Power as dark and as vast as the ocean.

Blood.

Death.

Color bled back into her surroundings. She shivered from a sudden wave of cold, fighting the urge to look beside her.

"What?" she choked out, registering that everyone in the room now stared at her.

"I'm taking attendance," Mr. Cummings snapped, irritated. "I take it you're here then, Miss Duvall, albeit not quite awake yet."

A few students snickered. Emma forced a nod. Beside her, the boy was deadly still. Not even his chest moved. The teacher called several other names, all of which were met with responses.

"Rowek Zennett." There was a pause.

"Here," the boy beside her replied at last. His voice was surprisingly deep, a rumbling sound that made something inside her stir. As if in...familiarity? As if she had heard it many times before but couldn't remember. Her attention shifted to his face, which was void of emotion.

Emma tried to take notes, doing her best to keep her eyes forward, but every so often, she glanced sidelong at the stranger. The boy called Rowek did not take notes. He didn't seem interested in hearing anything the teacher had to say. Emma couldn't help but frown at the oddity. Rowek reclined in his chair, his finger tracing the image on the closed textbook. It was another painfully slow class, but when the bell sounded Emma turned to fully face him.

"Two of the same classes," she said, trying to keep her voice from shaking. "What a coincidence."

He didn't answer or even look at her for several beats. She got to her feet as a burst of sudden anger flared inside her, shocking her.

Then he spoke. "Not in the slightest."

Her skin tingled at the way he said it. Like he knew a world full of secrets. Secrets that could be hers, if only she touched him again.

Wait, what? Had she just thought that?

There was an underlying hint of something else in his voice, though she couldn't place it. She stared at him for a moment.

"So, do you have American history next?" Part of her hoped he would say no, was begging the gods for him to say no. She had no idea how she would focus in any of the classes they shared as it was. But a small part of her, try as she might to dismiss it, wanted the opposite.

"I guess you'll find out in about five minutes."

He stood in one fluid, graceful movement, his textbook by his side, and sauntered out the door as if he had nowhere, in particular, he needed to be. Emma let out a shaky breath and followed. Once she was in the crowded corridor, however, Rowek was nowhere to be seen.

Emma entered the history classroom and found Adrianna. She waved Emma over to the desk she had reserved with her bookbag, shooting pointed glares at anyone who came near.

Before Emma was even seated, Adrianna began bragging about how Sean had carried her books for her after all. Emma listened while taking out her notebook and binder. Her heart gave a jolt, and she knew without looking up, who had just arrived.

Rowek's eyes flicked to where Emma sat, then they narrowed as anger flashed in them. Her heart jumped up in her throat as he walked toward the rows of desks. *Why was he mad?*

Her lungs constricted as he passed, his arm swinging dangerously close to Emma. She fought against the urge to lunge for him, to take whatever was inside him for herself, before he dropped into the chair behind her. She drew in a ragged breath.

Adrianna's eyes were wide as she gaped openly at him. Emma cleared her throat to try to divert her friend's gaze.

"Who is that?" she whispered, loud enough for him to hear. Emma shook her head to say she'd tell her later.

The class began with the energetic, mid-forties teacher who sported a well-groomed neck beard, skipping the standard first-day-protocol and diving straight into World War I. Emma appreciated his enthusiasm, having had him the previous year for world history. But the boy behind her kept her on edge... ever aware of the exact distance between them.

A folded piece of paper fell over her shoulder, landing in her lap. She stilled, staring down at it as if it were a bomb. Her fingers slowly worked to open the paper, careful to not make too much noise. The words written inside made Emma's stomach drop.

Meet me for lunch by the side doors next to the gym.

Emma stared down at the note. Was he insane? He looked at her like she was an insect, and now he wanted to have lunch with her?

Emma wrote back: *Can't. Eating with a friend.* Then she waited until the teacher had turned his back, scribbling a timeline animatedly, before she dropped the slip of paper over her shoulder.

The note didn't find its way back into her lap, and she began to be able to ignore the discomfort Rowek caused as she copied what the teacher had drawn on the board. He brushed his hands together, just as the bell sounded, white dust creating a cloud in the air.

The teacher hadn't even given his consent of dismissal before Rowek was out the door.

Adrianna spun in her chair. "Who is that?" she demanded again. Her tone was colored with awe and something else Emma chose to ignore. They stood, gathering their things.

"Rowek Zennett," Emma replied, trying to sound disinterested.

"He is hot with a capital 'h'!" She fanned herself with her hand for emphasis.

Emma scoffed. "He's such a typical bad boy. I'm not into that." The lie made her face hot, and she had to look away to keep Adrianna from seeing it.

"I'm way into it," she heard Adrianna mutter.

"He's in every one of my classes so far," Emma said to Adrianna, loud enough to be heard over the rustling papers and students shuffling through the rows. As they started for the door, Emma couldn't help but feel impressed at how well Adrianna maneuvered with her crutches.

"You say that like it's a bad thing."

Emma led her friend close to the wall to avoid being trampled and whispered, "There's something not quite right about him."

Adrianna gave her an odd look.

"You remember that night in the alley?" Emma asked.

Adrianna looked down, shifting uncomfortably. "You mean the night I broke my leg? Funnily enough, I do, yeah."

Emma forced herself not to flinch. "Well, those…things made me feel…cold and…i-it felt hard to breathe." Emma chewed her bottom lip. "Did you feel anything like that?"

Adrianna frowned. "No…just…bad, I guess."

Emma paused, considering her words. "And you didn't feel anything around Rowek?"

"You mean other than hot and bothered?" Adrianna asked

with a sly grin.

Emma punched her shoulder lightly. "I'm serious!"

"So am I...What do you feel around him?" Adrianna was still grinning, oblivious to Emma's irritation.

She managed a smile. "You know, it's probably nothing. I think I'm still a little jumpy from Saturday night."

Adrianna's smile faded. "I get it. That was some freaky crap."

Both girls arrived at their last class before lunch just after the tardy bell, earning them both a reproachful look from the short, gray-haired teacher at the front of the room. They found seats together, and Emma didn't bother hiding her smile at who was *not* present. It was a welcome relief to be able to concentrate and not feel like she was holding a live wire through the entire class. When the bell rang for lunch, Emma's stomach growled, making Adrianna laugh.

"Your stomach called. It said to tell you that you don't eat enough. Men like curves, ya know."

Emma snorted. "I have curves, thanks. And I do eat. All the time." Her stomach made another noise, as if in disagreement. Adrianna laughed.

The smells of the cafeteria made Emma's mouth water as they shuffled in. They were fortunate to have a café that served just about everything—no school lunch slop.

Emma grabbed herself a tray and was just about to grab another for Adrianna when a rich male voice said from behind them,

"May I be of service, milady?"

Emma turned to find Sean holding an empty tray for Adrianna.

Sean was definitely handsome, in a jock kind of way. His smile revealed brilliant white teeth. His hair styled with tidy black cornrows that crossed over his head. His basketball jersey hung loosely on his chest with his shorts worn low. Adrianna gave him a sultry smile before sending Emma a wink.

Emma filled her tray with a salad, a brownie, and a bottle of water. As she fished out some cash from her pocket, she heard Adrianna ordering half of everything on the menu. The girl liked to eat, and she was blessed with a metabolism that would puzzle doctors.

After the plump, surly-looking lady wearing a hairnet dumped Emma's change into her hand, Emma gestured to an empty table for Adrianna to see. She nodded before grabbing a bowl of mashed red Jell-O and added it to the heaping tray. Emma chuckled at Sean's wide eyes.

Emma set her tray down onto the table as a now familiar sensation surged in her chest. The hairs on the back of her neck stood on end, and she shivered. She took a slow, deep breath, forcing her lungs to fill with air.

A tray clattered onto the table next to her, making her jump.

"Cold?" Rowek asked. His voice made her stomach flutter.

"I'm fine." Her tone was harsher than she expected, but he didn't react. When she glanced over at him, his lips were tilted up in what she assumed was a permanent smirk. "Something funny?" she asked.

"Lots of things are funny. Have you been on YouTube recently?"

Emma stared, dumbfounded, while Sean placed Adrianna's tray on her other side. Once Adrianna plopped onto her seat, Emma saw her leaning forward to get a better look at Rowek. *Poor Sean.*

"You must be the new guy," Adrianna said.

Rowek's amber gaze slid from Emma to briefly glance at Adrianna.

"Yes, I am," he said, smile widening.

Emma glared down at her uncovered salad as she ripped the lid off. Beside her, Sean began chatting energetically to Adrianna about basketball. She saw Adrianna spear her fork into the massive plate of chili cheese fries, pretending to listen, though

Emma knew it wasn't Sean who held her attention.

"Not allergic to real food, are you?" Rowek's breath tickled her ear, making her drop her fork.

"What is that supposed to mean?" She turned to face him, anger simmering inside her. She wasn't sure why she was mad, but she didn't care. Rowek shrugged as he sipped his can of soda.

"I have something more important to ask you, actually," he said. His smile evaporated.

"And what's that?"

"Who are your parents?" Rowek asked, his voice low. From the silence to her right, she knew both Sean and Adrianna had stopped to listen.

"Erm, what?" Emma said, confused.

"Are they anyone I'd have heard of?" His tone was casual, but from the intensity of his gaze, Emma knew that there must be more to his simple question.

"No," Emma replied, stabbing at the browning lettuce with her fork. "I don't know who my dad is, and my mom's a surgeon."

"What's her name?"

Emma's heart stuttered, a sense of dread unfurling itself in her gut. She shot to her feet, her tray in hand, and started for the drop-off.

"Em!" Adrianna called after her, but Emma didn't stop until Rowek was in front of her. He grabbed her tray as she came to an abrupt halt, keeping it from upturning onto the floor.

"Hey, I'm sorry, I wasn't trying to freak you out," Rowek said. "You just look familiar, I thought maybe I knew you. You're new here too, right?"

Emma eyed him suspiciously. "How could you possibly know that?"

Rowek snorted a laugh. "You don't strike me as a true loner, which leads me to believe you just haven't had much time to make friends." He shrugged. "That, and people talk."

"Where *are* you from?" Emma asked with carefully leashed anger.

He looked surprised by her question. "All over. I've moved around a lot."

Her heart stuttered, and her shoulders slumped a little, the fire draining out of her. "Me too," Emma admitted.

His lips curved in a smile, though it lacked the arrogance he carried before. Emma felt herself smile back.

"I'm sorry if I freaked you out," he said, rubbing the back of his neck, almost shyly. "I get it. I'm not very good at making friends. You just have something about you…something different." His eyes were honest, the honey-colored depths pulling her closer. The tray pressed hard into her ribs, and only when he looked away, did she realize how close they were.

She took a step back, clearing her throat.

"It's okay," Emma said. "My mother has this thing about running away every time life gets uncomfortable." She winced at her harsh words.

Rowek laughed, unfazed. "I have a free period next. We could go get some real lunch, and you can unload all that pent-up frustration on me if you want. I'm a great listener."

Emma contemplated his offer. She didn't know anything about him, and while he was undeniably attractive, she wasn't sure she should trust him. The way she felt when he was near and what happened when he touched her made her hesitant.

She shook her head. "Thanks, but I'm going to get a head start on my homework."

After stepping around him, she hurried from the cafeteria to grab her books in case he decided to follow.

He didn't.

Emma found a spot beneath a willow tree to start on her calculus assignment and to text Adrianna, who had demanded to know why she had run off. She replied that she hadn't been feeling well, which wasn't entirely untrue.

A few minutes after the bell sounded for the end of her first free period, Adrianna ambled out the doors on her crutches and spotted Emma. She pretended to be busy reading her history book as Adrianna came to stand in front of her. The day was warm, the sun shining brightly. The scent of the final summer blooms floated around her shaded space.

"So, what's up?" Adrianna asked, still standing.

Emma glanced up. "Nothing, stomach ache."

"Yeah, because you threw your lunch away. Or rather, Rowek did. After you stormed out like he had just kicked your puppy."

"I did not," Emma argued.

Adrianna gave an exasperated sigh as she rested against the tree and slid down, her injured leg sticking out in front of her. Once she was on the ground, she dug through her backpack. With a satisfied noise, she tossed a pack of pop-tarts on Emma's textbook. Emma stared at the shiny foil pack for a moment, her pride and hunger at war. When her hunger decidedly won, she sighed.

"You have the best metabolism on the planet," Emma complained as she tore into the package.

Adrianna snorted. "You're the one eating them, not me."

Emma moaned as she reverently bit into the dry, sugary pastry.

Adrianna giggled. "I'll bring those more often, then."

Emma was thankful that Adrianna didn't ask any more about Rowek. They talked about their teachers and classes. Which boys got cute over the summer and who was sleeping with who. It was easy for Emma to feel normal again, if just for a few minutes. When free-period ended, they said their good-byes and Emma headed back up the stairs to the math department for her finance class.

Just outside the door, she felt her body react. Her heart skittered, her skin tingling, hot and cold warring inside her.

Rowek slouched down in his chair, his head bowed as he studied something in his hands. She swallowed hard, and her feet moved before she knew what she was doing. As she set her bag onto the desktop, she caught a ghost of a smirk playing on Rowek's lips.

The class was the same as the others had been, slow. Sitting beside Rowek felt like the room was pulsing with energy. She could almost see the currents arcing between them.

His hand twitched on the tabletop, mere inches from hers. *What would happen if I touched him again? Just brushed my fingers against his…*

She held her breath as her hand slid closer, trying to keep it from trembling. Anticipation swelled, and the air between them grew thick with it. Rowek didn't seem to notice her hand advancing until their skin brushed together. Warmth filled her fingertips, and they tingled.

No power to drain.

Her brow furrowed. Rowek looked at her questioningly. She gave him an embarrassed smile as she quickly withdrew her hand.

When the bell rang, Emma sprang out of her chair and raced for the door before Rowek could ask why she had randomly touched him.

Surely it wasn't just my imagination, she mused as she fought through the crowd to her last class of the day.

When Emma sank into her chair, feeling more exhausted than she had in a long time, she watched the door, worrying her bottom lip. People with plain faces that she paid no notice to filtered in. Even after the bell gave its shrill blast, she waited, wondering if he was just late.

Her mind wandered to this morning when Rowek had nudged her. The power she had felt from him had been real. And the hunger inside her had awoken, demanding more.

So why when she touched him again, was his power vacant? It was clear whenever he was in the room that he was something *other*. Not the same kind of evil she had experienced in the alley. But something more than just a seventeen-year-old boy.

When the final bell rang, Emma slung her bag over her shoulder and made her way out of the building. A flicker of disappointment surfaced when she realized she wouldn't be able to ask him anything until tomorrow.

In the parking lot, her mother's vehicle was nowhere to be seen. Emma pulled her phone out of her pocket and saw a text. **Won't be able to make it on time, I'll see you at home. Hope you had a great day. Be safe.**

Emma sighed as she shoved her phone back in her pocket. The events of the day just kept getting worse. Dark storm clouds rolled across the sky, the air thick with the smell of rain. *That would be just my luck*, Emma thought to herself as she set off for home. She didn't live more than twenty minutes away on foot, but that was plenty of time to get soaked if it did decide to rain.

When the first cold drop hit her nose, Emma sprinted the rest of the way. She slowed her pace as she reached the porch, stopping at the door to find her keys. The sound of the rain pelting the roof above her caused her to smile, despite her dampened state. Her hair dripped over her shoulders and down her back. She shivered.

As she slid the key into the lock, an eerie sensation of being watched crept over her. Her hands shook as she unlocked the door and stumbled inside.

A dark figure caught her attention as she turned to close the door, freezing her insides. Across the street, a man dressed in black stared in her direction, though his features were hazy through the sheet of rain. Heart thundering, she slammed the door shut and latched the deadbolt.

Her entire body shook as she wrung her damp hair out with a clean dish towel from the kitchen. She pushed the yellow floral curtain aside with a finger, peering out the window into the veil of rain. The man was gone, but she couldn't relax.

Something was very, very wrong.

EMMA

Emma's worry over the stranger in the rain slowly dwindled away the next morning. Rowek was absent, which made focusing easier, and she relaxed. The tension in her shoulders melted away as she and Adrianna entered the noisy cafeteria, giggling about Ms. Jules's cat sweater. They got their lunches before sitting at a table near the window.

The sky was still cloudy, but the sun was breaking through, casting a single pillar of light in the courtyard.

"So, no Sean today?" Emma asked.

"Nah, I think my eating habits scared him away." Adrianna glanced over at the loudest table in the room, her eyes shining with sadness. Guys laughed raucously, with tall cheerleaders either sitting in their laps or hanging off them with arms wrapped around their necks. Emma spotted Sean among them, laughing at something someone said. A rail-thin blond with no curves, straddled him in a dangerously short skirt as she ran a hand down his chest.

The girl's gaze fixed on Sean was less adoring and more… hungry. For his attention, and likely, his status. And Sean was either ignorant or impervious to it. He was fickle. Girls were little more than a conquest to guys like him. An ease of boredom. Emma doubted it was Adrianna's appetite that drove him away, but she didn't tell her friend that.

If he had pushed her, Adrianna didn't let on. If he desired

something from her, she wasn't willing to give…the sneer he sent in her direction was a pretty good indicator. Emma's fingernails bit into her palms as she forced herself to remain sitting.

"Well, screw him then," Emma bit out. "You can do much better."

Adrianna didn't respond, but as her gaze slid over Emma's shoulder, the unspent tears dried up. Emma didn't have to ask what caught her attention so completely. Recognition crept over her. Humming warmth spread in her veins, while her toes went numb. She inhaled sharply as a tray dropped onto the table beside her.

Rowek's light brown hair was perfectly styled. He smiled.

"Did you just wake up?" Emma asked, hoping she didn't sound as nervous as she felt.

Rowek smirked. "Maybe."

Emma huffed. "So you're one of those guys."

"I'm not *one of those guys*," Rowek replied with clear condescension. His smirk slipped, then he said, "It was a long night. My…dad made me work late with him. Nice shirt by the way." Amusement glittered in his eyes.

She glanced down at her faded Demon Hunter shirt. Her face heated, but she fought to ignore it. "I'm sorry. What does he do?"

Rowek took a bite of pizza, looking thoughtful. "He's in the military. But I help with recruitment."

That explained why he had to move around so often.

Adrianna cleared her throat, looking expectant. Before Emma could say anything, he extended his hand past Emma to her friend.

"I didn't get a chance to introduce myself yesterday, I'm Rowek," he said with a charming smile.

Emma could practically hear Adrianna swoon.

"Hi, I'm Adrianna," she said a bit breathlessly as she shook his hand.

"Adrianna." He rolled the syllables out on his tongue, tasting them. "Beautiful name. Have you lived here your whole life?"

She nodded, then little by little her expression changed to one of confusion. Adrianna's gaze flicked back and forth between Emma and Rowek. She blinked several times, then rubbed her eyes.

"You okay?" Emma asked her.

Adrianna rose from her seat and grabbed her crutches. "Uh, headache, I'll see you later."

Emma watched her friend go, feeling confused.

"Well that beats me trying to get you alone," Rowek chuckled deeply.

She turned to face him. "Huh?"

"I wanted to ask you about something."

She immediately thought about how she had touched his hand yesterday.

Emma's face flamed. "I'm sorry," she stammered.

Rowek looked puzzled. "For what?"

"I wasn't trying to hold your hand or anything, I—"

Rowek held up his hands to stop her. "Hey, you can hold my hand any time." He winked, and Emma's stomach flipped. "I actually was going to ask what you planned to do during your two free hours."

She blinked. "Oh. Uhm, when it's warm, I sit under the willow tree out by the football field. Adrianna usually joins me for sixth period."

Rowek nodded as he rose. "I'll meet you by the willow tree in twenty minutes."

Then he left too, leaving her alone at the table. She grabbed her chicken sandwich and stood.

After depositing the tray on the conveyer belt, she headed for her quiet spot, wondering what Rowek was up to.

The sun was now no longer hidden by the clouds. Its buttery warmth slipped through the low-hanging branches, warming her toes as she wiggled them in the grass. She closed her eyes, breathing in deeply. A breeze swept her wavy hair back, tossing it off her shoulders.

Her eyes flew open at the sudden tingle in her limbs. She searched around her, only spying people out on the field playing some sort of game that she didn't recognize.

"You look spooked."

Emma jumped. Rowek stood in front of her, a large coffee in each hand, his hair looking thoroughly windswept. His eyes were bright, the sun reflecting the golden hue within them. He held out a cup. The steam tickled her nose, and its bitter-sweet scent made her mouth water.

"Where did you get those?" Emma asked in amazement.

"Coffee shop down the street." He gestured over his shoulder. Emma reached out to grab the proffered beverage.

"Irish crème?" she asked, one brow raised.

He shrugged. "I found Adrianna in the hall and asked what you like."

She hadn't recalled ever sharing that information with Adrianna, but she smiled anyway. Before she had made it outside, she had received a message from Adrianna saying she was going home due to a migraine.

Emma made a mental note to send a message when she got home to see if Adrianna was doing any better.

"Mind if I sit?" He gestured to the grass in front of her.

She shook her head, then sipped her coffee as Rowek folded himself into a sitting position in front of her.

"Thanks for the coffee," Emma said.

He watched her take another drink and sigh, contentedly.

"So where were you born?" Rowek asked after a moment.

"Texas, Dallas, I think."

His head tilted slightly, as if he had expected a different answer.

"What about you?" Emma asked.

Rowek took his time, swigging from his cup, then looked out

at the field watching people run around with long sticks that had nets at the end, tossing a ball back and forth between each other.

"I don't know." Rowek met her incredulous gaze. "My father doesn't talk about my mother or anything to do with my birth. I'm just a tool to him."

Emma expected to find sadness in his eyes, but all she found was cold emptiness.

"I'm sorry," she whispered.

He shrugged. "Tell me about all the places you've lived."

A sense of trepidation sparked inside her. Emma knew her mother took precautions wherever they went so they couldn't be tracked. Since a very young age, Emma had been told to never answer questions about where they had last been or how many times they had moved, though she was never sure how she got each school she attended to accept her, or how she managed to find a new job within days of each new location.

She wrestled with herself, torn between wanting to tell him everything, and duty-bound to reveal nothing at all.

"Whoa, hey," Rowek laughed. "You don't have to look so frightened; we can talk about something else."

Emma's shoulders sagged in relief. "What's your favourite subject?" she asked, happy to deflect the awkwardness she felt.

He snorted. "They all have their perks." The way his eyes glinted mischievously made her think *she* was the perk he spoke of. Her cheeks burned at the thought.

They chatted about the teachers, about their favourite foods and other mindless topics that made Emma forget her near-panic episode. She enjoyed his company and his easy smiles, though still, something in his expression remained closed off.

"Do you have a ride home today?" he asked.

"Yeah. And when I don't, I walk." Emma took another sip of her drink, trying to hide her cringe. It felt too intimate for him to know that she lived within walking distance, but he just nodded as if he already knew that.

She tried to sound casual as she asked, "Why?"

"I just figured I'd offer to give you a lift home if you wanted it."

"I can't," Emma replied, shaking her head, "My mother would kill me."

"We don't have to tell her," Rowek winked.

"Ha. She knows everything. She has that crazy mom-telepathy that lets her know when I do anything she wouldn't approve of."

Rowek seemed to fight back a laugh, the corners of his lips twitching. "Believe me, your mother doesn't know nearly as much as you think she does."

Emma bristled, but Rowek continued, "If you change your mind, meet me by the side doors. You'll know my car when you see it."

And with that, he rose from his spot on the grass and went back inside just as the bell rang. She stood, stretching her legs and grabbed her bag. With an hour left to kill, she decided to take a walk.

Emma pulled her phone out and typed a quick message to Adrianna. The sun was pleasantly warm, beading sweat on the back of her neck. With fifteen minutes to spare, she re-entered the school grounds.

Her phone vibrated in her pocket, and she fished it out, hoping it was Adrianna. Instead, it was a message from her mother saying she wouldn't be able to pick her up again today. Emma huffed, feeling irritated. The hospital clearly needed to hire more surgeons so her mother could get a break.

I could always take Rowek up on his offer, Emma thought. She laughed out loud at the thought.

When Emma arrived in her finance class, ready to accept Rowek's offer, he wasn't there. Other students filled the empty seats and soon after Mr. Randall walked in, the bell rang. Emma couldn't help but feel a flutter of disappointment.

When he still didn't show in her last class of the day, Emma decided she would just walk.

After the last bell, Emma switched out her books at her

locker before glancing over at the side doors. Her hand gripped the cool metal tightly. *I'll just go see if I can spot his car. Maybe he was just skipping,* she told herself before she slammed the locker door closed and set off.

She scanned the parking lot, assessing every sports car she saw, trying to picture Rowek driving them. At last, she caught sight of a sleek, matte black Ferrari that was undoubtedly Rowek's. She started for it, deciding to wait beside it until he returned. Unless she chickened out first.

Two men stood by a cluster of trees next to the parking lot wearing black military-style clothing. She stumbled to a stop before she could fall face-first onto the sidewalk.

They were both freakishly tall with honey-kissed skin. The one on the left was built like a tank with black hair that was shaved on the sides with long, loose curls on top. Only his profile was visible with his head turned.

The other, with buzzed blond hair and a slightly crooked nose, like it had been broken one too many times, faced in her direction. They were both scanning the students filing out of the building, searching each face.

Something inside her shifted. A soothing warmth washed over her, and despite their intimidating looks, she walked briskly toward them. The blond's pale blue eyes snapped to her as if assessing a possible threat. Emma knew she should turn around, but her legs didn't stop.

The dark-haired male whirled to face her too, as if he sensed her presence. His striking features made Emma's heart leap into her throat. He had a strong, squared jaw and pale blue eyes that looked almost gray.

When she was close enough, she realized they both looked like they were only in their early twenties. Emma felt unable to swallow as she came to a stop several feet away from them. The magnetic pull was almost irresistible, but her stomach flipped nervously.

The dark-haired man stared at her with an unreadable

expression, his stormy gaze looking her over from head to toe. Emma barely looked at the intense blond man beside him. His head quirked to the side as if trying to piece together a puzzle.

Under their assessing looks, she felt stupid for so boldly approaching them. But her heart rate slowed, as if coaxed into a calm rhythm.

"Are you guys cops or something?" she asked.

The dark-haired man's lips twitched.

"No," the blond answered. "We're looking for someone." Emma detected a strong English accent. Without meaning to, her gaze roamed back to the dark-haired man. His curls looked as if he spent a great deal of time running his fingers through them, and for a brief moment, she wondered what it would be like to run her fingers through them too. If they felt as silky as they looked. Her cheeks heated as she mentally shook herself.

She averted her eyes and cleared her throat. "Who are you looking for?"

"A dangerous man we believe might be in this area," the dark-haired man said, and Emma tried not to swoon at the trace accent in his voice too.

She stood, unblinking at the devastatingly handsome man, while he reached into his black canvas jacket. He procured a photograph and held it out for Emma to see. She leaned forward, observing the grainy still.

Even with as low-resolution as it was, Emma still recognized the striking gold eyes. A tall, well-built man in an expensive suit. The recognition must have shown on her face because the blond said, "You've seen him?"

Her eyes flicked between the two men. She swallowed hard.

"I think so."

"When?" the blond demanded.

"Last weekend, when I was out shopping with my mom," she replied. The men exchanged a look of confirmation.

"You haven't seen him since then?" the dark-haired male asked. Emma shook her head. He frowned and her stomach dropped. Had her answer been disappointing? She wished she had more to offer them.

The blond turned as if to leave.

"What if I see him again?" she blurted out. They both stopped. "How can I get a hold of you?"

The blond opened his mouth, but the dark-haired man raised a hand to stop him. He rifled through an inner pocket in his jacket again, this time extending what looked like a business card for Emma to take.

She accepted it, looking down at the name first. *Blaze Thomas*. Beneath his name was a phone number.

He stepped closer, leaning down to whisper next to her ear. The smell of pine and warmth filled her senses.

"Stay safe, Emma."

He and his friend stalked off, leaving her rooted in place, feeling dazed.

As she walked home, Rowek's offer long forgotten, she felt a chill snake down her spine. The handsome dark-haired man— Blaze—had known her name.

Yet she never said it.

Later that night, Emma's mother brought Chinese food home as her way of apologizing for not being able to pick her up from school. As they ate, her mother questioned her about her classes. Emma momentarily considered telling her mother about Blaze and the other guy outside her school.

The conversation shifted when Emma told her mother about how several of the teachers mentioned the bombings. A school assembly was scheduled for later in the week to honor those affected and provide information about the increased security. Worry pinched her mother's lovely face.

"I've thought long and hard about you walking to and from school when I can't be there, and I've decided that it's too dangerous," her mother said as she pushed a cashew around her plate. Emma looked up, trying to keep her face neutral.

"It's almost your birthday," she continued.

As if Emma hadn't been counting down the days until she was eighteen.

Her mother sat straighter, a resignation in her expression that made Emma's heart leap. "I want to buy you a car."

Emma jumped up, her chair toppling backward to the floor with a crash. She squealed as she ran to hug her mother. Her lips were pursed in a tight smile, but she returned the embrace with rib-crushing strength.

"Thank you so much, Mom." Tears stung Emma's eyes. Her mother was not as physically affectionate as Emma. Usually flinching away from the simplest brushes, a haunted look in her seafoam green eyes. Emma suspected that her only daughter entering adulthood might have had something to do with the sudden change.

Her mother released her, eyes shining. She cleared her throat. "I thought we'd go car shopping this weekend."

Elation filled Emma. She didn't want to wait to call Adrianna, but since she had still not heard anything from her, she decided it could wait until morning.

Emma had a driver's license, and her mother let her drive often enough that she felt comfortable behind the wheel. It was little things like that, that made her feel as if her mother didn't mean to deprive her of normal, teenage life-events.

Emma gathered their dirty places and placed them in the sink, grinning from ear-to-ear. Behind her, her mother said,

"I also want you to carry this." She held out a pink stick of pepper spray attached to a key ring.

Emma gave a nervous laugh. "Why?"

"Because with the bombings and whatnot, you can't trust anyone. I can't very well send you to school with a gun, and you can't own one until you're twenty-one anyway."

"I don't think they'll allow that either." Emma nodded toward the small canister.

"Leave it in your car, then," her mother responded simply. Emma couldn't think of another response, so she accepted the tube.

An internal battle raged inside her, twisting her stomach into knots. She wanted to tell her mother about the dangerous golden-eyed man who had seemingly followed them, about the attack in the alley—all of it. But Emma knew how her mother would react.

If she didn't cart Emma off to a mental hospital right then and there, they would for sure be out of the state by midnight. The life she had grown so fond of would be ripped from her grasp yet again.

Her eyes prickled, and she blinked away the tears.

"Thanks, Mom." Emma placed a kiss on her cheek before heading up the stairs, feeling as if the weight of her isolation would crush her entirely.

LEVAROTH

The *freaks* had been outside the school. Their scent lingered in the air. They were circling. Either they had been looking for him, or they had been looking for *her*. The girl who smelled of sugar and radiated power like a walking sun.

He wondered how she would react if she saw him again. If he revealed himself to her. Would she flee like most humans did, or would her power ignite within her veins?

If it was true, then her power made her a weapon—her skin made her deadlier than any blade. He could be caught and bound, but only she would have the power to kill him. He needed to see her powers for himself. Then he needed to get her to trust him. If he earned her trust, then her power would be his. She would be his to control.

There was something about her that sang to his blood—to his own power like a siren. Like their beings were of a similar material, and he needed to be close to her.

It made him determined to get close. To push the boundaries between them. He needed to protect her. In the way one protected a possession. He would keep his vile pursuers from her.

From a distance, he trailed her. Levaroth had fought to control his need to reveal himself when the blond oaf followed her home yesterday. To rip his head clean off his shoulders. But the older one, Blaze, he recalled, was the real threat. Fortunately, he had managed to shake him.

He would keep himself hidden as long as he needed to. Feed further away to keep them guessing. Now that he knew Emma Duvall was on their radar, he would have to be watchful. If they discovered her power, they would do anything to possess her for themselves. Then they would destroy her. She would be too powerful for them to control. And whatever they couldn't control, they tortured—killed, if they could.

Levaroth heard a growl rumble up from his chest. They would not have her.

He sat atop the curling, brittle shingles of a roof on a lonely, roadside bar outside the city limits. Rowdy laughter and alcohol covered him like a suffocating blanket. Even the gentle breeze could not cleanse the air. He homed in on the sickly-sweet aromas of lust and pride, drinking of them deeply like a man in the desert stumbling upon fresh water.

He needed to feed after expending so much energy to keep his scent masked. His blood hummed with the need for bloodshed. A bunch of stumbling, loud drunks would have to do the trick. Not to mention it would lead his pursuers away from Seattle. But they already knew he could go anywhere. He didn't want to risk being away from the girl too long, in case they decided to take her.

The thought of them getting their hands on her made his muscles coil tight. A lion crouched and ready for the kill. He was in the mood for some theatrics. A wicked grin spread across his face as he leaped from the roof, landing on the gravel with the grace of a feline.

He pulled the door open. The smells of stale tobacco and marijuana smoke mixed with urine and sweat assaulted his nostrils. A hushed silence filled the room, and a few curious glances met him where he stood.

No one knew who he was or what he was capable of. That's what made the hunt so fun. Levaroth strode toward the bar, wearing an easy smile.

"What would you like?" the female bartender asked, her tone bored.

The woman was in her late forties, with bleached blonde hair and sallow skin. Her t-shirt had deliberately been cut with a low V-neck to display her surgically-enhanced breasts.

"What are you offering?" Levaroth laced his words with his least favourite capability. The woman shifted, the irritation dissipating from her wrinkled brow.

Women already fell at his feet, willing worshippers of his ethereal beauty. When he used his special ability, they had no choice in the matter. Tough, hardened men would happily slice open their veins if he willed it.

Several of the burly, biker-type men turned to face him, their slack-jawed expressions awaiting his instruction. The one closest to him swung around on the stool to face him, a thick, tattooed arm resting on his leg. A joint dangled between his lips. He didn't look ready to commit his unfailing loyalty. His graying mustache twitched with impending violence. Levaroth smirked at the man, daring him to make a move.

His gaze flitted back to the bartender. "A shot of whiskey," Levaroth said.

"Sure thing," she purred, puffing out her chest. Lust burned in her stare, the air around her reeked of it.

He wrestled against his body's natural reaction to break something. Her voice was harsh, no doubt from the countless years of smoke filling her lungs. The bartender poured a finger of amber liquid into a smudged glass, then slid it toward Levaroth. He plucked it up from the table and tossed it back, barely tasting it. Alcohol was weak compared to the drinks served where he came from.

Levaroth flung the glass at the woman, aiming just above her head. "Is there any part of you that's real anymore?" he shouted. His sudden burst of anger sent a wave of clarity through the room.

A trickle of blood ran down the wide-eyed woman's cheek; sliced by a shard of glass. "Now, excuse me—" her voice quaked.

The joint-smoking biker spoke. "All right asshole, that's enough. Get the hell out." He slid from his stool, pointing toward the door. The sagging skin made the tattoos covering his arms droop. Years of unchecked sun exposure and a human's natural aging had turned him into a wrinkled, leathery version of what had likely been a man worth fearing.

Levaroth didn't move. Though his wings twitched behind him, he kept them hidden from view. *No point in scaring them all to death in one go.* He tilted his head side to side, the bones cracking like gunshots in the tense silence that hung in the room. The man stalked forward a step to grab him, as Levaroth's hands lifted at his sides, palms up. His fingers curled into fists, and what little light there was, disappeared with an audible *pop.*

"What the—" several occupants shouted. A few stumbled over stools, tumbling to the ground with resounding thuds. Only Levaroth saw each scurrying prey with perfect clarity. He didn't need to light to see. He was made of shadows. Just as he didn't require physical touch to kill. It was the frantic rhythm of a pulse as it sputtered out that made him touch his victims.

Someone sprinted for the door, running blind. Levaroth intercepted him, grabbing him by the leather vest, and slammed him onto his back. The man choked on the air that was forced from his lungs. His terror coated the air as thick as molasses. Levaroth breathed it in with a sigh.

"W-what are you?" the man sputtered, his eyes squinting to try to make out Levaroth's form in his drunken state.

"I am many things," he whispered as he crouched over the man. "Nightmare. Monster. Beast. Death." His fingers itched to wrap themselves around the man's neck, to feel it snap like a dry twig.

The man sniffled, and Levaroth rolled his eyes. The bigger the man, the more they snivelled and begged for mercy when death approached. *Pathetic roaches. Humans are an infestation of creatures that seem to have forgotten their place in the universe.*

A light shone from behind the bar. Levaroth's jaw clenched. He'd have to make this quick.

He let his mind go; snapped the tether that held his inner beast. Fire flooded his veins, and his body welcomed it. He gripped sweaty flesh.

A sharp twist, and then a satisfying crack. The man went limp.

Levaroth moved like lightning, appearing behind the bar and grabbed the source of light from the bartender's shaking hands. She gasped.

"Technology just gets in the way these days, doesn't it?" He snapped her iPhone in half, but the 9-1-1 call was already made. He had less than nine minutes to finish what he had set out to do. "You ruined my fun," he growled, his voice more animal than human.

Grabbing the bartender's face with both hands, his nails dug into her soft flesh as she fought to back away. Her pulse beat wildly below his fingers like a drumroll. He focused on it.

Felt it.

Drank it.

Within a few seconds, her body hung lifeless in his grasp. He let her drop to the floor in a heap before stalking his next victim.

One-by-one, he cornered his scattering creatures and ripped their life-forces from their bodies, consuming them hungrily.

Sirens wailed in the distance. Levaroth stood, scanning the room. Not a single living thing remained. His beast was sated, his mind calm and content. As he closed his eyes, the bar disappeared. When they reopened, Washington was far behind.

By night he checked on Emma, keeping far enough away from her house to avoid her detection. Every evening, when darkness settled over Seattle, he watched her window. Her lean shadow silhouetted against the curtains. Every night, he stayed until her light went out.

He found himself wondering what would happen if he got closer. Imagined her waking with a jolt, searching for his presence. Would she come looking for him?

After a few days when those who hunt me realize I'm gone, they will leave, and I will be free to pursue the girl.

On Thursday, after every light in the house was extinguished, he gazed at her window, drawing closer. It was a dangerous game, he knew. He couldn't shake the urge to let her know that she was in his thoughts. That he watched out for her. Protected her.

It was well past two in the morning when his cell phone rang. He glared down at the screen, a brutal slash of anger surging through him at the interruption.

He paused at the name. This was not a call he'd receive unless there was news. In the day he searched for information regarding the girl that had caught his attention. Particularly her parentage.

For that reason, he at last, pulled himself away, sparing a final look at the sleeping street.

On the following afternoon, he decided he was done waiting. He brought himself to the school. After a thorough search of the area, he waited.

After the bell chimed its last, the air grew rife with excitement. Young, smiling faces poured out of the building, eager to begin the weekend.

Her presence lit the edge of his senses like a beacon. She followed a dark-skinned girl who descended the stairs on crutches, yammering away about something he couldn't quite hear.

But she froze, eyes flashing with surprise as she looked up, searching. Levaroth smiled to himself.

It was him she sensed.

EMMA

Emma halted on the stairs, blood rushing in her ears. Rowek leaned against his car, arms folded across his chest. His buttery brown eyes were locked on her.

He smiled, warm and dazzling.

Adrianna had stopped too, tracking her gaze to where Rowek stood.

"Mmmhmmm. Girl, you better go over there and see what he wants before I do."

Emma shook her head. "He's obviously not sick. He looks fine." So why had he missed several days of school?

"Better than fine," Adrianna murmured.

With a sigh, Emma started moving toward him, her body tingling with recognition. Her heart pumped harder, as if she had been running.

"You know school is a Monday through Friday gig, right?" Emma said placing a hand on her hip.

"I might have heard something about that," Rowek answered disinterestedly. The sun broke through the dark clouds, and he shut his eyes, leaning his head back to soak it up.

"I'll never understand how you got into calculus with *that* attitude."

He peeked at her from under a single eyelid. "Aw, were you worried about me?"

"You ditched me."

He flinched. "Something came up."

"Something that made you leave your car here?"

"Yeah, my dad and I had to go out of town for a few days. But I wanted to make it up to you. I thought we could go down to the Sound to talk, and then I'll take you home." Emma opened her mouth to decline, but Rowek held up a hand to stop her. "Adrianna was going to give you a ride home, right?"

"Yes." She shot a glance at her friend's idling car, parked on the other side of the lot.

"So text her and tell her where you'll be, and if at any point you want her to come pick you up, she can."

He opened the passenger side door in invitation. She stared into the car momentarily. The irrational anger she had felt when he had seemingly disappeared was gone. Now, she was looking forward to spending time with him again.

After several beats, she pulled out her phone to tap a message on the screen. When she was done, she stowed it inside her backpack and then slid into the car.

Rowek was behind the wheel before she could reconsider, the engine's sleek purr greeting them. Emma gnawed on her bottom lip nervously.

"Don't worry grandma, I'll go the speed limit," Rowek teased.

She forced herself to relax. Her mother would never know. The car cruised out of the parking lot, it's engine roaring as they picked up speed.

As they weaved through the afternoon traffic, a small smile curved her lips. She felt like a passenger in a race car, secretly wishing she could feel the engine's full power.

They reached Puget Sound in less than thirty minutes. Emma opened her door and climbed out, slinging her backpack over her shoulders.

"Shall we?" Rowek motioned toward the pathway around the waterfront. She nodded, looking around. They were the only two people around.

The sky was gray, the sun receding within the dark clouds. It was almost eerie, but Rowek looked unfazed.

He shoved his hands into his jean pockets as they started along the boardwalk. Docked boats creaked as they rocked, water slapping against the sides.

"It's probably going to rain," Emma observed, awkwardly trying to fill the silence.

"Not afraid of a little rain, are you?" His tone was light, but something about his rigid body language made the heaviness in her chest expand.

"No." Emma looked away from the docks toward the street in the distance. A mother hurriedly pushed her stroller, casting nervous glances at the sky as if trying to anticipate its first drops.

Emma's hands itched to fish her phone from her backpack.

"Chill, Emma, I won't let it rain on you." Rowek grinned as if he could truly prevent the impending deluge, and Emma forced a smile. *Relax*, she told herself

"Did you hear about that bar just south of Seattle?" Emma asked, spouting the first thing that came to mind.

Rowek's brow rose. "No, what happened?"

"Everyone inside was dead, and the wiring was completely fried." Emma relayed the information her mother had shared with her that morning. She had almost refused to let Emma go to school at all until Emma had convinced her mother that it was far enough away and that most schools were practically fortresses these days.

"Crazy," Rowek said. "What do they think happened?"

"Well the news says the building was struck by lightning, but some people are saying it's aliens." After the creatures she'd encountered in the alley, aliens almost seemed logical. Rowek paused his walking, his smile a mocking slash of white.

"And what do you think?" he asked. His honey-brown eyes pinned her to the spot, demanding an answer.

She sighed, choosing her words carefully. "I think there have been a lot of strange things happening lately."

"But aliens, though?"

Rowek's tone made her release a laugh.

It did sound ridiculous; but so did flesh-eating creatures that hunted in the shadows, weaving illusions to trap their prey.

"As fun as discussing the news is," Rowek resumed walking, "I'd rather talk about you. What kind of music do you like?"

"All kinds, I guess. Except for country…" Emma mused while looking back out at the bay, watching the seagulls soar through the air, spying their next meals. Her stomach felt like it was trying to work its way up her throat.

"What's your *favorite?*" he pressed.

Emma bit her lip and Rowek's brows shot up, then he groaned.

"Oh no, it's rap, isn't it?"

Emma laughed, "No, it's not rap."

"What is it then?" he asked, his eyes alight with amusement.

"It's rock," she muttered with a nonchalant shrug. "Some old, some new."

Rowek chuckled. His laughter, again, made something inside her stir. Like a slumbering animal twitching when its master spoke. She looked away from his face, knowing hers would be flushed.

"Okay, favorite band?" he asked, smiling. "Please don't say Demon Hunter."

"As I Lay Dying. And there is nothing wrong with Demon Hunter," she argued.

One moment Rowek was walking beside her, the next he was in front of her, stepping back as she walked forward. She stumbled a step, unsure of how she had missed his movement.

"That's a little heavy for you." He ignored her bemused expression.

"No it isn't," she countered in spite of herself. His grin grew, something sparking in his eyes that made Emma's heart skip a beat.

"Definitely didn't picture you as the screamo-loving type."

"Okay, what's your favorite kind of music, then?" Emma retorted.

Rowek sighed dramatically. "Well, while I can get into the whole head-banging thing, I'm more of an AC/DC, Metallica type guy."

"Respectable." Emma nodded. She inhaled the salty breeze that swept along her face, trying to loosen the knots in her stomach.

"Favorite movie?" Rowek asked. He turned back around and was walking beside her again, but this time he didn't seem to disappear and then reappear like before. Had she imagined it?

Emma thought for several moments, narrowing the choices down in her head. They stopped at the end of a dock, looking out over the Sound. The saltwater sloshed against the wooden posts, the briny scent thick in the air.

As Emma opened her mouth to answer, a familiar jingle that could make any child giddy made them both turn.

"Ah, ice cream truck." Rowek gave her a wink. "Be right back."

Her brows shot up. It was far too cold for ice cream. "It's okay, I don't need—" Emma started to say, but Rowek cut her off.

"My treat, I'll surprise you." He had begun jogging up the grassy slope to the street before Emma had time to protest further.

She frowned at his retreating form for a moment before turning to face the bay again. She loved the sounds of the water. Loved the mystery hidden within its dark depths. She sat on the edge of the dock, her feet dangling above the almost black surface. In the gloom, it was impossible to see more than a few inches deep.

A dark shape rose near the surface just under her feet. Emma leaned forward, trying to make it out. An invisible icy dagger ramrodded into her lungs. Gasping, she clutched her chest, and scooted herself back. She brought her legs up and stood, her knees knocking together. Her eyes scanned the area for Rowek, but he was nowhere to be seen. And so was the ice cream truck.

Where had he gone?

The ambient temperature plummeted, her breath curling in front of her in wispy white puffs. A shiver racked Emma's body as she wrapped her arms around herself.

She took a few steps toward the road, then stilled. The water behind her bubbled and gurgled. Fear sliced through her as she slowly spun on the spot just in time to see a sickly green, webbed hand grasp the dock. Emma froze in place, the weight in her chest making her breaths come in short, labored pants.

The creature pulled itself up. It had scaly skin. Seaweed hung off loose and chipped scales. It stood on two legs with webbed fins that resembled and acted like feet. Stringy, black hair hung from its bulbous head, its face pointed and amphibious in appearance. It stared at her with one entirely white eye and one pure black.

It took a floppy step forward, its fin smacking the wooden planks. Emma shrieked, backing away. When she turned, three more creatures, all identical, blocked her only way off the dock.

"Rowek!" she screamed, hoping he, or anyone, would hear her.

More bubbling broke the surface of the restless sea to her right. Emma turned just in time to see another creature begin to pull itself up. She spun. She was blocked in. Emma's eyes frantically searched for some way out. She remembered her backpack on her shoulders and mentally ran through its contents. *Nothing helpful, unless I can stab one with a pencil or lob the whole bag at one of them to try to knock it down,* she thought to herself. Anxiety threatened to choke her as they all drew closer.

She thought back to the night in the alley. All she had to do was touch the creature, and it died…or dissolved. Hoping to buy herself time to get close enough to one without the others attacking her, she spun her bag onto her chest. She unzipped the pocket as soundlessly as she could manage, then began rifling blindly through its contents. She grabbed a textbook and a pencil. *A makeshift sword and shield,* she thought grimly.

Not wanting the extra weight, she let the bag fall by her feet.

She knew how to defend herself in a human attack, but she had no idea what these creatures were capable of—how strong or fast they were. *Their size might be an advantage*, she considered. They were all roughly equal in height to herself.

She pivoted around, a mechanical pencil held firmly in her grip, the textbook hugged to her chest with her other arm.

As one stepped forward, a gap appeared, and Emma made her move. She lunged, thrusting the pencil at the nearest creature. The pencil cracked in half, the impact knocking it from her hand. It swung a webbed hand, narrowly missing her face as she ducked. Grasping the book tightly, she brought it up in an arc over her head. It hit with a wet *squelch*. Out of the corner of her eye, she saw its other arm swinging for her. She braced herself for the cold, slimy touch of a fish as she dropped her last weapon and clasped her hands around its arm, still crouched on the ground.

The surge of foreign energy jolted into her. It filled her veins, her muscles, her bones with a strength that made her want to roar. She looked up, its eyes bugging out of its head. A grin that felt out of place split her lips.

The creature's scaly flesh turned black. Ash rained down on her. Through the pounding of her heartbeat in her ears, she heard the other three monsters clicking and burbling. Communicating?

She stood, ready to take on the others when she felt something she hadn't before. It was new and not. Something to wield and control. Within her mind, she reached for it, and it told her what to do.

She spun toward the scaly face on her left. It stepped back, fear widening its mismatched eyes. She lunged, latching her hands onto either side of its face, not noticing that they were now the same temperature. The power inside her released.

The creature made a choked sound as water bubbled up out of its mouth, revealing several rows of tiny, needle-like teeth. She cocked her head to the side in equal parts fascination and giddy amusement.

Apparently fish can drown too.

In her peripheral vision, dark green figures advanced on her. More creatures lifted themselves onto the dock. Slick hands wrapped around her arms in a bone-crushing grip, tearing her away from the creature's face. She howled at the rumbling sky; at the monsters that broke her contact with her prey.

Though they touched her, their power no longer fed her.

Every ounce of energy and strength was leeched from her system. In its place, cold seeped into every fiber of her being. Her lungs filled with a salty, bitter fluid. She coughed, fighting to break free of the grip on her. Panic grew as she tried to breathe. Her lungs constricted, trying to expel the liquid. Water sprayed from her mouth, but air still evaded her.

She couldn't concentrate. Couldn't focus on pulling their power into herself. Only water filled her.

Stars danced in her vision as her body grew slack. She couldn't scream for help nor beg for mercy. She was drowning from the inside. The creatures that surrounded her grew blurry. She felt vaguely aware of more finned hands touching her, filling her with water until she dropped to the dock. Her forehead connected with the solid wood, but there were no sensations beyond the burning in her lungs. The pressure in her head. Even her skull was swelling with water. A balloon ready to burst.

Darkness started to close in on her, and she welcomed it. The pain eased. She heaved once, expelling the water from her lungs. Her head lifted. The creatures backed away from her, but they weren't looking at her. They were staring behind her. She choked out more water, her lungs stinging as she gulped down fresh air. Her head fell and her eyes closed. Exhaustion consumed her.

Shouts and sounds like sickening squelches rang out, but her eyes wouldn't open. Her ears still felt waterlogged, but she could vaguely hear sizzling, and at last wet thumps. She tried to move her arms to roll herself onto her back, but they shook in protest.

A large, masculine hand flipped her over in one smooth movement. She willed her eyes to open. They fluttered until finally, they split just wide enough to see a young, handsome face staring down at her. A few black curls hung across his forehead. His gray eyes that scanned her for injury, looked as threatening as the sky above.

"What the hell were you thinking? Are you stupid?" Blaze shouted at her, accent thicker than she had heard it before. Emma blinked, stunned. Why was he mad? She hadn't asked for those creatures to attack her. She hadn't asked to be nearly drowned. Sheer defiant anger gave her the energy to respond.

"Wow, asshole much?"

"Apparently walking up to strange men isn't risky enough for you. You get into random people's cars too?" His look of disgust made a burning sensation claw its way up her throat that was unrelated to the amount of saltwater she swallowed.

"Wait, what?" *Was he talking about Rowek?* "I'd have thought the green fish people were slightly more concerning."

His eyes narrowed, and a muscle in his jaw ticked. "Yes, and where is your so-called friend now?"

The blond guy she had seen with Blaze stopped at the edge of the dock, twin daggers fisted at his sides. "There's no sign of him, he must have masked his scent somehow. Jake and I will keep looking, he likely won't want to leave her for very long."

Emma felt the urge to burst into laughter. The seriousness of his words was lost to the sight of a grown man carrying knives like some ancient warrior.

"I'll join you as soon as I'm done here," Blaze called. He raked a hand through his hair, drawing it back away from his face. When the blond took off, Blaze looked back down. "Can you sit up?" he asked.

Her limbs protested as she tried to push herself up. A steady hand slid to her upper back, guiding her into a sitting position.

"What were those things?" she asked. Blaze gave a dry, harsh laugh. His eyes were scanning all around them.

He moved his intense stare to her. "Does your mother know what you can do?"

She swallowed, then winced. "What do you mean?"

"I saw what you did. I couldn't see your face, but for a moment you terrified them. Very little terrifies them." His voice was low as he held her gaze.

The way he looked at her, suggested he was not afraid of her. But she had seen terror in those creature's eyes too. Their power was—

She reached for it.

Gone.

The absence of their power to drown someone from the inside left a gaping hole inside her. An ugly emotion unspooled that she immediately forced down, hoping Blaze couldn't see it on her face.

"I don't know what I did, but it wasn't the first time." She looked down at her hands as her eyes burned.

Am I a monster too? There had to be something wrong with her. The greed for their power, the hunger for their death…it could only mean she was something far worse.

"When?" he demanded.

"Last Sunday. My friend and I were walking home when we were attacked. They were different though. They were tall and shadowy and—"

"Did they make you see things that seemed impossible?"

Emma's head snapped up. "Y-yes."

Blaze nodded, then sighed, running his fingers through his damp curls again. "It's better if you know," he muttered, more to himself than to Emma. "They're part of a race called the Shediem. Humans have created names for them in their lore. 'Demon' is the most common. They come in different shapes and sizes. The lower ranks are all you'll usually find. They're the foot soldiers if you will. From the sound of it, I'd guess the creatures you faced last week were Nybasses." He gestured to the slaughtered corpses on the dock. "And those are Nickor."

Emma blinked. Hysterical laughter built in her chest until it overflowed.

Demons? Emma believed in a higher power but never gave

much thought to a supernatural realm. Laughter erupted from low in her belly—the events of the last week that she had kept to herself released in a torrent.

Her savior scowled. Her chest tightened as her laughter turned into a fit of coughs. She wrapped her arms around her chest, trying to catch her breath. Blaze scanned the area again, searching for something.

When Emma fell silent, he said, "Finished?"

"Demons aren't real," she replied in a raspy voice.

Blaze rolled his eyes. "And yet, you can clearly see these aren't what you'd call normal."

"But…" She huffed in exasperation. "Wouldn't that mean there are angels and god and whatnot?"

"Yes, though their interactions on Earth are rare. That's why I'm here. There are hordes of Shediem that exist in *this city alone*, and it's my job to send them back to their realm." Emma opened her mouth to reply, but he continued. "I know it's a lot to process, but the fact is, you're a part of this realm whether you like it or not. In fact, no one has ever been able to do what you did. When we cut them down, we simply send them back. It buys us a few months. But what you did…I think when you touch them, you kill them."

Emma didn't answer. His words stunned her. Angels and demons—Shediem—not only existed, but she was the first person in history to *kill* them? Her head gave a painful throb.

She bit her lip to keep it from trembling. "What does that make you then?"

"I am a Giborim," Blaze answered with ease. "A descendant of a Fallen One from ancient times. Thousands of years ago a large number of Fallen Ones roamed the Earth and had… relations with human women. They impregnated them and created abominations like me. The one you call God, rid the Earth of most of the offspring with a flood, but some survived. We're faster and stronger than humans, which make us perfect soldiers.

"The Shediem have been waging war on the humans since the

beginning of time. The Giborim that remained after the Purge were allowed to exist, as long as they didn't breed with humans and kept the Shediem in line."

Her eyes widened. He was a descendant of fallen angels. "How did you know where I was?"

Blaze seemed to consider whether he should answer at all, when at last he said, "Let's just say, I'm looking out for you."

"Why?" Then she recalled that he had known her name without her giving it. "Is that how you knew my name?"

"Yes," he replied.

She moved to stand, ignoring the crushing sensation in her skull. Blaze offered his hand, and she hesitated before allowing him to pull her to her feet as if she weighed nothing. He didn't let go as she swayed, her muscles trembling. As her other hand rubbed her forehead, she kept her eyes closed for several seconds allowing the dizziness to pass.

When her eyes reopened, she said, "How do I know if I can trust you?"

"How do I make you feel?"

She considered his question. Both at the school and now, his presence was warm. Soothing. "Safe," she admitted.

Now that he was standing right in front of her, she took in the leather straps crisscrossing his chest and two hilts of what she imagined were swords peeking over his broad, corded shoulders. Sheathed daggers were strapped to his thighs. He was as deadly as he was otherworldly handsome.

He smiled, and the sight made her chest ache with how stunning it was. She wanted to make him smile all the time. Flustered, she shook her head as if to shake away her foolishness. *Too much salt water*, she thought.

"Your friend seemed to disappear as soon as you were attacked," Blaze said.

"He said he was getting ice cream, but he never came back." Had he seen the creatures attacking her and fled? He didn't strike her as a coward. Why hadn't he tried to help?

Blaze's expression was one of calculation. He was silent in his thoughts.

"Why were you following us?" she asked.

"The creature we're hunting left his scent in the area. We were already here when we saw you being attacked."

"The guy in the photo you showed me?"

Blaze let out a long breath. "Yes. It's tricky because he can change his form. Look like anyone."

She shuddered. A monster hiding in plain sight. "He's a Shediem I take it?"

Blaze nodded.

Emma hummed to herself as another wave of cold washed over her body. Every tremor that coursed through her made her muscles burn. "Why were you looking for him outside of my school?"

Blaze frowned at Emma's barely controlled shivers as if he was unable to feel the bone-chilling cold. "The Shediem we're after feeds on human emotions until their hearts give out." Emma's eyes widened. "But he also likes to kill just for the sake of it. It doesn't matter if he snaps their neck or feeds on their fear until their heart fails, he always leaves a trace. A signature of sorts." Blaze's accent grew thicker, and a wild glint flickered in his eyes as he spoke.

"All of his victims have charred fingertips. Like being near him burned them from the inside out."

Emma's stomach churned aggressively. "I still don't know why you were at my school." Her voice was as thin as the cardigan that clung to her damp skin.

Blaze looked out over the Sound. "He had several victims nearby. I convinced my brother, Axel, that I had caught his scent at the school. I wanted to be sure you were okay." Emma felt a ripple of surprise in learning the blond man was Blaze's brother. He still didn't look at her as he added, "I didn't think you'd walk right up to us."

Her brow knitted together, and she frowned. "How did you

know what I looked like?"

"I…didn't," Blaze answered, surprising her.

"So how did you—"

"I can't say," Blaze said firmly.

Emma swallowed hard. A moment of uncomfortable silence descended on them before Emma said, "The bar outside of town—the one with all those dead people inside—did they have blackened fingertips?"

Blaze nodded, his jaw clenched. "After seeing what you can do, I think he may be residing in the area. He may know about you." Her fear must have shown on her face, because he added, "It's probably a coincidence, but either way, we plan to catch him."

Her lungs were too tight, her breathing too shallow. "So you hunt these Shediem?"

He nodded again. "The one we're after is extremely powerful; a general. He's one of three war generals that serve the six princes of Sheol. We can't send generals back to Sheol like we can with the lower ranks, only capture and torture them."

She blinked, confused. "Princes? Sheol?"

"Yes, princes that rule the realm of the dead. Humans have all sorts of names for it, along with their ridiculous imagery. I assume you've heard of Hell, Hades? Lake of Fire?"

Emma gave a stiff nod. "You don't know if this general is after me though? Not for sure, anyway."

"No," Blaze admitted, and he sounded almost relieved about that fact.

"Do you have any powers like me?"

His jaw worked from side-to-side, as he seemed to consider his response. He was silent for so long that Emma thought he wasn't going to answer.

"No," he said at last.

She felt a pang of disappointment in her chest. Loneliness. Without a word, she stepped around him and tip-toed off the dock, careful not to step on anything she didn't recognize. A viscous green liquid that she guessed was blood was splattered in gruesome streaks across the wood. Emma's stomach roiled.

"Surely you have more questions," he said, walking beside her.

She stopped and faced him. Clutched in his hand at his side was her backpack. He held it out for her, and she swung it onto her back.

"Uh, yeah. Is that a sword?" She gestured to one of the weapons peeking over his shoulder.

He blinked. "Yes."

"Wouldn't a gun be more effective?"

"No." He paused. "Our swords are infused with the blood of the Righteous Ones. Even if we could do that with bullets, Shediem heal too quickly." Emma couldn't help but look behind her at the carnage strewn on the dock.

She wrapped her arms around herself as she started walking again, Blaze eating up the same amount of ground in half the steps. The cold had seeped into her bones, making her teeth chatter. Blaze glanced down at her, concerned.

"I'd offer you my jacket," he said. "But I don't have one."

Emma shook her head. "I'm okay," she lied. Her mind whirled and raced. There was too much to comprehend.

"Axel and I will clean that up," Blaze said with a nod toward the dock. He likely saw the question in her face—what would happen if someone saw the fish-like bodies with severed heads.

"There is something *I* want to know." When he halted, it was as if an invisible cord pulled tight, jerking her to a stop. Blaze crossed his arms over his muscled chest, his t-shirt pulled tautly.

She forced her gaze higher. "What do you want to know?"

"Can you sense Shediem?"

She nodded. "Yeah, I feel a cold weight in my chest." For a moment, she pondered asking about Rowek. The feeling of electricity pumping through her. What did that make him? Were there other supernatural beings beside Giborim and Shediem? Something inside her didn't want to know.

A look of relief crossed Blaze's face as he ran his fingers through his dark curls.

Emma recalled Axel mentioning the Shediem's scent, so she asked, "What do Shediem smell like?" Thinking back to every time she had faced a Shediem, in the alley, the Nybasses had just smelled of burnt, rotting corpses. The Nickor reeked of fish.

The scent of Rowek's cologne rose to her mind unbidden. Whatever he was, he didn't smell bad.

"Death," Blaze said without hesitation.

Emma's breath caught in her throat.

"Any other questions?"

Part of Emma wanted to go home and curl up in bed, and the other part wanted to find Rowek. To confront him. To ask why he didn't help her, and to ask what he was. The memory of his unimaginable power shot through her like a bolt of lightning. *It could be yours*, something inside her purred. *All you have to do is touch him.* But she had touched him, and nothing happened.

She shook herself mentally. "It's all a bit overwhelming," Emma said.

Blaze nodded, understanding in his gaze. "Can I give you a lift home?" he asked.

Emma shook her head again and pulled her phone out of her backpack. She groaned at the chip in the top right-hand corner of her screen. It didn't affect anything, but if her mother saw it, she would lecture her on being clumsy. The lie was much better than the truth.

"I have a friend I can call," Emma explained. She didn't feel like accepting rides from any more strangers, even if they did save her life. "Thank you, though."

He nodded. "I'll wait with you until your friend comes. I'll even keep my distance if that would make you feel more comfortable."

She gave him a small smile. "I'd feel better if you stayed close." In truth, the heat radiating from his body was soothing. She wasn't sure if she should trust him, but he had saved her and had offered an explanation for most of everything that had been going on. Even if the explanation was crazy and she didn't want to believe it. But somewhere, deep within her soul, she knew it was the truth. She couldn't explain it, but it was as if her very DNA confirmed it.

Now she had only to find out what her mother knew. Who was her father? What was Emma? Those answers would likely unlock the mystery of her strange power. And she knew exactly where to begin.

Adrianna pulled into the marina in twenty minutes flat. Blaze's expression darkened at the sight of her friend's car, which appeared to be held together with duct tape. Emma thanked Blaze, whose only response was a stiff nod. As soon as the door closed, Adrianna began questioning her at lightning speed.

"Who is *he*? Where is Rowek? Why are you wet? Are you hurt?"

Emma filled her in on as much as she could, explaining that Rowek had ditched her, which wasn't a lie; and that she had fallen into the water and that Blaze had saved her. Adrianna accepted her story with little effort.

"What a jerk, I'm so sorry, Em," Adrianna said sympathetically.

"Moral of the story, don't accept rides from random guys," Emma said, trying to sound light-hearted, but it came out bitter. Adrianna pursed her lips at Emma's attempted humor.

"You're taking this much better than I would have."

Emma stared out the window, watching Blaze's figure shrink in the wing mirror. "How are you?" she asked.

The heat pumping through the vents kept the chills away, but the bone-deep ache of cold remained. Adrianna shot Emma a tight smile. "I'm okay. I've been having lots of headaches lately."

Emma frowned. "You should see a doctor."

Her friend bobbed her head in non-committal agreement.

They arrived in front of Emma's house as the first drops of rain splashed on the window. She grimaced before pulling her bag into her lap.

"Do you want to come in for some coffee?" Emma asked.

Adrianna sighed heavily, looking out at the dreary sky. "No, I've got to get home before my dad. He's been threatening to take my car keys away again if I don't clean up my room."

Emma's heart sank, but she forced a smile. "Okay, well I'll see you tomorrow. And thanks for coming to my rescue."

"Anytime," Adrianna replied with a sympathetic smile. Then Emma climbed out into the rain.

LEVAROTH

H e had seen it with his own eyes. Emma Duvall had supernatural powers. By all accounts she was human. All but one. What she was, remained a mystery.

Levaroth wanted to keep her a secret from his master for now, until he was confident that she could be useful to their cause. If she was only a danger to his kind, then she would have to be eliminated.

Tonight's audience with his master was just the usual progress report, yet he was on edge.

The grand, sprawling throne room was pulsing with loud, exotic music. Its every beat hit deep in his chest, rattling his ribcage. Levaroth rolled his shoulders back, willing himself to look straight ahead as he walked beneath the dark, stone archway. It was high enough to accommodate his wings, but he kept them tucked firmly against his back anyway.

He stopped in front of a gossamer curtain where the silhouettes of female bodies were cast against it, swaying and moving like charmed snakes. *How accurate*, Levaroth thought to himself. The women that vied for the attention of a dark prince were snakes indeed, using the cruelest, sharpest tactics to ensure their place in his private chambers. They did so knowing they would not likely walk out again.

The beast that stood outside of the entrance to the throne room, was Geryon, personal guard to the prince.

He regarded Levaroth through black beady eyes that were narrowed into slits with the same level of distaste that he always did.

Geryon had two long, twisted horns that protruded from the top of his furry skull. He was covered in a thick, golden fur from his head to his torso, with a snout like a boar and broad shoulders. From the waist down, his fur was replaced with a dark blue hide that covered the hindquarters he stood on, his feet like that of a dragon. Every inch of him was honed muscle. Not that it was needed. The prince simply enjoyed his company, though Levaroth wasn't sure why. Geryon was an ill-natured brute who spoke mainly in the form of disapproving grunts.

"Come in, Levaroth," the deep, rumbling voice of his master boomed above the noise.

Geryon had either communicated his presence with his master through their telepathic link, or the prince had sensed Levaroth himself.

"Master, may we conduct our business in private?" Levaroth asked.

Geryon snorted contemptuously.

"Come in, Levaroth, surely one of these delectable creatures can entertain even you."

A giggle came from one of the women no doubt currently *entertaining* his master. Levaroth growled in frustration.

Pushing aside the curtain, he entered the festivities. The walls were lined with tables heaped with trays of food in front of dancing flames that gave off no heat. Plush cushions littered the floor. Shediem of every rank covered them, entwined with human men and women in various states of undress. Females of questionably young ages moved their bodies to the beat all around the stone platform.

And on the stone platform, perched atop a throne constructed entirely from human bones, was his prince. He was smaller in his human form, but still as intimidating as he was otherworldly. He lounged in the too-large seat, the buttons of his white shirt undone, revealing a smooth, alabaster chest. His jacket of black brocade adorned with swirls of ruby and gold threads hung behind him.

His blood-red eyes, bright with the consumption of the room's energy, tracked Levaroth as he weaved around the groups of sexual indulgence before lowering himself to one knee, his head bowed.

"Asmodeus." Levaroth's tone was reverent.

"Rise," the prince ordered. Levaroth obeyed. "How are things Earth-side, dear friend?"

"Everything is going according to plan. Better in fact. The humans scare like rodents." The disgust on his face wasn't faked. If the dancers heard his slight, they didn't show it.

Across the room, a pair of sapphire eyes caught his. A young girl with shimmering golden hair threaded through the throng with a tray of flutes. The assorted mix of magic-laced drinks encouraged the bystanders to join the pleasure-fest, giving them the endurance to last for days with little food or water.

The servant's gaze flicked up to his. She halted, expression turning cold. Obviously, she was not one of the volunteers. He extended his senses, blocking out the rife lust. Her scent reached him, and his eyes widened.

Asmodeus cleared his throat, drawing Levaroth's attention back to the task at hand. A smirk lifted the prince's lips as he looked out over his guests. His shadowed jaw, mussed hair and rumpled clothing told Levaroth he had recently participated in some of the party's more energetic activities.

Levaroth continued, "The Giborim have become quite active. They were able to trace me in Seattle—"

"How?" Asmodeus demanded, his red eyes flaring. The servant girl had moved closer and was openly watching them now. Levaroth caught a flicker of emotion in her crystal blue eyes—pride?

"An ex-member of the Russian mafia sold vital information to the Americans regarding our weapons manufacturing," Levaroth answered, keeping his tone even, "I was the one who questioned him. I made the mistake of getting too near their territory."

The serving girl wore the faintest of smirks, and his suspicion was confirmed. The only question was, did Asmodeus know? As Levaroth opened his mouth to reprimand her for eavesdropping, the prince spoke,

"You can have her when the party is over if you wish."

The girl's face went from stunned to red with outrage in less than a second. She started to advance toward them, her mouth opening to let loose whatever venom would likely result in her death.

Levaroth moved, blocking Asmodeus's view of her.

"No, thank you, my Prince." His head dipped in a show of respect. "I have training I wish to accomplish before I return. All work, no play I'm afraid." He gave an easy grin that the prince returned.

"Surely you can carve out an hour or two to…unwind." He motioned with his hand to the bunches of debauchery.

In truth, Levaroth craved a release, but he rarely allowed himself the opportunity. Usually, it was because no human man or woman, or even a plethora of them, had truly brought satisfaction. They were weak and small. They tired easily and were either too eager to please him or too insecure to let themselves find enjoyment.

One female, in particular, stirred a lust he had never known before. He dismissed the image of her that had surfaced in his mind. Thousands of years allowed him to control his sexual cravings.

He found his release in another pleasure.

The art of death he enjoyed above all else. With such fragile creatures, there was a thin line one walked to prolong their suffering. The slightest bit of excessive force would snuff them out. They had too many weaknesses, their healing was too slow. Any damage incurred had to be calculated. They could just as easily die from shock, toxemia, and infection as a bullet to the brain.

"Not this evening, master."

The prince's brow drew up, but he didn't offer again. "Very well. Get out of here, before you bore me with your stuffy personality." He waved Levaroth away as he rose to his feet. The prince's eyes were locked onto one of the dancers, consuming her with the gaze of a hungry lion.

Levaroth lowered his head again and strode out of the room, leaving the intoxicating scents and sounds behind. Before he let the curtain fall behind him, he risked a glance back at the girl who stared after him. If she valued her life, she would continue her duties without drawing any more attention to herself.

Something in her gaze had changed. She watched as Levaroth let the curtain fall. He wasn't sure if he imagined it or not, but he thought the burning hatred in her expression had been replaced with something softer. Gratitude?

When he was far enough away to not risk being heard by even Geryon, he huffed a sigh of relief. He needed to blow off some steam, and since using any of the humans as target practice was out of the question, he decided to train.

After several hours, he had put every formidable opponent in the ring that he could find and still he was not satisfied. He'd fought against spikes, talons, ice, and every weapon their training hall possessed. The few hits he took all stitched back together in a matter of moments.

He flattened his sore wings against the stone wall, his head coming to rest against it, eyes closed while his breathing slowed. Several lower-ranking Shediem huddled in a corner, casting glances in his direction while muttering to each other. Levaroth peeled one eye open, watching them, irritation churned with unrest. His caged beast was pacing, snarling, tugging on its chains. He needed to kill.

"Get back to work," he snapped at them. They exchanged annoyed looks as they broke apart and went back to their stations. He watched them for several more moments until the door to the hall flew open.

"General!" The club-headed Shax rushed toward him, all four of his ape-like arms swinging by his sides. Short, black horns protruded from his skull in a ring around the top of his head. A pair of matching tusks sat on either side of his bulbous nose.

Levaroth pushed off the wall, his long strides eating up the distance, meeting the creature halfway.

"Did you find something?" he asked in a low voice.

The Shediem nodded eagerly.

"Outside."

Levaroth spun him around and pushed him out onto the dusty path. The creature waited with his wide mouth clamped shut. One of his hairy arms reached up and scratched his bald head nervously with thick, sausage-like fingers.

When Levaroth was sure that no unwanted ears would hear their conversation, he spoke, "What did you find, Usik?"

The Shediem rocked back on its heels. "This level of secrecy is going to require double," it said in its eerily pleasant voice.

Levaroth's vision edged with red, his nostrils flaring. He lunged forward a step, his wings stretched out behind him in a show of dominance. He towered over the Shediem by more than double, but it didn't cower. What it lacked in size it made up for in cunning.

The Shax's mouth parted in a vicious grin. Thick, green fluid oozed from around its canines. The venom was only lethal to humans and animals, but it was still capable of causing extraordinary pain that would last at least a day for Levaroth's kind.

Levaroth gave a deceptively calm laugh. "How about I sweeten the deal?" He drew his wings back in. The Shediem narrowed its black eyes. "I'll give you triple for your silence. However," Levaroth bent closer to the creature, his tone menacing as he said, "if you ever try to threaten me again, I will ensure your silence remains eternal." The Shediem's eyes widened, fear flickering in them before it snapped its jaw closed and nodded.

"Thought so. Now, what did you find?"

The Shediem hesitated, considering its words. "Laura Duvall is the girl's biological mother and as far as I can find, a human. However, it's like the mother sprung up out of nowhere. Her records were particularly difficult to find as well. It's possible she is a criminal. I checked her birth records and the parents listed are fake identities. They never existed."

"What of the girl's father?"

Usik clasped his hands together in front of himself. "Still working on that, I'm afraid. Emma's birth certificate was issued by the state of Texas, but the hospital she was supposedly born in burned down a few months after her birth date, and none of the staff previously employed there have any records of her birth. Vital Records has nothing either. If I could get a hold of the mother—"

"Not yet," Levaroth replied, harsher than he meant to. "Let me know when you hit a wall, and I'll see what I can do."

Usik dipped his head before vanishing. Levaroth couldn't help but feel impressed at the thoroughness of the investigation, but irritation overrode the sensation. Whoever Emma Duvall was, her mother had gone to great lengths to keep her invisible. Numerous theories floated around in his mind, but few stuck.

Tension coiled inside him once again. He started back toward the training hall when a pair of sultry brown eyes met his. One of the dancers he had seen at Asmodeus's party leaned a hip against the stone building swathed in only a sheer, golden robe that hugged her curves, leaving nothing to the imagination. No doubt Asmodeus had sent her.

"You look like you could do with a break," she said, her voice a silky purr.

Levaroth chuckled. Her scent was rich and her lust intoxicating. She strode toward him, her hips swaying like they had several hours ago. But now they were almost within his reach.

"Surely you're the one who could do with a break," he replied huskily. Unable to stop himself, he stepped closer. He breathed her in as her hands slid up his chest. His blood heated as the covering slid off her shoulders and pooled on the ground at her feet.

"I don't tire easily," she said. It felt like a challenge. One that Levaroth was willing to accept.

"I'll be the judge of that," he growled.

Then they were in his private quarters, her back on the bed that was only ever used for similar occasions.

She had been right, but the aggression he poured out on her didn't subside. Every time he opened his eyes and saw her jet-black hair or deep brown eyes, a sense of wrongness filled the pit of his stomach. He tried to pretend the warm, supple body beneath him had sparkling green eyes and wild auburn waves, but the feel of her didn't fit his imaginings.

He tired of her. Of her demanding that he look at her. So he fed from her until her body grew limp.

Levaroth stared down at the woman's naked form. The glow of the candlelight on the wall made the graying hue of her skin even more sickly. A nagging sensation clawed in his gut like a wild animal. He had never felt it before, but he had tasted it on humans more times than he could ever count. It felt just as unpleasant as it tasted.

In an attempt to put it to rest, he summoned several human servants and ordered them to take her body and bury it. But long after the evidence was removed, the guilt remained.

EMMA

As promised, on Saturday, Emma and her mother went from one used car lot to another. She discovered that her mother knew a great deal about vehicles. She also learned that her mother could make men twice her size cower with just a look. After the third grown man stalked away in a huff, Emma was beginning to feel run down. One had even cried.

After a quick stop for lunch, they stopped at the fifth car lot. Finally, after forty-eight rejected vehicles—which included a deep blue, fully-restored 1970 Ford Mustang that her mother flat out refused—Emma climbed into the driver's seat of a metallic black Honda CR-V that smelled faintly of lemon upholstery cleaner.

Her mother fired questions at the tall, balding salesman until his forehead was covered in a fine sheen of sweat. Once it passed inspection by her usual mechanic, Emma drove it off the lot, grinning from ear to ear.

Emma tucked away her questions, promising herself she would ask them soon.

Her dreams were haunted by scaly-skinned creatures, waking her more than once, gasping for air. The memory of her lungs and throat bursting with water kept her awake, staring at the ceiling.

On the drive to school Monday morning Adrianna looked her over before commenting, "You look like crap, Em."

"Thanks," Emma replied dryly. "Haven't been sleeping well."

Adrianna gave her a sympathetic smile. "Me either," she whispered, almost too quietly for Emma to hear.

She opened her mouth to respond, but Adrianna turned the radio up, dancing in her seat. Emma wanted to tell Adrianna the truth about Friday afternoon, but even when Emma mentioned the attack in the alley, Adrianna was quick to change the subject. It was almost as if she had pushed it so far into the back of her mind, she was rejecting it as reality entirely. Emma didn't blame her. The bombings were enough to deal with. The possibility that the attacks were by supernatural beings complicated matters. Humans had weaknesses. They were changeable. But the creatures in the alley were not.

When a sad song came on, Adrianna turned it down. Emma opened her mouth to finally form the words, just as Adrianna began chattering about Aaron. Emma gripped the steering wheel tight, her body spiked hot with anger. Why were her emotions so out of control lately? She inhaled a deep breath to calm herself, loosening her grip on the wheel.

Emma listened as Adrianna told her she had given him her number after being rejected by Sean. That they had stayed up until one in the morning talking about music. She loved Adrianna and knew she deserved to be happy, but her own chest ached with the need to talk to someone. To share her burdens too.

They pulled into the school parking lot, and Emma smiled. She had a vehicle of her own.

Unable to stop herself, her eyes searched the parking lot for another vehicle, and her stomach dipped when she didn't find it.

"I slept with my dad."

"What?" Emma exclaimed.

"Finally," Adrianna sighed exasperatedly. "I've been rattling off a list of grotesque things to get your attention."

"Sorry," Emma replied sheepishly. "I was—"

"Looking for Rowek," she finished for her. Emma gave a small nod in reply, not daring to see her friend's expression. "It's okay.

I'd like to stick my fist through his face, too."

Emma laughed. The feeling was strange, but it helped calm her. She didn't tell her friend that she didn't want to punch him so much as demand answers from him. What he was and why she could sense him was at the top of her list.

They climbed out of the vehicle and swung their backpacks over their shoulders before starting for the door. Emma pushed all thoughts of Rowek from her mind as she entered the bustling entryway.

Adrianna waved. "See you in third period," she called over her shoulder before limping away to her first class. Emma went the opposite direction, her eyes scanning the homecoming banners and posters.

A smile lit her face. She hadn't been to a homecoming game or dance since they lived in Virginia when she was in ninth grade. She had managed to convince her mother to let her stay at a friend's house for the night. It had been her first ever sleepover and school dance.

The morning passed uneventfully. In the hallway, between classes, Emma received a small smile from the petite freshman girl she had practically trampled a week ago. She looked more at ease now, the timid look in her eyes, gone.

At lunch, Emma and Adrianna left to buy tacos with their spare pocket change. When they returned, Adrianna sighed dramatically before heading to class while Emma sat beneath her favourite willow tree and peeled open a book to read.

The wind whipped through the branches, tearing at the pages of Emma's book and she huffed. Then the wind stilled. Her fingers prickled and her heart felt as if it flipped over in her chest.

"Mind if I join you?" Rowek asked above her, startling her.

Emma looked up, her eyes narrowing to slits. "Why do you do that?"

His brows lifted. "Do what?"

"Only come to school when you feel like it? You'll fail your classes. If they don't kick you out first."

Rowek smiled, amused. "I'm not worried. I wasn't going to come at all, but I needed you to know I didn't just ditch you on Friday."

Her anger rose. "Then please, tell me what happened. Where did you go?"

He sat on the ground, not looking at her. "When I came back, I saw those…things. I wanted to help…but then I saw what you were doing to one of them." His eyes rose to meet hers, a glimmer of awe, or maybe fear in them that made Emma's stomach tighten.

"Your eyes glowed and then when you grabbed one of them, it crumbled into nothing. I was so freaked out; I didn't know what to do. Then when they crowded around you, I couldn't tell what was happening. I…It sounds awful, but I felt like I couldn't move." His head lowered, in shame, and Emma bit her lip.

"It's okay," she said.

When Rowek looked up again, his eyes were filled with anger. "No, it wasn't okay. I feel like such an idiot. When I saw three huge dudes with swords, I bolted. They didn't look like they were trying to hurt you, but it doesn't matter because I should have helped."

"What could you have done?" Emma asked.

Rowek stared at her for a moment, then sighed. "I have to tell you something…about myself. I think I can trust you now… because I think maybe, you might be like me."

Emma's heart beat harder, faster at his words. "Tell me."

He hesitated for a moment. "When our skin touched that first day, did you feel, like a shock or a jolt?"

She nodded slowly. "It was more like…I could feel power in you."

Rowek winced. "Yeah, well, that's because…I can do magic."

Emma blinked once. Twice. "Magic?"

Rowek gave a nervous laugh. "Yeah. I'm a Spellcaster, not a very good one. I've only just come into my powers, so it's a little unstable." He held out a fist, and one by one he opened his digits. Inside, dancing and twirling on his palm, was a small, bluish flame.

She gasped, staring at the flame, entranced by its beauty. Her own hand lifted, reaching to feel its heat. But there was none.

Rowek closed his hand, and the flame extinguished. When Emma met his smoldering gaze, her cheeks warmed. He drew her closer with just his intense expression. The two of them sharing an intimate secret.

Could she wield flame too? Was her power to turn those monstrous creatures to dust some type of special magic? And when she had killed the Nickor, she had taken its power for herself, though it didn't last long.

"Will I be able to do that too?" Emma asked.

Rowek's lips split into a wide smile. "I don't know. But I think what I saw was just the beginning of your powers. I can sense them in you too."

Emma frowned. "How is this possible? My mother doesn't have magic."

"Does your father?"

She shrugged. "I don't know."

Rowek stroked a single blade of grass. "I can help you try to find out. And maybe teach you what I know."

"Yes! Please!" she burst out. Rowek laughed as the bell rang. He looked around as the double doors flew open and people began to trickle out. Adrianna would come find her soon.

Rowek stood, as if sensing that fact.

"Tomorrow," he said. Then he started down the path that wrapped around the school, and out of view.

Emma's heart and mind raced as she tried to come to grips with this new fact. Perhaps she was not as dangerous as she had imagined. And this power inside her, it could be controlled.

Hope brought a smile to her face.

Her heart felt light in her chest as she and Adrianna discussed dress styles and colors for Homecoming as they weaved through the cars in the parking lot.

A soothing warmth washed over her. She felt at peace, her limbs light, and her mind carefree.

Scanning the parking lot, Emma's heart shot up in her throat when she spotted her car.

Blaze stood beside it, watching her.

"Whoa," Adrianna breathed, clearly seeing what she was seeing.

His eyes were glued to her as she and Adrianna made their way to him. The sun glinted off his eyes, giving them an icy blue look. A stark contrast to his dark hair.

He assessed her from head to toe as she stopped in front of him. As if satisfied to see she was unharmed, his gaze flicked to Adrianna.

"I don't believe I've had the pleasure." He extended his hand. Adrianna grinned as she shook it; her entire hand swallowed by his.

"Love the accent," Adrianna said. Blaze smiled, dazzling them both with perfectly straight, white teeth.

"I was just wondering if I could borrow Emma for a moment."

The spell his smile had cast over Adrianna evaporated instantly. She withdrew her hand to cross her arms over her chest, a hip thrown to the side.

"No offense, but anything you need to say to her you can say in front of me. The last guy I let cart her off, tossed her in the bay."

Blaze glanced at Emma with a single brow raised. Emma forced herself not to flinch. That wasn't exactly what she had told Adrianna, but when that girl was mad, everything became a fault in her eyes. She wanted to tell Adrianna the truth, and she would, she told herself. When the moment was right.

"It's okay, A," Emma assured her. "It'll just take a second. Here." Emma handed Adrianna her car keys. "You can pick the station."

Adrianna narrowed her eyes at Emma before switching her gaze back to Blaze, who held his hands up in mock surrender.

"There's no water around. I swear she'll be returned to you completely dry."

Adrianna sighed before snatching the keys dangling from Emma's fingers, muttering something she couldn't hear. Blaze made a noise that sounded like a laugh before it morphed into a cough.

"Lead the way," Emma said, ignoring the amused look on his face.

Blaze stalked toward the cluster of trees away from the parking lot. Emma hurried to keep up with his long strides, distracted by the way the muscles in his back moved under his shirt.

Without warning, he spun around. Before her face could collide with his chest, he had his hands on both of her shoulders. His scent washed over her, and she had to keep herself from breathing it in deeply.

Her cheeks heated as she stepped out of his grasp, letting the breeze clear her head.

"What did you want to talk about?"

"I came to warn you. You'll probably start to hear about it in the next two or three days, but hundreds of women have gone missing all over the country."

Surprise jolted through Emma. "Why?" she asked.

A muscle in his square jaw twitched. "I'm not sure yet. We have reason to believe the Shediem are behind the abductions."

"What would demons—uh, Shediem—want with women?" Her body went cold as she considered what they could be doing to them.

"It's not human women that are missing," he said. Emma felt the hairs on her arms stand on end. "It's Giborim females. Some are just children, and…" His gaze flashed, turning to steel. "I lost my mother and sister to those bastards."

Emma's lip parted on a sharp breath. "They were taken? When?"

Blaze looked out at the cars speeding away on the street.

"My mother was killed in an attack in our family home, but my sister…they took her." When his eyes met Emma's, the flare of unmasked rage made her breath catch in her throat. "I imagine she's dead now, but I can guarantee they made her suffer in all sorts of despicable ways. She was only eight." His throat bobbed, his accent thicker than she'd ever heard it.

Tears stung her eyes. "That's awful."

"Axel and I spent over a century tracking down every Shediem responsible. We've captured all except one."

Emma's eyes widened. "A century?"

"Yes." His expression seemed to change, as if realizing that she had little knowledge of his kind.

"How old are you?" She was practically shouting now.

"I'm two-hundred years old," he answered.

Emma gaped at him. "So you're immortal?" she asked. Her mind raced with questions.

"No. Giborim can live a long time. Our accelerated healing makes aging take a lot longer, but most of us die doing what we were commanded to do before old age ever reaches us."

The ease with which he spoke of aging and death was unnerving. Emma opened her mouth, but fear of having every question pour out at once made her close it again.

"Why come to warn me?" she asked. "I'm not a Giborim. I might not even be human."

Blaze studied her for a moment, opening his mouth then closing it again. At last he said, "They still might take an interest in you. I want you to be careful. We'll keep an eye out, but there's never been Shediem activity like this before. They're planning something, and it's not good."

Emma swayed, feeling suddenly nauseous. A very powerful Shediem could be lurking in the area, waiting to kill Emma, or worse, capture her. *At least I can kill anything that tries*, she told herself. Her chest heaved with uneven breaths.

As if he could read her thoughts, Blaze leaned closer to her. "You don't have to look so afraid. You're strong. You'll be okay."

103

Emma met his gaze and liquid warmth spread through her. "Do you think that general is still in the area?"

He straightened. "Levaroth. I think so, yes."

"So these abductions," Emma said. "They've been going on for a while then?"

"As long as humans have existed, but never to this magnitude. Something else is going on. In the past, it was mainly human abductions, but spread out over time. Likely to have a population of slaves. So many Giborim, and all females, tells me this was either a message of some kind, or they need them for something."

Emma's heart beat furiously. First the bombings, now people were being taken.

"Blaze," a sharp male voice shouted. Blaze's gaze grew more intense—as if he wanted to throw her over his shoulder and carry her away—before he slowly turned in the direction of a man jogging toward them.

Emma took in a steadying breath, shaking off the irrational loss she felt when Blaze had looked away. Every look, no matter how small, had her melting into a puddle at his feet. Even after she found out he was more than ten times her age. Emma reminded herself that though he only looked five or six years older than her, he was beyond entertaining the desires of a seventeen-year-old.

The male stopped ten or so feet away, his dark eyes flicked to her. He had short, dark hair and was dressed in the same military style clothing as Blaze. The man's lip curled up in disgust like he smelled something foul.

"Find anything?" Blaze asked. After several beats, the man dragged his cold stare away from Emma.

"No. If you're done here, we should keep searching." His tone was as frigid as the look he had given her.

"Carry on, I'll catch up with you guys," Blaze replied. The male didn't move. His hate-filled gaze made her want to shrivel up and let the ground swallow her whole. "Jake." Blaze's voice lowered in warning.

"I think you're getting attached, *mi hermano*."

"Leave, Jake. We'll discuss this later," Blaze said. The man's body stiffened.

Emma could feel heat rolling off Blaze in waves. Feeling fairly certain they were about to exchange blows she said, "I'm gonna go." Emma started to turn when both men replied in unison.

"Good idea."

"No."

Emma looked between them awkwardly. "It's no problem. I'll see you later."

This time Blaze didn't argue. Didn't look at her as she retreated from the trees.

Adrianna was standing outside the vehicle. Relief smoothed her furrowed brow and narrowed eyes when she saw Emma.

Emma could barely make out snippets of what the men were saying now.

"...a threat... needs to be dealt with..."

"...no idea what she is... handling it..."

Emma felt her stomach twisting into knots and sped up to get out of hearing range, but the next words stopped her in her tracks.

"...kill her or I will." Jake had raised his voice, and Emma knew it was so she could hear it too.

A scuffle broke out behind her, and she whirled around. Through a gap in the trees, she could see a blur of limbs. She hesitated for a moment before sprinting back toward them.

A crack of splintering wood sounded before the men came into view. Blaze had Jake by the collar of his jacket, his back pressed against one of the trees.

"Emma. Leave," Blaze said without looking at her. Jake glared at her. A trail of blood ran from his nose which now looked broken.

Anger bubbled up inside her, directed at Jake. "Look, I don't know what I've done to make you hate me so much, but whatever it is, get over it."

Emma had only just gotten the words out of her mouth

when Jake spat right at her. A deep growl sounded from Blaze as he whipped him forward before slamming him back against the tree. It groaned from the force.

"That's enough, Jake," Blaze ground out. "Apologize to the girl."

Emma felt as if the label "girl" should be offensive, but she supposed that was all she was in the face of men who had been alive for centuries.

The males glared at each other for a moment, and as if some unspoken conversation took place between them, Jake schooled his expression, tucking away the loathing she knew was still boiling inside him.

His gaze was still far from friendly as he bit out a single word. "Sorry."

Blaze unclenched his fists. Without a word, a blur of dark skin and black clothing sped away, leaving Blaze and Emma alone. Blaze didn't turn around as he sighed, then ran a hand through his jet-black hair.

Her eyes were wide. Were Giborim capable of moving as fast as the Flash?

"I'm sorry about my friend."

Emma opened her mouth to reply as the snap of a twig made her spin around. Adrianna limped toward them with an irritated look.

"What the hell, Emma?" she said.

A small breeze blew her hair away from her shoulders, and she craned her neck to see the spot where Blaze had been standing now empty.

"Sorry, I…" Emma racked her brain for an excuse. "I thought I saw an injured squirrel," she finished lamely.

Adrianna rose a thick, black brow, clearly not buying Emma's lie. "Where is that guy?" she asked, peering around Emma as if she could be hiding him. The thought almost brought a smile to Emma's face, but the lingering feeling of humiliation and confusion wouldn't let her.

"Oh, he left. He was just checking to see if I was okay after Friday."

The lies built, and Adrianna looked at her with an unreadable expression for a moment before heaving a sigh.

"We should go. We're pretty much the last ones here, and I have a popsicle-stick castle I need to build."

"Ooh, really? Can I help?"

Emma didn't have to feign interest as she followed Adrianna back to the SUV. She craved a distraction. As they walked, she felt as if every shadow hid a monster waiting to pounce. As if at any moment a terrifying Shediem general would appear before her and snatch her away for some reason she was certain she didn't want to know.

She pulled herself into the driver's seat and scanned the area one last time, unable to shake the chill that crept down her spine.

EMMA

"So you know all about Giborim and Shediem then?" Emma asked, setting aside another dusty, old book.

Rowek's fingers, which brushed along worn spines, paused for a fraction of a second. He turned, facing her. "Yeah. Spellcasters can sense them both."

"Have you seen either? Before Friday I mean."

Rowek looked back to the shelves lined with volumes that looked as though they hadn't been touched in decades. "No."

"Those guys you saw with swords, they're—"

"Giborim," Rowek said before Emma could. His voice was low.

Emma continued, "And the creatures on the dock, Blaze said they're called Nickor."

Rowek's expression darkened for a moment at the mention of Blaze's name, before he nodded. "I went home and looked them up. There are loads of Shediem types. It makes me want to be able to control my magic even more. You can't trust anyone but your own kind, you know?"

Emma bit her bottom lip. "I don't know, the Giborim don't seem bad. They keep the Shediem from completely taking over."

Rowek snorted but didn't reply.

"Look at this one," he said suddenly, holding out a book entitled *The Supernatural Realm: Separating Fact from Fiction.*

Emma reached up for it from her spot on the carpet and

sighed. "If none of the other thirty books we've looked through have anything to do with people that can turn monsters to ash, I doubt this one will either."

She flipped through the pages, spying drawn depictions of men, some stunningly beautiful, others with three animal-like faces, and all of them with wings. Angels. *The righteous ones.*

The Fallen Ones, who impregnated human women, resulting in superhuman children. Even the accounts of the offspring had elongated heads, standing at least eight feet tall. Blaze and his brother were tall, but only six and a half feet at a max.

Their incredible strength and speed were noted, but in almost every book she had seen so far, it claimed that their race was killed off.

But Emma knew they weren't.

"You know," Rowek said, contemplating. "I think I have a few books from my father about Spellcasters. We all inherit the *Book of Deeper Magic*, which is just really advanced spells, but I can look to see if any of the others say anything about it. I know that all Spellcasters have their own strengths. I'm an elemental, so water, fire, wind, and earth are easiest for me to manipulate, but really fire is my true speciality."

Emma nodded. "Okay."

Rowek had told her to meet him in the library after lunch, where they scoured for information on her power and how to control it.

"So your father is the Spellcaster?" she asked.

Rowek nodded. "I don't know if my mother was too, but when I didn't show any signs of having magic after my fourteenth birthday, my father tried all sorts of things to scare it out of me. He hated me; I could see it in his eyes.

"He uses his magic in wars, strengthening our army's weapons. He can make things indestructible. Not people though." He shrugged.

"How did he try to scare your magic out of you?"

Rowek gave a dry laugh. "He tried to drown me a couple

times, tried to run me over once or twice. One time, when he was teaching me how to fire multiple weapons at once, he made me run through the obstacle course while he fired at me because I missed. The point was to try to use wind to knock the bullets out of the air, or even to use a shield to protect myself."

Emma covered her mouth with her hands, eyes wide. "That's not just illegal, that's barbaric."

Rowek shrugged. "I was only shot once before I found the ability to throw fire around me. The bullets burned away to nothing. I thought he'd be impressed, but I don't think he even blinked."

A lump formed in Emma's throat; her eyes misty. "Wow, I'm really sorry."

"Don't be," Rowek replied. "He did what he had to do to prepare me for the future. I'm already one of the best soldier's my father has ever trained."

Her brow furrowed. "Have you already enlisted?"

Rowek paused. "Kind of."

A pang of sadness flared in her chest. Though she was thankful for every soldier that was willing to sacrifice their life for the country she loved, she couldn't help but wish that it wasn't Rowek. One day, he'd be sent away to war with no guarantee of returning.

With the way things were going in the world, Emma knew that day would be too soon. If it came to it, would she fight too?

She knew almost instantly the answer was yes.

"Do you know anything about the general, Levaroth?"

Rowek's eyes flashed with surprise, and something else she couldn't decipher. "I've heard of him. My father…has had some dealings with him."

Emma's heart thundered. "I think he's looking for me."

Rowek's laugh was harsh, bitter. "I hate to break it to you, Sunshine, but powerful Shediem don't *look* for people. They find them." His stare was blank, unfeeling. "If Levaroth wanted to find you, you'd already be found."

Emma released a shaky breath.

Rowek blinked, as if coming back to himself. He smiled lazily. "I wouldn't worry about it. Shediem trade favors with Spellcasters in exchange for what they can do, but you're too new, too inexperienced. And besides, you don't even belong to a coven."

Her mind spun. Spellcasters had covens? She wondered if she would need a black cat and a broomstick too.

"There's no, like, school for witches?"

Rowek threw his head back and laughed heartily, earning several angry shushes from nearby students.

"I take it that's a no," Emma grumbled.

Rowek chuckled as he sat down across from her, leaning against the frame of the wooden shelf. Stacks of books were scattered around them. Emma clutched the one in her lap tighter.

"First of all, don't call a Spellcaster a witch unless you want to be turned into an insect and crushed. Secondly, you can join a coven if you want. Often, they'll try to recruit you, especially if you have special powers. Some just go it alone, they're not as strong as they would be in a coven, but they also aren't bound by the coven's rules."

"So, I guess I'm not going to get accepted to Hogwarts anytime soon then." Emma sighed dramatically.

Rowek cocked his head to the side. "Hogwarts? That sounds like some kind of disease."

It was Emma's turn to laugh. "Okay, you lend me your witch-y books, and I'll lend you Harry Potter."

Rowek smiled, and it made Emma's stomach flutter. "I want to take you to dinner on Friday."

Emma sat, frozen for several moments. "What, like…a date?" she asked.

Rowek shrugged. "Whatever you want it to be."

Her face warmed, and she knew she must be blushing because Rowek smiled again.

"I don't think my mom will let me," she whispered, looking back down at the book in her hands.

The bell rang, and Rowek got to his feet. After helping her stand as well, he stuffed his hands into his pockets. "We won't tell her then," he said with a wink.

She felt her lips curving despite the way her stomach twisted with unease.

***

The next day in history class, Rowek tipped a note into her lap. When she opened it, she found a phone number scrawled inside and a time.

Emma made sure that her mother would be at work until late on Friday night before she finally typed a message to Rowek that morning with her address and the words: **see you tonight.**

The message showed as read, but he didn't reply.

They had spent the week looking through book after book, but there were no documented accounts of anyone, magical or not, that could kill Shediem by just touching them. Even reducing living creatures to ash didn't work on supernatural beings. Spellcasters had the power to "freeze" them, which was just wrapping threads of power around them and holding them in place. Only really powerful Spellcasters could do it. And the more powerful the Shediem was they were trying to freeze, the more Spellcasters it required to freeze them.

Emma had studied the spell late into the night. If she was able to freeze them, it would make using her power to kill them infinitely easier.

As Emma got ready for Rowek to pick her up, she felt jittery. She had no idea where he was taking her, but at lunch on Wednesday, he had whispered into her ear to wear a nice dress.

She stood in front of her wardrobe, biting her bottom lip nervously. Stuffed in the back corner was a short, gauzy red dress that her mother had bought her last year, though Emma didn't think there would ever be an occasion to wear it.

Now, however…

She pulled it out and carefully shimmied into it, then stared at her reflection. The hem fell to the middle of her milky white thighs, the fabric wrapped around her, hugging her curves. The top wrapped around one shoulder, leaving the other bare.

Despite how short it was, she felt pretty.

As she rifled through her closet for a pair of shoes to match, her eyes fell on her studded, ankle-high boots. She grinned.

After slipping them on, she headed into the bathroom to add some extra curl to her reddish waves and swiped on some mascara.

The doorbell chime sounded, and she stilled.

Emma's heart leapt up into her throat. Her eyes slid down. What was she thinking wearing a dress? She hated dresses.

Panic began to work its way up her throat, and she took several deep breaths, hoping her heart wouldn't rip right out of her chest.

The bell rang again, and she forced herself to leave the bathroom. She snatched a solid black clutch from her desk back in her room, before heading to the ground floor.

She felt a tingle work down her arms, and her fingertips grew hot as she neared the door. Her hand trembled as she gripped the handle and opened it. The sight before her knocked the oxygen from her lungs.

Rowek in a crisp black suit with a blood red tie, his hair styled into a leaning, upward sweep. He looked like a teenage mob boss. His amber eyes were dark, almost black in the dim lighting, and the moonless night seemed to cling to him. A shiver raced down her spine. His lips parted on an exhale as his gaze roamed over her.

"Don't you look delectable." His voice was low and husky. Her face heated.

"You—you look…" Emma's tongue felt swollen and heavy. "Nice."

Nice didn't even begin to describe how good he looked. The cool night air bit at her heated skin. Rowek didn't look the least bit bothered by it.

He chuckled. A sound filled with mischief. "Thanks, shall we go?" He jerked his head to the side, gesturing over his shoulder. Emma nodded, grabbing a black cardigan from the hook by the door, praying she didn't freeze to death in her tiny dress, before shutting it behind her.

Rowek walked to the sleek, black sports car and pullled the passenger side door open for her.

"Did your dad buy you this car?" she asked

Rowek chuckled. "No."

His laugh was contagious, causing her to grin as she slid into the car. She tried her best to drop onto the seat without her dress riding up. She tugged the hemline down vainly, noticing Rowek's gaze on her bare thighs. Her entire body flushed hot.

The car's engine roared to life, then a second later they were speeding away down the street. The journey was quiet, and she sensed they were both nervous. Each glance Rowek stole toward her made her regret her outfit choice more and more. She clenched her fists in her lap to keep from holding the fabric in place, and watched the passing city lights out her window.

Emma's jaw dropped at the sight of the elegant structure as it came into view. One side was paneled in solid glass that afforded a view of the bay. They cruised up the hill, the city glittering below, reflected off the dark, glassy water.

A boy in a uniform not much older than them came to the car. As she climbed out, careful to keep herself covered, she noticed Rowek lean close to the boy and whisper something to the valet. The boy's eyes became unfocused as he nodded and then drove the vehicle away at a snail's pace.

"I'm pretty sure they're used to rich guys bribing them to not take their cars out for joyrides," she teased.

Rowek arched his brow. "I didn't bribe him."

"What, did you threaten him?"

Rowek gave a laugh that didn't reach his eyes before gently placing a hand on her back, guiding her forward. Where his hand touched the thin fabric, her skin tingled, cold and hot all at once.

The chatter in the restaurant was quiet, the ambient music a light jazz tune that was only overshadowed by the occasional clink of dish wear.

The striking blonde-haired, blue-eyed hostess took Emma's cardigan and led them through the tables of ritzy looking diners into a private room along the bay view.

Emma's heart began to pound at the sight of the plush, velvet booth, intimate enough for two. The leggy blonde's heated gaze was locked on Rowek as she introduced herself, ignoring Emma completely. Rowek brushed her off with disinterest, gesturing for Emma to sit with a smile.

She sank onto the luxurious fabric as Rowek seated himself across from her. The hostess finally pried herself from the room, shutting Emma and Rowek in—cut off from watchful eyes.

"You look worried. You're not claustrophobic, are you?" Genuine concern shone in his gaze, and she softened slightly.

She shook her head. "No, I'm fine. I'm just confused. I've never been in a private room before."

Rowek glanced out at the view. "It had a nice view, but I also figured we could talk about whatever we wanted without being overheard."

She nodded. It made sense, she supposed. The aroma of the various sizzling plates of food that had wafted into the room before they were shut in, lingered. Her mouth watered.

"I'm starving," she said, before taking a sip of her water.

"You remember all those bombs that terrorized the parts of the world two weeks ago?"

She sobered, straightening in her seat. Then she nodded.

"No one has been able to give a logical explanation for them. There isn't any known terrorist group that could claim full responsibility."

Emma nodded again. These were all things she knew, things she and her mother had discussed.

The door to their room slid open, cool air washing over Emma that she breathed in deeply.

"Sorry for the wait." A tall, lanky server with short, rust-colored hair and a well-groomed goatee bustled into the room, smiling brightly. "The mayor decided last minute to dine with us tonight as well, so I was just getting him settled."

Rowek frowned. "The mayor is here right now?"

The waiter nodded energetically as he set a menu in front of each of them. "We weren't expecting him until next week, so it's been a bit of bustle, but no matter, we're very honored to have him here. He pulled his notepad out. "What drinks can I get you two?"

Rowek looked lost in thought, so Emma ordered hers first, then they both waited, staring at him expectantly.

"Water is fine," he said brusquely, waving the man away.

When the door closed again, Emma raised a questioning brow at Rowek.

After a few moments of Rowek still not speaking Emma said, "The bombs?"

Rowek appeared almost alarmed by Emma's words before he relaxed. "Right, yes. I was just thinking, maybe the bombs weren't done by humans at all. I've heard some rumblings that the Giborim could be using them to lower the human population."

His words struck Emma like a physical blow. "Why on earth would they do that?" Emma countered. "They protect the humans; they wouldn't try to kill them."

Rowek rolled his eyes. "You can't believe everything they tell you. And I imagine it's not that way for all of the Giborim, but I've heard they're sick of playing babysitter to a much weaker race. With the humans out of the way, the Shediem would have no one to control, and they'd leave Earth to the Giborim."

Emma looked down at the menu, trying to sort out her thoughts.

"What about the Giborim girls taken?"

His eyebrows climbed high up on his face. "What Giborim girls?"

"Blaze told me hundreds of Giborim girls were abducted

earlier this week."

Rowek's gaze darkened. "Did he also tell you about the hundreds of Spellcasters that have gone missing?"

Emma swallowed hard.

"What about the tens of thousands of humans taken over just the past century?" he asked.

"I knew about the humans," Emma said, though she felt foolish for even saying it.

Rowek sighed. "I wasn't trying to be an asshole. I just know that there are none who can claim complete innocence. And as I said, it's just rumors."

Emma gave a small smile. "I get it. Everything is crazy right now, and it's hard to trust anyone."

Rowek nodded. "I don't want to spoil tonight."

"Me either," she agreed.

The door reopened, and the waiter appeared with their drinks, then pulled out a notepad. Emma ordered the first thing she saw, her ears tuning out Rowek's brief exchange as she handed the waiter her menu. She stared out across the water, wondering what other horrifying creatures preyed on unsuspecting sailors. She doubted the Nickor were the most fearsome water-dwelling Shediem.

When they were alone again, her gaze snapped back to his. He watched her, his lips tugging to the side. His eyes were brighter, the golden hue shining through. Like a flame doused with gasoline.

"What's one thing you'd like to know about me?"

Emma thought for a moment. "What would happen if I touched you again."

His expression burned hotter as a wicked grin spread his lips. The invisible cord that drew her to him pulled tight, and she surrendered to it. A tendril of heat licked through her. Any fear or hesitation on her part was gone. She slid her hand across the table, lightly brushing her finger over the top of his hand. A spark crackled above their skin. She started, but she didn't withdraw her hand. Rowek didn't seem at all surprised, he just watched her.

Her fingertips trailed up the back of his hand, and his eyes flared in response. Gently, as if trying not to startle her, his hand grabbed hers. A jolt went through her, but it wasn't power. It was a heady sensation to be touched by him.

She let him pull her to her feet. Like she was in a trance, she let him guide her. His hands cupped her hips, and her heart galloped wildly. With little effort, he tugged her down onto him, her dress curling up her thighs as she straddled his lap. A fire stirred inside, every inch of her aware. Her hands ran up his chest, under the dark suit jacket. She could feel the toned muscle hidden beneath as her fingers brushed up to his tie and pulled it loose.

"What is your tattoo of?" Her voice was like silk.

"I'd show you all of it, but I'd have to take my shirt off." His hot breath tickled her neck.

She worked the first button open as his lips brushed against her skin, setting her on fire. Her fingers stilled, eyes fluttered closed, letting his touch consume her. Kisses trailed up her neck, and she shivered. His lips touched her jaw bone with feather-light delicacy.

"Is it a symbol?" she rasped, fighting to remain in control.

He made a noise in the back of his throat that sounded almost feral. Like he didn't want to stop kissing her.

"Yes," he replied, voice gruff.

Then he kissed her.

Inside, a deeper part of her felt the connection of their lips. At last, a uniting stronger than blood. His arms were her home. His tongue as it parted her lips, spoke of how he would protect her always.

Then he stilled.

The pause was just enough to cool her heated blood. Like a spell that had worn off, she felt dazed. Sense crashed down on her, and she shuddered. Had she really been unbuttoning his shirt? A flash of horror had her trying to move off his lap, but his grip on her hips tightened, his fingers digging in painfully. Panic cut through her like a blade.

"Shit." He was on his feet in a blink. He tossed her over his shoulder and sprinted for the door. Emma screamed as she tried to break his hold on her. Where was he taking her?

The room filled with oblivious diners all looked up from their meals with confused expressions as Rowek sped toward the exit in a blur. They barrelled through the first set of doors, passing staff who broke away from their idle chatting as the air stirred their hair.

Suddenly Emma's back slammed against a hard surface. Air whooshed from her lungs. Rowek's body pressed hard against her, shielding her right before the *boom*. A sharp jab of pain hit her leg, but she was too stunned to cry out.

Everything went silent. Seconds that felt like minutes passed while Emma tried to push Rowek off her. When she caught sight of his face, she realized his mouth was moving, but she couldn't hear a sound. He moved to the side just enough to show her the scene behind them.

White dust hung thick in the air. The door they had just come through was obliterated. Large chunks of the ceiling were crashing to the ground. Bits of debris fell from Rowek's shoulders as he moved back in front of her before she could catch a glimpse of what was left of the dining room.

The building is collapsing. Ringing started in her ears. Slowly, as if the sound was being turned back up, she could hear Rowek.

"...the fuck is responsible, but I swear I will make them pay..."

He grabbed her hand and ran with her. She looked down at their entwined fingers, feeling a swell of heat in her chest.

Cries and shouts chased them as they rushed out into the cold night. A sound escaped her as her leg gave a bark of pain. Rowek halted before swinging her up into his arms.

A wave of dizziness washed over her as Rowek sat her down. She looked around. They were inside his car. Nausea kept her mouth clamped closed, unable to ask what had just happened.

She didn't have time to look at what was left of the building before they were speeding away.

Her brain seemed unable to function, her vision swimming. Lights flashed past her window, making her nausea worsen, and she squeezed her eyes shut, leaning her head against the car door.

"How is your leg?" Rowek's rough voice made her start.

"Wh—" A burning sensation in her right calf made her look down. She stared at it for several moments, blinking at the warm, red liquid that ran down to her ankle, disappearing into her boot before she realized it was blood. "How did that happen?"

"Glass from the door," Rowek answered, his expression lethal.

Emma swallowed hard. "Oh." Her voice was a hoarse whisper. It didn't look serious, and she doubted she would need stitches.

Rowek's grip on the steering wheel tightened. His knuckles shone white in the light of a passing street lamp.

The car pulled into the parking lot of a hospital, and Emma's spine went rigid. She wasn't supposed to be here. She couldn't be seen entering the building with Rowek. What would she tell her mother? She was supposed to be at home, studying and eating Chinese food.

"I can't go in there," Emma said, looking at Rowek with wide, fearful eyes. "My mother works here. I can clean my wound at home and just bandage it up myself." The panic continued to swell inside her, her words rushing out in near hysteria.

Rowek faced her. "You need to be sure there isn't any glass in your leg." His words were clipped, almost irritated.

Emma felt a burning sensation in the back of her throat.

"I'll leave you here. You can tell them whatever you want."

Emma didn't say anything. She tried to slow her breathing as she unclipped her seatbelt and opened the door.

"I'm sorry, Emma, this isn't how I wanted things to go tonight."

She nodded, not looking at his face as she climbed out, keeping her weight on her uninjured leg. As soon as the door was closed, the car sped off. Instinctively she patted her hips for her phone, only to remember she was wearing hardly enough fabric to be considered a dress, and her phone had been left in the restaurant before the explosion.

She had no other choice but to tell her mother the truth...at least about tonight. She straightened herself up, her chin lifted, and took another step toward the building, then another. Before her courage had time to fade, she entered the emergency room. Several staff members rushed to greet her.

Before she knew it, she was seated on the crinkly paper covering a bed, and someone entered the room. Emma couldn't contain her grimace at the sight of her wide-eyed, red-faced mother.

LEVAROTH

"Asmodeus," Levaroth bellowed, storming through the vacant hall.

There was no curtain hung in the throne room this time. No wild party and no humans. The prince sat in his true form atop his throne made of bones. He was the size of a dragon, exuding lethal power; a sight that made all mortals tremble.

Even seated, he towered over Levaroth. With skin the color of red-hot, glowing coals, and charred symbols etched into his flesh that described his fall. His ever-faithful servant, Geryon, stood guard, beside Asmodeus. His posture shifted into defensive at Levaroth's palpable anger.

"Yes?" Asmodeus rumbled, smoke tendrils dancing from his nostrils. His blood red eyes were fixed on Levaroth who dipped into a partial bow, his body stiff with unspent wrath.

Levaroth's veins burned hot, his wings twitching behind him, begging to be used. He had devoured hundreds of souls in the middle of an ocean before sinking their cruise ship. His kills were not quick. They were not clean. Their blood coated him even now. The feel of it dried on his skin, and in his hair did nothing to sate his hunger for death.

But he knew he couldn't get the answers he needed while rage seared through him, more lethal than any drug. So he'd chosen humans whose deaths would be explained away by a fire that sunk the ship.

"Who sent Elbis to Seattle last night? The intended explosion took place a week early, apparently under his order!"

Levaroth had known she was at the restaurant before it exploded. Once he had made sure that Emma was safe, he'd gone back to the Sound area. Elbis' scent was everywhere. A marking for him to find. But when he had searched for him, to demand if he knew of Emma's existence, all traces were gone.

Asmodeus stared at him through narrowed eyes. A black, curved claw tapped against the side of his face.

"Do you not have command over all continents?" His words were spoken lazily but bore the hint of a challenge.

He lowered his eyes. "Yes, my prince."

"Then anything that goes amiss is a violation of your authority," Asmodeus said. "Do you suspect my brother has his own agenda?"

"It is difficult to say," Levaroth answered. In truth, it made sense that the overshadowed Prince of Greed would try to claim the glory of chaining the humans to the king's will for himself. And what better way to keep his hands clear of mutiny than by having his general do all the work?

The prince eyed him for another moment. "Keep watch on him, but don't let him know. Execute the traitors but bring Elbis to me if he is truly working against my orders."

Levaroth bowed. "Yes, master."

Asmodeus eyed him for long moments, assessing. Levaroth fought the urge to squirm, to even twitch under his master's gaze.

"There is something more. A spark of something I have not seen in many years." The prince's head titled this way and that. "This anger inside you is more than just disobedience. No, I see fear in your eyes."

Levaroth shook his head. "No, my prince. I fear nothing."

Asmodeus's laughter boomed like thunder through the grand hall. "Dare I venture to guess that there is someone whose life was endangered by this attack?"

His throat bobbed. "A girl I have been following was nearly

killed. She has the power to kill with a single touch. She absorbs their power, and she can use that power for herself. There's more in her that I sense. She is very powerful. Perhaps more powerful than any Spellcaster."

Asmodeus' eyes lit with interest. He was a collector of power, of strength. He had an army of spell-casters that did his bidding. "How do you know what she can do?"

Levaroth fought to control the surge of protectiveness that surfaced. He lifted his chin, readying himself for the consequences that would befall him. "I staged an attack with a small clan of Nickor. When she touched one, it to dust. Then she was able to wield their water powers."

"What of the rest of the clan?" His voice made the ground beneath Levaroth's feet tremble.

His spine stiffened. "The Giborim stepped in, sir."

Geryon stepped forward, ax drawn. Levaroth felt his fists clench.

Asmodeus' gaze was unblinking, thoughtful, even. "Is she working with the Giborim? She must know who and what you are." Asmodeus stroked his long chin, no doubt debating her annihilation.

"I don't believe she is working with them. However, the big, brutish son of the regional leader has taken an interest in her. I'm not certain of his motives, so I have worked to protect her from any attacks until I have heard from you about what you want to do with her."

She knows what I am. That worthless Giborim will have told her all about me. He will try to keep her from me. That thought made his vision spot with red, his wings flexing involuntarily. He couldn't understand why she had such a hold on him. *It doesn't matter, she'll be dead soon.*

"Bring her to me," Asmodeus thundered.

Surprise jolted through him.

"Whatever she is, she's not human. Perhaps a Spellcaster. I want to meet her. If she is as powerful as you say she is, then she could be of use to us." A chuckle rumbled through the prince's chest, the sound like mountains splitting open. "If she is of no use to me, then at least I shall be the one to end her."

"Yes, Master." Levaroth bowed low, then turned and let his wings carry him out.

As something deep inside him rebelled, he reminded himself that it was his duty to hand her over to the prince. *Time.* He needed time. She wouldn't trust him or agree to go with him. She would need to be persuaded to join them. To serve them. Then she wouldn't have to die.

What do I care? She is nothing. Just another mortal who will be gone in a blink.

He shook himself out, hoping to rid himself of his foolishness. Of her.

For many grueling hours after that, he trained until his body shook with exertion. Until several bones were broken. It numbed him. Let him forget for a while. When he left the training hall at last, he made another call to Usik, bringing a hefty bag of decaying human toes.

The greedy Shax munched noisily, fragments of nail and bone flying along with spittle as he agreed to look into Elbis' activities and Prince Belphegor.

Then Levaroth dusted off his suit jacket, excusing himself to get back to work. The Shediem nodded, waving him away, stuffing another fistful of rotting, disjointed toes into his wide mouth.

EMMA

The news called it a gas leak, which, much to Emma's relief, was what she had told her mother. Emma didn't believe it. Apparently, neither did her mother.

Her mother had grounded her. For life, she claimed. Emma would not be allowed out of the house except for school, and her mother had spoken with the neighbors on either side of them to keep an eye on Emma. It was like she was a middle-school student who couldn't be trusted not to burn the house down while her mother was away.

And to enforce that Emma got to and from school each day, her mother had filed for a brief leave of absence so she could drive her. *It could have been worse*, she reasoned. Emma had half expected to see boxes stacked throughout the house with a moving truck idling outside.

Her mother had shouted at her the entire time she pulled bits of glass from her leg and bandaged it up. Emma's focus faded in and out. She didn't have a phone to get a hold of Rowek, and she imagined that was the last thing she should bring up to her mother. He had seemed mad about the explosion. Like he knew more than he was letting on.

She wanted to assure him that she was okay. She wanted to find out what he knew, and she wanted him to help her develop her powers to help prevent this from happening again.

And a small part of her really just wanted to see him.

He had kissed her. She had kissed him back.

When Emma had told Adrianna what happened on Monday morning, as they walked into school, Adrianna had given Emma her own verbal lashing with a heavy dose of pride at Emma's "boldly reckless behavior". When Emma told her friend about her kiss with Rowek, Emma had nearly gone deaf with all the squealing. She had felt the heat course through her again at the memory. His soft lips on her neck, her jaw, her lips. Her face warmed as she recalled the way he gripped her like she was his air. All weekend she felt his phantom touch.

Bliss.

He was the type of guy that could kiss her into a dizzy, love-sick mess. But she didn't care. She wanted him to kiss her again. And soon.

The bell rang out, announcing the end of first period. She jolted, snapping her pencil tip. A frazzled-looking Ms. Farrars shouted the assignment over the scrapes of chairs on tile and crunching papers being shoved into bags. Emma scribbled it into her planner before gathering her belongings.

As she stuffed her textbook and binder into her bag, she noticed her calculus textbook was missing. She groaned at the prospect of going back downstairs to her locker as she shouldered her backpack and raced into the hallway.

She trudged through the throng of shuffling bodies on the staircase. With her head down, keeping track of where the landing began in between flights so she didn't stumble, a heavy weight slammed into her back.

The force sent her flying face-first into the students in front of her. With a cry, her hands went out, slapping onto the cold, dirty tile, keeping her face from impacting instead. A snigger made her snap her head up in time to see Sean flash her a malicious grin. His friends roared with laughter, several high-fiving as they continued down the stairs. The sea of students parted around her, but no one even seemed to glance in her direction as she got to her feet. She clenched her hands into fists, her palms stinging.

"Are you okay?" a small voice asked behind her.

Emma whirled around to find the freshman girl she had knocked to the ground on their first day looking at her with wide eyes, her brows creased with worry. She clutched a faded gray book tightly to her chest as if she was afraid it was going to be knocked out of her hands. Emma glimpsed the words, 'Guide' and 'Spells' on the spine before the girl shuffled her arms together to hide it, her cheeks flushing a delicate shade of pink.

"I'm fine," Emma replied. She pried her eyes away from the book, to brush a few blades of grass and some dirt from her Metallica t-shirt. "Guys are dicks."

The girl nodded with a small laugh. "Especially those ones."

"Well apparently a jersey entitles you to act as if all other humans are beneath you," Emma commented dryly.

"Yeah, I think I heard something about that." They both laughed.

"Sorry, my name is Emma by the way." She started to offer her hand, but then thought better of it, grasping the strap on her bag instead.

"Sara," the girl replied, smiling.

"Nice to meet you. You're heading to physical science, right?"

Sara nodded, her blonde hair bouncing in its ponytail. Just then, the bell rang, and Emma looked around at the near-empty staircase.

"Late for it, actually." Sara didn't sound upset about it in the least. Emma opened her mouth to ask about the book in her hands, but closed it, afraid of how she might sound.

"I'll let you get to it, then." Emma smiled.

Sara waved, then continued up a few stairs. Emma sighed, brushing herself off again. Sara spun, then said, "You know Adrianna, right?"

Emma looked up, confusion in her voice as she said, "Yeah."

"Do you think you'd be able to give her my number?" she bit down on her bottom lip, looking embarrassed.

"Sure," Emma replied.

Sara jogged back down to the center landing, reached into her bag and grabbed a pen and tore a chunk of paper out of a notebook. As she scrawled her number onto the paper, Emma glanced the full title of the book: *Beginner's Guide To Advanced Spells*.

"Interesting reading material," Emma remarked, then immediately wished she hadn't, because Sara's face turned a deep red. "I didn't—" she started. "What I meant was I've been looking for similar material. A friend and I have been doing some research."

Sara's eyes widened. "Adrianna?"

"Erm…no," Emma said.

"Well, I should get to class, please tell her to call me." She held out the paper and Emma took it, before Sara bounded up the rest of the stairs without a backward glance.

Emma sighed.

On the ground floor, a cold tingle danced down her spine. She was just about to round the corner when she came to a grinding halt. Her heart beat faster, and her limbs prickled with awareness.

Leaning against the wall, she heard a clank that sounded like something heavy hitting metal. It echoed through the hall. Then a deep, rumbling voice reached her ears. She peeked around the corner and found Sean up against the wall of lockers with Rowek's face inches from his, his expression calm and focused.

"You will apologize to Emma, and then you will go home, climb up on your roof, and jump off as many times as it takes to break your leg," he said slowly. Menacingly.

Emma expected Sean to laugh it off, to break Rowek's hold on his jersey, but he didn't. Instead, he nodded. Then Rowek let him go and stepped back to let Sean pass. Emma stepped into the corridor, catching Rowek and Sean's attention.

Rowek's burning gaze revealed not even a flicker of surprise at her appearance as Sean approached her. His chocolate brown eyes were blank and unfocused.

"I'm sorry I pushed you down the stairs, Emma," Sean said.

His voice didn't carry the laughing quality it normally did. It sounded flat. Robotic.

Emma's brows knitted together. She grabbed Sean's shoulders, but he looked past her as if she wasn't there and moved out of her grip. Emma stared after him in stunned silence for a moment. Then she felt Rowek behind her and spun to face him.

"What did you do?" Emma asked.

He searched her face for a moment before saying, "I... *persuaded* him to do what I want."

A memory rose unbidden in her mind of a young valet's face going blank. Whatever Rowek had done to Sean, he'd also done to the valet. How many others had he done that to?

"How?"

Rowek gave a single-shouldered shrug. "With magic."

"Why?"

Anger flashed in his eyes. "He hurt you."

"But I...I didn't see you in class."

"I got here just as that jackass shoved you."

Emma eyed him. Maybe he had been standing too far for her to sense. "I see."

"How is your leg?" he asked, running a hand through his perfect hair.

"Good," she hedged. She didn't want to tell him that it had healed overnight. Not until he explained how he could move so quickly. "Lucky you were able to get me out so fast."

He nodded. "Yes." Shifting his stance, he said, "Come take a walk with me."

"Have you ever done that to me? Mind-wiped me or whatever that was?" she waved a hand at the spot Sean and Rowek had been.

"No. I'd never do that to you." His voice was sincere, and she believed him, letting her shoulders sag in relief.

"You can't take away people's wills like that. Even though Sean totally deserves it. It's wrong."

A small smile curved his lips. The same lips that ignited a

flame within her. He held out his hand. An invitation, and a silent question.

The urge to take his hand was nearly overwhelming. "I have to go to class," she forced herself to say.

"Skip," he replied with a wink.

To keep herself from leaning into him, she took a step back. "I can't. I have to—*we* have to go to class."

He sighed. "I know, I just wanted to talk to you about the explosion at the restaurant. I know who did it."

Emma's eyes widened. "Really? Who?"

"It was a band of rogue Shediem. For some reason, they're no longer happy serving their king."

Emma's jaw dropped. "Wow, that's not good. Do you know why they targeted the restaurant?"

Rowek glanced around. "Can we talk about this outside?"

"There's no one here." Emma gestured to the empty corridor.

He pulled his shoulders back, looking uncomfortable. "There are cameras."

Emma sighed as she grabbed his hand and pulled him out the side door. Once she was under the willow tree, she let his hand drop, missing it almost as soon as it was gone.

"Do you remember when the waiter told us the mayor was supposed to be coming a week later than he did?"

She nodded.

"Well I have some…uh…friends who followed some leads to a group of rogues that are trying to start something with the other Shediem."

But why, she wondered.

"I wonder if Levaroth is in the area because of that, then. Maybe now he'll move on." She worried her bottom lip as she thought. "We have to try to stop any more bombs from going off—"

Rowek cupped her face and pressed his lips to hers. She sighed as she wrapped her arms around his neck and pulled him closer.

When they broke apart, Rowek's eyes were bright. "I couldn't wait any longer to do that."

She hummed in agreement, her mind fuzzy. "I need to go to class."

Rowek released a long breath. "Okay, Sunshine. I'll catch up with you at lunch."

Emma stepped out of his embrace and went back inside, feeling giddy.

***

In history, Emma gave Adrianna Sara's phone number. She swayed, looking ready to spill her breakfast all over her desk.

"What's wrong?" Emma whispered.

Adrianna stared at Emma with a stunned expression, before grabbing Emma's wrist, and lifting her arm, inspecting it.

Emma pulled away, casting her friend a concerned look.

"I think I have a brain tumor," she announced, loudly to the whole class. The teacher stopped mid-sentence, and every pair of eyes swivelled to Adrianna.

"Excuse me?" Mr. Patterson said, blinking.

Adrianna's mouth fell open as she realized she had practically shouted. She jumped to her feet, grabbed her crutches and hobbled out of the room as fast as one could in a cast.

Emma felt like sprinting after her, but instead she slid down in her seat, trying to hide from the curious eyes. When everyone had gone back to focusing on the teacher's lecture, she slid her phone out of her pocket and messaged Adrianna to see if she was okay.

At the end of the school day, she had still not received a message from Adrianna. Rowek had eaten pizza with Emma at lunch and they spent her open periods under the willow tree, talking and stealing kisses. He tried to get her to stir the leaves and pull water up from the soil, but nothing happened. Rowek assured her that it was normal to not be able to do it on her first try, but still she couldn't help her disappointment. She wanted to impress him.

Her lips were red and swollen as she walked into finance class, grinning like an idiot. But Rowek didn't come to class.

She wondered if his father somehow kept forcing him to leave school, and hoped that Rowek wouldn't get in too much trouble when his tardiness came into question.

She met her mother outside after the last bell. As she opened the door of her mother's car, she felt a cold, hard weight punch her in the chest. She gasped, spinning around.

Her mother said something, but all Emma could her was her pulse thundering in her ears.

There, between the copse of trees, less than fifty feet away, was a dangerously gorgeous man dressed in a black suit. His eyes blazed a fiery gold. She couldn't breathe.

"Emma!" her mother shouted.

She whirled around and saw her mother's wide eyes.

"I'm okay," she said shakily as she got into the car. She looked back to the trees.

A few fallen leaves, twirling in the breeze fell to the ground where Levaroth had been standing.

EMMA

"Get started on your homework," her mother said when they were inside, and Emma heard the strain in her voice.

She paused with one foot on the first stair, then turned.

"Mom," Emma began, choosing her words with care, "I know it doesn't help, and I'm not trying to get out of my punishment, but I want you to know I really am sorry I disobeyed you. I'm sorry you have to take time off work to babysit me and I'm sorry I broke your trust." Emma's voice cracked.

Her mother gave her a small smile. "Thank you for saying that Emma, but it doesn't change my mind about anything. You could have died."

Emma nodded again. A tear slipped down her cheek that she hastily brushed away. "I know," she replied softly. "I just wanted you to know."

A little over an hour later, a knock came at her door.

"Come in," Emma said, not bothering to turn around.

"I'm running to the store to get more tortillas; ours are stale. Do you need anything?" Her mother's voice was noticeably warmer than before. The chokehold of guilt eased a fraction.

Emma twisted in her chair to face her mother. "I could go for a Yoo-Hoo."

Her mother smiled. "Okay."

She started to close the door before swinging it back open. Her expression became serious again as she said, "Stay. In. The. House." Her finger jabbed the air in front of her as she stressed each word.

Emma nodded vigorously. Then her mother shut the door. After hearing the front door close, Emma went back to staring at her freehand world map that still needed to be color-coded and labeled.

Her mother's car had only pulled from the driveway and drove away a moment before the doorbell rang. She froze, her pen hovering above the paper. Slowly, she laid it down and rose from her chair.

The chime sounded again as she took the stairs two at a time. At the window, she pulled the curtain back enough to see who stood on the porch.

Surprise shot through her and she flung the door open. Blaze gave her a once-over, relief flashing in his stormy eyes, before stepping into the house.

"You can't be here. My mother is going to be back soon. How did you even know where I live?"

"Axel and I followed you when you walked home to make sure you got home safely."

Emma recalled the figure standing in the rain that one day. The figure wasn't as built as Blaze, but Axel…

Blaze crossed his arms over his chest, stretching his tight shirt to near bursting. "I needed to be sure you were okay after what happened at the restaurant."

Emma blinked. "How did you know about that?"

Blaze huffed, impatient. "I told you I was keeping an eye out for you." He paused. "I was just checking the perimeter but then I smelled at least twenty Shediem, mostly just Nysroghs—lower ranking Shediem," Blaze offered before Emma could ask. "I had to take them out. But as I got closer to the building, the Shediem went up in rank. It was only then that I realized they

135

were protecting something."

Emma knew where this was going. Images flashed in her mind, screams and crying echoed in her ears. Emma's leg gave a phantom twinge at the memory of the glass slicing into her. She still wore the bandage so her mother didn't know it was already healed. She had gaped at the smooth, unscarred skin for at least a full minute, prodding it as if trying to be sure it wasn't some illusion.

Had she known she could heal so rapidly, she wouldn't have bothered walking into the hospital at all, but Rowek had insisted, and at the time she could barely form a cohesive thought. It was just confirmation that she wasn't fully human like she had thought her entire life. She made a mental note to ask Rowek if all Spellcasters could heal quickly. Would she be able to move fast like him too?

"I tried to neutralize the bomb—even tried to get it away from the building—but I was too late. I tried to go in after you to get you out, but I jumped through the window right as the bomb detonated and I was tossed out. By the time I was back on my feet and searching for you among the bodies…" He ground his teeth as his arms fell to his sides.

He had thought she died in the blast. Without a thought of how he'd respond, Emma reached out, resting a hand on his arm. His eyes met hers, a storm raging within them.

He cleared his throat. "Jake and Axel were able to catch your scent at the hospital and since it was clear you were being cared for, they went off to track the other Shediem involved. This wasn't Levaroth, there was only a trace from a different general."

Emma's lips parted, a sickening sensation of dread unfurling in her gut. There was more than one general in the area? Did they know she existed too?

"Anyway, I'm glad you're unharmed. You should stay home as much as possible. It's not safe."

Emma gave a choked laugh. Safe was a distant memory. "Don't worry, my mother has grounded me until the end of time.

Maybe even beyond that."

Blaze smiled sadly. "Your mother loves you very much. She may seem overprotective, but everything she does is to keep you safe. You should open up to her. I think you'll be surprised what you'd find out."

Her breath hitched. How did he know her mother?

Blaze opened the door, giving Emma a final once-over before pulling it shut with a soft click.

Tell her mother? She wasn't sure how her mother would react to know Emma had been attacked by Shediem twice, and that she had some kind of magic in her that gave her the power to kill Shediem. Even if she omitted that the power was more of a craving, she doubted her mother would respond by revealing whatever secrets she kept so closely guarded. If the reason they were always moving had to do with Shediem in the area, then she had no doubt her mother would do something far more drastic if she learned the truth.

An engine idled just outside, snapping Emma from her thoughts. She raced up the stairs and threw herself back down into her chair just as she heard the door open, bags rustling.

Moments later, her mother poked her head into the room.

"Can you come downstairs and help me make dinner?" she asked. "There's something I want to discuss."

She tried to swallow her growing nervousness. "Sure."

Emma finished outlining New Zealand with her green highlighter, then went back down to the main level where her mother was washing the peppers.

"What's up?" Emma asked, schooling her expression to one of calm as she took the washed peppers and began carving out the tops. She willed her hands not to shake, her breathing to remain even as she worked up the courage to tell her mother everything that was going on.

Her mother stacked the last pepper on the pile and dried her hands with the faded '#1 Mom' hand towel Emma had gotten her for Mother's Day when she was ten.

"I've been thinking about your grounding," her mother said, leaning against the wooden counter-top.

Emma looked up. *Not what I was expecting.*

"You'll be eighteen in two weeks, and while I know I've been a bit overprotective, I've tried to not smother you as best I can, and I think we have a pretty good relationship."

"We do," Emma confirmed with a touch of curiosity.

"I don't want you to spend your last few weeks resenting me, and have you take off at the first chance you get."

Emma put the knife and pepper down, wiping her hands on the stained towel. "Mom, I could never resent you. And I'm not just going to take off."

Her mother wrapped her arms around Emma, and she relaxed into her. The crushing weight of the secrets and the questions that weighed on her seemed to melt away for the short moment that her mother held her in her embrace.

There were many times during her childhood, when her mother was always moving them from one place to another, never settling down, that Emma had begun to resent her. Every friend she had made was left behind, and she was forced to start fresh over and over.

But as she got older, her mother loosened her grip little by little. They would hang out together on the weekends, baking and watching movies. She became the only friend Emma didn't have to say goodbye to every time they uprooted their lives.

"Mom," Emma started.

Her mother let her go, smiling. "So," she continued, ignoring Emma. She walked to the table where her beige purse sat and rummaged through it. She pulled out a little black flip phone and her car keys. "You may have these if you promise to not lie to me again."

Emma nodded, smiling weakly. "I promise."

Could she tell her mother now? After she had extended Emma freedom so unreservedly? Emma sighed. *It can wait a little longer,* she told herself.

Her mother held them out for Emma to take. "It's not a smartphone, obviously; it can only call and send text messages. Perhaps in two weeks you'll get something a little nicer." She winked, making Emma laugh.

"Thank you, Mom," Emma said, throwing her arms around her again.

She promised herself that when the moment was right, she'd ask. For now, she'd pretend to be a normal seventeen-year-old girl, hanging out with her mother.

Emma woke before her alarm, alert and content, deciding to sneak downstairs to make pancakes. Humming a random tune, Emma flipped yet another bubbling pancake. The smell of maple and blueberries brought a smile to her face like little else could.

"Smells delicious," her mother said as she entered the kitchen. When Emma turned around, she saw the formal pantsuit, which could only mean one thing.

"Going to work?" Emma asked as she slid the last pancake onto a heaping plate on the table. Her mother eyed the spread with a smile before glancing down at her watch.

"The board is supposed to be meeting today and it's mandatory that I attend." She sat down across from Emma, picked two pancakes off the pile and began to coat them with butter.

"Sounds like fun," Emma said dryly.

Her mother watched her with a small smile. "Thank you for making breakfast."

Just as Emma opened her mouth to respond, her mother's phone rang. She glanced down at the screen, frowning as she pushed back her chair and stood.

"I've got to go. Have a great day at school sweetheart."

Emma's heart sank. "Thanks, love you," she called to her mother's back.

She heard her mother say, "Hi, I'm just walking out the door."

Then the door clicked shut.

Emma heaved a sigh, staring at the empty seat in front of her while she finished her breakfast. The rest of the stack she gathered into a container that she placed in the fridge before heading to school.

As soon as Emma got out of her car, she was nearly tackled by an excited, squealing Adrianna.

"You got your car back?"

"And a temporary phone." Emma held up the piece of ancient technology. Adrianna wrinkled her nose in disgust, causing Emma to laugh. "It's just until my birthday," she explained.

In front of her, Adrianna was practically vibrating with excitement.

"What?" Emma asked.

"Guess who asked me to the homecoming dance?"

Emma felt her stomach sink. "Who?" She tried and failed to keep her tone light.

"Aaron!" Adrianna squealed. Emma's gut twisted. She and Adrianna had discussed going to homecoming together only a few days ago, but the joy that shone in her eyes was undeniable.

Emma smiled as she said, "That's great, A!" There was a tiny spark of satisfaction in knowing Adrianna would be with a guy that truly adored her. He may not be solid, lean muscle like Sean, but Emma believed he was a good guy from the few short months she'd known him.

"Oh, don't look so smug," Adrianna admonished playfully. "I haven't said yes yet."

"Why not?" Emma asked.

They began walking toward the building when Emma caught sight of a miserable-looking Sean...whose leg from thigh to toe was covered in a cast. He leaned into the support of the crutches under his arms, scowling at the curve-less blond who was speaking into his ear.

Emma felt cold as she stared. "Sean broke his leg." Her voice was paper thin.

"Yep," Adrianna replied with a satisfied smirk. "Won't be able to play sports at all this year, I heard."

As if he could hear them from across the lawn, his gaze flicked to them. Loathing coated his every feature. Emma rushed into the building, tugging Adrianna behind her before her guilt made her lose her breakfast.

"So, what do you think I should tell Aaron? I obviously can't go with him since you and I are going together," Adrianna said.

Emma's mind reeled. She pushed the disturbing sight of Sean from her mind, swallowing down the lump that had formed in her throat.

She had planned to go with Adrianna because there was no way her mother would agree to let her go with a guy, but she wouldn't even consider letting her friend reject the boy she liked.

"No, go with him," Emma said without a shred of self-pity.

"I can't. Who would you go with?" Adrianna asked. "Oooh! I know!" she laughed. "Go with Rowek!"

Emma shook her head. "That's so not his scene. Besides, my mother would never let me go with a guy."

Adrianna pouted. "Can't you just tell her you're going with me and have him meet you at the dance or something?"

Emma bit her lip, considering.

"At least ask Rowek. If he says no, then it can be just us girls." Her smile was so bright for the first time in what felt like weeks, and Emma didn't have the heart to argue.

Emma nodded. "But if Rowek says no, I still want you to go with Aaron. You deserve it."

Adrianna appeared torn. "That would be lame for you though."

Emma laughed, though it sounded as forced as it felt. "I'd be fine. When he tries to put the moves on you, I'll just follow you to his car and sit between you two, so he doesn't get any ideas about getting lucky."

Adrianna cackled with laughter. "Okay, well we have to go dress shopping this weekend! My budget isn't very much but I might be able to convince my dad to give me a little extra if I offer to help out at his office for a few hours."

Emma still didn't know if her mother would even agree to let her go but she nodded anyway. The idea filled her with a rush of excitement.

At lunch that day, Adrianna, Aaron, Emma and Rowek all sat at a table. Aaron talked to Adrianna about music, and she rested her chin in her hands, staring at him as if he were the ultimate source of knowledge.

Rowek had been quiet all day, contemplative.

"What's up?" Emma asked him, nudging him with her shoulder.

He hadn't touched his pizza, and he pushed the tray away to face her.

"I suppose you want to go to that dance thing, right?"

Emma's spine straightened, her eyes wide. "Um, yeah, but I get it if that's not—you don't have to—"

"I want to," Rowek said, but the crease between his brows said otherwise.

"Uhm," Emma cleared her throat. "Are you sure?"

Rowek nodded, then he smirked. "There's a long list of things I'd endure to see you in a dress again."

Emma choked on her sip of water, coughing and sputtering. His brows drew together again, and she blushed. Partly because she remembered the red dress she wore to the restaurant and how it slid up her thighs when she sat on his lap, but also because she was now choking for air.

He patted her on the back as she wheezed in another breath. Adrianna and Aaron were watching her, both with looks of concern.

"Are you guys going to the game too?" Aaron asked, looking between Emma and Rowek.

Emma wrinkled her nose. Football was not her thing. "No," she said, and Rowek chuckled, low in his throat.

"Oh this is so perfect!" Adrianna clapped her hands together, bouncing in her seat. "We're all going to homecoming together!

For the rest of the lunch period and at every possible moment that week, she and Adrianna looked at pictures of dresses from magazines, and on Adrianna's phone, comparing styles and arguing about which ones would match their body types.

By Friday evening Emma still hadn't talked to her mother. Every time she saw her, her mother was either in a hurry or flustered. Emma kept telling herself that was the only reason she kept deferring the conversation.

After dinner, as she was washing the dishes, which she had been doing at every opportunity to try to lessen her mother's stress load, along with laundry, vacuuming and even scrubbing the toilet, Emma finally worked up the courage.

"Hey, Mom?"

"Hmm?" Her mother was reading yet another text message with her brows scrunched together in concentration.

"So, I know you and I usually hang out on Saturdays, but I was hoping you would be okay with me going dress shopping with Adrianna because Aaron asked her to the homecoming dance and I really want to go with them and—"

"Sure," her mother said.

Emma blinked, stunned. "Really?"

Her mother looked up from her phone screen. "Did someone ask you to the homecoming dance?"

Her cheeks heated. "Yes."

Her mother smiled brightly. "Not surprising! You're a stunningly beautiful young woman. I wondered why the house was so clean." She laughed.

Emma sat, unblinking, unable to process her question as her mother placed her phone down on the table.

"Tell me about him, what's his name?"

"Rowek."

"How old is Rowek?"

Emma thought she could feel sweat begin to bead on her temples. Her mother's interrogation was only made worse by the fact that she seemed genuinely interested to learn about him. In learning about him, Emma worried she'd somehow blurt out that he has magic and ruin her mother's enthusiasm.

"Seventeen," Emma said, and then she thought, *he is seventeen, right?* Why hadn't she thought to ask him?

"Can I meet him?" her mother asked. "Just for a minute before you two take off for the dance?" she added, noting Emma's terrified expression. "I'll have to work, I'm sure, but you two can stop by the hospital just so I can say hi."

Emma nodded stiffly. There was no point in trying to fight her mother's wishes. Not when she was being so...relaxed.

She noticed a bit of a glow coming from her mother. Her skin was vibrant and youthful. And when was the last time she had seen her smile so much?

Emma couldn't recall.

"Great! You'll need a dress." Her mother grabbed her purse from the table and pulled it into her lap. She fished out a wad of bills and handed them to Emma. "This should cover it."

Emma took the money, staring at it with eyes as big as golf balls. "I don't think even wedding dresses cost this much."

She laughed. "Oh, they do. Ten times more than that usually. Get lunch with Adrianna and keep the rest for dinner or something the night of the dance."

Emma nodded, feeling a little disoriented. Then she rushed up the stairs to her room and called Adrianna to tell her the good news.

———

"I told you the purple would look good on you," Adrianna said, observing the rhinestone-covered dress that clung to Emma's body.

"It's way too short," Emma complained as she observed her reflection in the triple-mirrors. Images of herself in a particular red dress flooded her mind, and her body flushed with heat.

"There's no such thing," Adrianna disagreed, gesturing down

at the black and red number that squeezed her chest up, cinched in her already tiny waist, then flared out at the hips in swaths of tulle.

"You better wear a slip or shorts underneath that," Emma told her.

But Adrianna wasn't listening. She was too busy twirling in the mirror, watching the skirt's movement. "How much is this one?" she asked, standing still long enough for Emma to grab the tag.

Emma gulped. "They clearly don't price these things in accordance with the amount of fabric they use."

"Come on, how much?" Adrianna prodded.

"Four-fifty," Emma answered. Her eyes met Adrianna's as they filled with disappointment. "How much did you get from your dad?"

"Two-hundred," Adrianna groaned.

Emma bit her bottom lip. "I'll give you the other two-fifty."

Adrianna's eyes widened. "No, don't worry about it, I'll find something else." She stepped off the platform, heading to her changing room. Emma grabbed her arm.

"It's non-negotiable," she said firmly. "My mom gave me more than enough. I'll get that navy blue one. It's only a hundred."

Adrianna scrunched her nose. "The floor-length one? You'll have to have it altered which will be at least another hundred and fifty," she pointed out.

"I'd still have enough."

Adrianna's eyes bugged. "Can I have your mom?"

Emma snorted. She still mused at her mother's strange behavior. But it was a good strange. Emma wondered if her mother was trying to show just how "cool" she could be, in an attempt to keep her living at home while she went to college.

There were several universities in Seattle that offered the degrees Emma was considering, but every time she started to fill out an application, she couldn't bring herself to finish it. Nothing felt quite right yet.

They left the shop after paying for their dresses. Emma left hers with the seamstress who agreed to hem the length so she didn't trip, and told her it would be ready for pick-up on Wednesday.

"You hungry?" Emma asked. "My treat." Adrianna opened her mouth to protest, but Emma held a hand up. "My mother told me to buy us both lunch."

"And my dress?" she quipped.

"Half of your dress," Emma corrected her.

"Over half."

"Oh, hush," Emma said. "I'm hungry, what do you want?"

"Anything." Adrianna glanced away, looking embarrassed. Emma eyed her with confusion. In the time she had known her, Adrianna had never been ashamed of her appetite, but Emma didn't pry.

They walked down the street, passing restaurant after restaurant, their smells wafting out to greet them. The scent of butter and garlic made Emma inhale deeply.

"Mmm, I haven't had Italian food in forever," Emma said.

Adrianna was practically drooling. "Me either."

They turned to walk toward the quaint little restaurant when Emma felt a brick of ice lodge itself between her lungs. She whipped around, searching for a pair of golden eyes. Instead, a man in a stained brown trench coat with blond, greasy hair and arctic blue eyes stormed toward them.

"Murderer!" he screamed. His voice sounded like grinding gears. The faint clatters and voices from inside the restaurant fell silent.

Emma gasped, stumbling back as he leapt for her. His hands gripped her throat, cold and strong. Her back hit the cool glass table behind her. It rocked, groaning with their combined weight as she tried to breathe.

Heat shot through her as her power flared to life. The man's eyes flicked down to his hands as if he was experiencing discomfort. A warm trickle of energy seeped into her skin, so faint, it was hardly noticeable

"How dare you," he snarled as his grip tightened. Her hands clamped around his bony wrists, and she pulled, but he didn't budge. "You can't kill me without killing my host."

Host? Her mind fumbled over the word. Neither Blaze nor Rowek had mentioned people being possessed by Shediem, but the power she felt was so much less than any other Shediem she had touched before. The man had to be possessed.

Stars danced in her vision as she struggled to draw in a breath. *Plan B.* She dug her thumbs into his eyes. He jerked back far enough for her to get her knee between his legs. She rammed it into him. Her thoughts were hazy but air—blessed air—filled her lungs again.

He didn't so much as flinch as his mouth spread into a demented grin, revealing a decaying and chipped smile. The Shediem inside him had likely been there for a long time. Her gut twisted at his wrongness as she rubbed at her sore throat. He stepped toward her again. She braced herself for the feel of his cold, dead hands on her.

"What's going on here?" a man shouted behind them. Emma heard Adrianna say something in a panic-stricken voice.

"Get lost, buddy!" The beefy man stepped into Emma's peripheral vision, waving the Shediem-possessed guy off, but he didn't move. If anything, his grin grew.

"Rougot!" a deep male voice shouted.

It knocked into her, nearly bringing her to her knees as a cold tingle spread down her arms. A man came into view, his golden eyes burning with rage.

Was this man Levaroth?

In less than a second, he had her attacker pressed against the brick building. Several people shouted. Out of the corner of her eye, Adrianna shuffled next to Emma, gripping her arm with trembling hands.

"Get outta here, all'a yous!" the restaurant worker shouted.

"Shediem killer! Murderer!" her attacker roared in Levaroth's face, but his crazed eyes were on Emma. He flailed against Levaroth's grip, fighting to wrap his hands around her throat again. Instinctively, she retreated a step, preparing to run.

The insane man laughed; a sound that made Emma want to grind her teeth.

Levaroth pulled him close, their faces inches apart, and in a voice so low Emma could barely make out the words, he said, "You will leave this city and never come back, or I will personally be the one to end you."

Fear extinguished his fight. The man glared in defiance but didn't utter another word. When Levaroth let him drop to his feet, the man sneered over his shoulder at Emma before jogging away. When the man was out of sight, Levaroth turned to Emma and Adrianna.

"Are you okay?" His eyes were fixed on Emma as he spoke.

"Yeah," Adrianna squeaked. Her eyes were wide, taking in the man before her.

His muscular frame was clothed in a pristine black suit, his face was angular—as sharp as his gaze that bored into Emma with a raw emotion that made her unable to breathe.

Protectiveness.

Possession.

She trembled from head to toe. So this was it. He was going to kill her now. She took a step back, fearful.

"You have nothing to fear from me, Emma."

Her name on his lips was so beautiful, her eyes filled with tears.

He was power and strength.

Darkness and beauty.

Emma turned and ran, pulling Adrianna with her. She knew without a doubt if he wanted to catch her, he could. She was mouse underneath the cat's claws.

But he had released her. Whatever his sick game was, she feared it was far from over.

EMMA

The music thumped loudly in the gymnasium. Lights flashed and pulsed in time to the rhythm.

Adrianna was chatting loudly to Aaron behind her and Rowek. He reached down and grabbed her hand as she paused just outside the door. She looked up at him and smiled. The smile he returned held no shortage of desire and she blushed.

He looked so good in his suit, his perfectly styled hair. Too good. Almost inhuman.

Her mother had insisted they visit her at the hospital, and she had taken pictures of the two of them, telling everyone that walked by that her daughter's boyfriend was taking her to the homecoming dance. Emma had made some ridiculous sound, trying to warn her mother away from that term.

He hadn't said he was her boyfriend, and she didn't want to assume.

But he had just smiled, complimenting Emma's mother on how youthful she looked. He even asked how long she had been a surgeon and if she liked the profession. As soon as her mother heard that he was considering the medical field, she had walked around with heart-eyes. Emma snorted a laugh to herself. If Rowek didn't get his school attendance up, he would be lucky to be accepted to a community college.

"Ready?" she asked, giving his hand a light squeeze.

He didn't answer, simply led her into the gymnasium,

Adrianna and Aaron just behind them.

Her friend threw her fist in the air and shouted, "Dance time!" before pulling a nervous-looking Aaron out onto the dancefloor.

Rowek led her into the undulating crowd, the music so loud, it blocked out everything else.

She was slow to let herself get lost in it, and she swayed for a while until Rowek pulled her close.

They moved as one body, Rowek spinning her away and back to him once or twice. The rest of the time, his hands held her hips, and slid up her sides.

Emma glanced over and saw Adrianna and Aaron grinding on each other like there wasn't any clothing between them, and she looked away, feeling as though their intimacy wasn't something she should ogle.

Track after track played and she loosened in Rowek's skilful arms, beginning to feel slick with sweat.

When a slow song played, Emma started to walk away, to get a drink, but Rowek grabbed her hand, grinning.

He twirled her to him, her hands landing on his firm chest. He waltzed with her, somehow keeping her upright, even though she tripped on her own feet more than once. He slowed, noticing her lack of dancing skills, and she rested her head on his chest. His arms wrapped around her shoulders, squeezing her to him.

"You're so perfect," he whispered against her ear.

She looked up as he leaned down, pressing his lips to hers. It was bliss.

"Just think," she said, absently tracing a finger down his lapel. "If everything goes according to plan, you can take me to prom too. My mother already loves you."

Rowek's eyes shuttered as something crossed his expression, too briefly to assess. He gave a feeble smile. "Yeah, probably."

Her heart suddenly ached, wondering if she had been too forward. "I'm sorry," she said. "I wasn't trying to be...I just..."

He shushed her, pulling her against him again. "My father

may not let me stay here much longer. But I'll do whatever I can to buy us more time."

Her throat grew thick and her eyes burned. He was going to leave?

She was finally so completely and utterly happy, despite the terror of the future. She hadn't forgotten about Levaroth or the fact that a supernatural war could be looming on the horizon.

But this. Here with him was perfection.

And she didn't want it to ever end.

Distantly, someone screamed. Rowek froze, and so did Emma, breaking away from his intoxicating heat. A cold weight of ice settled between her lungs. *Shediem.*

"Emma, you need to run," Rowek said urgently.

"What? No!"

More screams sounded and the music screeched to a halt.

Then all hell broke loose as nightmarish monsters poured in through the double doors. The crowd began screaming and running away. Bodies tugged at Emma, trying to pull her from Rowek's grip.

"You have to go," he hissed in her ear and pushed her along with the crowd. She lurched forward, nearly falling into the stampede, but she managed to right herself.

Her eyes scanned for Adrianna and Aaron, but they were nowhere to be seen. An alarm shrieked as the fire exit was thrown open to give way to the fleeing people.

Emma turned, trying to find Rowek, but she couldn't see him anywhere. A short, bulbous monster with elongated canines like a saber-tooth tiger began to sing a hauntingly beautiful tune. All around her, people stopped and turned toward the sound. Mindlessly they trampled over one another to get to the ugly beast.

A woman with gray, leathery skin that wrapped around her skeletal frame, with long black hair, lifted an almost normal-looking hand. Then claws shot from her fingertips, sharp and glinting in the light before she began to slice into the prey that had walked willingly to their death. Emma pulled on those that still passed her by, oblivious to the slaughter.

"No," she cried, losing her grip on a young, dark-haired girl. "Stop!" she shouted.

Some of the monsters picked up their victims and began to tear them apart with their sharp teeth. Some looked like they were kissing them, then dropped their limp bodies like discarded juice boxes.

Hundreds of students, and some adults, all tried to get to the Shediem. Her heart pounded. She couldn't run up and try to kill them all, there were too many.

Had Rowek succumbed to the song like the rest of them? Why hadn't she? She hoped that whatever made her immune, also made him immune.

A blast shook the school, and men with swords and blades rushed in, some crashing through the ceiling.

Emma recognized Blaze among them. His eyes scanned the sea of people waiting their turn to be killed, finally spotting Emma, frozen in terror between the monsters and her exit. He sagged in obvious relief, but he couldn't fight his way to her. Too many innocent people stood in his way.

Giborim sliced through the Shediem, who had turned to fight their opponents. One who appeared to be hidden in the center of them, was a winged man, tall with dark, cruel eyes. He had two twisting ram's horns that protruded from his skull, his skin a bronze color that shimmered.

His gaze also locked onto Emma and his mouth twisted in a wicked smile that made her blood run cold.

He began walking toward her and she stumbled back, screaming at herself to run. As she turned to do just that, she heard the flapping of wings.

She screamed as the man pummelled into her back. She hit the floor with a gasp, the air knocked from her lungs.

"So you're the worthless bitch my brother is so obsessed with?" he sneered at her.

Brother?

Out of the corner of her eye, she saw Blaze fighting harder, screaming her name, though she couldn't hear it.

A pop sounded, and a man stood behind her, hauling her to her feet.

Her power hummed in her veins, burning hot. She lunged from whoever had grabbed her, toward the cruel-eyed monster, hungry for his power.

She was caught around the waist and hauled back by strong arms. The scent of woodsmoke and cloves washed over her, and she stilled.

"Hold still," Levaroth growled in her ear. She felt it rumble in his chest, and through her body. Her breath hitched.

He held her carefully, her arms pinned at her sides so as not to touch her skin.

A feral snarl erupted from her lips and she heard him chuckle. *He chuckled.*

The bronze-skinned man looked on with amusement. "Why not show your true self, Levaroth? I don't think she'd fight so hard if she knew what you truly looked like."

"Elbis, stop this. You have no command here. Go back to your prince and both of you beg our king for mercy. He may spare you."

The beast-like man—Elbis—made a strange clicking noise that she thought might have been a laugh.

"You'll never be able to keep her. She belongs to our king."

"She belongs to me," Levaroth hissed.

Emma's mind whirled.

Just as Elbis opened his mouth to respond, Blaze broke through the throng and charged at them all. Elbis flashed a smile at Emma, then he disappeared.

"Let her go, Levaroth!" Blaze roared. His eyes were wild. Crazed. And for a moment, Emma feared him.

His brother, Axel, came charging over too, and Levaroth gripped her harder to him. Their blades were coated in something black and oily.

In an instant, the floor fell out from under her and she screamed. Her vision went black. Then she was standing further from Blaze and Axel, Levaroth still holding her. Nausea crashed into her like a tidal wave.

She gasped. Had he just disappeared with her?

"Sorry, darling," Levaroth whispered against her ear, like a lover. He slid one hand up her belly, against the thin blue fabric, and over her chest. Her blood was hot with a million sensations. His palm stopped just above the swell of her breast. Her heart raced beneath his touch.

The Giborim brothers stepped forward in unison, only to stop abruptly. They knew they wouldn't be able to get to him without the possibility of injuring Emma.

With a jolt energy shot into her, searing her skin. She gave a tiny a whimper, and he twitched, as if her pain hurt him too.

"As a precaution," he added before sending another powerful blast into her that made her go limp and darkness swallowed her whole.

EMMA

A *booming dubstep track made her body swing and pulse. She kept her eyes closed, letting her heart pump with the beat. The music was alive inside her. She brushed her hair from her sweat-slicked face then threw her hands up, cheering with the crowd. The bass sent vibrations through her feet and up her legs.*

Large hands were on her, gliding across her hips and chest, worshipping her body. She ached for his touch. Longed for it.

"That's it, Emma, dance for me."

Her eyes flew open and she spun, looking up at Levaroth's molten gold eyes. They were hungry. Possessive. She backed away, but he moved toward her with the slow, lazy stride of a predator.

Her back hit the wall and his hands came up on either side of her, caging her in. His eyes turned cold, his expression deadly. She tried to scream, but his hand covered her mouth.

"I own you, Emma," he purred with his silky voice.

"No!" Emma sat bolt upright in her bed. She was cold and damp with sweat. Looking around, wildly, she realized she was in her bed. Alone. A shiver raced up her arms and she rubbed them, trying to warm herself. Her alarm clock read two minutes until six. It was still dark outside.

Emma ran a hand through her wild tangles. She stared down at the now rumpled fabric of her dress. Her mind raced, replaying the nights events. What had happened after Levaroth grabbed her? She kicked off her comforter and staggered into the hall, still bleary-eyed. Her mother's door was closed, though she didn't know if that meant she was at work or in bed. Slipping into the bathroom, she turned the shower on.

Steam spilled out from above the shower curtain, and she began to undress. As she worked the dress off her sweat-soaked body, a wave of grief hit her. Unbidden tears stung her eyes and sob broke free.

How many people died last night?

Were Adrianna and Aaron and Rowek okay?

Her body shook violently.

Where was her phone? She needed to be sure they were okay.

She stumbled back into the hall, naked, to find her phone. Sitting on her desk, was her clutch and her phone. Her breaths were jagged, and her lungs burned. How had her things gotten there? Had Rowek dropped them off? Last she knew, they had been in his car.

She grabbed her phone and headed back to the bathroom.

Her fingers shook as she scrolled through texts from Adrianna and Rowek.

Relief flooded her so completely, her knees knocked together. They were both okay. Rowek said he dropped her purse and phone off at her house. *Mom must have found them and brought them in.* His last message said to text him as soon as she awoke.

Adrianna's messages were just as panicked as Rowek's, freaked out about what had happened, but they just said: **I have something I really need to tell you, please call me.**

Emma sent a text that said she was safe and that she would call soon.

Emma set her phone onto the counter and stared at her reflection. Steam billowed out behind her, and her eyes widened at the sight of a red, inflamed mark on her chest. It looked like she had been branded with a cattle iron.

The center was no more than an inch long, like a diamond on its side and a cat-like slit in the middle. *An eye,* she realized as a chill snaked down her spine. From all four points of the eye, thin, deep purple lines branched out like veins. Anxiety rose up inside her. Her fingers trembled as she traced the outline. *What is it? Am I dying?*

Emma heard a door close, and she started. She climbed into the shower and washed herself quickly, ignoring the throbbing coming from the mark on her chest.

After she towel-dried her hair and brushed her teeth, she wrapped the damp towel around herself again. She peeked back down at the mark and saw the spidery-like veins peeking above the cloth. She snatched her dress from the floor and held it to her chest. She made sure the mark was fully covered before she stepped into the hallway.

"Morning," her mother greeted her, looking flawless as usual. It was Saturday, so she was dressed casually, her shiny strawberry-blond hair bone-straight, framing her slender face. Emma wanted to complain to the universe about how bitterly unfair it was that her mother looked fresh out of a style magazine at six-thirty in the morning.

"Morning," Emma replied. She forced a smile onto her face as she scurried back to her room. Somehow, her mother clearly had no idea about the Shediem attack at the school last night. Weren't people dead? Surely it would be in the news. And she had been at the hospital at the time where the wounded would have been treated.

She puzzled as she stood in front of her full-length mirror, staring at the angry-looking mark while worrying her lower lip. What had Levaroth done to her? Did the mark do something? Her stomach knotted painfully. She closed her eyes and shook her head, hoping that whatever it was would go away on its own.

She didn't waste any time getting dressed, choosing a sweater that perfectly hid the flaming red mark. Downstairs, the smell of bacon lured her into the kitchen, even though her stomach felt filled with lead. She doubted she'd be able to eat.

Her mother was humming a tune to herself, swaying to whatever beat was in her head when Emma entered the room.

She definitely didn't know about the attack.

"How do you have so much energy this early?" Emma asked begrudgingly as she dropped into a chair and poured herself a glass of apple juice.

"Coffee," her mother replied cheerfully.

Emma's brow arched. "Do you have a secret coffeepot in your room that I don't know about?"

Her mother laughed—a sound Emma didn't hear often, and it tugged at her lips. But her heart was too heavy to smile.

"Don't be silly, I was up at five." Her mother set a plate heaped with bacon, eggs and a single Belgian waffle. Emma's stomach grumbled threateningly. "You look as if you didn't sleep so well," her mother added as she sat across from Emma with a plate that had about half of what Emma's did.

She thought about confessing about the attack but stopped. How would she explain how she got home? How she got away unscathed.

Emma shook her head. "Nightmares."

Her mother gave her a sympathetic look over her steaming mug. "Well, it's the weekend, you could always take a nap later. Although, I was hoping you could help me tackle that flowerbed outside. It looks positively dreadful."

"If by dreadful, you mean overrun with weeds that are as tall as I am, then yes, I guess you're right." Emma stabbed the scrambled eggs with her fork. "I might try to lie down later, but I don't mind helping pull a few weeds first."

Her mother beamed as she plucked a strip of bacon from her plate and bit into it. Emma nibbled a piece of waffle, hoping her stomach would accept it as a peace offering.

After the little breakfast Emma could stomach, she went out into the front lawn and knelt beside her mother who handed her a pair of gloves. The sun was completely hidden in the gray, cloudy sky. A small pile of excessively tall weeds sat between them. Emma wrapped her hand around the base of a thorny cabbage grass and shimmied it, to loosen the roots' hold on the

158

soil. Then she pulled it out, roots and all, smiling at her success.

"Well done," her mother praised. She huffed as an extra-long dandelion snapped at the base. "So, how was the homecoming dance?" she asked as Emma pulled another weed free.

Her stomach flipped, threatening to expel what little food she had consumed.

"It was okay," Emma replied with a stiff shrug. "I felt sick after an hour or two, so I ended up coming home and going to bed."

"You were probably dehydrated."

Emma wished she could tell her mother the truth. Instead she bit the inside of her lip, hard enough to hurt. "Maybe," she replied.

"Rowek seems very nice. And he's certainly handsome."

Emma nodded, swallowing thickly. "We had a lovely time." Even though it wasn't an outright lie, the words tasted sour on her tongue.

Remembering Adrianna's panic, Emma stood. "I'm going to go call Adrianna. I didn't get to say goodbye before I left last night."

Her mother nodded as Emma hurried inside.

Once she was in her bedroom with the door closed, she dialed Adrianna's number. She answered on the first ring.

"Hello?" her voice was panicked.

"What's wrong?" Emma asked, concerned.

"Emma, something weird is going on. Last night when those things busted in—"

"They're called Shediem," Emma offered, trying to sound gentle.

Adrianna paused. "What?"

"They're like demons, I guess," she explained, wishing they could talk face-to-face.

Emma heard Adrianna try to muffle a sob. Her heart cracked at the sound, but she waited for her friend to regain her composure.

"Aaron and I got away, so we didn't really see what happened, but then this morning when I called him, he remembered going to the dance but not how we ran for our lives."

Emma's body went cold.

That's how it hadn't gotten into the news.

"Emma, I'm not crazy right? That really happened?"

"Yeah," she said, hoarse.

Adrianna continued, but Emma wasn't listening. "And there's the hazy colors floating around people, and I get these headaches all the time—"

"I'll call you back, A." Emma hung up and sat on her bed, unmoving.

Someone had wiped people's memories.

LEVAROTH

Usik had sent a message of summons in the dead of night. The small, leathery creature, no bigger than a bat had offered its leg, the note clutched in its talons. Once it dropped the message into his hand, the veemuris erupted into flames, leaving not a trace behind.

Levaroth read the note then tossed it away just before it too burned into nothing. He collected the Shax's payment and appeared outside the Shediem's door. It opened before Levaroth could raise his fist.

"Caught a whiff of a place I thought you might like to check out," he said in his sing-song voice as he offered another folded slip of parchment. Levaroth took it with a single nod.

Usik's eyes narrowed on the bag clutched in Levaroth's fist. "My payment?"

Levaroth tossed it to the Shax who made an eager noise in his throat.

"I also have some information about the girl."

Levaroth's back straightened. "What did you find?"

Usik moaned as he crammed a fistful of toes into his mouth. "I'm waiting on confirmation of one last inquiry," he replied, his mouth full.

Levaroth's lip curled.

"Take care of that." He nodded to the slip in Levaroth's hand. "Then come back. I should have everything I need by then."

Levaroth gritted his teeth, irritation sparking inside him. The door slammed closed as Levaroth unfolded the paper. A single address.

He closed his eyes and Sheol was gone.

When he opened them, he was in an abandoned building, the walls and ceiling blackened from fire damage. He crossed the bottom landing, stepping lightly and tucked his wings in tightly to keep them from scraping against anything.

Voices carried up the flight of stairs, but the words were indistinguishable, even with his heightened sense of hearing. He could sense at least ten of his brethren, but if they could sense him, they didn't reveal it.

He knew there was no way he would be able to maintain the element of surprise, so he opted for the act of casual interest. He stepped down the stairs, a bit louder than was necessary, ducking his head under the lintel.

No less than twelve Shediem scowled from their seats. There were various ranks amongst them: two Shax, one Drude, and four Djinns. The rest were Nysroghs.

"What, are we having an AA meeting in here? Why wasn't I invited?" Levaroth asked the silent room.

"You're not welcome here, traitor," the Drude said at last. Drude Shediem were always female in appearance, with gray, leathery skin, snake-like facial features and long, flowing black hair.

Levaroth's fists clenched. "Traitor?" he ground out.

"We know about you protecting the girl," one of the bulbous-headed Shax said with a rich, melodious voice.

The accusation made his veins run hot. "If any of you thick-headed toadstools had bothered to ask, I would have briefed you on my mission," Levaroth seethed. "She is a valuable asset—"

"We don't care," one of the Djinn snapped. "You and your master are wrong, always working everything to your own gain and we've had enough. *Our* mission is to stir the pot, strike fear into the humans' hearts. Belphegor is the leader we need. That wench you are so obsessed with has killed many of us. She's as much the enemy as the Giborim and should be slaughtered without mercy."

Red dots enveloped his vision as he fought to control his now burning rage. "Leave this place and remember that *I* am your Master while you are on Earth," he warned. His voice no longer sounded human.

"We do not answer to you, traitor, we serve Elbis!" a Nysrogh shouted. *Elbis. Belphegor's general. He would risk annihilation to see the prince he so closely serves take Nakosh's place as King?*

A pang of emotion hit him, the taste of it metallic and pitiful. Sadness was of little use to Shediem. He pushed it away. If Elbis, his brother in arms, chose to throw in his lot with the rebellious prince, he deserved death.

"There are many more of us that stand against you!" said another.

Chairs toppled over. The room rang out in a chorus of "Traitor!"

His wrath snapped free, and in a blur of motion his hands thrashed and spun with his blades. Each thrust and movement was met with flesh and bone. The Djinn brought two long blades down with crushing force that collided with his knives in a deafening ring. The Djinn were intelligent—human legends said they could predict your next moves—but Levaroth had trained them all. Remembered every weakness.

He wrapped a wing behind the Shediem's back and sliced, his talon-like claw making purchase. The Djinn's eyes widened as it let loose a blood-curdling scream. Levaroth felt the flesh sever. He sliced again with his other wing, at the same time, driving his knives up into its chest.

"You slaughter your own kind, and for what?" the Shediem gurgled. Thick, black, oily blood bubbled up from its lips.

"Conspiring against your General and your King is treason. I have dealt your punishment."

"Elbis is our General. Belphegor is our King." The Djinn gave

163

a garbled laugh as more blood oozed over its chin. "That girl has rendered your loyalties untrustworthy. She will be your death. I just wish I could watch as—"

Levaroth slashed a blade across its throat before the Djinn could finish. Its head hit the floor with a wet *thump*.

His breathing was uneven as he glanced around at the room, but it had nothing to do with physical exertion. He had just performed an execution of his kind. The pain of their deaths resonated in every cell. A wretched, horrible sound ripped from his throat.

He fell to his knees on the dusty floor. There he remained, though he didn't know how long. Unmoving, not bothering to draw breath.

When at last he found the strength to stand, he called forth his flame, which danced and curled like a living thing in his palms. He dragged them on the walls as he climbed the stairs. The dry wood caught instantly, and before he was out the door of the shack, the basement was engulfed in flames.

He turned and watched from the outside as the structure succumbed to his destruction, covering his murderous outburst. Levaroth could rationalize their deaths to his prince by revealing their plot, their loyalty, but the truth lingered. Twelve of his comrades fell to his rage that only burned so hot, because of *her*. They bombed the restaurant that could have killed her. They threatened her life and had to be punished.

She was a sickness that had infected him, her scent of purity and goodness a drug he didn't care if he overdosed on.

What was coming soon, what he would be forced to do, she would not survive as she was. Did he want her to remain as she was? *No*, he thought. *She'll desire another as long as she is good.*

I'll turn her. I'll blacken her heart and then she'll be mine.

When the ashes of his sin were carried away on the wind, he took flight into the darkness where he knew he belonged.

EMMA

E mma fell asleep, too exhausted to comprehend any more. She had called Rowek to ask what he remembered. He replayed the Shediem pouring in exactly as she remembered it. The crowd being entranced by the bulbous creature that he told her was called a Shax. He had been one of the unaffected ones, but he'd gotten caught in the stampede and was knocked unconscious. When he came to, the gymnasium was empty.

When she told him what Adrianna had relayed to her, he had gone silent.

"So those that lived forgot it happened, but what about those that didn't live?" he'd said. "Were their family's memories tampered with too? How is anyone going to be able to cover up a bunch of people suddenly missing?"

They talked for several more minutes until Emma had yawned for the third time.

"Hey, get some sleep. Message me when you wake up."

Emma agreed and hung up. Her eyelids were too heavy to keep open long enough to change into something more comfortable, and she was asleep almost instantly.

Sometime later, the mattress dipped by her hip. Slender fingers stroked her hair, and Emma thought she detected a slight tremble in the movement. She tried to pry open her eyes, but they were leaden.

A warm droplet hit her cheek. Was her mother crying? But sleep, heavy and consuming, pulled her back under before she could ask.

She didn't remember feeling the weight lift from her bed, but once she was able to open a single eye, she knew she was alone. Light beat against the drawn curtains, leaking from all sides and casting a warm glow within the room. She craned her neck around to the bedside table. The time on the alarm clock read a few minutes after eight. She had slept the rest of the day and through the night.

Emma scrambled out of the bed. Across the hall, she saw the door to her mother's room open, and descended the stairs. The house was quiet. In the kitchen, Emma's gaze caught on the note hanging from the fridge.

Emma,

Went to work for a bit. Be back before morning.

Love you, xoxo

Emma's heart constricted. She had left that note sometime last night, and still she was not home. Phone in hand, Emma tried calling her mother's cell. Her mother's voice filled the speaker with her voicemail message.

Don't panic, she's probably in surgery. She tried again an hour later. Still nothing. She debated calling the hospital and decided if she still couldn't reach her by noon, she would call her work.

Noon came and gone, and at two in the afternoon she called her mother's cell again. Still it went straight to voicemail.

She chewed on her lip as she found the hospital's number. After being directed to the correct floor, Emma got the receptionist.

"Hi, I'm just wondering if Laura Duvall is still there? I'm her daughter."

The woman paused. "She hasn't been in all day."

Her heart missed a beat. Like missing a step and suddenly falling. "Are you sure? She might be in the E.R."

"Hold, on let me check." Emma heard the distinct sounds

of tapping. "No, sorry, she was last in on Friday night, it says she left at two a.m."

"Oh," Emma's voice cracked. "Okay, my mistake." She hung up, her heart pounding.

She slumped onto the couch, her mind running a million miles an hour. What if her mother was in danger? Or had intended to go to the hospital but got into a terrible accident on the way there?

If she was okay, then where was she really? Did she have someone she visited? A friend?

A lover?

Emma stood, her spine ramrod straight as she climbed the stairs. Instead of turning left on the landing to go to her room, she turned right.

Her mother's door was already cracked open as Emma pushed her way into the room. *If she won't offer up answers, I'll find them.* Her determination wavered as she flicked on the light and looked around the room.

Tidy was an understatement. The décor was minimal. A queen-sized bed, a side-table with a lamp, a tallboy, and a beautifully carved armoire. The bed was carefully made, the entire room looking like a display at a furniture store.

Emma pulled open the top drawer of the side table. Dainty glass vials rolled to the front, clinking together. Some of them were filled with shimmering silver liquid, others a murky green that looked like grass and dirt sediment mixed with water. *Potions?* The idea nearly made her laugh out loud.

Her fingers brushed along them curiously. They were warm to the touch.

Emma closed the drawer and pulled open the next one. Notepads and papers were stacked neatly inside. But the one on top caught her attention.

It was a handwritten note in elegant scrawling letters that only some, Emma recognized. *Russian?* She didn't know for sure, and she couldn't read the signature at the bottom.

Is this who Emma's mother was with right now?

A car door shut outside, and she stilled.

The front door opened, and Emma slid the drawer shut quietly. She flicked the light off and pulled the door partially closed.

"What are you doing?" her mother asked from behind her.

Emma's stomach dropped as she turned.

Her mother looked exhausted, her hair a wild tangle on top of her head.

"Where were you?" Emma asked, folding her arms across her chest.

Her mother looked at her, blinking blankly. Then she cleared her throat. "Work."

"I called the hospital, they said you weren't there."

Her mother sighed heavily. "Well I was, now if you don't mind, I've been up for over twenty-four hours and I'd very much like a bath." She moved toward her room.

"Where were you really, Mom?" her voice was gentler, and she tried to meet her mother's gaze. "If you have a boyfriend or something, you don't have to keep it a secret. I'm a big girl I can handle—"

"Emma!" her mother shouted, cutting her off.

Emma fell silent, her eyes wide at the palpable anger on her mother's face.

"I am a grown woman. I do not need to tell my seventeen-year-old daughter anything!" She pushed past Emma into her room and slammed the door.

On Monday morning, Emma's eyelids flew open, as her alarm clock blared. She glared at the noisy box, slamming her fist on it a little more forcefully than was necessary. After untangling herself from the duvet, she climbed out of bed—a bit reluctantly—and began her morning routine.

Downstairs, a store-bought cinnamon roll sat on the

countertop next to another note from her mother saying she was needed back at the hospital and that she would see her after school. Emma balled up the piece of paper and tossed it into the trash with a scoff. She ignored the gooey, cinnamon-flavored attempt at an apology, filled her travel mug with coffee, and left for school.

With a few minutes to spare, Emma hastened through the hall. As she arrived at her first class, she spied Rowek, who half-smiled when she entered. She took her seat, noting at least a handful of empty chairs, including Jared's.

Sick, she wondered? Or victims of the Shediem attack?

Her stomach clenched as nausea rose up inside her.

Ms. Farrars entered just before the bell rang, beginning class, but she didn't seem to notice the missing students.

No one seemed to notice.

Her second and third classes were the same, holes in usually full classes, and Adrianna looked panicked as she looked around.

As the history lecture stretched on, Adrianna scribbled furiously on a piece of paper. Emma tried to crane around her to see what she was writing. Adrianna was a decent student, but not an avid note-taker.

Finally, she fed the paper through a gap under her arm, and Emma grabbed it.

There were names. At least twenty.

People missing.

One was a teacher, and Adrianna had written in parentheses that a boring old woman had taken over her Greek Mythology class with no mention of the previous teacher.

Emma wrote down Jared's name too and tried to recall the names of each person that wasn't already on the list, though she didn't know as many people as Adrianna.

When she was finished, she passed the paper back up to Adrianna. Her eyes were shining with tears as she gave a sad smile over her shoulder to Emma.

Rowek shuffled in his seat behind her, and she felt a zing of electricity course through her as his lips brushed her ear. She shivered.

"There's too many people involved in this. The cover-up is too complex. If whoever did this made a mistake, we'll find it. They may have overlooked a distant relative or something. We'll figure it out."

Her chest ached at his words.

Who needed to keep the massacre a secret? Why not broadcast it and let everyone tremble with fear?

At lunch, Emma, Adrianna and Rowek sat down for lunch. Aaron, Adrianna had explained, was at home sick per her request.

"It took some convincing," she said, taking a bite of raspberry brownie, "especially since he doesn't think there is any danger. But I told him he could stay home and play Xbox all day. He didn't fight me very hard after that."

Rowek snorted a laugh.

Emma felt unable to smile, let alone laugh. "What I want to know, is why the three of us can remember everything, and if there is anyone else that can too."

The freshman girl, Sara, sat down across from them at that exact moment. "Yes," she said simply.

Her eyes lingered on Rowek, as if puzzled by him. He stared back at her, unabashed.

Emma's eyes widened. "You were there last night too?"

She nodded.

Adrianna shifted in her seat.

"One of my best friends was killed in the attack. When I saw her sister this morning, she acted like she didn't have a sister." Her eyes glistened with unshed tears, but her face remained hardened. Angry.

Emma's lips parted on a sharp inhale. Beside her, Rowek and Adrianna were silent.

"Do you think you can make a list of people that have their memories, and a list of those missing in your classes? It's not right for all of those people to just be completely wiped from history."

Sara chewed on her bottom lip for a minute, considering, before saying, "I can try." She looked at Adrianna for a long moment, who shifted again. "I'll get back to you."

Emma smiled. "Thanks, Sara."

"Yeah, thanks, Sara," Rowek's low timbre was almost too quiet to hear.

Once Sara was gone, Adrianna looked down at her remaining lunch with a sickened expression. She pushed the tray away, folding her arms around herself.

"You okay?" Emma asked.

She nodded, though she looked unable to speak.

Rowek stood suddenly, drawing both their attentions. Emma gave him a questioning look, to which he responded, "I have to go check on something, I'll meet up with you later." He pressed a kiss to the top of her head before stalking out of the cafeteria.

"What if whoever did this finds out that we still remember? Will they come get rid of us too?" Adrianna asked.

"I don't know, A." A lump lodged itself in her throat that Emma couldn't swallow down. Then a thought struck her. "I'll see you later," she said, then hurried away, through the empty halls and out into the blinding sunshine.

⸻

"Hello?" Blaze answered on the second ring.

"Uhm, hi, this is Emma." She paused for a second. "Duvall." As if that would help him better remember her.

"Are you okay?" he asked, his tone urgent.

She swallowed. "You remember the night of the dance, right?"

"Of course."

Relief flooded her as words poured from her in a torrent. "Everyone has forgotten—or almost everyone—people are dead, and no one even knows they lost someone, it's as if they never existed. I don't know what's going on!"

"Wait, slow down. Who forgot who?"

"The people that died, the attack, no one remembers

anything. The families of the deceased don't even remember them."

Blaze let out a low whistle. "After Levaroth left with you, he came back and said you were home safe. The next thing I knew, the hall was completely cleaned up and everyone disappeared."

Emma released a breath. "Like, in front of your eyes?"

"Yes."

She shook her head. A sharp pain lanced along the back of her skull. Too much was going on, and none of it was making sense.

"So Levaroth somehow removed several hundred people in the blink of an eye except you and your...people as well as making it look like a bunch of people hadn't been slaughtered?"

"Well, not exactly," Blaze amended. "Me and a few other guys were suddenly outside the school. Others were transported further away."

Emma recalled how Levaroth had moved them instantly, and how it had made her dizzy. But he had been touching her when he did that.

"Maybe, when he isn't touching the people he transports, he doesn't have as much control over where they end up," she mused.

"I'm not sure. It was a first for me. I went by your house to make sure you were safe, but you must have been asleep."

"Yeah," she said absently, her mind still trying to process everything. "Why did he let me go?"

She hadn't realized she had said the words out loud until Blaze responded. "I don't know, but it's clear that he knows who you are and what you're capable of. I have a constant posting of guards around your school and your home, but it won't be enough..."

His words fizzled out and she was sure she knew why. *It won't be enough if he decides he wants me.*

"We have to do something," she said firmly. "People have to know what happened."

"How do you think that would play out?" he asked, his accent growing thicker with the emotion coating his voice.

"Who is going to believe us if we tell people they had another son or daughter? Who would listen?"

A burning sensation crept up her throat. "Then what do we do? Innocent people died and there's no one to remember them."

Blaze sighed. When he spoke again, his words were tender. "We will remember them. I'll ask around to see if there is any way to reverse the effects, but that may not necessarily be better. At least this way, they don't have to be in pain. There's no grief."

Emma nodded, even though Blaze couldn't see it. A tear slipped out and she wiped it away. "I have to do something. The bombs didn't have anything to do with me, but the attack at the school felt like it was directed at me. That other General, Elbis or something, he was looking for me. None of this would be happening if I—" her voice broke and she sobbed.

"No, Emma. It was never your fault. Shediem kill. It's the only thing they're capable of."

Emma took a deep, steadying breath.

"You'd be much safer if you stayed with me."

She blinked. "What?"

"My house, it has protections that make it so Shediem can't enter. You should think about coming to live here. At least until things die down."

"I…I couldn't. My mother would never let me."

"She would be welcome too."

Emma laughed. "Yeah I don't think I can just walk up to her and say, 'Hey so let's go move in with some Giborim. You know, descendants of angels that are superhuman warriors that protect the human race.'" She laughed harder, somehow finding the idea far funnier than Blaze, who was silent.

"Just think about it," he said. Then he hung up.

Her face flamed with shame. She considered calling him back and apologizing. Her outburst of hysteria had been involuntary, but no less rude.

Deciding against calling him back to make an even bigger fool of herself, she got out of her car and headed back inside.

EMMA

From the second Emma's eyes peeled open, she felt as if something wasn't quite right. The very atmosphere was charged with tension.

In the mirror she grimaced at the mark on her chest, the spider-like veins webbing from the top of it had curled up the ridge of her collarbone. If they spread any further, then she'd have to wear a turtleneck.

She wanted to ask Rowek about it, to see if he could tell her how to remove it, or at least stop it from growing.

Every part of her was on high alert, nearly shooting out of her seat when her mother dropped the sugar spoon into the sink, earning a raised brow.

When she arrived at school, Adrianna limped over to her without her crutches. She didn't look as terrified as she did the day before, though her normal level of cheer was far from sight.

"Hey," Adrianna said.

"Hey," Emma replied, feeling too worn out for smiles.

"How are you?"

Emma shrugged. Without another word, they wrapped their arms around each other, offering what little comfort they could. Tears pricked her eyes, but she swallowed them down.

"We should hang out after school today," Emma offered when they broke apart.

"Sure," Adrianna nodded, wiping away her tears. "I was supposed to meet up with Sara, but I can cancel."

Emma frowned. "Meet up for what?"

Adrianna shuffled her feet. "She's been trying to get me to meet up with her for a week or two. She said that whatever has been going on with me—the headaches and the vision problems—they're not migraines, like I thought."

Her frown deepened. "Then what are they?"

She bit her lip. "I don't know. I was going to find out."

The warning bell sounded for their first class and the two embraced each other quickly before departing to their classes. Emma promised to text her.

In truth she wondered about Sara. The spellbook she tried to hide had made her think she might also be a Spellcaster.

She rushed into the classroom, forcing her thoughts away. Once the test was passed out and the teacher sat down, reading something on her desk, Emma typed a message to Rowek, asking where he was.

"Miss Duvall!" Ms. Farrars snapped from the front. She stood, her eyes narrowed as she marched toward Emma's desk.

Her face was hot as Ms. Farrars held her hand open for Emma's phone. She relinquished it with a whispered apology.

"You can get it back at the end of the school day from the Principal's office.

She shrank down in her chair, acutely aware of more than two dozen sets of eyes fixed on her.

Her test was taken too, and she would have to schedule a time to retake it later in the week for a lowered grade.

The sense of dread that lingered in her gut only grew as the minutes ticked by to the end of the class period.

When the bell rang, Emma slung her bag over her shoulder and stomped out, into the hallway, eyes fixed straight ahead as she walked with the flow. The traffic kept pushing her closer and closer to the wall. Her sweater snagged on the bricks several times, but no matter how much she tried to push away, the crowd kept her pinned. Mild claustrophobia made her heart beat faster.

Without warning, the entire school trembled violently, the floor beneath her shoes vibrating. Emma leaned against the wall, suppressing a scream as students around her swayed and stumbled. Then the shaking stopped. A thunderous boom followed, and Emma's heart began hammering frantically in her chest. Alarmed shouts filled the corridor.

"Not an earthquake," several people shouted. Then the school became deafening, everyone yelling to each other. She pushed off from the wall and forced her way through the sea of bodies.

Some people ran, and it took everything in Emma not to allow herself to be knocked down. She was numb.

She knew what had happened. Why everyone was racing to get outside.

Seattle had been hit.

Once the cool morning air hit her, she managed to break away from where the staff was attempting to wrangle everyone together and walked to her car. People shouted and pointed; some cried. Emma paused with her hand gripping the door. High in the air, off in the distance, was a gigantic gray cloud hovering around the tops of buildings.

Emma leapt into her vehicle. The engine roared to life and she threw it into gear before speeding out of the parking lot before anyone could stop her. She raced through town, the ominous cloud of dust hanging in the air like a beacon. She weaved through cars that had stopped; their drivers out taking photos of the scene. Emma scoffed angrily.

Once she was closer to the heart of Seattle, all traffic was stopped. She pulled her car onto the sidewalk and killed the engine. She sprinted on foot, her heart pounding as she made her way into the thick, debris-filled air.

Nothing could have prepared her for what she saw once the wreckage was in sight. The Seattle Space Needle was obliterated. Huge hunks of shredded metal lay in the streets; smoke plumed from the ground every few feet. The buildings in the area had been hit by the shrapnel, chunks of the architecture gone.

Everywhere, people were huddled. There were those who wailed with heart-breaking sobs and those who stared straight ahead, silent and numb. First responders were busy tending to the wounded. Fire trucks were dousing fires and police were keeping bystanders calm. Emma easily slipped past the police tape, unseen.

She walked over toward a young, female paramedic who was bandaging a head wound.

"Is Laura Duvall here?" Emma asked.

She glanced up briefly. Her honey-colored hair was tightly braided, her hazel eyes filled with the determination of her duty. "We don't have a list of the wounded available yet, sorry hon."

"No, she's a surgeon. She works at the hospital near here."

The woman didn't glance up at her again as she answered, "Then she probably stayed there to receive the critically wounded. Heaven knows there will be plenty of them."

Emma nodded. "Well, is there anything I can do to help?"

This time the woman did look at her. Really looked at her. "There are bandages and cleaning supplies over there. Just tend to the minor injuries."

"Great, thanks." Emma stalked over to the crates the woman pointed to. She gathered an armful of things and made her way to a man sitting on the ground. Blood seeped from a long gash in his leg. Emma swallowed. It looked more serious than what could be considered 'minor' but he was losing a lot of blood, his skin a sickly pallor.

She knelt before him and he looked into her eyes as if she were some kind of angel. Above the wound, a strip of cloth had been tied to stanch the blood flow.

"What's your name?" she asked him. Keeping him conscious was priority—something she remembered from health class.

"Andrew," he said in a pained whisper.

"Hi, Andrew, I'm Emma. Mind if I look at your leg?"

He shook his head. She doused her hands in the alcohol

solution she had to sanitize them before she picked up the medical scissors. With surprisingly steady hands, she pulled the blood-soaked fabric away from his leg, inserting the scissors below the wound, and made a cut long enough to peel it away. It was difficult to see beneath the layer of blood, she let out a sigh of relief when she saw that the wound was not quite as bad as she had anticipated.

She soaked a square of gauze in antiseptic solution before gently wiping away the sticky fluid that was beginning to dry and crust around the edges. Fresh blood bubbled up and streamed through her fingers, warm and thick. Her heart dropped. He was going to need sutures. Her head whipped to the woman who was now accompanied by another paramedic. They were performing CPR on a little girl, who looked no more than eight years old. Tears burned her eyes. She looked around for any other paramedics who could stitch the wound but all around, they worked on their own patients, all of them seeming severe.

"Can you stitch it up?" he asked, his voice thin. His eyes were closed. She needed to act now. A woman a few feet away who was cradling an arm that was very clearly broken limped toward her.

"I'll help you," she whispered. Emma looked into the woman's dark, kind eyes. She smiled reassuringly.

"Yes," Emma told the man. She sorted through her materials, feeling her mind go blank. The woman pointed with her other hand to the wrapped packages. She removed the plastic coverings from the needle holders, pronged forceps, and the needle kit.

The woman walked her through each step, even how to hold each instrument.

"Now insert the needle at a ninety-degree angle. Make sure the bite is even on both sides."

Emma did as the woman instructed. She held her breath as the needle pierced the flesh. The man winced, an indication that he wasn't yet unconscious. The tip reappeared on the other side and she exhaled.

"Good work," the woman praised. "Now pull it through so

you have enough of a tail to make the knot.

Emma pulled gently, a slight tremor starting in her hands. The woman gave her in depth instructions on how to tie the knot. Emma worked with her brows scrunched together in concentration. A bead of sweat glided down her forehead as she pulled the needle holder through the loop and the first knot was made. She sighed with relief.

"Now do that about fifteen more times," the woman said.

Emma glanced up at her with uncertainty.

The woman gave a sympathetic smile. "You're doing great, kiddo."

Emma was able to stitch the rest of the wound shut, and though she knew it would leave a noticeable scar, the bleeding had stopped.

She thanked the woman profusely, who gave her a one-armed hug. "The world needs more people like you," the woman whispered into her hair and Emma couldn't stop the tears that spilled over.

After she cleared away her supplies, dropping the used tools into a large bio-hazard container, she found bottles of water that she handed out, starting with the man, who thanked her.

Shortly after, more paramedics arrived, and she happily let them do their jobs while she cleaned minor scrapes and gave out bottles of water.

When it looked as if she had done all she could, she walked back to the ambulance. As she grabbed a bottle of water for herself, she paused. The female paramedic she had first seen was sitting with her back to Emma. It shook as she shed silent tears. Emma climbed into the truck.

"Are you okay?" Emma asked her.

The woman turned around and Emma's heart ached at the sight of her tear-stained face. Her eyes were red and swollen. "We…couldn't…s-save her," she said through strangled sobs.

Emma remembered the little girl, she had seen receiving chest compressions and her heart rose up in her throat. Emma held her unopened bottle of water to the woman, who took it. Emma sat beside her, saying nothing for a moment as the woman drank the water.

"I'm so sorry," Emma whispered.

The woman wiped her face. "I'm new. I've never had anyone die before."

Emma couldn't think of anything to say that could be of comfort. She didn't know what it was like. All she could think about was how, somewhere out there, someone was now grieving the loss of a daughter. There were countless people just outside the ambulance, grieving. So many people were dead. Emma couldn't wrap her head around it, and silently, her own tears fell. For the little girl. For everyone who would go to bed that night with an aching, all-consuming hole in their hearts where their loved ones once were.

"I saw you stitching up that guy," the woman said beside her after Emma wiped away the last of her tears.

"I had help," Emma answered. "Everyone looked busy; he was losing a lot of blood—"

"Hey," the woman laid a hand on her arm. "Thank you."

Emma looked at the woman, giving her as much of a smile as she could muster. "My mother is a surgeon. I knew almost instantly it was a bomb. I just acted. I knew I needed to see if there was anything I could do."

The woman smiled in understanding. "You'd make a great paramedic."

Emma wanted to say that she didn't think she could ever give CPR to a little girl and find the strength to walk away when her body went cold in front of her. But instead she said, "Thanks."

The woman patted her arm and then she got to her feet. "I should get back to it."

Emma nodded. The woman shot her another small smile before she hopped out of the truck. When Emma was alone, she patted her pockets, searching for her phone.

Only to remember it was still at the school.

She'd have to find some other way to get a hold of her mom and let her know that she was okay. The school would likely be all locked up, with everyone rushing home to their families.

She'd try to get it tomorrow.

Emma slid out of the vehicle and started back toward her car. Her mother would likely be at the hospital so Emma would just leave a message for her.

"Emma!"

She spun toward the direction of Rowek's voice. He raced toward her between the labyrinth of abandoned vehicles, his expression drawn with concern.

Emma started toward him, closing the distance. His arms wrapped around her, squeezing the air from her lungs. She snaked her arms around his neck, feeling the pain of the past few hours slam into her at full force.

He gripped her shoulders, pulling her back to examine her. "What in blazing hell did you think you were doing?"

Emma swallowed back her tears. "I just had to come see if I could help."

A choked noise sounded in his throat as he hugged her again. "You shouldn't be here."

She drew back to look at him. "I had to."

He smiled. "I know you did. Come on, let me take you home." Wrapping an arm around her shoulders, he began to steer her away from the destruction. The mark on her chest gave a sharp burst of pain, and she hissed between her teeth.

He stopped, looking down at her with creased brows. "What's wrong?"

She tugged the neck of her shirt down, revealing the mark to Rowek.

He swallowed audibly and his eyes flashed. "A protection of some kind," he said.

Her eyes widened. "You've seen this before?"

Rowek ran a hand through his honey-colored hair. "I've heard about them. Read about them. They're unique to whoever places

181

it on you. Who gave you yours?"

"Levaroth."

Again, something crossed his expression, too quickly to read. "I see. Well I wouldn't worry about it too much. From what I know of them, they keep you invisible to Shediem."

She raised a single brow. "All of them? Why would Levaroth make me invisible to himself?"

Rowek opened his mouth, then closed it again. "I think whoever places the mark can track the wearer."

She released the hem of her shirt, gasping as if it had burned her.

He marked her like she was his possession. Making her only visible to him. Anger shot through her making her blood hot.

Rowek held up his hands. "Hey, don't kill the bearer of certain random knowledge." His words were light, his voice playful.

"Emma!" another voice called. She peered around Rowek as he spun to see who trotted up to them.

Blaze, armed to the teeth with more blades than an armory, slowed to a stop in front of them. Rowek moved to the side, blocking Blaze's view of Emma. She placed a hand on his arm.

"It's okay, I know him."

After a moment of hesitation that she could feel in his bunched muscles, he stepped to the side.

Blaze stared at Rowek, as if trying to see beneath his skin. Then his gaze snapped to Emma.

"You're not safe here, Emma. You need to come with me."

"Like hell is she going anywhere with you!" Rowek spat.

Emma's brows shot up at the vehemence in his tone. "It's fine, I was just heading home."

Blaze shook his head, his dark curls swishing side to side. "It's not safe there either. These bombs were a diversion—"

"What would you know about it?" Rowek scoffed.

Blaze ignored him. "Emma, you have to trust me. There's a meeting that I want you to attend. You deserve to know the whole truth."

Her lips parted. "Truth about what?"

Blaze glanced at Rowek, as if unsure whether he should hear what Blaze was about to say. "About who you are."

Emma's eyes widened, but Rowek grabbed her by the bicep. Hard.

"She doesn't need you to tell her who she is. She already knows, don't you Emma?"

She bit her lip, looking down at Rowek's tight grip. He loosened it slightly. Then she looked to Blaze.

"Can't you just tell me right now?"

He shook his head again. "Please, come with me. We can offer you complete protection."

She thought about the mark on her chest. If she was invisible to Shediem, what more protection did she need? But Levaroth could still find her, and it was only a matter of time before he did.

If Blaze had answers, like who her father was, then she didn't have a choice. She shot Rowek a small smile.

"It's okay. I'll call you. Go home and stay safe."

His eyes widened in shock, then filled with anger as he turned to Blaze. "Be very careful, Giborim. And don't touch what doesn't belong to you." He released her arm and pressed a kiss to her temple. Emma stood there in shock at his words.

Don't touch what doesn't belong to you.

She didn't *belong* to Rowek or to anyone.

Blaze stared daggers at Rowek's back as he stormed away.

"Your boyfriend has control issues."

Emma didn't respond. Her lips felt glued together.

For the first time since they had kissed, she wondered if Rowek was dangerous.

EMMA

As she stepped up into a black Range Rover, Axel turned around in the passenger seat, flashing her a grin. Emma forced a small smile in return.

Blaze shut the door for her before climbing into the driver's seat and then they were driving. The city was congested with such a large portion being blocked off, but no one seemed to have the sense to stay home.

"How did you know where I was?"

"Whenever there is a threat, it's our job to check it out."

She nodded.

"So the bombs were a diversion? How? I mean," she licked her lips, her tongue like sandpaper. Her mouth was dry. She had cried what little moisture her body could muster, and she had given her bottle of water to the EMT. "What was the real intent then?"

Blaze's stormy gray eyes flicked up to the rear-view mirror. "More abductions. Giborim compounds were attacked. The Shediem know if they bomb human structures, the Giborim forces will be diverted to offer aid and try to hunt the Shediem responsible. That leaves the fortresses with less protection in the event of an attack. Seattle wasn't the only place hit. It's everywhere."

Perhaps she was too numb to feel the weight of what he had said, because no surge of horror rose up in her as it should have. Instead she just rasped, "Oh."

In the front seat, Axel unzipped something Emma couldn't see, and her heart shot up into her throat. Then he turned and handed her a bottle of water. The outside was frosty with cold. Emma swallowed hard and took it with a grateful smile. She gulped it down greedily, welcoming the stinging cold in her throat and the ache it left in her skull. Axel wordlessly passed another cool bottle back to her which she accepted with a small, "Thanks."

The cityscape faded behind them, replaced with trees and foliage. Leaves of gold, burnt orange and deep red rained down from the branches, blanketing the road. Ahead of them, the Cascades shot high into the air. Already their tops were blanketed in white.

"Where are we going?" Emma asked.

"I guess you can say it's my house. There's going to be a meeting with Giborim from all over once we get there."

"How far away is it? I need to be back before my mother."

Axel chuckled. "Don't worry, sweets, we're almost there."

Emma sat back and tried to relax, unsuccessfully, as every bump made her muscles tense. Everything felt like it was going sideways; now, even Seattle was marked unsafe. Emma wouldn't be surprised if her mother tried to move her into some underground bunker. Nowhere in the world was safe, and it felt like all hope was crumbling along with the shattered sense of security. And the way she and Rowek had parted left her insides twisted and unsettled.

They turned onto a dirt road, hardly worn. Blaze drove with a certainty that was just as clear as if they were on a visible track. The terrain turned rocky, and they had to slow. Emma gripped the overhead handle as the vehicle rocked and bounced up a steep, mountainous incline. When at last she felt what little breakfast she had consumed, threatening to escape, it leveled out again. She blew out a long breath.

"You okay?" Blaze asked gruffly. Emma nodded.

"You aren't going to chuck up in my car, are you?" Axel groaned.

Emma gave a soft laugh. "No, I'm okay," she assured them, but Blaze's gaze remained on her in the mirror for several beats and she stared back into his unreadable gray-blue eyes.

Emma looked out into the distance to see a tall, metal fence, as well as two figures guarding an ornate steel gate that twisted and curved, ending with spear-shaped spikes at the top. A fortress it most certainly was. The closer they got, the tighter Blaze's grip on the steering wheel became.

"Is this like a military base?" Emma asked.

"No," Blaze replied with a hint of irritation that Emma didn't think was aimed toward her. "It just has a lot of Giborim in it right now, so the security was amped up."

"Oh," Emma answered.

At last they were in front of the gate and the two men dressed in a similar, full-black military style uniform that Axel and Blaze wore, approached the vehicle. They were holding large, intimidating rifles as they came to either window, which the males obligingly rolled down.

"Morning, Garret," Blaze said to the olive-skinned man who had dark, slanted eyes that searched behind Blaze to where Emma sat. "This is Emma, I'll introduce her later at the meeting," Blaze explained.

Axel laughed about something the other guard had said, though she paid little attention to either of them.

Garret gave a single nod. "Welcome home, sir," he spoke with a somber voice. Blaze nodded in reply before rolling his window up. Axel saluted the guard on his side before rolling his window shut as well. Garret tapped the side of his helmet and spoke, though Emma couldn't read his lips. The gate swung inwards, and the guards gestured them in. As the car rolled through, a weird sensation ignited within her that was both pushing and pulling her in opposite directions. Her breath caught in her throat. Abruptly, it stopped, leaving a lingering sense of nausea.

"Welcome to my home," Blaze said. His voice contained a touch of pride, but also a touch of something like sadness.

Emma's gaze traveled from the mirror where she had curiously observed the change in his eyes, to the view in front of her, and her lips parted in surprise.

The "house" was anything but. Like a castle, the chateau-esque architecture was grand and fit for housing at least fifty people. The grounds surrounding the manor held an elaborate garden filled with rose bushes and hedges that Emma suspected were kept so tidy by a team of gardeners.

A sound of awe escaped her as the vehicle pulled along a paved driveway that looped in front of the house. When the car came to a stop, a tall man in a tailcoat and top hat walked out onto the wide front porch. He looked like he had stepped out of the early nineteen-hundreds, his hands crammed into the tiny front pockets of his coat, a hard stare and dark, bristly moustache to match. Axel gave a semi-audible groan as they opened their doors and stepped out of the vehicle.

"Boys," the man said in a tone that sounded almost like reproach.

"Uncle, this is Emma Duvall." Blaze placed a hand on her back and guided her forward. She fought the urge to dig her heels into the pavement. The man's nose wrinkled as if he smelled something foul. "She'll be sitting in on the meeting," Blaze said in a way that left no room for argument. The man gave a stiff nod by way of greeting.

"Nice to meet you," Emma said, trying to keep her tone from reflecting any of the disdain she felt.

"Shall we go in?" he asked. Emma couldn't help but wonder if he owned the house by the way he acted. She could hear a slight accent in his clipped, nasally voice. It wasn't like Axel or Blaze's which left her puzzled.

Axel and Blaze exchanged a look over Emma's head as Blaze took the lead and they entered the magnificent building.

As elegant and grand the outside was, the inside was doubly so. Emma sighed a sound of awestruck wonder at the historic décor and a glassy marble staircase that curved up along the wall to her left, leading to the next level which she could see glimpses of through the railing above. Where she stood, rooted to the tiled floor, her head tilted back to admire the high ceiling that had been carved with an ornate design of flourishes and swirls.

She could have stared for hours just at the details in the foyer, but the men ahead of her were waiting for no one. They strode through the hall, passing several closed doors on the right, and even a door beneath the staircase on the left, which Emma was dying to peek into.

A warm, garlicky and buttery smell tantalized her as she passed an open archway on her left, through which she spied a full kitchen where a dozen or so people were all busy working. Her stomach gurgled loudly which was amplified by the structure of the house. Blaze glanced back at her, brows creased. Axel chuckled.

They came to a wide, open door. Blaze was the first to enter and Emma could hear the people within fall into hushed silence. The room was large, with three long, sturdy, wooden tables pushed together in one long row. At the table, were at least fifty wooden chairs. All but four were filled.

Dozens of faces scanned along the procession, falling on Emma. Each set of eyes were dazzling and mesmerizing in their own way. Her cheeks flamed as she snapped her attention to Blaze, who took his seat at the head of the table. His uncle seated himself on his right, Axel selected the seat on his left, leaving Emma the seat between Axel and a girl who looked to be around her age. She was just as beautiful as every other person in the room. Her pale ivory skin was flawless. Her blonde hair hung in elegant waves with not a single hair out of place and was so light it was almost white; her full lips appeared to be rose-kissed. Emma felt like an ugly smudge among their beauty.

As Emma sat, the girl gave her a quizzical look. Emma's

face burned with embarrassment and she glanced toward Blaze, hoping that the deafening silence in the room would soon be broken.

Blaze's gaze was already studying her, and after a beat, he stood. Everyone's attention in the room shifted back to Blaze. With the exception of his uncle, they all regarded him with respect and authority.

"Good afternoon," Blaze spoke. His confidence and ease in the presence of his own kind was evident. "Late last night, and earlier this morning, all around the world, our women were abducted during a time of vulnerability. Our most precious asset to the survival of our race, stolen." Emma's hands began to tremble. "I know you all have questions, and that each of you has either lost someone, or knows someone who has." He paused, his eyes briefly passing to his brother, and Emma saw the tiniest flicker of emotion flash in his eyes. She thought of their mother and sister.

"I swear to you, we will do everything we can to get your loved ones back. And for those of you who have brought your wives and daughters here today, I offer them protection and solace. You are all welcome to stay in my home. As you can see, it is plenty spacious for you all."

"Who is the girl?" a tall, gangly man with short, tight brown curls asked before Blaze could continue.

Emma felt her cheeks warm yet again under the scrutinizing gazes of the entire room.

"I'm coming to that," Blaze answered. His eyes bored into the man, who looked as if he wanted to argue but thought better of it. "As you all know, we wouldn't usually ask our women to hide and leave the fighting to the men, but in this instance, I think we can all agree it is best to keep them protected. In doing so, we will all band together and finish this war. We have a new player to add." He paused, allowing whispers to fill his silence. "The Shediem now have a new enemy to fear." The room grew quiet.

Emma felt herself go cold. The eyes of nearly everyone in

the room burned into her. Blaze addressed the room as if she were not in it. Panic flooded her, robbing her body of the ability to move, to speak.

"Emma Duvall is that enemy. Her touch is lethal to Shediem." Whispers broke out again, but Blaze pushed on. "She can absorb their life-energy. With her help, the higher ranks of Shediem can be annihilated. We can make certain our loved ones are never again taken by them."

The room was in uproar before he finished, and Emma wanted to shove her fingers into her ears to stop herself from hearing their protests.

"How can we trust her?"

"What if she turns on us?"

"Who is she?"

"What is she?"

Tears of humiliation burned her eyes, and when she looked at Blaze again, it was with anger. Beside him, his uncle was red-faced, shouting. Blaze's gaze searched the table, skipping over her. It all became a roar in her ears as she blocked it out. Among those contributing to the cacophony was a face that leered directly at her. His familiarity made her stomach drop, remembering when he had spit at her. Triumph lit Jake's face. A room full of centuries-old warriors who all saw her as a threat.

"Enough!" Blaze roared, and the room fell silent. But Jake continued to look at Emma with utter contempt even as Blaze spoke again. "As I said, I know you may have questions or even some concerns, I don't have all the answers, but Miss Duvall is the answer to ending this once and for all. She has a love for humanity that should inspire us all."

Blaze finally looked toward Emma, and this time he held her gaze for several moments for the whole room to see. A respect shone there that surprised her.

"To the question of who she is—she is Emma Duvall and that's all you need to know. As for what she is, as you all undoubtedly want to know, it is not for me to say. She is not a threat, and I want you all to treat her with the respect she is due. She is a great ally and a fiercely compassionate person."

Warmth spread through her, her lips betraying the slightest of smiles. The room remained unmoved. The silence was deafening. It felt strange to her that in the moment disaster struck Seattle, she had been able to work alongside those with higher education and training but had been viewed as an equal. Yet here in a room filled with people who knew little about her, she was being treated not only like their enemy, but their inferior. It was the look in Blaze's eyes that said she was just as capable as everyone else seated at the table.

"Now, the chef has prepared a meal for all of you. You are welcome to dine here in this hall, or you take it to your rooms once we've gotten you all settled," Blaze finished, and then he sat. His gaze flicked to hers again for a moment, with an expression she couldn't quite make out.

Then the room began to disperse. Emma sat, frozen in place, unsure of what to do with herself. Several men, all young, and well-built flocked to Blaze blocking him from view, when a voice beside her spoke.

"Hi, I'm Emerelda," the girl beside her said in a thick accent. She extended a pale, slim hand to Emma and after a brief pause, she took it.

"I'm Emma…obviously."

The girls wide, blue-green eyes reminded Emma of her mother, though her hair was a pale honey color.

"You feel familiar to me," she said as her gaze searched Emma's.

"Oh?" Emma said with forced lightness.

"What are your parents' names?" she asked conversationally.

"Laura Duvall is my mother, but I don't know my father's name," Emma replied.

"Hmmm," the girl said, tapping her chin with a finger. "There is something about you that looks very familiar." Her accent was almost too thick to understand. Russian, Emma realized.

"Well, you don't sound like you're from around here," Emma remarked.

The girl smiled a sad smile, her eyes casting a stern look toward Blaze and Axel's uncle who was leaning close to Blaze, deep in conversation. From the way Blaze's brows were drawn together, Emma guessed it wasn't light conversation.

"My godfather insisted I come here, for my own protection."

Emma looked from Blaze's uncle to Emerelda. "He's your godfather?" she asked with surprise.

Emerelda nodded. "My parents died years ago, but my godfather keeps a watchful eye on me."

Emma fought back a snort. *I bet he does.*

"I'm sorry to hear that."

The girl waved a delicately boned hand. "They lived long lives." Emma glanced back at Blaze's uncle, curiosity bubbling up before she could stop herself.

"How old is he?"

Emerelda shrugged. "He is over five hundred and fifty, last I checked."

Emma felt her eyes widen and the girl laughed.

"So how old are you, then?"

The girl gave her a wry smile. "Eighty-eight."

"But you look so young!"

Emerelda laughed again, a rich, melodious sound that drew all three male's attention. Blaze's curious gaze went from Emerelda to Emma, where it lingered. He rose, interrupting his uncle mid-sentence, and strode toward them.

Emerelda became silent as Blaze stopped behind them. Emma craned her head to look over her shoulder at him.

"Emerelda." He nodded to her. An endearing shade of pink coloured her cheeks, her lashes lowered.

When she spoke, her accent was noticeably thicker. "We meet again, warrior."

Though the words were harmless, the way she spoke them sounded more like a proposition. It made sense that Blaze would prefer the likes of the flawless female beside her to Emma who was just a "girl", age aside.

"I hope you are finding Washington to your liking," he said, seemingly unaffected by the woman's bedroom eyes.

"I am, thank you. It is very kind of you to allow us to stay here," she replied. Her eyes shifted for a moment to where Axel still sat.

Emma suddenly found the room too warm and stood. As she did, Blaze looked toward her, but she side-stepped him and fled from the room with a muttered, "I need some air."

Emma found the foyer empty as she stalked through it toward the door. Outside, the brisk, fragrant air caressed her face and she inhaled it deeply.

A dark form shot out from the side of her vision. Large hands wrapped around her throat as her back struck an unforgiving brick wall.

LEVAROTH

He knew the instant she became untraceable. The invisible cord that bound them didn't sever, as it would if she had died. No.

It pulled taut, then released. She was cloaked.

Hidden from him.

After the bombing, he'd felt her go directly into the hot zone. So he followed her. He'd watched her help the wounded from afar, too enraptured by her goodness to pull himself away. She cared like she couldn't help herself. Like caring for humans was written in her genetic code.

It was fascinating. To see her emotions worn so plainly.

It was cruel that he would have to snuff that out of her.

But he would so she would be his forever.

He had lingered in the shadows when the pathetic Giborim warrior had convinced her to go with him.

She trusted so easily, he wanted to wring her delicious, slender little neck. But a bone-deep ache grew inside him, knowing she would not so easily lend her trust to his kind. Not their truest forms, anyway.

He followed them until the cloaking charms swallowed them whole. Their destination was invisible unless he got close enough to sound the alarm.

Even knowing he wouldn't be able to feel her. To caress the thread that secured her to him. It was agony. Clawing, gnashing panic filled him when she disappeared.

He'd wait for her as long as he was able. Pacing back and forth, snarling like a wild animal.

His rage scorched his veins even as his entire body shook with exhaustion. It had been too long since he'd last fed. He couldn't feed when he was constantly watching his new little pet, making sure that the Giborim didn't steal her away, or worse, kill her.

But now she was in their claws. He could have stopped it. He knew he should have. Something inside him had taken root. A desire not to cause her pain. Only her willingness to go prevented him from tearing the Giborim's throats out. The look she gave him that night at her school function was emblazoned in his mind.

Terror.

Hatred.

Disgust.

He'd seen them all before. But her wide, emerald eyes had nearly split him in two.

Levaroth forced himself away from the Giborim stronghold, reasoning with his insanity that he'd come for her when he was at full strength.

He just hoped the Giborim would show their true colors by then.

***

The French Quarter of New Orleans was as vibrant and lively as ever. It was a hub he frequented. A few murders here and there were an everyday occurrence. Humans here, being superstitious and riddled with occult members, would easily look the other way while he drank his fill.

Upbeat jazz music could be heard on many of the streets, and people gathered to watch the live musicians. Everyone was focused on taking videos and photos with their phones; no one noticed when he selected his prey.

A young woman in her early twenties with blonde hair that hung over her shoulders and draped down her back like a golden curtain was his first. He stood behind her and gently brushed a hand along her lower back.

She spun, startled by a stranger's touch. Her eyes narrowed in accusation. *A feisty one*, he thought gleefully.

"My apologies," Levaroth said with a look of sincerity. Her expression softened. He held her attention with his golden eyes as he said, in a low, commanding voice, "Don't move, don't make a sound."

Obediently she stood still as his hand wrapped around her thin wrist. He could drink a human's life-force anywhere on the body, but the arteries and the heart were the quickest.

She didn't taste like much, those that were mind-blocked never did. Their emotions were what gave the flavor, and without emotion, the energy was plain and unsatisfying. Her pulse slowed beneath his touch. She collapsed within a minute, and as she fell, the crowd became aware of her, grabbing for her to stop the fall.

He disappeared before anyone could check her pulse. He carried on through the crowds. The heat would be blamed for the number of fatalities, but what he truly wanted was a cold-blooded kill. His rage was merely coated with desperation. He needed to hurry so he could get back to Emma.

In his current condition, he couldn't be around her. It would be all too tempting to feed off her, and that was the last thing he wanted to do. He knew that once his beast had a taste of her, it wouldn't let him stop.

At last, he found a victim who made his pulse quicken with delight. Like the first, this one was female but with short, spiked, vibrant purple hair. The look of her said she was spoiling for a fight, which was exactly what he wanted.

She seemed to be placed directly in his path as if by design. The street he followed her on was one of the more unkempt within the city. Humans wreaking of urine and vomit, strung out on their drug of choice were slumped against walls every few feet. His prey walked through the thick of it, entirely sober. The only emotion he could taste from her was disgust.

He trailed her at a distance, but it didn't take long for him to realize she was looking for something, or someone. She found it, or rather him, passed out near a dumpster. A mangled sound of anger and sadness came from her lips as she pressed them tightly together and crouched beside him.

Levaroth moved himself into the shadows as he watched, grinding his jaw with rage. He could spring out and spill her blood in this alley. Leave her to die with all the other bottom-feeding scum.

He would. He'd taste her blood after he fed off her vibrant life-force.

As he took a silent step forward, a sharp voice cut through the thick, humid air.

"Why are you following me, Shediem?"

Levaroth paused. Few could sense him through his disguises. Even the Giborim couldn't.

It took an incredibly powerful supernatural being to see the monster beneath the sleek, male face he wore.

He looked closer, studying her pixie-like features. "And what are you wild one?"

The girl rose, leaving the boy. Her eyes changed from a tempting, espresso brown to the color of her hair, and in the instant that they flared with light, Levaroth knew.

"Ah."

"Go and leave this city alone," she commanded.

Levaroth laughed. "I don't think so, Spellcaster."

Only a second before she moved, he saw the glint of metal in her hands. Excitement surged through him, stoking the flames of his rage. She rushed toward him, blades flicking open. Levaroth closed the space between them in an instant, palm up, ready to stun.

At the last moment, the blades fell from her hands. Blinding, cold light shot from her. He realized too late, it had been a ruse.

When his skin made contact, his body went rigid and he dropped to the ground.

She had used his bloodlust against him.

"Haven't you heard the expression 'never bring a knife to a magic fight'?" Her smile was a flash of white. "Nothing personal, demon. I just need to be able to get my brother out of here without you following me."

He was encased in icy, shimmering light.

She loomed over him, and all he felt was the flood of his wrath burning every inch of his stiff body. Internally he was roaring, but his lips wouldn't so much as twitch.

He could do nothing as he watched her struggle to gather the filthy, unconscious heap that bore little resemblance to her. His eyes caught on a long, purplish scar that wrapped around her toned bicep. The boy weighed at least double what she did. Her lips barely moved as she breathed an incantation before hoisting him up over her slim shoulder, dragging him past Levaroth and out of the alley.

EMMA

er windpipe was being crushed beneath a pair of firm hands. When her head crashed against the brick, white flashed across her vision, cutting off her view of her attacker.

"I know what you're up to, you filthy, half-blooded whore and I will not let it happen." Jake's breath was hot against her cheek. He pulled her off the wall, and it gave her the momentum she needed to drive her hands up between his wrists and break his hold.

She gasped as she sucked in air. Coughing, she stumbled away, rubbing her throat and trying to keep out of his striking zone until her vision cleared.

"God, what is it with everyone trying to choke me?" she wheezed.

"Jake!" Blaze's voice was lethal. His large outline stepped into her line of sight, blocking Jake's advances.

"Get out of my way, *Hermano*," Jake ordered.

Blaze folded his arms over his chest.

"You will not harm her," Blaze commanded. His voice was low and menacing.

"You're not fooling anyone. She isn't here under your protection because she's an asset to our cause. She has put a spell on you—"

"Jake," Blaze warned.

"She's one of them, and you know it! Our DNA is hardwired to sense them, and my instincts are telling me to kill."

One of them. She knew what he was saying.

No. Emma ground her teeth painfully. She didn't want to hear this. She couldn't hear it. *I'm not a Shediem. I'm a Spellcaster, I have magic. I am good.*

"Look at her, Jacob," Blaze growled. "Does she *look* like our enemy? Does she *act* like our enemy? She is the only being alive that can *kill* Shediem."

"She's just showing you what she wants you to see! They're all the same!"

"Let's get one thing clear, *Brother*," Blaze said through gritted teeth. "I am under no delusions. She has put no spell on me. As for her scent, she only gives off a trace of it. She managed to pass through the wards, and I know you can also sense the familiarity." His voice lowered when he spoke the last part, and Emma froze, gaze sliding from Blaze's back to the deadly expression Jake still wore and back.

"She's an abomination," Jake spat after a moment. Then he stalked off the porch, shooting a glare in her direction before breaking into a sprint toward the gate. Silence hung in the air, thick with tension.

"What am I?" she asked, her voice small.

Blaze stood still for several moments before heaving a sigh, then he turned to face her, running a hand through his hair.

"I swore I wouldn't say," he said.

Emma huffed, throwing her hands up. "By who?"

"I can't tell you that either."

Her blood grew hot, her hands clenching into fists at her sides. "Why not?" Her voice was thin.

"Because I don't go back on my word." His look implored her to drop it, but she wouldn't. She couldn't.

"The Giborim all seem to think I'm some kind of monster. So tell me," she snapped. "What. Am. I?"

Blaze sighed again. "What's your mother's name?"

Emma's mouth turned down. "Laura Duvall, why?"

Blaze stared out at the dark tree line, mist crept through the massive trunks. "That's not her real name."

She started. "What are you talking about?"

Blaze searched her face, his gray eyes like rolling storm clouds before he spoke again. "Walk with me."

Emma followed him off the porch and through the maze of hedges and rose bushes. She couldn't help but admire the beauty of both the landscape and the one who owned it. They paused along a row of exceptional roses that started out a vibrant yellow where the flower wound tight, each petal opening into a burning orange, then finally, red at the tips—*like little fire blossoms*, she thought.

Blaze continued, "The Giborim were commanded to only breed with other Giborim in order to keep the bloodline pure." Emma felt confusion at the turn in conversation, but he held up a hand as if to say *bear with me*. "Those that were caught breeding with humans were cast out from our ranks in disgrace. It wasn't common, but it happened. We all knew that we needed to do our part to keep our numbers strong, so we kept our distance from humans to avoid any emotional attachments.

"In Russia during the early 1700s, Albert Ivankov, who was a descendant in a long line of strong, dedicated Giborim, fell in love with a human. He was cast out, disgraced and excommunicated. His wife, Anna, bore him four children. One of whom, was James Ivankov, who in turn, married a human and they had two daughters. Nadia Ivankov was the eldest."

Emma's brow furrowed. "What does this have to do with me?"

"Nadia knew about the Giborim, or more importantly, the Giborim knew about her. Every child with Giborim blood, no matter how small, is kept track of to help keep the existence of our kind a secret. We live far longer than humans, so certain precautions have to be taken so as to not raise suspicion. The

201

record of Nadia ended when her family home burned to the ground." He paused, searching Emma's face, as if she might indicate knowing more than she was letting on. "Nadia was pregnant out of wedlock and she feared her family's wrath. So, one night, when her family had gone out, she started the fire, making it to look as though she had perished in it."

Emma shook her head. "If you're trying to say my mother is Nadia Iva-kov or whatever, she's not. Her name is Laura, she was born and raised in Texas." Her voice was filled with uncertainty.

Blaze glanced sidelong at her. "They found a body, burned beyond all recognition—"

"Well, there you go then," Emma interrupted, but he continued.

"She has a friend that hid her until she too gave birth to a little girl almost eighteen years ago. Then she moved to the states. With you."

Emma scoffed. "Then why doesn't my mother sound Russian?"

"Let's just say, her friend has made her nearly untraceable. It's the reason your mother is able to find jobs as a surgeon everywhere she goes. She has eluded everyone who had ties to her family, moving each time a group of Giborim set up permanent residence nearby."

Emma's hand fell away from the delicate rosebud she had held in her grasp. She faced Blaze and was split somewhere between wanting to burst out in laughter and telling him he was crazy. She decided on the latter. "My mother is Laura Duvall. She isn't from Russia and if anything, she's a Spellcaster, not a Giborim."

Blaze tilted his head. "Spellcaster? Why do you say that?"

"I found vials of some weird liquids in her nightstand. And, maybe this power I have that can kill Shediem is my form of magic."

He pondered her words for a moment. "The friend I spoke of is a mutual friend of mine and your mother's. His name is

Sergei. He is a Spellcaster. They are close, though I do not believe him to be your father."

"What are you saying?" Emma asked, folding her arms over her chest.

"I do not pretend to know your mother's secrets. My relationship with Sergei is mostly business. Spellcasters are generally for hire, but he asked me to keep an eye on you for your mother. What I know of her is what Sergei has told me, and also what is documented in Giborim history."

"And what about what Jake said?" she prompted.

He sighed heavily. "You carry a faint Shediem scent. But that does not mean you are one. Spellcasters can cloak themselves to appear human to Giborim, and Shediem. Until they learn to do so, their scent is similar to that of a Shediem. It is possible that Levaroth's presence near you has temporarily altered your scent, or just that your scent is similar to one."

Emma wrinkled her nose. "Great, so I stink."

Blaze gave a warm laugh and stepped toward her. Her body hummed with awareness.

"You smell fine," he said, his head tilting towards hers, a smile tugging at his lips. "Like warm sugar and spring." His hand lifted slowly, tucking a stray strand of hair behind her ear. His touch was almost hot, the heat spreading through her. "I know what you are Emma, and a monster is not it." His accent was thick. "You help people in need without a second thought of the risk to yourself. You're the most caring and selfless person I have ever met."

Emma's heart pounded. She swallowed hard, letting herself get lost in the depths of his stormy gaze as he leaned closer.

A sudden rustle came from a bush behind them. Emma whipped around to find a large, black bird perched atop a thorny branch. It cocked its head to the side, watching them with eerie curiosity.

"Damn birds," Blaze huffed.

She cleared her throat. "So, is this, Nadia's family still alive?"

Blaze took a step back as he said, "Just her sister. She lives in Russia."

Again, Emma contemplated his words. "My mother doesn't have a sister. She was an only child. And if she were a Giborim, wouldn't she still look like she was, like, nineteen?"

Blaze met her gaze for a moment before looking back toward the mansion. "She will age only slightly slower than a human since her blood is so diluted. Her lifespan will likely be only a few decades longer than that of a human." Emma wondered how long she would live—if she would live longer than a human too. The answer came down to who her father was.

A chilled breeze reached them, and Emma shivered.

"Let's go back inside, shall we? I imagine you're hungry." The mention of it made her stomach clench. She felt ravenous. The bird cawed loudly, then took flight, its wings batting the roses. A cold chill dripped down her spine as she watched it disappear into the cloudy sky.

"Sure." Emma followed him back to the house.

Once they were back inside the large meeting room, Blaze had two meals brought out. A plump, gray-haired woman began eagerly setting dishes of finger sandwiches and bowls of creamy, garlicky soup in front of them while chattering away animatedly to Blaze about her grandson's soccer team. He smiled fondly at the woman and agreed to watch him play later in the week. Emma felt a sense of warmth at their interaction, and also a sadness.

Emma had never met her grandparents; her mother had only said they died before she was born.

The woman, whose name, she discovered, was Gertrude—Gertie for short—was the first person in the house to not only smile, but to chat at length with her. Emma mentioned that she also enjoyed cooking, which sparked a lively conversation about her favorite foods and what Emma liked to cook. Several times she caught Blaze looking at her. There was a warmth in his eyes that made her heart stumble.

Stop it, she scolded herself. *You're with Rowek!*

When Emma was certain she couldn't eat another bite, she thanked Gertie and they stood. She offered to help clean up, but Gertie shooed them out as staff came in to clear the empty dishes away.

Blaze cleared his throat. "Would you take another walk outside with me?" he asked.

Emma nodded, smiling. She knew she should be getting home, even though her mother would likely work well into the night.

"One second," he said, standing up from the table and disappearing from the room.

Emma walked back into the foyer, spying a massive crystal chandelier above the staircase. She watched the light twinkle on the crystals, sending rainbows of color in all directions.

Blaze jogged down the marble steps near soundlessly, drawing her gaze back to him. When he reached her, he extended a large black sweatshirt. She took it, her smile spreading as his scent reached her, and she slipped it on.

"Thanks."

Blaze nodded, his eyes flashing with an emotion she couldn't place.

They strolled through the winding maze of gardens again, further from the house. Emma was enraptured with the beauty of the property. She wanted to stop and study every type of flower that was miraculously still in bloom, but to do so would require more hours than she had to spend.

"You like the gardens, I take it?" Blaze asked with a hint of amusement.

Emma nodded enthusiastically. "How many people do you hire to keep it so immaculate?"

Blaze gave a low, throaty chuckle. "Would you believe me if I said only one?"

Emma turned to look at him, disbelief written plainly on her face. Blaze nodded. A brightness lit his eyes that made him look younger. His entire countenance seemed more at ease here.

"I tend to most of it myself. I employ only Gertie and the caretaker my father hired. They both live here and care for the house when Axel and I are away."

"Where is your father?" As soon as the words were out of her mouth she winced at her insensitivity. "Sorry, I didn't mean to—"

"Don't worry," Blaze replied. His lips tugged up in a small smile. "He stayed in London after my mother's death."

Emma nodded in understanding. "I'm sorry," she said again.

"No harm done," he said. "I'm glad you like this place so much. I hope you will come to think of it as home. It is entirely safe."

Emma lifted her face from the pink speckled rose she had been smelling, to gape at Blaze.

"I can't," she said, a little too forcefully. "Even if my mother *is* a Giborim, she'd never allow it."

"If I went to her, told her who I was, I'm sure she would agree. She knows that the our kind can protect you better than—"

"No," Emma cut him off. "Thank you, but no. Besides, if it's so safe, why are Giborim females being abducted? Shouldn't that be impossible?" She hadn't meant the words to come out sounding so harsh. *Idiot*, she scolded herself.

A muscle in his jaw flexed. "Giborim protect their homes with wards and spells that only Spellcasters can provide. Most Giborim aren't fond of their practices. Especially because their loyalty lies only with the highest bidder. They provide our wards, but in the cases of the strongholds that were compromised, the Spellcasters were obviously offered a higher price to remove them."

"And what makes you so sure your Spellcaster won't be bought out from under you?" Emma asked.

Blaze gave an uncharacteristic grin. "Well, I happen to know she's rather fond of me."

Emma's brows knitted together. Then it hit. Emma's eyes widened with surprise. "Gertie is a Spellcaster!"

Blaze chuckled. "A well-practiced one too. She's been

providing us protection for almost fifty years."

"Wow," was all Emma could think to say.

"She can sense both Giborim and Shediem—not all Spellcasters can. The fact that she took to you right away is just proof that you could never be anything other than good."

Blaze was close again, his body projecting a heat that was intoxicating and inviting in the cold, damp air. His warm, earthy scent filled her senses as her gaze met his. Her brain felt muddled. Hazy. Tentatively, slowly, his fingertips brushed a stray strand of her hair from her face. The simple action felt intimate and unexpected. A strange sensation snaked through her, and she couldn't remember why she shouldn't be this close to Blaze. Her breath caught in her throat as his fingers slid down her jaw brushing like the touch of a feather on her neck, then they slid around to the nape of her neck.

Heat spread through her, and as if of its own volition, her own hand came to rest on the plane of his chest, feeling the hard-earned muscles beneath her fingertips. Before she could process what she was doing, she raised herself up on her tip-toes as he leaned down, guiding her lips to his. With less than a breath separating them, he paused, looking into her eyes, a question in them.

She felt the desire to jerk away.

But why, she wondered. *Perhaps he is seeing me as more than just a girl.*

As she stared back, her heart beating like the clap of a racehorse's hoofs, a shrill siren sounded, jerking them apart.

She blinked, dazed. Her stomach dropped, realizing she almost kissed Blaze. Not Rowek.

Blaze's expression transformed, becoming cold and calculating. His eyes churned with wildness as he growled, "Shediem."

LEVAROTH

It took over an hour for the Spellcaster's hex to wear off. The girl and her brother were long gone. Levaroth's energy was almost completely spent and his skin felt as if it were being melted off from the inside. His rage was a living thing inside him, always burning, always pushing its way to the surface. And right now, his bloodlust was boiling. A walking disaster waiting to happen.

He crawled—actually crawled—to an unconscious body. Their life was hanging on by a thread, and he barely had to touch the filthy human before he sucked it up. It was a drop of water in a blistering desert. Even with so little energy, he had one purpose in mind as he staggered to his feet.

He was back at the entrance to the Giborim layer, panting from the heat that rippled under his skin. His feet carried him unsteadily forward, pushing through the wall of sticky protections.

Sweat coated his brow and he broke through. Their scent knocked into him, turning his stomach violently. Like sunshine coating the deepest part of the forest. It was disgusting.

The gate wasn't far, and he shuffled toward it. In the distance he saw her. More specifically, the big, brutish Giborim with his hands on her, his mouth seeking hers, and Levaroth lunged for the gate with a roar that was wholly his beast.

His veins seared, and he let out a choked laugh. *I'll kill him.*

The taste of his blood would be vile, but ripping out Blaze's spine and delivering it to his prince would be his greatest reward.

Sirens sounded, a high-pitched wail that made him want to grind his teeth, but he grinned, wide and wicked. *Let them come*, he thought, *I'll kill them all.*

In a moment, the other side of the gate was filled with armed Giborim, snarling and ready for a fight. Emma pushed her way through the warriors. Some shot her looks filled with loathing and his grin spread. He could use this to his advantage. A moment later, the Giborim he most wanted to slash into a thousand pieces moved through the wall of soldiers. Unlike when Emma passed, his comrades wore looks of respect and adoration. He was armed, swords drawn, wearing a look that oozed with brutality.

"Come out, come out, little warrior," Levaroth taunted, his face between the iron rungs, ignoring the searing pain the wards inflicted. His inner beast was in control and ready to at last be fulfilled.

"Why are you here?" Emma demanded, her voice like a knife, cutting a hole through his rage that only she could do.

"I'm here for you, of course," he said. The crowd shifted with unease.

Emma narrowed her eyes at him, arms crossed. "I'm not leaving with you."

"I think you will when you hear what I have to offer." His voice was giddy and sounded strange to his ears. The beast was reveling in the upper hand.

"Enough of this," Blaze growled. "Cut him down!"

His minions all moved in obedience. The gate lurched and swung inward, all filing around it like robots, but no one crossed the border. They were safe within the wards, and they knew it.

"Wait!" Emma shouted just as the front lines started to advance. Everyone halted—in surprise rather than loyalty.

The warrior glanced sidelong at her, but her eyes were fixed on Levaroth. "Emma, don't," he said softly.

"What could you possibly have to offer, *demon?*" she asked.

Levaroth's mouth spilt into a grin again, and his head cocked to the side as the beast took her in appreciatively. *Yours*, it hissed.

"We're not bargaining with him," Blaze growled.

Emma looked up at the warrior with a tenderness that drew forth a rumbling deep in Levaroth's chest. *Mine*, his beast wanted to roar at the male standing too close to what he wanted most.

"He won't hurt me, Blaze, and you need to find your lost people." She turned back to face Levaroth. "What can you offer?"

The Giborim started to protest, but Levaroth cut him off.

"The exact locations of Shediem of varying ranks. And I can tell you who is stealing the Giborim females." He had killed the twelve that posed the biggest risk, but they were not Belphegor's only followers by any means.

Sounds of shock and disbelief rippled through the Giborim. Blaze eyed him with suspicion.

"And why would you do that?" he asked, despite a few whispered warnings from several of his people. One such soldier was his fair-haired brother whose name he couldn't recall.

Levaroth shrugged. "They are set for execution anyway. You'd be doing me a favor, really. The name I offer you will not save those you've lost. But will help prepare those that remain."

"We don't do favors for your kind," the brother spat.

But Blaze's face was utterly haunted. Ripples went through the gathered Giborim as his words set in. Those that had been taken were beyond saving. And more was yet to come. They could only guess what was coming. But Levaroth knew. It was why his eyes slid to the girl who was not human. To the girl with undiscovered power pulsing through her veins. What her role would be in it all.

"Then I'll let them continue to tear Seattle down, piece by piece," Levaroth replied with another shrug.

A flash of pain crossed Emma's face. Her lips parted as she inhaled sharply. He immediately regretted causing her pain, but it was too late. The damage was done.

"Locations of Shediem and a name is of little value. Tell us why we should agree," Blaze said.

"I know how you Giborim can't resist killing, even if you rationalize it by calling us evil. The name you need is a kindness far greater than you deserve."

"But why betray your own?"

"*They* are the traitors. Death by my hands is too quick. Capture and torture by your kind is the lowest punishment I can offer them. And as I said before. The name itself will not save anyone."

"We agree to your terms," Emma said before Blaze or his brother could object.

Chaos rung out. The Giborim behind them were all shouting at once as Blaze grabbed her, spinning her toward him. His wings were not visible, but he felt them twitch with the desire to spread them wide and take flight. To soar over this blasted gate and grab Emma. The Giborim needed to have his hands removed, since he was incapable of keeping them to himself.

"You cannot leave with him, Emma! He didn't offer to take you home and let you live your life. His offer was just that you leave with him!"

Levaroth smiled. The disappointment of walking away without a fight settled into a deeper sense of victory at what he was about to gain. It wasn't yet time to present her to his master, but he could prevent the bond between the warrior and Emma from forming. Not when she had another option.

"I vow to take Emma home, warrior. No harm will befall her by my hands," he shouted over the cacophony. He made intersecting slashes over his heart in the form of an 'X'.

Emma glanced at him over her shoulder. "See, I'll be fine," she said with feigned lightness. Blaze looked ready to drag her away from the fence, but reluctantly, he released his hold on her arm. The Giborim fell into a stunned silence.

She reached for Blaze's hand, giving it a reassuring squeeze. "I don't want to get stuck in traffic, can we hurry this up?"

Levaroth said, rolling his eyes.

Emma huffed a sighed and then she stepped over the manor's protection, her body tensing as if the sensation was uncomfortable. Then she was in front of him.

"I'll have the name and those locations now," Blaze demanded.

"Oh, right," Levaroth said with a wicked flash of his teeth, as if he had merely been forgetful. Then he grabbed Emma's arm tightly, and before they disappeared, he said, "For every day you do not contact Emma in any way, I will deliver a location to you. You will get the name when you have captured every Shediem I give you."

EMMA

They were in her room. Nausea gripped Emma and she swayed. Levaroth pulled her to him, steadying her. Emma pushed herself away as the weight of her decision crashed down on her.

She had almost kissed Blaze, which now felt foolish and like a betrayal to Rowek. But now she didn't know if or when she would see him agin. Angry tears stung her eyes. Levaroth stepped toward her, eyes bright, and she stepped back.

"Get away from me."

Levaroth held his hands up as he froze. "I just saved you from being his next chew toy. A little gratitude wouldn't hurt."

"You don't know anything about me or my life," Emma snapped.

His lips twisted to one side. "Oh, that's right, don't you already have a boyfriend? Rowek, or something?" He tsked. "How do you think he'd feel to know you let another man's lips anywhere near you?"

"Get out of my house!" Emma shouted. She turned, picked up a book from her bed, and by the time she had spun back around to throw it, Levaroth was in front of her. His hand gripped her wrist, stopping it in mid-swing. It fell from her hand, flopping to the floor. His grip was gone the moment her power surged to life, only the faintest trickle flowing into her. Gone before it truly began.

In the next instant, her body landed on the bed, wrapped tightly in her duvet. She yelped as Levaroth kept her pinned, the fabric cutting off her power.

Shrieking, she tried to free an arm, but he was as solid as a brick wall.

He ground his teeth together before leaning down. "Just stop fighting me for a second," he hissed near her ear.

Her heart hammered wildly in her chest. Reflected in his molten gold eyes was the faint greenish glow of her own. Her power was flowing through her, hungry for his energy.

"Emma stop, I don't want to hurt you. I need to feed, and if you attack me, I can easily overpower you," Levaroth said, his face contorted in pain. Their faces were so close. She moved her lips toward him, but he flew back before she could make contact. Anger and a flash of hurt flooded his face.

"I'd like to see you try," she drawled as she freed herself.

"Emma," Levaroth warned. His voice had dropped, sounding guttural and no longer human. She paused. "You can be pissed at me all you want. You don't belong with them—with *him*. They will only let you live long enough to serve their cause and then they'll kill you."

Emma rolled her eyes. "You don't know anything about them. You kill people. That sounds to me like we're enemies."

Levaroth's jaw clenched. "I've been around a lot longer than you, and once you become who you really are, they will turn on you."

He appeared directly in front of her again. Her eyes went wide as his lips planted a gentle kiss on her cheek.

Then he was gone.

The contact was so subtle and brief that she barely felt a spark of energy. It felt familiar somehow. But as she stared at the place he had been standing, she wondered if it was even her power at all.

Her mother arrived home less than an hour after Emma

had. Panicked, and looking near collapsing, she threw her arms around Emma.

"I've been calling and calling you!"

Emma gasped. "Oh, I totally forgot to get a message to you. My phone is at the school."

Her mother shook her head, tears falling freely. Emma's heart ached at the sight. "I couldn't get away, but all I could think about was that you were dead.

"I'm really sorry, Mom," Emma said, crying too. "I went to see if they needed help, then a…friend brought me home. I'll have to go get my car tomorrow. Hopefully it hasn't already been towed away."

"Okay," her mother put her hand on her forehead, brows pinched. "We'll go get it first thing in the morning."

Emma nodded, hugging her mother once more before her mother climbed the stairs and shut herself in the bathroom. Emma made a sandwich for her that she left in her room.

Emma didn't see or hear from her mother the rest of the night, and almost as soon as her head touched the pillow, she too fell into a deep, dreamless sleep.

School had been cancelled in memoriam for Monday and Tuesday, with the plan of reopening on Wednesday. They assured the parents that counsellors would be onsite should anyone who was grieving need it.

"These are troubling times. But it is the wish of terrorists to keep us hidden in our houses, cowering, too scared to live life. We must not give them their wish. We must be strong and power through, letting them know we will not be broken." That's what the officials of Washington state all said.

If only they knew the terrorists that they spoke of were not simple humans who would be caught if and when they made a mistake. The world was under attack by crazed supernatural beings who could tip the scales into anarchy at any moment.

Emma went to school on Wednesday, even though her mother had expressed her concern with her doing so.

Rowek made an appearance in every one of her classes that day. She hadn't even known he was in all her classes since he skipped so often. Things were awkward between them, and she felt as if her almost-mistake was somehow written on her face. But he brought her coffee and kissed her gently, with a hint of desperation as he wrapped his arms around her, as if deciding to never let her go.

A sickening feeling sat heavily in her gut. More than just guilt for almost kissing Blaze. It was his possessive words playing over and over in her mind. And the way he took to sitting in silence beside her at lunch and during her free periods. They didn't speak about much of anything, but he watched her.

Always watched her.

She felt alone. Like being in a tiny box, feeling around for a hole to suck in fresh air. Adrianna didn't come to school on Wednesday. After grabbing her phone from the office, Emma had called her, and Adrianna told her she had another migraine, but her voice shook like she had been crying. Emma knew not to push her friend. Adrianna would talk to her about it when she was ready.

In American history on Thursday morning, a folded slip of paper tumbled over her shoulder, into her open textbook. Emma unfolded it discreetly. *You look beautiful*, it said.

It was a sweet gesture, she supposed. And perhaps he was trying to strike up conversation, but she couldn't shake the feeling that the hidden message was *you're all mine*. And being his wouldn't be so bad, because he was also hers, but something in him seemed to have shifted.

His presence was darker. Dimmer. His eyes looked almost black. Darkness radiated from him like a disease.

On Friday morning, before school, Adrianna showed Emma the compiled list of everyone that had ceased to exist last weekend. Her eyes were wide, her hair mussed. Like she hadn't slept.

"I talked to Sara yesterday and she said four others maintained their memories." She looked around then leaned in closer to Emma and whispered, "She called me like ten minutes ago. They don't remember anything now. She apparently got their testimonies of the attack a few days ago, but when she spoke to them individually last night, they had no idea what she was talking about. They said the dance went off without a hitch."

Emma's lungs constricted. If Levaroth was the one that wiped everyone's memories, he must have discovered those that he missed. She wondered how long it would be before he tampered with Sara's and Adrianna's memories.

Ugly, vile hate filled her. She couldn't swallow it down.

She would let it fuel her. The next time she saw him, she'd kill him.

That evening, after finishing her homework, Emma put together dinner and waited at the table for her mother to arrive. She stabbed moodily at her baked potato with a fork, glancing down at her phone every couple of minutes. At ten minutes past eight, her mother's car pulled into the driveway, headlights flashing across the living room window.

Her mother walked through the door, moving straight past the kitchen doorway. Emma jumped up from her chair.

"Mom," she called, heading into the hallway.

Her mother froze on the first step. "Yeah, babe?" She didn't turn around.

Emma blinked, confusion and hurt stabbing her in the chest. Had she known Emma was in the kitchen and avoided her? "I made you some dinner."

"Thanks, just stick it in the fridge. I'm going to take a shower. I'll have it later."

Tears welled up in her eyes. "What's going on?" Emma asked. "You seem to be avoiding me. Are you going to be around tomorrow?"

Tomorrow was Emma's eighteenth birthday.

Her mother turned around. Guilt slashed across her features. Then it was gone. Her eyes were brighter, clearer. Her hair tousled.

"Yes, honey, of course I'll be here tomorrow." Her mother smiled.

Had she imagined her mother's look of guilt? The hospital was likely filled with people needing life-saving surgeries, and she had selfishly been mad at her mother for neglecting her. Her shoulders slumped.

"Okay, I love you."

Her mother gave her a watery-eyed smile. "I love you too."

She didn't move right away, looking at Emma as if taking her last look at her seventeen-year-old before she became an adult. Emma swallowed the growing lump in her throat.

Then her mother turned and climbed the stairs. Emma heard the bathroom door shut as she wrapped her mother's plate in cling wrap and stuck it in the fridge. After she washed the dirty dishes, she trudged up to her room, the aching hole of loneliness burrowing itself deep into her chest.

Silent tears fell, soaking her pillow until sleep claimed her.

***

"Rise and shine!" Her mother's voice stirred her awake. Emma peered up at her through bleary eyes. A flame danced on a single, pink, glittery candle that was stuck into a large, glazed cinnamon roll. The warm, sweet cinnamon scent made her stomach rumble.

"Happy birthday!" her mother said excitedly as Emma sat up, rubbing her eyes. "Quick, blow out the candle."

Emma smiled. She didn't believe in wishes, but she found herself wishing for today. A day with just her mother, before she blew out a breath. A tendril of smoke danced up from the extinguished wick before her mother waved it away. She held the plate out to Emma.

"Thanks, Mom," Emma said as she tore a chunk of the pastry off and popped it into her mouth. She didn't bother stifling her groan at the delicious treat. Her mother laughed.

"Get dressed, I have big plans for us today." Her mother winked and left Emma to devour the rest of the pastry. A paper cup sat on her bedside table. Steam curled up from the hole and the tight knot in her chest unfurled. Everything felt right again, if just for a moment.

She clambered into the shower a little while later, her hands sticky and her belly full. Once she was dressed and back downstairs, she could hear her mother speaking in the kitchen. Emma came in just as her mother tossed her phone down on the table, her head tilted back, eyes closed and huffed an exasperated sigh. The ache in Emma's chest hit her full force; her smile evaporated.

"Please tell me you don't have to go to work," she whispered, fighting back the tears that sprang forth.

"I'm so sorry Emma." Her mother met her stare and she looked torn. "It's literally reopening an incision and draining the—"

"Make someone else do it," Emma said, hating how childish she sounded. *Today is the one day I'm supposed to be allowed to get my mom all to myself, right?* Deep down, she knew the answer to that.

She shook her head. "Jerry and Alex are helping at the other hospitals. This patient will die if I don't go right now."

Emma's shoulders drooped but she nodded. "Fine, go."

Her mother brushed a kiss on her forehead. "I'll be three hours, tops. Then I swear, you have me for the rest of the day."

Emma nodded, biting down on her lip to keep from saying something she'd regret.

"I love you, Emma. You can open your present while I'm gone," her mother said as she threw on her coat and headed out the door.

Emma stared at the pale pink wrapping paper, spotted with shiny, gold splotches. The shape of the box told Emma right away what it was. She stared at it with an empty sadness for several moments before she picked it up and stripped away the wrapping. Her eyes were fixed on the brand-new smart phone box, her face void of emotion.

Deciding she might as well start getting it set up, she took it up to her room and booted up her laptop. The phone charged as she loaded all her apps and settings onto it.

She flicked through old pictures, deciding which ones to keep. Several of her and Adrianna making silly faces, made her smile.

The doorbell sounded.

Her brow creased as she rose from her desk and set off downstairs.

Peering, out the side window, surprise, and perhaps a thread of dread filled her. Her limbs tingled with his nearness.

"Did you already eat?" Rowek asked when she opened the door. He held two coffee cups and offered her one.

"What are you doing here?"

Rowek cocked his head to the side in confusion. "It's your birthday, I thought you might like some company. Or at least your liquid caffeine addiction."

Emma snatched the cup from him, ignoring the burning hot coffee that sloshed out onto her hand. "It is not an addiction."

Rowek laughed his silky-smooth laugh. "Well, you grabbed that awfully fast for it not to be an addiction. It's not your first this morning, either."

Emma stilled with the lid against her lips. "How do you know that?"

Rowek shrugged. "You smell like coffee."

"Thank you for the coffee, but I don't want you here right now," Emma said firmly.

"Look, I know things have been weird," Rowek stepped into the house, forcing her to step back, "but you have to understand how it looks when you decide to run off with some big, muscly dude."

A spark of guilt ignited inside her. She closed the door and sat on the couch. Rowek followed suit. "Yeah, well it didn't help that you were all 'I own you.'" She said the last part in her best creepy voice.

Rowek fought a smile. "I didn't mean to make you feel that way. But we belong to each other, don't we?"

Emma let out a long breath. "I don't know. I just—we're not items, you know?"

Rowek nodded. "I won't say it like that then."

She smiled, feeling her chest loosen.

Rowek sat straighter, his face going stony.

The doorbell chimed again.

"Expecting someone?"

Emma scoffed. "No."

She headed for the door, Rowek following closely. When she opened the door, a sweet-smelling aroma hit her. A large wicker basket with at least a hundred vibrant, multi-colored roses was held up by a pair of large, wrinkled hands, the man behind it hidden from the waist up. She recalled the scent with ease, and her face lit up with a smile.

"Emma Duvall?" the man said from behind the avalanche of flowers.

"That's me," Emma replied gleefully.

"Do you want me to bring these in for you?" he asked. Emma giggled, not sure how he could see to bring them in, but she held the door open for him.

"Sure, come on in." She helped direct him to the kitchen table where he placed the basket. A card poked out from the top. Emma reached for it, when a hand plucked it from the holder. She spun around.

"Hey!" Emma said. The elderly man who had carried in the flowers, stepped away uncomfortably. Emma wondered if he was the magnificent grounds-keeper at Blaze's manor, but before she could ask him, Rowek had him lifted off the ground by his throat.

A surge of blistering rage blasted through her veins as Emma sprang into action. She yanked at Rowek's shoulders, his arms, clawing and screaming at him to stop. But Rowek was immovable. The man's feet kicked wildly, his face red and eyes bulging.

"Put him down!" she screamed, her throat burning.

Rowek released the man's throat with one hand, then grabbed Emma's arm. The contact dropped her to her knees. Pain blasted through her skull, fixed behind her eyes. Her vision blackened, and she thought she would lose consciousness. Then the pain receded. She scrambled back up to her feet, her body shaking. *He used his magic on me.* Her anger burned hotter.

The man choked, his face flowing from red to purple. Doing the only thing she could think to do, she clapped her palms over Rowek's ears, hoping the burst of pain would loosen his grip. Giddiness surged through her as rich, dark energy flowed through her. She gasped, each cell filling with power.

The man fell to the floor in a heap. Her anger was a rolling high tide that threatened to crash down on her and Rowek both. She didn't want to let go, but the new foreign darkness roared for violence. Emma drove a fist into Rowek's solid stomach, and he doubled over as she tackled him to the ground. She straddled him as her fists rained down, pummeling his face. He tried to block, but every time their skin met, she was fed a rush of his power. It weakened him, making him slower while fueling her. She screamed down at him, letting the craving for his blood sing its haunting melody in her ear. A few of her blows he ducked and blocked, others connected with thick cracks. His flesh split open in several places. Blood, thick and dark, oozed from the wounds. Then they stitched closed right before her eyes.

Make him bleed and take his power.

"That's it, Emma, give in," Rowek rasped. He was grinning.

She froze, a fist raised in mid-air. Her limbs shook with the effort not to fall onto him and drain him of his power. For long moments she stared down at him. As the fog of violence lifted, shame replaced her anger and she leapt off him. What was he? Was she absorbing his magic? It had been so dark. So old. He wiped away a trickle of blood from where his lip had split. The tissue and skin knitted itself back together neatly.

The elderly man gave a choked cough from the floor beside her and she rushed to his side. He slid away, cowering from her touch and Emma was transported back to when she had seen her friend react similarly.

She gave a broken sob. "I'm not going to hurt you." Her voice was hoarse. She didn't try to move any closer to the man. "I'm so sorry," she whispered as tears flowed down her face. She hung her head and cried as the man pulled himself up to his feet, using the table. No one said anymore as the man fled through the door, slamming it closed behind him.

She felt a hand brush her shoulder and she spun toward Rowek with a snarl. "Get away from me."

Rowek stared down at her with a dark expression.

Her head throbbed. "What are you?" she asked in a whisper.

He rolled his eyes. "I told you, I'm a Spellcaster."

She shook her head. "No. Whatever is inside you has been around for thousands of years. I felt it. It's evil."

His cold expression faltered. "No, Emma, you know me." He crouched down in front of her. "You know me."

Her eyes were wide as chills wracked her body. "I don't know the boy that almost killed him over *flowers*."

"That Giborim keeps getting in the way," he hissed. Rowek paused, seeming to consider something.

With a flick of his wrist, her eyelids became too heavy, and she slumped to the floor, enveloped in darkness.

EMMA

Golden orange light blanketed her. Emma rolled over, feeling excessively warm, she worked her legs to bunch the duvet down at her feet.

Why were her legs so sore?

Flashes of Rowek holding an elderly man by the throat, her fighting against him, filled her mind.

And power.

Heat swept through her as she recalled his power. Sweat dotted her forehead and she wiped it away, panting. *More.*

More.

Need more.

Emma shook her head, trying to clear it. She imagined this is what a drug addict felt like when coming down from a high.

She both hoped for and dreaded her mother's return. Her questions couldn't go unanswered any longer. Emma was exhausted by the lies. Her magic, her ability needed controlling. Perhaps who her father was would help bring clarity and make Emma feel a little less alone.

She dozed in and out of sleep until the squeak of hinges forced her eyes open. The room was dark; the day had passed. Her mother sat on her bed, placing a warm hand on her shoulder. The touch burned into her.

"Emma, are you okay?" she asked. Her voice sounded as tired as Emma felt.

"I'm fine," she replied. Her voice was scratchy. She cleared her throat, trying to push back the bile that forced its way up.

"Why are you in bed so early?"

"Headache," Emma answered. She was so tired.

"I brought home Chinese food, if you're feeling up to it. We could watch a movie?" her mother suggested.

Emma warred with herself, wanting to reject her like she had been rejected, but knowing it wasn't her mother's fault. And she missed her mother. Whatever was left of the day, she didn't want to spend it alone. She needed to get answers.

"Sure." Emma sat up shakily and her mother wrapped her up in a bone-crushing hug.

"I'm so, so sorry Emma. I promise I'll make it up to you tomorrow," her mother whispered against Emma's hair.

Emma melted into the hug, trying to absorb the love and warmth she was craving.

***

They ate while watching a comedy. Emma tried to laugh as if she hadn't a care in the world. Both of them smiled but the air felt weighted.

When it ended, her mother turned her body to face Emma.

"I've missed this," her mother said with a sparkly-eyed smile.

"Me too," Emma admitted.

While she had her mother's attention, she asked, "How did your parents die?"

Her mother had never discussed them, Emma had never seen pictures of them, and all the secrets only solidified Blaze's theory about who her mother really was.

Her mother let out a long sigh, her smile gone. She rubbed the bridge of her nose as she said, "They died in a car accident."

"Where did they live?"

"Why all these questions all of a sudden?" her mother asked. Her tone was sharp, but Emma couldn't stop now. She kept digging.

225

"I'm an adult now," Emma said, selecting her words with caution. "I know basically nothing about my past, I don't even know where our ancestors are from. I've never seen a picture of my only grandparents—I don't even know my father's name."

The last part made her mother's expression harden. "We're not talking about him." She rose from the couch, collecting their dirty plates, and strode into the kitchen. Emma rushed after her.

"Why?" Emma folded her arms over her chest. "You didn't think about asking his name the entire time you were naked together? Because that seems a little far-fetched to me." Emma's voice rose steadily, and she didn't quite know why she was angry.

The dishes slammed into the sink. "Yeah, sure, I thought about it, but none of this is something I'm proud of. I got pregnant at eighteen. I had to go to college while working full time *and* raising a child." Her mother's voice quaked with a thread of fear.

"Did you run away from home?" Emma asked coolly.

Shock colored her mother's face. "What?"

"Did you run away from home because you got pregnant?" Emma repeated.

Her mother seemed unsure of how to respond, opening her mouth and then closing it again.

"Well?" Emma demanded.

"Yes."

Emma felt as if her stomach dropped out of her completely.

"My parents were very strict. My dad was an abusive, drunken asshole and on more than one occasion, he said that if I ever got pregnant out of wedlock, I would be better off not coming home at all. So one night, I left and didn't go back." Her mother's arms were folded over her chest, her eyes swimming with the anguish of re-surfaced memories.

"I'm sorry," Emma whispered. "I didn't mean to bring up bad memories, I was just—"

"Curious," her mother finished for her. Emma nodded solemnly.

"Well, can I ask what my dad looked like? He must have been handsome," Emma prodded gently.

A sad smile curved her mother's lips, her gaze faraway. "He was the most gorgeous man I had ever seen. Dark curls and the most captivating emerald eyes—" she glanced at Emma, her eyes glistening— "a face that looked like it had been sculpted by an angel."

She shivered. "How did you two meet?"

"I was at a house party hosted by a bunch of college-aged kids. I saw him, he saw me, and the next thing I knew, I was staring down at two pink lines." The tremor in her hands betrayed that there was more to it than that, causing Emma's brows to draw together.

Given how protective her mother was, Emma found it hard to believe she had ever been a part of the partying scene, but she didn't pry.

"What was your mother like?" Emma asked.

Her mother's icy blue eyes darkened. "I think we should probably get to bed."

"Why? It's not a hard question," Emma said.

Her eyes narrowed, brows angling down. "I don't want to talk about my parents, Emma, end of story." Then she stormed out of the kitchen, Emma close on her heels.

"I get that your dad was a jerk, but I'm sure your mom loved you."

Her mother halted, spinning around just before Emma knocked into her. She stepped back.

"I don't want to talk about my family," she repeated, stressing each word like Emma was a child.

"Just help me understand, then. Do you have any pictures? Give me something, Mom!" Emma was shouting. Even though her head was telling her to stop, her heart wanted answers. Most of all, she wanted her mother to deny that she was Nadia Ivankov. She needed to tell her mother about her magic, about the Shediem. Emma needed to tell her mother about Levaroth and find out if her father really was a Spellcaster.

"No. End of discussion, goodnight!" her mother fumed, pointing toward the stairs.

"I get that they hurt you and forced you to live a harder life than—" Emma started.

"Just go!" her mother bellowed, her eyes shining with tears.

"Why are you pushing me away? Why are we always moving? Who are you running from? Is my dad still alive? Did he hurt you?"

"Not another word! Go to your room!"

"Fine!" Emma threw her hands up before stomping up the stairs, then slammed the door closed.

Hot, angry tears streamed down Emma's face as she threw herself onto her bed. She landed on something hard with an *oomph*. Sitting up, she spied a small, plain black box. A narrow, red satin ribbon was tied around it, knotted at the top.

Emma slipped off the ribbon and pulled the top of the box off, setting it aside. Inside was a small white card. Scrawled in handwriting she had seen before, the note read:

Happy Birthday. Her heartbeat sped up. She flipped over the card and saw another message: *Look under the paper.*

Emma lifted the red paper and her heart stopped. Her lips parted in awe of the glittering jewel beneath, resting against plush black velvet. A dazzling emerald in the shape of a tear-drop surrounded by small, shining diamonds hung from a simple, silver chain. She held it up and the light danced off it, casting multicolored streaks across her wall.

It was beautiful. But also from Rowek, who she didn't want to see ever again. *He must have left it on my bed when he carried me up here,* she thought. Then paused, frowning. But she had awoken on her bed and there had been no box. She dropped the necklace back into the box and replaced the lid.

This is the worst birthday ever.

Emma groaned, hiding her face in her hands. She knew she needed to apologize to her mother. She hated when they argued, and she knew she shouldn't have pushed her mother so hard. Her secrets were her own and if she ever decided to share them with Emma, she would.

The day can't end like this, she thought as she jumped off her bed.

She cracked the door open, listening for her mother to ascertain if she was still downstairs. A muffled whisper reached her. Emma tiptoed into the hallway, pausing at the top of the landing.

"Yes, rental fee from Seattle to Pensacola," her mother said.

Emma's stomach plummeted. *Moving again? Why?* Anger flared up inside her, warming her from head to toe. Her mother had never looked so happy, nor taken an interest in gardening before. Emma had truly believed this would be their forever home.

Fueled by the injustice of being forced to uproot her entire life yet again, she stormed down the stairs just as she heard her mother say,

"Yes, Monday is fine...thank you."

Her mother froze with her phone in her hand as Emma glared down at her from the last step.

"Leaving again, are you?"

"We both are," her mother said through tight lips.

"There is no way I am moving to Florida with you," Emma spat. "I'm applying to colleges here. My friends are here. I'm staying *here*." She almost felt like stomping to emphasize her point but knew that she already looked like a spoiled child throwing a tantrum.

"We've leaving Monday morning and that's final. I don't care if you're an adult now; you're my daughter and you'll do as I say." Her mother's eyes narrowed, her expression challenging.

"I'm not leaving with you!" Emma yelled, tears spilling over onto her cheeks as she turned and ran back up to her room. She slammed the door with a frustrated cry. Pausing, Emma looked for her phone. She picked it up off her desk and scrolled through the contacts. Her thumb hovered above Adrianna's name. Her dad wouldn't like it if Emma just showed up; so, she scrolled. Rowek's name appeared.

She didn't want to see him, but she missed being able to talk to him. For a brief moment she considered calling him just to vent but decided against it.

She scrolled back up, seeing Blaze's contact. If Levaroth viewed him sending flowers as a breach of their agreement, she would know by now, wouldn't she? And if their agreement wasn't already dissolved, her begging him for a place to stay would surely end it.

She hit enter before sense could stop her.

"Are you okay? I've been trying to get a hold of you all day," Blaze said after only one ring.

For a moment, she sat, speechless. Then she remembered the flowers, which her mother hadn't even remarked on. She remembered the sweet man who had carried them in and Rowek's jealous rage that almost killed him.

"How is he? The guy that delivered those flowers?" Emma asked guiltily.

"He's fine," Blaze said in a low voice.

More tears spilled down her face as she said, "I'm so sorry. You were right, Rowek just suddenly got so jealous that he—"

"Yeah, Gus told me."

"I'm so sorry," Emma repeated. "I would have called but... Rowek...Made me unconscious or something. I slept most of the day."

"He what?" Blaze growled.

Emma swallowed hard. "We fought. I was just trying to break Rowek's grip so I grabbed him, but then I started taking his power or something—"

"Hold on," Blaze said loudly. "Power, what power?"

"He's a Spellcaster."

Blaze paused. "A Spellcaster...what coven is he bound to?"

Emma opened her mouth, stopping. "I don't actually know. I think he and his dad are just loners or whatever."

Blaze made a noise, but she wasn't sure if it was a laugh or a scoff.

"Can you pick me up?" Emma asked.

A pause. "Sure. Where?"

"Meet me at the high school."

She packed lightly, not sure how long she intended to stay. After stuffing a week's worth of clothing into her bag, she threw open her window.

Emma looked down at the sodden grass more than ten feet beneath her, panic swelling up in her throat. Swallowing it down she reminded herself that worse case, she healed quickly. Then she closed her eyes and jumped.

She landed easily on her feet and almost cheered, catching herself just in time. Then, with only a single backward glance over her shoulder, she ran. The shadows cast by the darkness allowed her to move quickly. She navigated the streets with ease, making it to the school in less than twenty minutes.

The parking lot was empty, so she waited by the copse of trees, leaning against the rough, gnarled bark to slow her rapid breathing. Panic began to set in. Somewhere in the distance an owl hooted, startling her. Her breath puffed in visible clouds in front of her face, and she folded her arms across her chest in an effort to conserve her body heat.

It was too late for remorse or a change of heart. Though she knew her mother would be upset, she couldn't bring herself to turn around and face yet another moving truck. Another new school, when she had just gotten used to her current one. It was her senior year, and she wanted to finish it out with Adrianna. She wanted to talk about colleges and boys with her. Rowek's face flashed in her mind and she dismissed it. They were over. Even if they weren't, he said he wasn't likely to stay in the area for much longer.

A mixture of sadness and guilt swirled like a brewing storm, but before she could change her mind, a pair of headlights flashed as a vehicle pulled into the parking lot.

EMMA

B laze didn't say much as they drove out of the city. He glanced in her direction occasionally, but she stared out the window in silence, her forehead resting against the cool glass. She was grateful that he didn't ask questions. She wasn't ready to talk about her fight with her mother.

The long drive gave her time to think. Her thoughts shifted as the silence became awkward. Remembering their almost-kiss warmed her cheeks, which she was glad he couldn't see in the dark.

They pulled up to the large metal gate, and Garrett greeted Blaze at the window. His sharp gaze looked Emma over with curiosity. When he seemed satisfied, the gate swung open. Blaze parked inside the gravel loop and then turned to face Emma.

"Are you sure about this?" he asked, his eyes searching hers in the dim lighting cast by the porch light.

"If it's an inconvenience, I can—"

"No," Blaze interjected. "You are more than welcome to stay here for as long as you like. I just meant, are you sure you want to leave things with your mother the way they are?"

Emma looked at him quizzically, cocking her head to the side. "How do you know things are bad?"

Blaze chuckled. "When I offered for you to stay earlier this week you said your mother would never allow it. Then you call me at eleven o'clock at night and have me pick you up at the high school, carrying a bag that looks like you fit everything but your bed inside it. Just a guess." He smiled. The effect made her stomach flip.

"Right, yeah. Of course."

"So, are you?"

Emma thought for a moment about how upset her mother would be, and though it made her ache with guilt, she knew. She nodded.

Blaze looked at her approvingly. "Okay, let me show you to your room." He grabbed her bag from the backseat, and they headed into the grand manor.

Her steps echoed loudly across the shining marble floor of the foyer. Flashes of light poured out from a room to the right. Voices spoke loudly, and Emma realized there was a movie playing. She glimpsed several rows of chairs all filled with women ranging from preteen to early twenties, which was apparently when they stopped aging for a good portion of their lives.

Blaze marched up the stairs in front of her and Emma followed, staring up at the breath-taking crystal chandelier directly above them. It was purely ornamental, but light from the sconces on the wall refracted off its jewels, like a thousand drops of burning crystal. She had been so busy admiring its beauty that she didn't see Blaze spin to face her at the top of the staircase, and she collided with his solid muscled chest. Her arms flailed as her body tipped backward, an embarrassing shriek escaping her.

He grabbed her hands, pulling her safely to the top landing. A grin tilted his lips.

"Distracted?" he asked.

"The chandelier," Emma pointed up at it, hoping to keep him from seeing her face catch fire.

"Yes, beautiful," he replied, his eyes never leaving hers.

Emma sucked in a slow breath, trying to keep her heartrate under control. As if remembering himself, Blaze pivoted and turned right down a long, wide corridor. Emma wasn't sure how many doors they passed as they walked along, but she felt like she was in a grand hotel rather than a house.

At the end of the hallway there was a door, and one to the left. Blaze opened the one on the left and stepped inside. Emma followed, her jaw dropping as she took in the plush, vintage décor. The bed was at least twice the size of the one she had at home. Another door to the side was ajar an inch or two. White tile started at the doorway and Emma guessed it was a bathroom.

"Sorry, this is the only room left," Blaze said, and when she whirled around, her face still set with awe, she noticed his look of discomfort.

"Why are you sorry?" she asked.

"I don't want you think it a bit forward." He nodded to a door beside the bed that Emma hadn't noticed before. Her brows knitted together.

"A closet?" she asked, confused.

Blaze cleared his throat nervously. "No, that leads to my bedroom."

Her face flamed again. "Oh, I see." Not knowing what else to say, she stood still, unable to look away from the door.

"Don't worry," he added. "It locks from your side too."

Emma forced her gaze from the door and nodded. "Thank you."

"It's my pleasure," Blaze replied. "I hope you sleep well, and I'll see you tomorrow." He spun on his heel and was out the door before Emma could reply.

She marveled at the golden accents in the intricately designed claw-foot bathtub and matching sink as she hurriedly brushed her teeth and readied herself for bed. As she walked back to the four-poster bed, she paused by the door that led to Blaze's room. She couldn't help but wonder what his room looked like, or if the entire house was one style.

She couldn't picture such a manly guy enjoying every shade of pink ever stitched into a rug, decorating *his* floor. Or the drapes on his bed being the same baroque textured weave that hung from the one Emma climbed into.

She felt a comfort and safety knowing he was near. A pleasant warmth remained inside her throughout the night and it soothed her into a deep sleep.

A gentle rapping on her door roused Emma from what had been the best night's sleep she had ever had. She sat up groggily, expecting her mother to poke her head around the door and tell her breakfast was ready. She glanced beside her to check her alarm clock and felt a stunned confusion at her surroundings. Then, slowly, it all came flowing back and she felt her stomach knot itself back up.

The knock came again, and she lunged out of the bed, almost tumbling onto her face in the tight cocoon of blankets that she was tangled in. She freed herself and pulled the door open, forgetting she was only wearing a long, baggy As I Lay Dying t-shirt.

Blaze stood in her doorway, bare-chested and holding a tray with several assorted plates of delicious-smelling foods that she ignored entirely to gape at his perfectly chiseled muscles. A light sheen coated them as though he had just finished whatever brutal workout kept him so fit.

"Thought you might be hungry," he said, holding out the tray.

Emma took it, reluctantly shifting her gaze up to his face, noticing that his eyes were sliding in the opposite direction.

"Thanks," Emma squeaked. She cleared her throat. His gaze on her bare legs reminded her of her attire. In a burst of humiliation, she kicked the door shut in his face.

She stood staring at the closed door, blinking rapidly.

"Let me get dressed," she called.

His warm presence didn't shift, though the realization that she could *sense* him was abandoned to the low muttered response uttered on the other side of the door.

"What?"

"I said, sure," he answered. His tone held a hint of laughter.

She didn't feel like pointing out that whatever he had said was not "sure". Groaning internally, she deposited the tray onto the bed, still feeling flushed.

She changed into a black ruffled top and skinny jeans, then opened the door again. The hallway was empty, but she could feel him nearby. She turned toward that soothing warmth when a soft knock came from the door connecting their rooms.

She walked over to it apprehensively, pausing as her fingers gripped the lock, then she slid it free and swung the door open.

Blaze scanned her again, smirking. "I quite liked the band t-shirt," he said. Blaze had also put on a shirt, Emma noted with a slight frown, though it still accentuated every inch of his rippling chest.

Emma gave a choked laugh. "Well, I thought this might be a little more appropriate."

"The jeans help, I suppose."

Emma nodded before looking away.

"I thought you and I could do a training session after you finished your breakfast," Blaze explained as he leaned against the doorframe, his arms crossed over his chest.

"Train, how?" she asked incredulously.

He grinned. "I have a special something in mind."

Emma dreaded what that could mean. Images of them running thirty miles flashed in her mind.

"I'll let you eat. Just knock when you're ready."

After she attempted to stomach a few bites of dry toast, Emma changed into the only thing that could be considered workout-appropriate attire. She stood outside the joint space for several moments, working up the courage to lift her fist. After knocking softly on the door, she folded her arms over her chest.

The door opened soundlessly, and he stepped into the shared space between their rooms. She caught the briefest of glimpses of the décor in his room. Nothing pink.

"Shall we?" he gestured behind her.

The outside air felt as if she had been transported into the dead of winter, the sun concealed within the dull gray sky.

"Where are we going?" Emma asked as Blaze led her away from the splendor of the gardens. They walked around to the back of the manor.

"Cells," he answered simply.

Startled, Emma stumbled. Blaze's warm hands caught her by the shoulders, hauling her back to her feet.

"Did you say cells?" she asked. His hands fell away, and the cold wind burned in the absence of his touch.

He started walking again. "Yes."

Emma wasn't sure she wanted to know why, but she followed him anyway.

At the back of the house, across a long stretch of bumpy, grassy land, stood Axel, leaning against a small brick building that appeared to be a shed and biting into something that looked like an apple. He gave Emma a wink when they neared.

"Sleep well, luv?" he asked suggestively. He chomped into the crisp flesh of the green apple. The heat that spread through her body gave momentary reprieve from the biting cold.

Blaze sighed. "If you're done flirting," he shot his brother a glare, "then we can get started. Are you feeling up for this?"

She still didn't know what "this" was, but she nodded.

Axel tossed the remainder of the fruit aside before turning to slide a key into the lock of the steel door. Each bolt that he slid aside rattled and clanged, the sounds echoing deep within Emma's chest. She cast a nervous glance in Blaze's direction, but his eyes were narrowed in focus. Unblinking, he stared after his brother, who descended a set of stairs into darkness below.

Scraping and several thumps made their way up to them and Emma started forward instinctively. Blaze caught her with an outstretched arm. Moments later, a cold heavy weight punched between her lungs, making her gasp. Blaze watched her, gauging her reaction as she tried to keep her breathing even.

A chill shot through her from the inside out as a sickly thin female with leathery gray skin was pushed up the stairs, arms bound behind her back. Emma had seen this creature before at the school

The Shediem was naked, and her mouth was bound with a thick leather strip. It was secured with buckles that went around her head like a barbaric muzzle. What hair had been on her elongated head had been shaved off. Her eyes were entirely white with the exception of thin, yellow, cat-like slits.

When her unnatural eyes stopped on Emma, her expression became smug and defiant. Emma's throat tightened with nervousness.

"What is she?" Emma felt herself ask.

"A Drude. They leech oxygen from the room, suffocating their victims. Which is why we are outside," Blaze said.

"And what are we doing with it?"

"You're going to kill it."

The bitter cold seeped into her bones, paralyzing her. "Wh-why?" she stammered.

Blaze leveled his gaze to hers. "For training."

Something twisted inside her. The idea felt wrong for reasons Emma couldn't understand. The creature seemed to smile beneath its gag.

"How did it get here? Aren't the wards supposed to keep them out?" Emma asked.

"Gertie lowers a portion of the shield to let them through."

"Hurts like hell too," Axel added, his face serious. "Or at least we think so, if their screams are any indication."

"Oh," Emma muttered, wishing she hadn't asked. "Well, are you going to give her back her hands, at least?"

Blaze raised a brow. "Why would I do that?"

Emma worried her bottom lip. "It doesn't feel right to just kill her."

"First of all, Emma, I know it looks like a woman, but it's not. Second, this creature helped blow up the Space Needle. It's responsible for thousands of deaths, and not just the ones last week."

She knew she should feel a burning anger toward the creature standing before her for the murders it caused, but somehow… all she felt was sick. She moved in front of the Drude, searching its face for a hint of remorse. A glint of wicked delight shone in the creature's eyes, and it sparked the anger she had been missing. She laid a palm on the Shediem's arm, her skin tingling with anticipation. But no energy fed her. All she felt was cold, sticky skin.

Her brows furrowed in confusion. Then a thought struck her. Every time she was able to feed off Shediem's energy, it was when she was in danger or felt scared.

"I need her to attack me."

The amusement in the Shediem's eyes grew as Blaze stepped in front of her, arms crossed over his chest.

"Absolutely not," he ground out.

Emma folded her own arms. "It's the only way it'll work. It's a defensive measure."

He looked down at her in almost a challenge. "The point of this training is to turn it on and off at will. It's an unnecessary risk to allow the scum to defend itself."

Emma sighed. "Sure, but I'm trying, and nothing is happening. We can try it my way first. Nothing is going to happen to me. You can take the Drude out if things get out of hand."

Axel piped up, "The two of us can keep this one in check, brother." Blaze whipped toward his brother, anger lit his eyes, making them look almost silver.

"It will try to kill her!" His tone was protective, but Emma thought she detected a cord of desperation that gave his expression an almost unhinged quality.

"We won't let it," Axel replied calmly. Blaze seethed in silence for several moments. Emma risked a glance at the Drude, which grinned beneath its binding. Triumph lit its eerie eyes and Emma wondered if she was completely insane.

"Fine." Blaze motioned to Axel, who pulled a long, curved

sword from over his back. It sailed through the air to Blaze, who caught it with smooth, practiced grace. Then Blaze nodded to his brother. A clank of metal sounded as the manacles fell into a pile on the crisp grass. The Shediem's hands sprung free.

Behind the gag, a grin curved its cheeks up high, it's snake-like nostrils flaring as its papery skin pulled tight over its skull. Emma raised her fists nervously, hoping her little knowledge of hand-to-hand combat would be enough. The Drude lunged, elongated black claws shooting from its fingertips. It swiped at her throat and Emma stepped back, stunned. Out of the corner of her eye, she saw Blaze, sword raised, close enough to kill.

"No! Not yet," Emma shouted.

A flash of black rushed toward her and she stepped back. Pain bloomed in her cheek. Instinctively her hand touched her face. When she pulled her fingers away, they were stained red. The creature moved again, this time ramming its bony shoulder into her stomach. Emma flew back, landing onto the icy ground, the air forced from her lungs.

She gasped for air, her chest struggling to rise as the Shediem stared down at her, its eyes mocking. Blaze and Axel shouted something before charging forward. The Drude spun. Emma leapt to her feet, her fingertips just a breath from the Drude's skin as it spun out with its leg, knocking her to her back once again. She grunted as pain shot through her limbs.

The Giborim circled the Shediem, but its gaze was locked on her. It was toying with her. Taunting her.

When she got to her feet again, she stepped toward the Shediem, her skin burning as anger filled her. Her power thrummed with eagerness. Awareness lit its eyes and it sauntered toward her, fearless.

"Come get me," Emma said, her voice low.

The creature lunged, both set of claws flying for her face, and she moved to the side. She was faster now. A growl rumbled in its throat as it swung again. Emma crouched, driving her foot into its knobby knee. A sickening crack drove the creature to its hands.

Muffled panting came from behind the covering on its mouth as Emma brought both palms up on each side of the Drude's face.

Dark, raw energy filled her veins. It warmed her, coated her blood with its power. An elated laugh bubbled up out of her throat. *Yes.* The creature's body became stiff as it looked up into her eyes. Relief shone in its face. It closed its eyes and exhaled. The creature crumbled. Like ash, it coated her hands, the wind swirling the Drude's remains.

Emma rose to her feet, every muscle tight with unspent energy. Her fists clenched as she tilted her head back, inhaling deeply. When she opened her eyes again, intense, steel gray eyes looked back at her. She blinked.

A warm, gentle hand stroked her cheek, and she realized he had been speaking.

"What?" Emma said. The power flushed itself slowly out of her system, replacing every cell with ice. She leaned toward the warmth that radiated from him.

"I asked if you were all right," Blaze replied.

"I'm fine. You're so warm." She fought the urge to rub against him like a cat.

A chuckle came from over Blaze's shoulder, and she peered around him to see Axel watching them. Embarrassed, Emma took a step back, the cold air consuming her. She shivered.

"That was brilliant," Axel praised as he walked over to them. *Clap. Clap. Clap.*

Blaze and Axel whirled to face the newcomer. Emma saw Blaze and Axel's uncle standing less than twenty feet away from them. He offered Emma a smile, twisting his wide, thin lips so he looked like the Cheshire cat.

"Brilliant, indeed," the man said, still smiling. "I wonder if you would honor us with another. I'm curious if all Shediem succumb to you at the same rate."

"Maybe later," Emma answered, her teeth chattering. Blaze narrowed a concerned look toward her before facing his uncle.

"Perhaps she can go again after lunch," Blaze suggested.

His uncle's smile became brittle. "But what is one more really?"

"I said no!" Emma started to push past Blaze, catching his uncle give him a pointed look. She didn't want to stick around and find out what it was about.

Blaze jogged up next to her. "Let me carry you inside so you can warm up."

"I'm g-great." Her teeth knocked together, and she bit into her tongue with a groan.

They walked side-by-side in silence until they rounded the manor's front. The gardens looked perfectly preserved despite the cold.

Blaze pulled the large door open for her and she scurried inside, rubbing her arms to try to keep warm.

"I'll have Gertie make you some tea," he said.

Emma nodded gratefully as Blaze walked ahead.

"There you are!" A heavily accented voice trilled through the open foyer. Emerelda bounded down the stairs like a gazelle, her honey-blond hair bouncing over her shoulders. Emma fought back the bitter taste of annoyance that rose up inside her.

"Hello, Emerelda," Blaze said. "I'm just in the middle of something, can we talk later?" he asked politely, though his tone was clipped. Her face fell, her gaze sweeping over to observe Emma.

"Of course, I'll be in my room." Her lids lowered suggestively at Blaze before she started back up the stairs, her graceful leaps replaced with hurried marching. Blaze grabbed Emma's hand, jolting her with surprise as he pulled her toward the kitchen. Warmth spread from his hand to hers and when he released it, the warmth evaporated. They entered the pristine kitchen; steel shelves lined the wall beside them. Stacked silver bowls and assorted wooden cutting boards filled each shelf.

Bouncing gray curls appeared from the other end.

"Ohhh," the plump, elderly woman squealed happily, wiping her hands on her stained apron. She dashed over to Blaze and wrapped her arms around his neck, he obligingly leaned down to hug her back.

"Hey Gertie, I was wondering if you could fix us a pot of tea. I'd do it myself, but I never know where you keep anything in here."

"Of course, of course!" she exclaimed, and before anyone could say another word, she shooed then out of the kitchen. Blaze chuckled as he led Emma back into the large, empty meeting room. He pulled out a chair for her and then took the seat opposite.

Emma's teeth were no longer chattering, and the chills had subsided, but the cold still lingered deep in her bones.

"How are you feeling now?" he asked.

"Fine," Emma lied.

Blaze's gaze bored into hers for several moments, broken only when Gertie carried the tray into the room. Blaze took the tray from her, placing a kiss on her cheek. She slapped his arm playfully, casting Emma a private smile that she returned. She had felt trepidation before walking into the kitchen, but that was put to rest when Gertie didn't look at her the way Gus had.

Blaze poured Emma a steaming cup of tea that smelled like peppermint. She took the glazed stone cup, inhaling the soothing scent.

"You did well with that Drude," Blaze told her as he poured tea into his own mug, though he didn't touch it.

Emma gave a dry laugh.

"Considering you are untrained and were unarmed, you did quite well."

"If you guys hadn't been there, I'd have gotten my butt kicked," Emma said.

"I don't know if you're brave or stupid," he muttered, sipping his tea. "Why did you want it to be able to defend itself when it deserved a swift death?"

Emma thought for a moment. She studied the tendrils of steam rising from her cup, her voice a whisper as she said, "I knew it had taken innocent lives, but for some reason, I just felt like an executioner. A murderer."

Blaze rose abruptly from his seat, grabbing the cup of tea from her hands and setting it onto the table. "I want to show you something."

She wanted to protest the loss of its heat, but instead she rose from her seat and followed him to the end of the long room. He stopped in front of a door she hadn't noticed before.

A large, dimly lit room sprawled out before them. The floor was gold with white symbols curving into shapes Emma didn't recognize. Swords, daggers, guns, and a vast assortment of things she had never seen before lined the walls. Blaze walked along the wall to her right, his hands clasped behind his back. Emma followed, observing everything with fascination. She craned her neck to stare at a row of blades shaped like crescent moons as she passed them, her mouth slack. Colliding with a hard wall that was Blaze's chest, his arms shot out to steady her, a deep, rumbling laugh escaping him.

"Do you run into anyone else this much?" Blaze smirked down at her.

Emma's cheeks burned. "No, pretty much just you," she mumbled.

"I'm honored."

"Is this what you wanted to show me?" Emma asked, looking around the room. "Your armory?"

Blaze thrust his fingers through his hair, his lips tilted up in what looked like a nervous smile. "No, I figured it would be the quietest place to talk."

Emma's heart picked up speed. "About what?"

His gaze swept over the wall. "When we were in the garden."

Her heart pounded harder. "What about it?"

He ran his hand through his hair again as he huffed a sigh. "I've seen a kindness in you, as well as a fierce bravery that I find… enchanting. You're beautiful and so much wiser than your age."

Emma made an involuntary noise in the back of her throat,

recalling Emerelda's natural and confident beauty. He stopped. After a moment's pause, Blaze ate up the distance between them in two strides, and then he was there in front of her. Their faces close, their breaths mingling.

"I do not care what you are, Emma. No one could ever convince me that there is darkness within you." Blaze cupped her face with both of his large hands.

Her hands rested against his chest, feeling the steady rhythm of his heart. Though Rowek was out of the picture, it didn't feel right to be having this conversation. She didn't know Blaze, and though his physique was intriguing, she wasn't ready for anything more. Besides, weren't Giborim only supposed to breed with pure-blooded Giborim?

"We can't do this," Emma whispered.

Blaze's brow creased, but before he could respond, a loud bang from the other side of the door made them both leap back. Emma's heart hammered wildly. Blaze swore, so low Emma could hardly hear it. Then the door swung open and Axel's back appeared, with two slender hands searching and grasping, tugging his shirt up. Blaze cleared his throat loudly, and Axel broke contact to look over his shoulder at his brother. He gave them both a lopsided grin. A slender blonde peered around his shoulder and Emma made a choking noise at Emerelda's red, swollen lips. She smiled bashfully at them both.

"Brother," Axel drawled lazily.

"Rekindling old flames, I see." Blaze folded his arms over his chest, glaring at his brother as if he were about to tell him off.

"Had the same idea, I see," Axel countered, waggling his brows at Emma. She was thankful for the dim lighting to hide her embarrassment.

"I was giving Emma a tour of the compound," Blaze replied coolly.

Axel barked a laugh. "Not what it looks like, mate, but I'm not judging." He held his hands up in mock surrender.

Emma fled, brushing past Axel and Emerelda.

"Emma," Blaze called after her.

She stopped in the middle of the echoing foyer and turned to face him.

"I'm sorry," he said when he reached her. "You're right. You're still upset about that Rowek kid—"

She shook her head. "It's fine," she muttered, though her heart ached.

Deep down, she had wanted him to kiss her. And that revelation only made her feel worse. Rowek had been right to be jealous, though it still didn't give him the right to nearly kill someone.

But even if Rowek hadn't been a part of her life, the situation with Blaze wasn't like Axel and Emerelda's. They could get caught with their faces glued together; they were both Giborim. She was…whatever she was, and Blaze was a respected and vital person in the community of Giborim. A relationship between them would have consequences that would be catastrophic to his status and way of life. She couldn't allow herself to form an attachment.

"I shouldn't have come here. I need to go home." Her eyes drilled a hole in one of the intricately carved balusters of the hand-rail.

"What?" Blaze said, his tone forcing her to meet his steely stare. "What's brought this on?"

"I think it's best that we accept that nothing can happen between us," she bit out the words, and they burned her tongue like acid. A swell of threatening tears filled her eyes, blurring her vision.

"And why is that?"

"Because I'm not like you." She turned toward the wide staircase and Blaze grabbed her arm. She jerked her arm away with a sudden jolt of anger. As his hand fell away, it caught the top of her shirt, exposing her collarbone.

Then he was in front of her, his hands painfully gripping her shoulders. "What is that?" he demanded. His eyes were on her shoulder, and the mark that she had momentarily forgotten about, burned as if in painful reminder.

"Nothing," she answered hastily.

Blaze's gaze was narrowed, brimming with deadly anger. "Emma, what is that?" he growled, tugging the material aside to take in the mark fully.

Emma tried to pull herself out of his grasp, but he held fast. "Let go of me," she snapped.

His nostrils flared as he reluctantly unclasped her shoulders. "You can't go home. Levaroth and God knows how many other Shediem can find you there. You're safe here."

Emma straightened, refusing to cower under his stare. She stepped around him, climbing several stairs when he spoke again, "Did you get that on the night of your school dance?"

As if her mouth operated of its own volition, she said, "Yes."

"Come here." His voice was a rumble of barely-leashed rage.

Her back stiffened for a moment, before she faced him. Blaze extended his hand. She lifted her chin, ignoring it.

"Why?"

"Just come with me, please." He spoke softer, though there was still an edge.

With a heavy sigh, Emma followed Blaze back outside, the cool air stinging her cheeks. He didn't lead her around the back of the manor like she expected. Instead, he stalked toward the gate. As he approached, the steel doors swung inward, exposing the compound.

Emma swallowed nervously, stopping beside him at the threshold. He looked at the two guards.

"Close this gate behind us and stay in the manor until we return."

The two men wore so much gear, Emma couldn't see their faces. They glanced at each other before they nodded and set off inside.

Heat rolled off him and Emma felt the urge to cling to him in order to get warm. His hands were fists at his sides as he took a step forward, then another. Emma followed suit, feeling like her stomach was being forced up her throat, her body tingling from head to toe.

Then it stopped.

"Why are you so mad?" Emma asked as they stood in the cold.

Blaze gave a humorless laugh. "Do you know what that mark does?"

"It allows him to find me?" Emma guessed.

"Which led him to the stronghold! If one Shediem can find it, then they all can."

Emma felt bile rise up in her throat. "I didn't think." She had unknowingly led a Shediem general to the place where at least thirty females were hidden for their protection. "So what are we doing here?"

"Waiting."

Realization hit her. "What? We're waiting for Levaroth to come to us? Why?" she shouted, panic beginning to claw through her. Was he giving her back to him?

Blaze stared straight ahead, not speaking. His jaw worked from side-to-side.

The punch of cold ramrodded between her lungs before she even saw him. Then, out of nowhere, he stood less than ten feet from them, hands in his pockets, looking casual and slightly amused.

"Sick of her already, Warrior?"

"Take it off her," Blaze growled, and Emma realized he was talking about the mark.

"I can't. It's for her own good, and besides," Levaroth said, lowering his voice, "I like it."

"She is not your property!" Blaze snarled, and the ferocity on his face was practically feral.

"You're just jealous you didn't mark her first."

Emma felt her stomach twist and nausea gripped her.

"I don't *mark* women," Blaze said. "I'm confident in my ability to keep them satisfied without needing to piss on them like a dog."

Levaroth's lip drew up in sneer. "You Giborim males are like a bunch of animals with how you treat your women."

"You don't know what you're talking about, Shediem filth."

"Remove the mark," Emma said, snapping both males' focus on her.

Levaroth looked her over slowly, thoroughly, and she glared back. "Even if I could, I wouldn't," he told her. "There are rogue Shediem who are acting under another prince's banner, and taking you out is their priority. That mark conceals your presence. If one were to pass you in the streets, you would appear to be a normal human. I'm the only one who can find you now."

Emma's eyes widened in surprise. Rowek had been right.

"Lies," Blaze hissed.

Levaroth leveled his stare on Blaze, his molten gold eyes burning with disdain. "Think what you want, Muscles. I've done more for her safety than you have."

Emma stepped in front of Blaze right as he lurched forward. "Why?" she asked Levaroth.

His smile changed, appearing almost tender. If demons could be tender. "Because you're worth it."

Blaze made a noise that sounded like another growl as he pushed her aside.

"Blaze, don't," Emma pleaded.

Blaze never faltered as he rushed toward Levaroth, who welcomed the attack by springing forward. Emma felt shock ripple through her when the first fist, thrown by Levaroth, landed with a gut-clenching crunch. Blow after blow flew, both of them blurs of motion. Snarls and grunts came from the tornado of limbs, but Emma couldn't tell who made what sound.

Blaze spun for a kick, but Levaroth anticipated it and leapt over him in a perfect arc. She saw his arm wind back, but before he could launch his fist into Blaze's jaw, she stepped forward.

"No!" she screamed. Tears burned her eyes.

The males froze, the sound splitting them apart. Blaze's

expression was drawn in concern, but his eyes were wide. Levaroth's was something darker. Her soul-crushing scream had ultimately been for Blaze, not him. His jaw clenched, rage burning bright in his eyes. Both of their chests rose and fell in heavy breaths.

Blaze wiped blood from his face with the back of his hand.

"Just this once, Muscles," Levaroth said. Then he was gone.

Emma rushed to Blaze's side. "Are you hurt?" she asked, noting a bruise already beginning to form around one of his eyes.

He straightened. "I'm fine. Let's get inside." Blaze pulled a phone from one of his pockets and punched something in on the screen.

The gate opened, and Blaze grabbed her arm, pulling her inside with him.

Neither spoke as they made their way back to the house, the gate swinging closed behind them.

LEVAROTH

She chose him.
She cares for him.
Why do I care?
I don't care about anything.
But she belongs with me.
The prince won't be happy with her disobedience.
I will win her over.
She will be mine.

Levaroth's mind was plagued with unending thoughts. He brought himself to a small village deep within a forest. In the dark, he crept, silent, as he drank away the lives of those that slumbered. When he was sated, he created chaos, letting those that were left fill his mind with their terrified screams until her face was blotted from his focus. He coated his hands in their blood, touching the crimson to his tongue.

If she believed him too evil to love, he would be his most wicked self. Let her surrender to him when he slaughtered without mercy. *She will do anything to save these pathetic humans, and I'll do whatever it takes to make her mine.*

When dawn broke, the sky aglow in red, orange and gold, he stood, staring out at the sea of broken and lifeless bodies. He wanted to revel in his destruction, bask in the atrocity that would secure Emma's fealty. Instead, a scream tore itself from his throat as he fell to his knees. His body shook violently as he fought to control the anguish within his wretched beating heart.

EMMA

"Another!" Blaze shouted.

Axel cast Emma a smirk before descending the stairs to collect the next Shediem. She bent over, her hands on her knees, panting. She had already fought two Shax. After her success with the Drude the previous day, Blaze had allowed the next one a pair of hands, but the second one, he insisted she try to turn her power on without being attacked.

It was easier than she had expected, despite the crowd of Giborim that had come outside to watch. Blaze and Axel's uncle was of course, among the faces observing her power.

Once she had a taste of the Shax's energy, she became ravenous for more. The first one had been allowed enough of its own power to remove her sight.

She had screamed, going down on her knees as everything went black. It moved silently. Only its vile, acidic scent alerted her to its proximity. She swung blindly, only meeting air with her fists. Cold metal chains dug into her throat, pulling her back. With a fierce grunt, she clawed behind her. Finally, her hands found thick, leathery flesh.

Her sight had only returned when the creature had been reduced to dust, coating her hands and hair. But like with the Nickor, she had felt a new piece of her caressing the edges of her mind, instructing her on how to use it. The applause from her audience had felt like her ear drums were being grated and she had snarled at them to stop. When Blaze started toward her, she held up a hand, warning him away. But like a challenge, he stepped toward her slowly.

The power that swirled inside her was still in control and raised its hackles at the approaching threat. She struggled to break through, but a moment too late. She lunged toward him and with the mighty strength of a panther, she knocked him to the ground. Axel was there in an instant, trying to lift her off. Then he fell to his knees behind them, his hands clamped over his eyes.

The shocked sounds from the onlookers broke through to her, and she realized as they all shakily removed their hands from their eyes, that she had blinded them too.

Blaze stared up at her in wonderment. She suddenly became aware that she was still on top of him and leapt to her feet.

"You can use their powers," he said with awe. Axel got to his feet. Emma opened her mouth, an apology loaded on the tip of her tongue, until his face split in a wide grin.

"That was bloody brilliant!"

Emma blinked in stunned confusion. Blaze stood, his face set in determination. She glanced at the crowd. Some looked horrified, fearful, and some, like Blaze's uncle, looked impressed.

"Again."

When Axel pushed the second Shax out of the doorway, it had the good sense to look a bit frightened.

"Why can't it blind me right now? Why does it wait?" Emma asked, steeling herself for what was to come.

"The shackles are infused with magic that dampens their powers," Blaze had explained.

"Which is why they should stay on," Axel added with a pointed look.

Emma opened her mouth to tell him to take them off, but Blaze's uncle interjected. "Attempt to use you power without the instigation of a fight."

Surprisingly, the Shediem simply tried to scurry away, past

Emma, its stumpy legs working furiously within the chained length it was allowed. Emma jumped into its path.

She reached for it, but it leapt away, moving faster than she thought possible.

As she intercepted the creature, it headbutted her in the abdomen, sending her sprawling in the grass with a pained grunt.

It jumped on top of her, ramming its head into her jaw, her cheeks, her nose, though her arms tried to protect her. With a snap the gag over its mouth split in two. Its mouth opened wide and a thick, snot-like liquid oozed around its tusks.

"Their venom is poisonous!" Blaze shouted.

Emma bucked the creature off, carefully avoiding the fluid that dripped from its mouth. The grass sizzled, blackening. The Shax tried to make a run for it again. Boiling hot anger rose up inside her. She loosed a roar and lunged for it, wrapping her arms around its middle, between its two sets of arms. It gave a shrill squeak as they fell to the ground. Its body stiffened, and energy flooded her like a tidal wave. She squeezed, wanting more of it. *More. More. More.* Its flesh grew brittle, cracking beneath her grasp. A wail escaped her as the breeze broke it apart, wrapping another layer of gray dust on her. The ashy taste filled her mouth.

Blaze stood directly in front of her and the hot ripple of power inside her lashed out like a whip. Blaze's eyes became unfocused. Axel appeared in front of her and she let out an inhuman hiss and he grunted.

"Try to hold it, Emma," Blaze said through gritted teeth. "Don't fight it."

The power seemed to stretch on forever inside her, unending, but to keep both Giborim blinded took effort. Inside, her muscles burned. Her blood rushed through her like molten lava. She clenched her jaw against the pain.

She wasn't sure if it had been seconds, minutes, or hours, though it certainly felt like the latter when she slumped over, supporting her hands on her knees and breathing heavily. More clapping had sounded, but she ignored it. Ignored the faces that stared at her like some kind of lab rat.

She had been only vaguely aware of Blaze giving the order to bring out another Shediem when Axel had given her his infuriating smirk before disappearing into the ground.

"Good," Blaze whispered to Emma. "That was very good."

She couldn't reply. The blistering cold chilled the sweat on her forehead and neck. She shivered. *More*, her body pleaded.

Another bound prisoner shuffled out in its chains. A slow smirk stretched the Shediem's taut-looking skin. This one was not gagged. It had an eerily rich purple gaze that was fixed on her. This one was different, as tall as Axel at least, since she could only see his broad shoulders poking out from behind the creature. It looked almost human, muscled and naked, its skin a midnight blue.

"Hello, traitor," it said.

"This is a Djinn. It's a shapeshifter. It can see your loved ones and appear to be them, in voice and looks," Blaze warned.

"It's also ridiculously clever," Axel added.

"Thanks for the heads up," Emma said.

"Why don't you let me out of these horribly uncomfortable chains little girl?" It grinned wickedly.

"Nice try, trickster," Axel said dryly.

"Go ahead," Blaze said. "Kill it."

"Take the chains off." Her eyes never left the Djinn's. A flash of satisfaction glinted in its amethyst-colored eyes.

Axel gaped while Blaze turned to stone beside her.

"Are you out of your mind?" Axel asked incredulously. "Do you have any idea how many Giborim it took to catch this thing?"

Emma shot him a sharp look. "And there are plenty here if I can't handle it."

Axel looked to his brother for instruction. But it was his uncle that spoke.

"Let her have it her way. I find it fascinating to see her fight them."

Blaze shot his uncle a glare and opened his mouth to tell

him off.

"Let me show you who your heart truly lies with," the creature taunted.

Emma thought of Rowek, but dismissed the image of him in her mind, even as a pang of longing went through her.

With a sigh Axel slid the key into the lock. It clicked open, the manacles falling with a *chink* to the grass. The Djinn didn't waste a single breath before slamming its bony elbow into Axel's face. He bellowed as he stumbled backwards.

Blaze had his weapons drawn and rushed swiftly toward the Djinn, who spun out of his reach, and was in front of Emma before she could blink.

The unsettling purple eyes changed to gold, then to seafoam green, making her heart stutter. Silky, strawberry-blond hair tied up in a flawless bun, high cheek-bones and thin red lips, and a gray-pinstriped pantsuit that was all too familiar.

"Emma." Her mother's worried tone made her breath hitch. "Come home," she pleaded.

Tears stung Emma's eyes.

"Emma, it's not real!" Blaze shouted. "Kill it!"

A look of horror transformed her mother's face. "Kill me?"

Then her mother's face became cold and unfeeling as Emma lifted a shaking hand. "You're a killer, Emma." The words twisted her insides. She knew it wasn't real, that her mother wasn't standing in front of her, but she couldn't shake how real it looked and sounded. The edges of her mother's form flickered, revealing the hideous form beneath.

But she had hesitated too long. Her mother's arm swung out in a backhand. Pain exploded in her cheek, making spots fill her vision. A bitter tang reached her tongue when another blow came to her chest. She felt the crack in her ribs as pain shot through her, blinding her. She couldn't draw air into her lungs. Her back hit the ground, her eyes closed as pain radiated through her spine. She gasped, vaguely aware of shouts all around her.

Two hands wrapped around her throat and her eyes snapped open to see smooth dark skin and chocolate brown eyes.

Adrianna's tight, black curls fanned out around her face as she bent over Emma and hissed, "You disgust me."

Darkness crept around her vision. She felt her power wrap around the hands that grasped her throat and it drank greedily. *More.* Adrianna's face faded, and wide, amber eyes replaced them. Rowek's face flickered in and out, his body going rigid. A choked sob escaped her.

"I'm sorry," she said. Then Emma wrapped her hands around its bony wrists, prying its grip from her throat while still feeding. *More.*

It jerked against her grasp and she twisted its arm. It snapped at the elbow and the Djinn shrieked. The last tide of power crashed into her and the Shediem crumbled to dust.

She stayed on her back, the heady surge pulsing in her mind. *More,* it demanded. The pain that had been in her chest and face was gone, but still she drew in labored breaths.

"Emma," a voice said cautiously. Her attention snapped to the male approaching. An image of a young girl with honey-kissed curls and sapphire blue eyes flashed in her mind.

Whatever happened next made more than one person suck in a sharp breath. She tried to access the image again and when she did, she held onto it. Memorizing the young girl's joyous, round face, her bright smile and the twinkle in her eyes. It was a memory she realized after a moment. Then she realized who the girl looked like and the image slipped away.

Blaze was staring at her, wide-eyed and ashen faced. Axel walked forward, drawn to whatever he had seen, his eyes glossy.

"What?" Emma asked, perplexed.

"Haddie," Axel said, his voice cracking.

Her mind reeled for several moments, then guilt flooded her.

"I'm so sorry," Emma said, looking at Blaze, who was still staring at her as if his little sister sat before him, looking the way she had when he last saw her. She felt her heart ache for both men. And for the beautiful young girl whose face still clouded her mind. Surrounding her, every face looked stunned, but it was Blaze's uncle's face, that stopped her. His skin was tinged green, his entire body shaking.

Blaze shook his head, as if coming back to reality. "We're done for today," he said stiffly. No one protested as he pulled Emma to her feet and then stalked back toward the manor alone. Emma hurried to catch up, ignoring the shivers from the bone-deep chill, but his quick strides put distance between them. The sun was setting in the distance and the air was rapidly getting colder.

"Don't worry about it," Axel said from behind her, stopping her in her tracks. She turned. He gave her a half smile. "Neither of us have seen her in over a hundred and fifty years, and you managed to perfectly replicate her. It was a bit spooky, actually."

Emma bit the inside of her lip. "I know," she whispered. "I'm sorry you both had to relive that."

Axel shrugged. "I've made peace with her passing, but I think my brother still hopes that she's alive."

Emma nodded in understanding. It was easier to hold onto hope than to accept what she might have suffered at the hands of the monsters that took her. Axel gave her another small, reassuring smile before he jogged ahead of her.

When she made it up to her room, she couldn't help but pull her phone out of her bag and power it on.

A flood of texts and voicemails came through. She scrolled through the texts, noticing several from Adrianna and a few from Rowek.

Her phone vibrated as her mother's contact filled the screen. Emma sucked in a sharp breath. She wasn't sure if it was the effects of facing the Djinn that made her accept the call, or just the ache in her chest that had been there since she had climbed out of her window two days ago.

"Hello?" Emma said tentatively.

"Emma!" her mother's voice choked out. "Are you okay? Please come home!"

"Calm down," Emma said as a single tear rolled down her face. Her mother's panicked tone broke her. "I'm safe, I'm great, actually." If you didn't consider that less than thirty minutes ago, she had been fighting Shediem.

"Where are you?"

Emma hesitated. "I can't tell you."

A sob echoed through the line and Emma's heart squeezed painfully.

"Please, baby," her mother begged. "I'm so sorry, just come home."

This time Emma sobbed as the dam that held back her tears shattered. "I can't."

"Are you being held there against your will?"

She took a steadying breath as she wiped the dampness from her cheeks. "No."

"I'm sorry for what I said. I was mad, I shouldn't have reacted that way."

"It's okay, Mom. I love you," she said.

Her mother sniffled. "Then please come home."

Her resolve cracked. She had both bags over each shoulder and was out the door before she could think clearly. In her haste she collided face-first with Blaze.

"Going somewhere?" he asked.

Emma huffed. "Home. My mother needs me."

Blaze's brows drew together. "If this is because I pushed you too hard or—"

"It's not," Emma interrupted him. "I've stayed too long. My mom and I need to patch things up."

Blaze ran a hand through his hair, and several strands fell back against his forehead. "It isn't safe. Levaroth will have full access to you."

She focused on a spot over his shoulder as she spoke, her voice soft. "I don't care. I have to go."

He was silent for several moments, and her heart pounded as she waited for his reply. "I'll have Axel drive you," he said. Then he spun on his heel, heading down the other side of the long corridor.

Emma hurried down the stairs, her throat burning as she went out into the cold, dark night to wait for Axel.

EMMA

The car rolled to a stop a few blocks away from her house and Emma thanked Axel before grabbing her bags and closing the door. The idling car followed at a distance as she walked to her house, all the while preparing herself for what she would say and how she would act.

She stood at the bottom of the wooden steps, staring at the door when it flew open and her mother barreled out, throwing her arms around Emma's neck. Emma returned the embrace, letting the ache inside her chest melt away. The knots in her stomach remained as she waited for her mother's stern words.

Her mother released her, holding her at arm's length to inspect her for damage. If only she knew that Emma's wounds healed in minutes.

"You're okay," she said, relieved. She continued to stare at her, as if unable to comprehend that she was uninjured.

"I told you I was safe," Emma replied gently. She didn't want her words to stir up whatever anger she knew her mother was harboring, however deep it was buried.

Her mother nodded with a teary-eyed smile. Then she led her inside, out of the crisp autumnal air. Her mother took her bags, tossing them under the coat hooks. Dozens of fragrant aromas met her at the door; cooking was a stress habit for her mother.

"Are you hungry?" her mother asked, rushing into the kitchen. When Emma didn't answer right away, she peered back into the entryway, as if making sure she hadn't disappeared again.

"Uh, yeah," Emma said. She had left before Gertie had a chance to feed her dinner, and while she would miss her comforting foods, she loved her mother's cooking.

A perfectly baked lasagna sat in the middle of the table, along with an entire loaf of garlic bread. Emma smiled and sat down. But the knots in her stomach wouldn't let her get more than a few bites down. Emma looked into her mother's eyes, waiting.

Her mother sighed. "I'm not going to yell."

"Why not?" Emma asked. "I can see that you want to."

Her mother gave a soft laugh. "Would it do any good? Would you run away again if I yelled?" Her words were like a sharp knife to the heart, but they were legitimate questions.

"It would make me feel better. And no, I won't run away again."

Her mother's eyes brimmed with tears again. "How can I trust you?" she asked softly.

Emma shook her head, swallowing the lump that rose up in her throat. Tears burned her eyes. "I'm so sorry," she said.

Her mother nodded. "I know." She gave a heavy sigh. "But I'm not going to yell. You are an adult, you may come and go as you please. All I ask is that you stay safe and don't sneak out. I'd prefer it if you still told me where you were at all times and who you were with, but I realize that may be overreaching."

"I'll do my best," Emma said. Her mother smiled.

"There is something else I did want to discuss with you." Emma sat up straighter. "You asked about my mother before…" Her voice trailed off and Emma nodded.

"She was a delicate woman. She loved cooking and baking. My father was nicer to her than he was to me, but she always stood by him, no matter how he treated either of us. It wasn't that she was weak, it was that she loved him so much, she somehow convinced herself that it must be her fault or my fault when he hit us."

Emma's stomach rolled. It made sense now why her mother

had run away. And why she never mentioned them.

"I'm sorry," she whispered.

Her mother gave a half smile. "It's okay. There are many children with far more tragic stories than mine, but I hoped that you would understand why I don't speak of them.

Emma nodded. She chewed the inside of her cheek for several moments, debating asking the question plaguing her.

As if reading Emma's mind, she spoke. "It's okay," her mother said. "Ask whatever you want."

"Are you an only child?"

A flash of surprise lit her mother's features before she schooled her expression. "Yes, I am," she replied stiffly.

Another lie, Emma thought.

"You should probably get some sleep since you have school in the morning," her mother said. Emma nodded, rising from her seat. Her mother wrapped her arms around Emma, squeezing almost painfully.

"I love you," her mother whispered. Emma could feel her worry and fear drain away between them.

Emma trudged up the stairs with her bags, her belly full, her mind fatigued with more questions, more lies, and more secrets.

Her mother had taken the day off to take Emma to and from school. She felt guilty about the broken trust, but not as guilty after her mother had blatantly lied about being an only child.

Rowek and Adrianna were both absent from school. Adrianna had messaged, saying she wasn't feeling well.

At her lunch break, Emma had been eating alone, reading a book when her phone vibrated. She pulled it out and read the message from Rowek: **I miss you.**

She couldn't swallow her bite of pizza and nearly choked on it. Well if he missed her so much, why wasn't he at school? She had typed those exact words several times and erased them every time.

Her mind was muddled through the rest of the day. When she got home, Emma's mother made her a warm cup of coffee that Emma held to her chest while doing research on her laptop for her history paper. Her mother tidied up the house, peeking her head back into the living room occasionally to be sure Emma hadn't moved. Rain battered the house, and she smiled, content.

She glanced at her phone for what felt like the hundredth time. Nothing more from Rowek. Nothing from Blaze either.

She stretched, setting her empty mug and laptop beside her on the sofa. She glanced at the time on the computer, making her stomach growl. Her mother walked in just in time to hear it.

She laughed. "I was just going to ask what you wanted for dinner."

"Anything," Emma replied with a shrug.

"Pizza?" her mother offered. Emma nodded with a grin. Her mother was on the phone to the delivery place before Emma had climbed the flight of stairs. She placed her laptop on her desk and then slid her phone from her pocket.

She stared at the screen as what sounded like a loud thunderclap shook the house. The following tremor that rocked the house made her heart turn inside out. She rushed from her room, meeting her mother on the staircase. The stunned look on her face had Emma running down the stairs past her mother and grabbing her coat from the hook. The shock subsided and her mother raced after her.

"Where do you think you're going?" she asked.

"Same place you're going." Emma tossed her mother's jacket to her and grabbed the keys. They started out the door without any further discussion.

Rain fell in thick sheets. It was too dark to see where the bomb had gone off, but the volume of it and the way it shook the ground said it wasn't far.

"We don't know where it is," her mother protested as Emma threw the SUV into reverse and then peeled off down the slick road.

"Call the hospital, EMTs would have been sent out," Emma said, but she hadn't needed to. Her mother was speaking to someone when Emma's phone vibrated. Blaze's number flashed on the screen.

"Where was it?" Emma asked.

"The Seahawks Stadium," he replied, then his voice lowered. "Stay home, okay? We can handle this." Emma cast her mother a sidelong look that her mother returned with raised brows.

"Too late." She hung up and spun around, heading for the stadium. First responders were quicker this time, having blocked the area off at least a mile away. Emma parked on a curb, and she and her mother raced toward the line of security holding onlookers back.

There were no lights except for the sparse few that had been brought in and were running off generators. Emma could see the destruction; chunks of shattered brick and twisted, charred pieces of steel lay out like a sea of debris. The stadium's coverings had collapsed, and the walls had exploded outward. Teams of firefighters and EMTs were wading through the wreckage, scouring for bodies. If anyone was still alive and needing medical attention, Emma imagined the chances were slim.

"Sorry, no one is allowed in. This may have been an act of terrorism, and we need to treat it as such," a nasally officer said as they approached.

"I'm a surgeon." Her mother flashed her ID at the officer. "This is my assistant." She gestured to Emma.

The officer eyed them with hesitation.

"Please," her mother said in a low voice. "We can help."

The officer lifted the tape and they ducked underneath. Her mother spotted the head paramedic and introduced Emma. He was tall and looked to be in his mid-to-late fifties, his forehead heavily creased, his short hair beginning to gray. They didn't exchange pleasantries, but it was clear they knew each other.

"What do we know so far, Bill?" her mother asked. She was in full surgeon mode.

"Not a lot," the man answered. "There was a game going on, so the stadium was almost to capacity. Nearly everyone within the blast radius that survived is being taken to Virginia Mason, and those with less serious injuries are being treated over there." He pointed to what looked like a large marquee on the far side of the stadium's parking lot.

"What can I do?" her mother asked.

"You can either catch a ride over to the hospital or you can help in the tent."

Her mother nodded. Then she turned to face Emma. "Head over to the tent and see if you can help there, okay?"

Emma swallowed hard, then nodded. Her mother placed a gentle kiss on her rain-soaked forehead before Emma jogged over to the tent, ducking out of the cold and wet.

She didn't know if it was a good or a bad thing that the majority of the injured in the tents were all things she could help with. She relieved a paramedic who looked ready to pass out, whom she later discovered had been on the job for fourteen hours before the explosion. When another paramedic came to take Emma's place, she did rounds with bottles of water and helped clear away used supplies, and the night passed by in a blur.

Somewhere in the early hours of morning, a hand rested on her shoulder, causing her to spin. Stormy gray eyes met hers.

"You've done all you can here," Blaze said gently.

Emma nodded, her eyelids heavy.

"I'll drive you home."

She didn't argue as they walked back to her mother's SUV. She wondered how long it would be before her mother would get to sleep.

"You okay?" Blaze asked gruffly.

Emma nodded, slumped in the passenger seat, fighting to stay awake. He didn't say any more and she hadn't even noticed she had closed her eyes, let alone fallen asleep, when she felt a hand tuck a strand of hair behind her ear. She stirred, looking up at Blaze.

"We're here?" she asked groggily.

Blaze gave a small chuckle. "Yes."

Emma fumbled for the latch on her seatbelt. With a click, the clasp sprung free and Emma pulled it over her head, moving slower than she meant to. Her entire body ached from the cold, and she wasn't sure how she would make it up the stairs.

She vaguely heard Blaze say, "Hold on." Then her door opened, and he lifted her out. Her lips lazily mumbled a protest that was met with a rumbling in Blaze's chest as her head rested against it.

The next thing she knew, she was in her bed with a solid, soothingly warm body pressed up against her back. She tried to turn her head, but all she heard was, "Shhh, go to sleep."

She obeyed.

When she awoke the following morning, the absence of warmth left a chill that no number of blankets could ease. Sunlight streamed in through the window, and Emma balked at the idea of the sun shining when the world was covered in the gloom of tragedy. Reluctantly, she angled her face up to look at the time and ripped off the covers. She stopped at the edge of the bed. *Would there even be school today?* It seemed an odd thing, to go to school when yesterday Seattle had been attacked again.

She picked up her phone, noting the missed calls and texts from Adrianna with dread and relief. *At least she's okay.* She sent a message saying she would call later, but before she hit send, she quickly added: **glad you're safe.**

Soft footsteps creaked on the stairs and she waited. A moment later, her door opened and her mother's face peered in. Her eyes were lined with purple, her hair mussed.

"Hey," her mother said, her voice raspy.

"Did you just get home?" Emma asked. Her mother's arms folded over her chest as she moved into the doorway.

"About an hour ago," she replied. Her eyes brimmed with a sadness that made Emma's chest ache.

"How bad is it?" she whispered.

"Sixty thousand estimated dead, at least twenty-five-hundred wounded, many of them critical." Her mother's voice cracked toward the end and Emma gasped. For several moments, Emma watched tears fall down her mother's cheeks, unable to think or move, or breathe. *Sixty thousand*. Bile rose up in her throat.

"I don't even know what to say," Emma said, dumbfounded.

"Me either," her mother said as she tried to suppress a yawn.

"You should get some sleep," Emma suggested. Her mother nodded.

"There's no school today, by the way," her mother added before turning and closing the door behind her.

Emma fell back onto the bed, her stomach clenched and heart aching. At some point, she drifted back to sleep, awaking again just before noon. She checked the news. Seattle had ground almost entirely to a halt, in memoriam of the dead.

After a late breakfast that consisted of toast with peanut butter and an extra strong cup of coffee, she grabbed her laptop and settled herself back on the couch, planning to do some more research when her phone rang.

Her heartrate quickened when she looked down at the screen.

"Hey," Emma said.

"Come outside," was all Blaze said before the call disconnected. Emma's brows creased as she set the laptop aside and padded across the carpet. She slipped outside, a chill snaking down her spine as the bright, sunny day did little to warm the air.

Blaze stood on the porch, hands shoved into a pair of faded denim jeans that hung low on his hips, the fabric of his navy-blue t-shirt stretched across his firm chest. He looked as though he hadn't slept yet, his eyes red-rimmed. The casual attire he wore made him appear younger.

"That's also a great band." He nodded to her chest and she felt her face flame. She had forgotten what she was wearing. She glanced down at the faded Demon Hunter t-shirt that was paired with a pair of plain, gray sweatpants that had more than one mysterious stain adorning the legs.

"Thanks," Emma mumbled. She fought the urge to wrap her arms around herself as she said, "You look exhausted, have you slept yet?"

Blaze ran his fingers through his silky black hair as he shook his head, disbelieving. "We pulled so many bodies from the wreckage last night, I just keep seeing their faces."

She nodded, a bitter taste in her throat. Her eyes prickled.

"You were so brave and selfless last night. Every time I remind myself that you're so young, you surprise me by acting ten times your age."

Her stomach dipped. "Thank you," she said quietly.

Blaze gave a gentle smile. "You're a warrior at heart, Emma. We'd be lucky to have you among our numbers."

"Did you come here to recruit me?"

He laughed, a rich, beautiful sound that made her heart race. "My uncle sent me here to recruit you, as you put it, but that's not why I'm here. Axel and I will be away for a few days, I just wanted you to know."

Confusion drew her brows together again. "You came all the way into Seattle to tell me you're leaving?" she asked.

"I had a Tohsia stone made, I've put it under your window."

She blinked. "What's a Tohsia stone?"

"A protection that wards against Shediem. They only work for small areas and they have to be replaced every month or two, but I wanted to do what I could to make sure Levaroth couldn't get to you."

"Thank you," she said again, her head spinning slightly.

Blaze's gaze searched her face. "Be safe, okay?" he said, low and gentle as he took a step toward her. His eyes were bright, his warm, earthy scent drawing her closer. His hand came up, cupping her cheek. His thumb stroked it gently.

Her mouth was dry when she said, "I'll try."

He smiled before bringing his mouth down onto hers. The touch of his lips sent a shiver through her. His hand slid to the nape of her neck, weaving his fingers into her hair as she wrapped her arms around his neck and pulled him closer.

Their kiss grew in intensity, their bodies flush.

With a groan, Blaze pulled away, his irises dark with desire. Emma bit the inside of her lip, wondering if she had been too eager.

"Finally," he said, his voice husky.

Emma's cheeks warmed. Now that there was space between them, the cold returned, wrapping around her like a blanket. She folded her arms around herself.

"I'll…" She hesitated, unsure if she should finish the sentence, but then it came out in a rush before she could stop it. "I'll miss you."

A smile touched his lips. Then both of his hands were on either side of her face, his lips pressing against hers in a firm kiss. When he pulled away, she felt a bit breathless.

Then, Blaze jogged down the steps, off the lawn and was gone from sight. Heat burned within her that could not be quenched by the cool breeze. She carried it with her through the evening and into the night.

LEVAROTH

The master's summons felt like hooks deep inside his chest ripping him from Earth. In a blink, he was standing before the prince, both of them in their true forms. He lowered himself onto one knee, bowing his head.

"Stand, Levaroth," Asmodeus said, wisps of smoke curling up from his nostrils.

Levaroth stood. "You summoned, Master?"

"Time is up. Bring the girl to me; by force if you have to." His long, black onyx claws flashed as he tapped them in succession on the bones he sat upon. "My brothers will travel to us. Belphegor's betrayal must be dealt with."

Levaroth gave a tight nod before he disappeared. Too much time had been wasted; he was now forced to act while she trusted him no more than the day they met.

School didn't operate for a week, so he waited, unmoving. Fresh protection spells kept him from just appearing in her house.

At last he saw Emma to leave for school. Her mother's car drove down the street, with Emma in the passenger seat. He couldn't believe what he was about to do, but he waited with preternatural stillness until she was out of the way. When her mother's car pulled back into the driveway, he changed, making himself look harmless.

She climbed out of the vehicle and strode up the porch, exhaustion weighting her shoulders. Levaroth stepped out of the bushes and walked across the street as she fumbled with her keys.

He stood behind her, and she turned with a startled yelp, dropping her keys to the ground. Levaroth stooped over and snatched them up.

"Sorry, I didn't mean to frighten you," he said in his best innocent voice.

A look of suspicion lined her face as she slowly extended her hand out for her keys. Levaroth smiled. Then he grasped her hand and they disappeared.

Her scream echoed through the dimly lit chamber, stopping abruptly when her eyes opened. She clutched her stomach, her skin turning a shade of green from the transportation. Geryon stepped defensively in front of Asmodeus who was back in human form. Levaroth felt his throat burn with bile. The prince's eyes were not the red of bloodshed he was accustomed to. They were the same glittering emerald green as Emma's. He shook away his own unfamiliar feeling of regret for what he had done. And for what he was about to do.

Recognition flashed in Laura's eyes, her lips parting in surprise.

"You," she breathed.

Asmodeus's eyes bled back to red, swallowing the whites of his eyes and eliminating the last semblance of humanity in his face. The look he gave her said he recognized her as well. He waved Geryon to the side, and reluctantly, he stepped back beside the throne.

"So you're the Giborim bitch that I slept with," he spat in disgust.

The woman seemed to recoil at his words. "You're a prince?"

Asmodeus rolled his eyes. "Yes, yes, are you in fact a Giborim?"

Laura swallowed audibly. "Yes. I'm not a pureblood, though, or whatever they call them—"

Asmodeus gave a snort. "Clearly."

"What do you want with me?" she turned around, having just noticed the Shediem general who stood behind her, at least seven feet tall, with wings partially stretched out. She gaped. "Where is my daughter?" she addressed the prince and then spun to face Levaroth again. "Where is Emma?"

Asmodeus spoke with mirth, his fingers steepled under his chin, "Emma will be joining us shortly."

EMMA

Emma had only made it through her first class before the pounding in her head made her dizzy. Rowek was still absent, and she hadn't received another text from him. The bell rang, signaling the start of second period just as she stepped out into the brisk morning air, inhaling the breeze in hopes of easing the headache. After several moments, a wave of nausea crashed into her.

She leaned her shoulder against the cool bricks, steadying herself. The parking lot before her swam. Her mother would likely be catching up on much-needed rest and Emma didn't want to bother her. She staggered down the paved steps, setting off in the direction of her house.

The world spun and she stumbled, catching herself before her face hit the pavement. After several blocks, she stopped along a row of bushes where her breakfast forced its way up, coating the dry, brittle leaves. She whimpered as she wiped her mouth clean with the back of her hand. She dropped to her hands and knees on the sidewalk, bowing her head against the cool pavement, relenting at last to call her mother.

The line rang once. Twice. Three times. Then her voicemail. She hung up, groaning and massaging her temples. When the nausea began to subside, she climbed to her feet and started walking again. Little by little, her vision righted itself.

She made it several more blocks when the feeling of unease unspooled itself in her gut. A piece of paper hung on the door, and the last few yards she took at a sprint. She ripped the paper off the door and flipped it over. An address was typed on the middle of the sheet as well as a time.

Her hands shook as she freed her set of keys from her bookbag, fumbling with them before getting the door unlocked. She shoved it open, racing up the stairs. Her mother's bedroom was empty. Untouched. She ran through the house, calling for her until her voice became hoarse.

Tears flooded her eyes, cascading down her face as a wail racked her body. She cried, screamed, letting the pooled emotions flow freely until she was empty. Hollow. Then, she dialed Blaze's number.

"Emma?" Blaze's voice was laced with concern.

"They have my mom," she rasped.

There was a pause. "Who has your mom, Emma?"

She didn't know if she could say it, if she could voice the words. She wasn't even entirely certain, but she had a pretty good guess.

"The Shediem." Her voice was a crackly whisper.

"How do you know?" Blaze's voice was fierce, and it made Emma's eyes sting, her eyes too dry to shed any more tears.

"They left a place and time. No demands, though—" And as if saying it out loud was all she needed to fit the last piece of the puzzle, her body went cold. She was the demand.

Levaroth.

Blaze seemed to realize it at the same time as he shouted, "No! Absolutely not. I'm coming home right now, I'll be there first thing tomorrow, Emma, and I swear to you, we will figure this out."

"Yeah," she said numbly, her ears not fully listening. The time said tonight at seven o'clock. Tomorrow would be too late. "I'll see you in the morning," she whispered, and as she hung up, she could hear Blaze's protests.

She couldn't move from her spot in the middle of the floor, staring at the front door, half expecting her mother to walk through it. Her brain wouldn't process what needed to be done. Every time she began to think of another way to save her mother, her mind went blank. So she stared at the door, unmoving, hardly even breathing.

Another thought occurred to her. She picked up her phone and called Rowek.

"Hello?" he answered.

"They have my mom," she said, her voice even.

A pause. "Who does, Sunshine?"

She hated that he called her that when her whole world was falling apart. "Levaroth."

His swallow was audible. "What do you need?"

"I have to go get her by seven tonight. I want you to come with to make sure she gets out safely."

"Why call me? Surely your Giborim can help." his tone seemed off, but she wondered if it was just the surprise that Emma would call him instead.

"He's out of the country. Can you meet me or not?"

"Text me the address," Rowek said. Then Emma hung up.

The light from the window had begun to dwindle, and with a sigh, she rose to her feet. She sent the address to Rowek as a gust of guilt filled her. She was the reason her mother was probably tied up in some horrid building. She couldn't let herself picture the horrific things they were most likely doing to her without nausea washing over her and making her retch.

In anguish, she launched her phone at the wall. It ricocheted off in several pieces, but she didn't care. She ignored the device, before grabbing the paper and heading for the door.

Tomorrow would be too late, and she wasn't going to wait for Blaze to show up. If wherever her mother was, was filled with Shediem all thirsting for her blood, then it would make even less sense bringing Giborim along. If her mother was truly Nadia Ivankov, then Emma had messed up her mother's entire life by simply existing. She wanted to show the same level of sacrifice her mother showed her every day.

She got in her car, typed the address into her mother's GPS and pulled onto the street, praying to whoever was listening that her mother would still be okay by the time she got there.

The drive was painfully long in the evening traffic, and Emma kept glancing at the clock, bouncing her left leg to keep her anxiety from tightening its grip any further. The GPS led her out of Seattle as the last light of day sank below the horizon. She turned onto a gravel road that led out to a derelict farmhouse that looked as if it hadn't been occupied in years.

In the headlights, she could see boarded-up windows and entire sections of shingles missing from the roof. Wild vines scaled the sides of the house, clinging to the decomposing structure and winding their way through cracks and crevices. Rowek's sleek black car was parked off the gravel road, and it didn't look like he was still inside. Emma killed the engine but left the headlights on. With no phone, she would have no lighting. *Stupid!*

Her footsteps were light as she approached the house. Structurally, it didn't look stable enough to have fifty or more Shediem lurking and waiting inside. It was silent. Empty.

"Rowek," Emma whispered loudly, hoping he stayed close. It wouldn't make sense for him to already be inside, but the closer she got, the more she figured that he must be.

The silence was eerie. Not even the insects made a peep.

Fear kept her rooted to the spot for several moments until she heard a cry.

"Emma!" It was her mother's voice that propelled her forward.

She sprinted through the waist-high weeds that had grown over the walkway. The front door swung open and closed only a few inches in the wind. She launched her foot into it, sending it shooting open, the dry, rotting wood splintering. Inside, she found herself in a house that looked almost frozen in time despite the cobwebs and dust.

Her stomach flipped as the musty scent of decay assaulted her. Something else lingered in the air too. Something she couldn't quite place. But everywhere her eyes scanned was empty.

"Mom?" Emma called. She hoped Rowek was nearby.

A muffled sob reached her, and she froze. It came again and her feet moved, pulling her in the direction of the sound. She passed threadbare settees and armchairs covered with crocheted throws. A cold, empty fireplace groaned as the wind filled it. The floorboards creaked beneath her steps as she located a set of stairs that led down into a basement. Light flickered up, illuminating the stairs. Terror consumed her, but the sounds of her weeping mother led her down, down into the frigid depths of the rickety house. Ice filled her veins with each step, lodging between her lungs.

"Mom? Rowek?"

"Down here, come quick," Rowek's voice called, but it sounded wrong.

As she reached the final step, the scent of bleach burned her nostrils. Her eyes searched the room, waiting for the attack. Her brows knitted themselves together as she looked around. The room was empty. She spun, noticing a table with various tools, and started toward it.

Then a rich, seductive purr came from behind her.

"Hello, Emma."

EMMA

Emma whirled around. Rowek watched her, his amber eyes shining golden in the single light from above in the dingy space.

"I wasn't sure you'd actually come," he said, as if she were late to a party.

Her pulse roared in her ears. "Where is my mom?" she asked.

"She is perfectly safe. I will take you to her." He reached for her hand, but she stepped back. He sent her an impatient look.

"I told you to meet me here. Where is she? Who took her?" Emma repeated.

Rowek heaved an exaggerated sigh. "Not here. I wanted more time to ease you into things, to show you that you can trust me. There's someone who wants to meet you and—"

"You have two seconds to answer my question before I *make* you tell me."

Rowek's brows rose, pride lighting his features. "That's the kind of potential I want to help you unlock." He stepped toward her eagerly. "You have so much raw potential. The blood that runs through your veins is a potent cocktail of supernatural power. The things you can do..."

Horror swept through her. "You're working with them, aren't you?"

Rowek paused. Then his body shifted, became taller, his

shoulders broader, his face became older, his eyes changed to gold.

All the air in Emma's lungs left her as if he had struck her in the chest.

"Levaroth," she breathed.

"Yes. I almost blew my cover on more than one occasion. I didn't think you'd learn to trust me as this form of myself," he gestured to himself. "So I became Rowek."

"Why?" she shouted, her blood hot. "Why go through all this trouble if you're just going to kill me?"

Levaroth laughed, the sound a sultry caress against her body. "I don't want to kill you, Sunshine. I mean, on that first day, I just wanted to see who you were. What you were. When I touched you, I could see, as well as feel you drinking my power. You were suspicious of me. I had to expend my energy daily as well as have a Spellcaster bind it so you couldn't sense it just so I could touch you and be near you."

The memory of his hands on her—of his lips—made her face burn. Her hands fisted at her sides and a tremor started through her.

"I staged the attack with the Nickor clan to see your powers in action. I found myself drawn to you for reasons I still don't understand. I searched for information on who your parents were for weeks. Then that bloody Giborim bastard got in the way. Just as you were beginning to trust me and let me in."

She couldn't speak. Her mouth hung open, listening to him continue.

"Again, everything was almost ruined that night at the school dance when Elbis and his band of rogues found you. Dozens were killed, and while I could have let it slide, there was one thing I needed to protect. Time. If word got out that Shediem had attacked the humans so publicly, you'd have been pulled from school. Your mother's little boyfriend would have figured out some way to cloak you both long enough to disappear. I would have had to start all over as someone else, gain your trust, get you to desire me—"

"Desire you?" she bellowed. "Are you insane? You're a Shediem! A monster!"

He didn't even flinch. "You did desire me Emma. I tasted it on your skin. I heard your heartbeat speed up every time I neared."

She swallowed hard. She had desired him. His laughter, his smiles. His kisses. Her face burned as her heart squeezed painfully.

"All those people, not only died, but you wiped them from existence!" Hot tears streamed down her face. "They won't be grieved or remembered! And you played along, acting like we'd figure out who did it and try to undo it."

"I can undo it, Emma." His eyes locked onto hers, intense and heated. "Say the word and I can do it."

She scoffed. "You're disgusting. I should have guessed when I felt your power again on my birthday. I thought maybe it was your magic I was feeling, but it wasn't. It was you. A Shediem." Emma laughed, cold and cruel. She wiped away her tears, determined not to shed any more for him. "Give me back my mother and stay away from me."

Levaroth shook his head, his dark hair swaying. "If you come with me, then she will be returned."

"Why? My powers kill your kind. Doesn't that make me a threat?"

"Yes. But the extent of your powers is a bottomless well. We want to help you unlock them. Become who you were truly meant to be."

Emma couldn't listen anymore. She leapt forward with a roar of anger, her power simmering to life, hungry and strong. Levaroth disappeared as she sailed through the space where his body had once been, summersaulting to her back on the damp, concrete floor.

She pulled herself back up to her feet in time to see him materialize to her right, and she sprinted towards him.

"If you want to see your mother again, come with me right now," Levaroth said with urgency.

She halted mere feet from him. "How do I know you aren't lying?"

"She isn't here, Emma. Let me take you to her." He held out his hand with a look that burned into her soul. She could feel his sincerity, feel his *truth*.

"But I heard her…"

Levaroth shook his head. "You heard what I wanted you to hear. I needed to make sure you would come inside."

She hesitated for a moment, hoping to give her brain time to catch up with her actions. Her hand lifted in automatic surrender as thunderous footsteps sounded on the floor above them. Whipping her head toward the stairs, she heard Blaze calling her name.

Three figures leapt to the bottom of the stairs, one of them a man she didn't know. The last thing she saw was Blaze's face contorted in horror, his eyes swimming with agony.

Levaroth lunged for her hand as Blaze roared through the decrepit house, filling her mind as her body was whisked away.

EMMA

All her senses felt as if they were going haywire. Her eyes struggled to adjust, her ears roared with the sound of her thundering pulse. All at once she felt a sense of warming excitement and the sensation of her skin being pierced with a thousand shards of ice. She drew in a few shuddering breaths as things came into focus, her heartbeat slowing. Nausea crashed into her as she took in her surroundings.

A darkened hall stretched out on either side of Emma, the only light coming from flames that appeared to erupt from the stone floor and danced up at least six feet high. Her body was thrust toward one of the flame-covered walls and she screamed. A large hand clamped firmly over her mouth. The flames parted around her, licking near her skin, but they gave off no heat.

Burning golden eyes drilled into her. But the face that contained the eyes was not that of a mid-thirties man. This creature was much taller, with far more lean muscle. His face was a more perfect version of Rowek's. All sharp angles and stunningly beautiful.

"Quiet," the face growled. "Do everything he tells you to do." The voice was different too. Deeper, raspier. *Older.* Sandy blond hair slid to one side. Heat poured off him, and Emma realized his shirt was gone. Thick black whorls and markings that looked like some ancient language decorated every inch of his bare chest and biceps, wrapping around his back.

Her eyes followed the lines of his impressive body, discovering the reason his shirt lay shredded to ribbons on the stone floor at his feet. Massive bat-like wings stretched out around both of them, blocking her view of the hall. *Or blocking anyone nearby from seeing them.* Realization dawned on her as she felt the raw power radiating from him.

"Levaroth," she breathed.

The Shediem general. Not a teenage boy. Nor an intimidating man in a suit. No, this was his true form—terrifying and haunting. Beautiful yet dangerous. For the first time, he truly frightened her.

His eyes glinted, his pupils dilating. Like a void smothering flame. But he stepped away from her, as if he sensed her fear.

"This way," he said. Unsure of what else to do, she followed. He led the way through the winding tunnels that were as stifling without natural light as a tomb. Were they underground? Emma lost track of every corner they turned and began to feel as if the walls were getting closer. They turned again, and another long hall lay before them, with more dark-gray stone, and flames flickered along the walls, making her dizzy.

"Don't question him. Bow until he says you can stand, and be respectful," the general rumbled out of the corner of his mouth. Emma wanted to ask who 'he' was, but before she had the chance, a monstrous creature came into view. It looked like a minotaur with a boar's head and long, thick brown hair that covered him from his head to his strong, muscled torso. Long, curved spikes protruded from the tops of his shoulders and a set of spiraling horns decorated his skull, at least two feet long. His legs bent backwards like a canine's but were a deep blue and the rough, textured skin of an alligator.

His black, empty eyes made Emma shiver, and her steps became smaller as she tried to tuck in behind Levaroth, if only to escape the dead stare the creature was giving her. She wondered if this was who she was supposed to be seeing.

"Hey there, Geryon," Levaroth said conversationally with

the same arrogant manner she had seen on Rowek. The beast grunted. "Right, thanks, yes, we'll just go right in then." Another grunt.

Levaroth shot Emma a familiar smirk over his shoulder, but on this new face, it was alarming.

They walked down another corridor. Levaroth snaked a bare, muscular arm around Emma and pushed her in front of him as they passed under a wide archway.

The room was massive and bare. A handsome human figure lounged within a much-too-big seat. Was this who Levaroth was talking about? He didn't look much older than mid-to-late-twenties. As they drew closer his eyes made her very soul quiver. From corner to corner, eyes as red as blood tracked her every step. A recognition bloomed like a flower within her, but she faltered as her lungs squeezed, making her gasp softly. Her mind screamed in protest with every step she took, but she forced herself to keep going, following Levaroth. When they came within a few feet of the bottom stone stair that led to the man sitting in his throne, Levaroth dropped to one knee, bowing low.

"Asmodeus, my Prince."

"Levaroth." The man's voice was not of a man at all. It was the sound of rolling thunder, or of a mighty avalanche.

Emma felt her mind telling her to bow, but her eyes were fixed on the crafted throne. With the rise of a burning sensation in her throat came the jolt of recognition.

Bones.

Human bones. A mockery of mankind. A morbid display of dominance and disregard for the living and the dead.

A deeply sensual laugh came from the man's throat. "My, you are a pretty, little thing, aren't you? So very like your mother."

A tidal wave of rage rose up inside her. "Where is she?" The strength in her voice surprised even her. A smile split the prince's face. He was…*pleased* with her?

"She's right where she should be," he replied, pushing himself upright. He glanced over to where Levaroth was still kneeling.

"Rise, Levaroth."

He obediently rose, throwing daggers with his eyes in Emma's direction.

"I have a proposition for you. I will release your mother, drop her back in her little oasis in Seattle, if you agree to my terms." The prince moved toward her with lazy, unhurried strides and she wondered if he was stupid enough to get close to her.

Anger still rolled through her as she said, "What terms?"

A brow rose, disappearing beneath his mane of shaggy curls. "I'm sure you can guess, *Shediem-slayer*." Emma's skin prickled uncomfortably as every little hair stood on end. A knowing smile lit the man's terrifying face. "That's what they call you. My daughter: the killer of her own blood."

Every molecule in her body froze as horror consumed her. Her vision blurred, and a shout reached her ears a moment before she realized it was her own. "Liar!" *Daughter? His* daughter? Her *father?* A Shediem prince? A *demon?* That couldn't be right.

The prince gave a chuckle that rumbled so low, she felt it in her own chest. It knocked against her lungs, reminding her to breathe.

"Yes. Levaroth, here, was so kind as to do all the grueling research for me but when he brought Laura to me, or should I say, *Nadia*, it was confirmed."

Emma shook her head, but deep down, she had known. The hope Blaze and Rowek had given her made it easier to ignore, but the truth stood before her with eyes that burned like red-hot embers.

Her father wasn't a Spellcaster. She was a Shediem—or half-Shediem, anyway. And her mother was a Giborim. That fact she had accepted, though the concept felt strange. Try as she might, she couldn't fathom how her father could be a Shediem. And her power killed only Shediem, so what did that mean?

"I don't understand," Emma croaked.

"I'm sure Levaroth can explain how all of that works—"

"I know how babies are made," Emma snapped, and a flash

of anger flared in the prince's eyes, making her spine stiffen.

He waved off Emma's remark with a flick of his wrist. "None of that matters. I don't think you need proof. You know what I say is true, you just want to believe you're not tainted by the blood that flows within you. My blood. You are capable of more than what you are right this second, and here in my palace, we will help you unlock that. Make your Shediem blood become dominant. The world will see the level of destruction you are capable of." His red eyes burned with excitement.

"No thanks."

A slow, sadistic grin crept onto his face before he said, "Then your mother will die." He drew closer.

Emma's brain worked furiously. Out of the corner of her eye, she saw Levaroth's features morph into a look of warning. Ignoring it, she lurched for the prince's face. Like a wisp, he was smoke between her fingers. She landed hard on the stone floor. Pain bit into her knees, but she ignored it. She leapt back to her feet.

"Now, now, play nice," the prince's silky voice said behind her. She spun and lunged again, her teeth gritting in frustration. He was gone again before her hands could make purchase. Arms wrapped around her waist, crushing her arms against her sides. A powerful surge shot through her; every nerve ending charged with energy. It was glorious. The strong grip released her, and a sound ripped itself from her throat. A desperate cry for more.

"Emma, stop," Levaroth growled. She whipped around with a hiss. The dark energy she had absorbed trickled away like water held in her hands.

Asmodeus sat back on his throne, lounging with one leg draped over the side, his mouth curved in a wicked smile.

"I'm willing to overlook your narrowmindedness," he said, his eyes void of amusement. "Levaroth will show you to your chambers and we'll have another chat tomorrow. There is something I want you to see before you make your final decision."

Emma knew that nothing could sway her, but Levaroth

pulled her away by her shirt before Emma's argument could spill out of her mouth. The look in her father's eyes said whatever tomorrow brought would somehow change her mind, but she let him see the determination in hers as she let herself be led from the room.

EMMA

Levaroth disappeared without a word at the top of a tower, the wooden door open. She didn't know how many stairs they had climbed to make it to the room, but the burn in her legs had distracted her from the cold dread that filled her.

She stepped into the room. The minimal décor was drab and unwelcoming, especially after the grandeur of the suite in Blaze's mansion. Everything was colorless. Lifeless. The only light came from two candelabras; one that was attached to the wall, and one on a table at the foot of the bed. The space was small. A chamber off to the right held a rancid-smelling toilet, where the contents appeared to drop straight through the floor, and a cubicle for showering. It was practically medieval.

An ache festered in her chest as she sat on the thin mattress, covered by a worn, patched blanket.

My mother is a captive of a Shediem prince. That prince is my father. The boy I liked is really a Shediem general.

She covered her face with her hands, fighting back tears until the dam broke. A strangled sob escaped as the tears poured down her face. Her body shook as defeat and helplessness consumed her.

Growing up without a father had been hard at times, but as she got older, she realized her mother didn't talk about him because he was not a good guy. She must have known who he was. Her father was Asmodeus. Her mother was a Giborim.

And Emma's power was useless against a creature that became smoke as soon as she got close. How was she supposed to free her mother and kill the Shediem? War between the Giborim and the Shediem was imminent, and everyone left on Earth was in danger. Adrianna, and the faces of others she had known from her previous homes, flashed in her mind. If war broke out, using the streets of Seattle and the rest of the world as their battlefield, they would all die. She had to find a way to stop it.

I can fight, a voice inside her said. She lifted her head, drying her face as a spark of courage turned to flame.

She started as a knock rapped at the door. A tall, rail-thin girl with golden-brown hair who looked only a few years older than Emma, cautiously swung the door open, bearing a tray in her arms. Her bright blue eyes took in Emma without a hint of fear.

"Hello, Miss," the girl said. "Thought you might be hungry." She nodded to the tray.

Though Emma couldn't possibly entertain the idea of food, she nodded. "Thank you."

The girl dipped her head in reply, setting the tray on the small, round table. Curiosity got the best of Emma and she asked, "Are you a slave?"

The girl gave her an odd look, then she seemed to consider it. "I suppose I am."

Emma felt her throat tighten. "I'm sorry," she whispered.

The girl looked surprised by Emma's response. Then her features softened. "Thank you."

Emma gestured to the seat across from her. "You can sit if you like."

She shook her head fervently. "Oh, no, I'm supposed to be—"

"It's okay, I won't tell," Emma said. The girl let a smile tug at her lips before she dropped into the seat with a low hiss. Emma guessed she didn't spend much time sitting.

"How long have you been here?" Emma asked, picking up what looked like a cherry tomato and popped it into her mouth.

A sadness dulled the brightness of her blue eyes. "I don't know anymore. A very long time."

Emma felt the ache in her chest deepen.

"Out!" a booming voice said from the doorway and both girls jumped. Levaroth's voice was still so new to her, Emma hadn't recognized it. The servant girl leapt to her feet and scurried out, her head bowed.

"What did you do that for?" Emma shouted angrily. Levaroth's expression remained hard.

"I might ask why you attacked your own father, your master."

Emma scoffed. "He may be my father, but he is most definitely *not* my master. He is an evil, despicable monster. How do I know he hasn't already murdered my mother? Or that she isn't in some dark, leaky dungeon somewhere, bruised and bleeding?"

Levaroth stepped into the room, dwarfing the space with his sheer size and instinct took over, forcing her back. He stopped, looking pained. "Why do you fear me now? Because of my form?"

In truth, that was part of it. "You're a liar and a murderer."

He exhaled. "Your mother is fine. Fed, even."

Emma's anger slipped for a split second. Distantly, the reminder that a basic necessity such as being fed was not kindness. Not in this place. Her eyes narrowed. "She should be at home."

Levaroth looked ready to retort, then he paused. His weight shifted from one foot to the other. "Eat. I'll see you tomorrow." Then the place he had been standing was empty, the doorway deserted. What time was it here? Did time move the same in this place? She knew it had been at least several hours since she had left Washington. Her heart constricted painfully in her chest as she recalled the rage and pain in Blaze's eyes. Would she ever see him again, she wondered? *Yes, you will*, she told herself fiercely. She yawned, eyeing the tray of food.

Emma picked at the bits that looked familiar, pushing away the rest before attempting to wash herself in the shower cubicle that was motion activated, and obviously only one temperature. She was shivering uncontrollably by the time she was done, grabbing what looked like an old rag to squeeze the excess water from her hair and pat her body dry before she ran to the bed, ripped back the blanket and crawled under. It was too thin to provide any warmth, but soon, exhaustion consumed her, pulling her into a fitful sleep.

She awoke to pitch blackness. A large hand stilled against her face.

"I didn't mean to wake you." Levaroth's voice was low and husky. Emma shot upright, clutching the paper-thin blanket to her chest. Her mouth opened to speak, to yell, but a pair of soft lips crushed themselves against hers, his tongue slipping inside. Her abdomen tightened with both shock and pleasure. He kissed her like Rowek kissed her. All sensual heat and desire.

As if coming to herself, she flung back, unaware of where the mattress ended until she slipped off. Her back collided with the cold, stone floor and she groaned. Every muscle in her body was aching and tense.

Several bursts of flame erupted on the tips of the candles in her room, casting a soft glow. Levaroth stood beside her, looking down at her as if he wasn't sure whether to help her off the floor or not.

"What are you doing in here? Creeping on me while I sleep?" She glared.

"I was checking to see if you were still awake, but I saw the candles extinguished. You were shivering so hard, I could hear your teeth chattering. I only sat beside you to warm you up and you stopped. So I stayed."

"And that made it okay to *kiss* me?" She got to her feet, keeping the blanket wrapped around her.

Levaroth's molten gaze was locked on hers in determination. "You used to enjoy my kisses." He smiled. "You made this little noise when I stopped, like you were begging for more." His eyes flared with lust.

"Anyone that's ever tasted your lips would be addicted. Not to mention you're the most beautiful creature I've ever seen;

powerful and strong. My every thought is consumed with you, and I know you feel for me too. This place is not all bad, Emma, and once you've had time to think about it, you'll want to join us. You will find who you were truly meant to be here among your own kind, and though it's never been done before, you and I, we could be…" His voice trailed off.

Emma's lips parted, her eyes widening. She blinked, unable to process his words. Was he saying he wanted a *relationship*? A Shediem? A murderer…

She gave a bark of laughter. "You're a monster, the lowest scum ever created. I would never and could never be with you. You are more unlovable than the most evil and corrupt human. You pretended to be a normal guy, then you lied to me about what I was."

He stared at her for several moments, his gaze burning, and for a second, she wasn't sure if it was the candlelight, or if flames truly danced within his eyes.

"That Giborim scum already managed to win your loyalty? He has killed too! Humans, Spellcasters. He just passes his kills off as righteous; but his hands may be just as bloody as mine." Emma opened her mouth to scream, to tell him just how wrong he was. Then Levaroth said, "The servant will bring some more blankets." His gaze dipped to where the blanket stopped on her chest before adding, "And some clothing." Then he vanished.

Her anger had her body burning hot by the time the servant girl rushed into the room, holding a large stack of thick, newer-looking blankets and what appeared to be similar drab garments to what she wore.

"There you are, Miss," The girl bowed hastily then slipped from the room again. Emma picked up the thickest-looking blanket and tossed it on the bed, though now she felt too warm for it. Then she slipped into a basic, knee-length nightgown and sank back beneath the covers. Her mind raced and her heart pounded until the candles burned low, and at last sleep reclaimed her.

EMMA

S he felt as though she had merely blinked when a soft knock at the door startled her from her sleep. It came again, this time louder. She looked around, remembering the night's events. The candles were taller, as if newly replaced. She sat up, feeling the ache settle into her chest again.

"Are you awake, Miss?" a gentle voice called.

"Yes, sorry." Emma unwrapped the blankets that had twisted around her limbs.

"May I come in?"

Emma bounded over to the door, throwing it open for the girl. A pleasant warmth washed over her.

A small smile greeted her, the servant's brilliant blue eyes hidden beneath her lowered lashes. "Good morning, Miss." She held out a tray with more food, steam curling off the platter of crinkled bacon and linked sausages that made Emma's stomach growl audibly.

"Thank you." Emma took the tray. A sudden flare of loneliness gripped her as the girl curtsied, then turned to go. She wasn't sure if it was because she was the only friendly face she had seen in this horrible place, or if it was the comforting sensation she had when she was near. Her eyes were familiar, and though they held years of pain and sadness, she didn't look beat down by it. Whatever the reason, Emma found herself saying, "I need your opinion on something."

The girl turned, her eyes flicking up, a brightness shining in them for a fraction of a second before she shook her head. "I can't, Miss. I have chores that need doing and—"

"Emma."

The girl stopped short. "What?"

"My name is Emma," she clarified. "I don't like being called 'Miss.'"

The girl dipped her head, then she turned to go. Emma grabbed her arm, not wanting to be left alone. She flinched, and Emma let go, guilt pressing in.

"What's yours?" Emma asked gently.

Something like understanding dawned on the girl's face. She gave a small smile. "What was it you wanted my opinion on?"

Emma returned the smile with gratitude.

They sat at the table as Emma tried to eat the food slowly, though her body was screaming at her to eat faster.

"My name is Hadessa," the servant girl said after a few moments. Her eyes flicked to the tray of food every few minutes. Sensing her apparent hunger, Emma pushed the plate of bacon and sausage toward her. She hesitated for several moments, then at last, she picked up a strip of bacon and nibbled the edge.

Emma drained an entire glass of orange juice before saying, "How old are you, if you don't mind my asking?"

The sadness returned to Hadessa's eyes. "I have been here for too long to know for sure. As you may have guessed, time is a little different in Sheol."

Emma's fork froze on the path to her mouth, a piece of egg sliding off the tines. She set it down. "I'm sorry." It didn't seem like answer enough, what words could possibly lessen the hardship endured in a place like this?

They sat in silence for a few moments, Emma couldn't help but study the girl's familiar features before she managed to ask, "How did you get here?"

Hadessa blinked. "I don't remember."

Emma swallowed a bite of toast. "Do you have any siblings?"

A myriad of emotions crossed her face. "Two brothers."

"What are their names?"

Hadessa seemed to be recalling deeply buried memories while her eyes unfocused for a moment. "William and Andrew," she said at last, her tone colored with an unmistakable fondness.

Emma's heart sank.

"You seem disappointed with that answer."

Emma shook her head. "I thought you might be someone that I…" She paused. "A friend of mine lost his sister many years ago."

Hadessa grabbed another slice of bacon. "There are a lot of us here. Girls who were taken. It's been going on as long as the human race has populated the earth. Some were sold by their parents or guardians. Others, like me, were just a bonus on an assassination."

Emma furrowed her brows. "What do you mean?" she asked.

Hadessa didn't reply right away as she chewed the last bite of bacon, looking longingly at the remainder of the eggs. Noticing her gaze, Emma pushed the plate toward Hadessa.

"The last thing I remember was our house being broken into. My mum was in the early months of pregnancy and was always tired. When the Shediem broke in, they were looking for my father, but he was away on a mission. My two brothers, who were both quite young themselves, fought to protect me and my mother. She just wasn't fast enough and there were too many… they killed her. The next thing I knew, I was here. They didn't exactly know what to do with me. I was only a child myself. I've served in the kitchens and waited on Asmodeus's many guests."

Emma listened with tears stinging the backs of her eyes. "I think I know your brothers."

Hope sparked in her sapphire eyes. "You know Andrew and William?"

Emma nodded slowly. "I think so. They don't go by those names, though. Blaze, my… friend, told me of a similar story. His mother was killed and his younger sister, Haddie, was captured." Emma didn't tell Hadessa that both men suspected she was dead.

Or that she had been missing for over a century and a half.

Her eyes sparkled with tears. "They used to call me Haddie."

Emma felt her chest swell with emotion as the girl's tears overflowed, streaking down her cheeks. "They're alive," she murmured. Emma grabbed her hand from across the table and squeezed. Emma let Hadessa cry, her own tears falling with joy at the sight of Blaze and Axel's long-lost sister. She was alive, and though she had likely seen and heard unspeakable things, she looked healthy, though perhaps a little malnourished.

When the girl's tears turned to melodious, joyful laughter, which Emma imagined had not been practiced by the slight hint of hysteria in it, Emma laughed too, wiping away her own tears. Her mind recalled the image of the girl, no more than eight years of age, and she couldn't help but feel the ache in her chest lessen.

She leaned toward Hadessa. "I swear to you, I will get you out of here," Emma promised. "I will take you home to be with your family."

EMMA

Hadessa left after Emma had her explain the various plain garments that were brought to her. With a flustered sigh, she asked that her jeans and t-shirt be washed and returned to her, and Hadessa agreed, though her distaste for the garments was apparent.

Shortly after, Levaroth came to retrieve her. She stared at the tattoos that covered his back, and words spoken by Rowek came flooding back to her. *I'd show you all of it, but I'd have to take my shirt off.* Even as Rowek he kept a part of his true self, and she wondered why as he led her back through the maze of stone halls and into the main chamber where her father sat.

His roguish face twisted into a smile as they entered. Levaroth bowed just as before while Emma stood, arms crossed.

"Sleep well?"

"Where's my mother?" Emma returned.

Irritation wiped away his smile. "Still fine," he replied. Then he rose to his feet. "I want to show you something. Follow me."

The beast that guarded Asmodeus kept himself positioned between them, but they didn't walk like Emma thought they would. Instead, the chamber disappeared and was replaced with a hallway that they were squeezed into.

Up ahead, a door swung inward, and Emma tentatively followed, Levaroth pushing in closely behind her. He spared her a quick glance as they filed into a long, cold stone room. Emma's jaw dropped. From one end of the room to the other was what looked like glass, but as Emma stepped closer, she noticed how the surface shimmered. On the other side, Emma could see rows and rows of small rooms. Looking from a side angle, as if their view was from a camera, each room held at least four beds placed up against the walls. Beautiful young women either sat or laid atop them. Some paced the small chambers as their hands rubbed their swollen bellies. Some were just beginning to show, others looked ready to explode. Bile rose up in Emma's throat. She lifted a hand to touch the glass and a stab of pain hit her palm. She winced, looking down at her hand. A small red welt had formed on the pad below her thumb.

Her father stood beside her, looking on at what was in the rooms with something like pride in his eerie red eyes.

"What is this?"

"My breeding program. For many years I tried to figure out how to raise my own army of Shediem, and now, you are proof that I was only missing one element." He gave her a pointed look.

The women in the rooms are all Giborim. Her stomach flipped and nausea gripping her. But it didn't make sense that some of them looked nine months pregnant when the mass abductions only started a few weeks ago.

"All of these women are the Giborim you have been abducting," she whispered. Her fists clenched; her jaw locked. "How are some of them almost due when they were only stolen a few weeks ago?"

"Well, my brother took it upon himself to take Giborim females to execute as a way of sending a message. When I discovered the secret to hybrids like you, I began collecting them here. I use some of my resident Spellcasters to speed up the process."

Emma felt her breakfast working its way back up. As she backed away, shaking her head, her eyes searched for her mother somewhere in the labyrinth of women being used as incubators. She didn't think the prince would tell her if her mother was amongst them, but Emma didn't see her.

"Why are you doing this?" Her voice shook with anger. "You have a kingdom, thousands of Shediem bowing to you. What more do you need?" She couldn't voice the rest. *Why are you bombing earth? Why are you killing hundreds of thousands of humans?*

Asmodeus turned to look back at the maze of rooms, stacked on top of each other like cages for animal testing.

"We are setting the stage, if you will. Sending the human race into chaos so that when the choice comes, they will choose to save their pitiful lives and fight against the Giborim. We will build a far greater kingdom on earth and none of us will have to hide what we truly are there. We won't be hunted anymore."

Emma took a step back. Then another. Before anyone could stop her, she fled the room. She had no idea where she was going, but her bare feet slapped the cold stone, carrying her as far away as she could manage. Her flimsy dress rode up her thighs as she sprinted, but she didn't care. Selecting turns at random, she climbed up several levels of stairs until she broke through to what looked like the main entry hall. Orange light poured in through slits at the top of the stone walls and Emma sobbed in relief. She raced to the exit, pushing open the wide, ornate, golden set of doors, feeling excitement rising inside her at the prospect of feeling the sun on her face.

But what she saw outside was unlike anything she had ever seen before. The ground was burnt orange and chalky. Plumes of the dusty mineral burst up around her with each step she took. The sky was cloudless and an ominous shade between orange and red. A bustling city of stone architecture lay before her. Creatures that haunted every child's nightmares flew above or shuffled about in dark stone streets. Most of them were armed, and every single one in close proximity, stopped to stare at her.

A few uttered whispers, a few shouted. But they all said the same word. "Killer."

Before Emma could back away, Levaroth appeared in front

of her, his face contorted with rage. He grabbed her arms, his nails digging in painfully, and then she was back in the dreary room she loathed. He released her instantly, the sudden flood of his dark energy cut off. It left her cold and wanting more, but she forced herself not to lean into him.

"What were you thinking?" he shouted.

"Are you insane?" Emma asked. "Those women are forced to carry little demon babies! And for what? Why does he want to replicate this?" Her hands motioned to herself. "Why would he want a bunch of hybrids that can kill him?"

A muscle in Levaroth's jaw flexed. "There is a possibility that others will manifest powers that will work against our enemy. It's possible you have undiscovered powers. It's not as bad as you think; we will allow them all to care for the children until they reach an age that is suitable for training."

Emma blinked, dumbfounded. Then she scoffed. "You're sick," she spat vehemently. "Get out."

"Give it time, Emma. You'll see that this is a smart move."

Then he was gone. Emma wanted to scream and throw things, but besides her clothes, which had been neatly folded and sat upon the table, there was nothing she could hurl at the walls until she finally felt better.

When Hadessa brought dinner later that evening, Emma told her what she had seen. By the time she was finished, the color had drained from Hadessa's face and her hands noticeably trembled. They both knew what that could mean for her, though neither felt capable of voicing it.

"We need to try to escape. Tonight." Emma kept her voice low, in case anyone overheard them, though she knew it wasn't likely.

"How?" Haddie asked.

Emma bit her bottom lip. "I don't know yet," she admitted.

"As far as I know, the only ones who can leave here are Shediem."

"Well then, we escape the castle. Hide out somewhere until

we can figure out how to get home. Anywhere is better than here."

Hadessa didn't look convinced. "Without food and water, we'll die. And they will just set the Gargolosck on us as soon as they notice we're gone."

Emma rose a single brow. "What's a Gargolosck?"

Hadessa gave a somber smile. "They're great big beasts like wolves that lock onto your scent and either kill or retrieve, depending on the order. But even if they're meant to retrieve, they aren't gentle about it. There was a servant girl who ran away, and they sent a Gargolosck to retrieve her. There was hardly anything left of her." She paused to clear her throat. Her eyes shone. "I tried to treat her wounds, but they were so bad…She died in the end."

A chill ran up Emma's back. But she felt resolve fill her even more. Her chin lifted. "You don't have to come with me, but I have to go. Do you have any idea where my mother is being held?"

Hadessa stared at Emma for several moments before saying, "I'll come to you after the last kitchen workers have all gone to bed. Your mother isn't far."

Emma smiled widely. "Thank you so much."

Hadessa dipped her head in reply, then left Emma alone with her dinner. Nervous energy kept her from consuming more than a few salad pieces, leaving the suspicious ball of meat untouched.

The candles, as Emma discovered, cycled by magic or whatever force powered them. They burned all the way down, and when the last drop hit the floor, the pool of hardened wax would lift back into the holders, relit as full candles. Watching them was the only thing that kept Emma from pacing.

Her door creaked open a fraction after she felt her lids grow heavy and Emma got to her feet. *No going back. It's now or never.* Emma admitted to herself that it was probably a suicide mission, but the spark of hope led her out the door.

Haddie led her silently down the spiral tower, their pace making her dizzy. On the bottom step, the golden-haired girl peered around, making sure the coast was clear. She waved her forward and Emma followed her into a wide hall that had the familiar wall of flames dancing up toward the high ceiling.

They tip-toed down it, keeping close to the heatless fire. Emma's heart felt like it was working its way up her throat. A large shadow came into view on the floor before them and they stilled. Her blood rushed in her ears as the shadow became more distinguishable. Horns and the broad set shoulders that looked like the beast Levaroth had called Geryon.

Emma glanced behind her. The stairs they had come down were too far away. Panic flooded her as the beast's footfalls became audible. Haddie tugged her toward the flames that licked her arm, and instinctively, Emma jerked away until she saw what Hadessa had done. A doorway was opened within the stone wall. Hadessa stood in the flames, seemingly unaffected. Emma followed her into the space, flinching as she passed through the flames. When she was inside, the stones rolled back into place, enclosing them in darkness.

"What is this place?" Emma whispered, her eyes adjusted as much as they could, but still she could barely make out Haddie's outline.

"Servant's passageways. This route will take a little longer, but it'll be safer."

"How are we supposed to see?" Emma asked.

"That's another reason why I didn't want to use these halls. The candles don't light until the prince wants them to."

Emma's heart sunk. Hadessa's hand grabbed Emma's, her palm rough and calloused from her work. It was clear she knew the path by heart, guiding Emma through the labyrinth. Their light steps on the stone floor seemed loud in the otherwise dead silence.

They came to a stop and Haddie released her.

"Stay here," she said. Flickering light split from a crack as the faux wall opened, and Hadessa squeezed her slender body through. Then Emma was plunged into darkness once more.

Silence stretched so thin, Emma's ears strained to hear

anything. She leaned against the wall and waited. And waited. The lump in her throat rose further, and she swallowed hard against it. What was taking so long?

At last, the wall parted and Haddie's thin face peered in. She motioned Emma out.

They were back in another hallway, this one narrower than the last, and instead of fire lining the walls, there were candelabras with burning candles like in Emma's room. The dim lighting was just enough for Emma to see Hadessa as she headed into the room ahead. The darkness inside swallowed her whole. Instinctively, Emma's arms went out in front of her to keep from bumping into anything.

Vague outlines were visible, of countertops and what she assumed were cooktops. She kept her footfalls soft and glanced up to look for Hadessa. Movement caught her eye, and too late, her leg collided with something cold and smooth. It fell, shattering against the stone floor with a deafening crash. Her shoes crunched over the smashed item as a slim hand grabbed her wrist and then she was being tugged at a run from the room.

"What was that?" Emma asked shakily.

"A bowl, I'd imagine."

"Crap."

Haddie released her wrist and another wall was split open. What little she had been able to see before was completely gone.

Haddie pulled her into the tight corridor, then the wall closed behind them. They shuffled through, only turning twice before Haddie pushed the wall open again. She peeked her head out, then flattened herself back against the wall, the light catching the look of shock on her face. Emma opened her mouth to ask what she saw, but Haddie only shook her head. The corridor remained quiet; she hadn't been seen.

After a moment, Hadessa peered back out, this time more slowly. She beckoned Emma to follow her. Emma jumped through the wall of orange and red flames, still not trusting its inability to burn, landing softly on the balls of her feet.

Emma took in her surroundings, her skin prickling. Another wide, grand hall, the fires of light parting only for the few doors tucked along the walls. At the end of the hall, double doors glinted solid gold. She knew who was behind the doors and a voice inside her head whispered for her to go inside. It urged her forward, to end the prince while he slept. Her fists were balled tightly at her sides and a rage simmered under her skin. She ground to a halt just as the doors creaked open. Emma felt her breath hitch.

Hadessa jerked her arm, moving her into a small alcove. Emma glanced around the rugged stone. A scantily-clad female giggled as she slipped out into the corridor, then two more followed her. A rumbling voice echoed into the wide hall, but the words were lost to Emma's ears. Another round of sultry giggles escaped the three girls and then they retreated behind separate doors. Emma's stomach clenched. The prince wasn't sleeping, then.

Haddie nudged her out of the small space and then took the lead again. They only had a short distance to go before they turned left, and she pointed at a door across the way. A jolt of excitement coursed through her. Her mother was on the other side of that door, she could feel it.

Her heart sank at the sight of a shiny metal lock. She cast an anxious glance at Haddie who procured a key from her dress. Emma's brows lifted in question but Haddie silently slipped the long, brass key into the hole. It ratcheted softly as she turned it. When at last the lock sprung open, Emma's heart pounded as she pushed the door open.

The room was laid out much like Emma's, if only a little bigger, the bed sturdier. Atop the mattress, covered by a thick, red duvet, was her mother's thin frame. She was facing away from the door. Her chest rose and fell in a steady rhythm. Her strawberry blond hair was mussed, lacking its usual lustrous quality.

Emma ran to the bed and gently shook her mother's shoulder. "Mom, wake up, we need to go."

Her mother slowly turned over, "Emma?" she croaked.

Sudden tears flooded her eyes. "Yeah, Mom. Come on, get up; we need to go."

Her mother's eyes searched Emma's face for a moment, as if trying to decipher if she was really there. "You're okay."

Emma nodded. "I'm going to get you out of here."

Her mother sobbed. "I should have told you. I should have told you everything."

Emma shushed her gently, casting a nervous glance at the door. Haddie met Emma's gaze with a gentle urgency in her eyes.

"Help me get her up," she said to Haddie, who nodded. Together, they tugged her to her feet as tears flowed down her sunken cheeks.

"I was so young. I hated them all, so I ran. That's all I've ever done is run. Every time I feel afraid, I run—"

"Mom, it's okay, we can talk about this when we get home okay?"

Her mother jerked back out of their grasp. "No, I have to tell you now." Emma checked the door again, wondering how long they had before they were discovered. "My real name is Nadia Ivankov. I was born in Shlisselburg, Russia. Sergei helped me escape, he has helped keep us safe all these years. I love him. We wanted to tell you, I'm not always at work, sometimes I go to be with him. Your father—by the time I discovered he was a Shediem, he wouldn't let me go. I hid you from them, I was so scared. I know you know about Giborim. He told me you were at their compound, but Emma, you can't trust them. I'm just so sorry I never told you—"

"I know," Emma whispered. "I'm being careful." Emma wondered why her mother said she couldn't trust the Giborim, but they didn't have time. She glanced sidelong at Haddie to see if she was listening, but Haddie didn't react.

Her mother looked her over for several moments, then hung her head. "I'm sorry I lied to you, I'm sorry we moved around so much. I'm sorry you never knew my family…I have a younger sister." She lifted her head again, tears shining in her eyes. "When you get home, I want you to find Sergei. He'll protect you—"

A *boom* shook the floor and walls. They stood frozen for a moment. Panic tightened around her throat like an invisible hand, squeezing. Haddie started for the door and Emma pulled her mother toward it. After searching in both directions, she beckoned Emma and her mother to follow. They padded into the hallway as voices began shouting, and from the way her lungs constricted, she knew there were a lot of Shediem close by.

Haddie paused, stopping all three of them before spinning Emma. She grabbed her hand and pulled her in the opposite direction they had come, her mother jogging beside Emma. Footsteps behind them sounded like a stampede, but Emma could hardly hear them above the blood rushing in her ears.

"Isn't there another servant passageway somewhere?" Emma asked Haddie desperately. The weight in her chest made it hard to get the words out.

"Up here," she said, pointing to a spot at least thirty feet from them. They ran harder, sprinting as fast as they could.

"Emma, stop!" Levaroth boomed from behind her. The menacing tone made the hairs on the back of her neck stand on end.

Her throat burned, panic choking her. They reached the spot Haddie had pointed to. Her hands gripped the stone and pulled, but it didn't budge. She pulled harder, visibly straining. Emma grabbed the wall and pulled too, her nails scraping across the stone as she lost her grip. A cry escaped her lips.

"It's no use, Emma. The passages are sealed." Levaroth's voice was directly behind her. She spun. Several more figures were marching down the corridor toward them, and Emma felt sick. She grabbed Haddie's arm.

"Go, get out of here. I'll tell them it was my fault. You weren't a part of this," Emma told her fiercely.

Haddie's eyes held a sadness, but also a peace that Emma couldn't understand. She covered Emma's hand with her own and squeezed gently.

"It's okay," she said.

Emma tried again to swallow the lump in her throat. She spun toward her mother.

"I'm so sorry," her voice cracked.

In her mother's eyes, she found the same heart-breaking devastation that she felt. "I love you," she whispered, pulling Emma into a tight hug.

When Emma whipped back to face Levaroth, her eyes were narrowed, and she allowed hatred to burn in them.

"You did this," she spat.

He didn't reply, but there was a confirmation in his expression that made a chill skate across her skin. It almost looked like regret, but it was gone before she could analyse it further.

Asmodeus stopped before them, a mirthless smile on his face. "Geryon, please return Nadia to her room," he said. A grunt was Geryon's only response as he started for Emma's mother. Emma stepped in front of her.

"I've had enough of this," Emma snarled. "Let my mother go."

Cruel, unreachable eyes flicked to her. "You're in no position to make demands, daughter mine. After this stunt you've just pulled, you make me wonder what your worth to me really is. If I had Levaroth snap your neck, you would no longer be a nuisance to me, nor a threat."

"Don't you dare touch her," Emma's mother said. It was with the type of calm tone a mother used that guaranteed an unfathomable level of danger should you not heed her words. The young, handsome prince smiled, his face transforming with a look that made Emma's stomach flip with unease. Geryon had her mother's arms behind her back before Emma could blink.

"Find Sergei. He'll help you," she whispered against Emma's ear before the beast pulled her away. Emma's heart raced, rage spreading through her body like a toxic venom as she watched her mother's only chance at freedom fade away.

"Levaroth," Asmodeus said. The winged soldier snapped

to attention. "Take her to the dungeon." He snapped orders to another creature that resembled the Shax she had killed back at Blaze's compound and it leapt for the girl, but she didn't fight it. Hadessa was being dragged away but Emma couldn't hear anything above her own screaming.

Hands were on her, trying to bind her. She fought against them, fought with every ounce of her strength, but no foreign energy fueled her. She raged, her eyes burning into her father's. Then a sharp pain erupted in her temples, and the world went black.

LEVAROTH

He stood outside the cell door for several moments, watching her through the bars, unable pull himself away. His eyes traced her features, which were softened in her unconscious state. They lingered on her full lips; parted by a breath. He shook his head, as if trying to clear away his foolishness. She began to stir, her eyelids fluttering. He stiffened, casting a final glance at her slumbering cellmate, before disappearing. *She can defend herself*, he assured himself.

He was back in the training hall. A few startled glances came his way; many of the soldiers straightened up, training with renewed vigor. Wordlessly, he walked around, checking form and selecting warriors at random to spar against him.

"You look like you could use a decent opponent," a familiar voice said behind him. Levaroth released the squirming Nickor from his fatal hold. It wheezed, shooting Levaroth a reproachful look before hurriedly scuttling from the ring.

"When did you arrive, Tlahaz?" Levaroth asked, turning to face the hardened warrior standing outside the ring. He was his equal in size and power, created for the same purpose as Levaroth: to lead legions of Shediem into battle.

His gray skin was studded with spikes from the top of his head to his thighs, each one ivory in color at the base, but blackened at the top, as if each was charred. He had wings similar to Levaroth's, though they were feathered in a myriad of grays.

Levaroth pulled the two short swords from their sheaths across his back before he leapt with skillful grace at Tlahaz who flew at him in a blur. His blood heated as the thrill of a good fight jolted through him. The other soldiers in the hall became still as their superiors exchanged blows and slashes. Jeers and shouts spurred them on, both grinning at the sport. Levaroth gave himself over to the violence, holding nothing back, but Tlahaz was just as quick and deadly.

"You're a bit rusty," Tlahaz goaded, swiping his arm out, narrowly avoiding Levaroth's cheek. Tlahaz's entire body was a crafted blade, every inch of him sharpened to lethal points.

"Distractions are for those lacking in skill." Levaroth drove his blade down, its tip grazing Tlahaz's shoulder. Tlahaz barked a noise that resembled a laugh. Levaroth's mind filled with Emma—the way her smile lit her wide, almond-shaped eyes and the refreshing sound of her laughter. Like musical bells.

A sharp, searing pain lanced through his right wing and he hissed.

"Clearly it worked." Tlahaz frowned.

"Don't stop!" He sliced across with his sword that glanced off Tlahaz's well armored chest. He needed this, craved this. The burn in his wing as it repaired itself reminded him of who he was. A general in Sheol's army. Not some lovesick human. He gritted his teeth as he spun, swinging both blades out as a distraction while the claw on the tip of his wing dug into his opponent's wing. He sliced down, stripping the skin and slicing through tendons as if they were tissue paper. Feathers floated to the ground and Tlahaz laughed, unaffected by the wound.

"Is this to the death, comrade?"

Levaroth kept his offensive position, lunging, turning, slashing, dodging. "Your tactics won't work, Tlahaz."

A flap of gray feathers flung out, knocking Levaroth back. He brought his sword up, preparing to drive it through the general's wing, when he faltered. The split second of indecision brought a burst of pain to his left wing. He winced, and his blades were knocked from his hands.

White eyes, with black slits so small, they were almost invisible glared down at him. "I think we're done, Levaroth." Palpable anger rolled off him, driving the temperature up further.

"Too much for you, Tlahaz?"

"You were foolish and put too much energy into your attacks. What has you so distracted?"

Levaroth rolled his shoulders, stepping out from his comrade's scrutinizing gaze. "Nothing, I have been on Earth too long, brother. We should train more while you are here." He stowed his swords back into their sheaths, already missing them, like extensions of himself.

Tlahaz watched him as Levaroth stepped out of the ring. "Yes, I agree."

Levaroth clapped him firmly on the back before taking his leave, feeling the general's eyes on him even after he left the training hall.

Once he was back in the palace, he roamed the halls. Asmodeus wouldn't need him until later that evening, and his private quarters held nothing of interest for him. He told himself that he would simply patrol the wing, at first wondering if Elbis had come too. If Nakosh sent Tlahaz from the pit, then war was close. Consumed with his thoughts, he descended deep into the darkest part of the castle.

He hadn't fully comprehended that he had made it to the dungeons until an ear-splitting scream made his body jolt. A pained hiss and then the sound of fabric ripping had him bursting into the cell in an explosion of stone and shredded metal. His blood screamed in his ears when he saw the Nybbas crouched low over Emma. Whatever illusion it forced her to see had her arms flailing above her head, keeping her from making contact with the thin creature.

Its long, forked tongue ran up her exposed chest, where it had ripped open her t-shirt. Her body bucked wildly, her eyes wide as she tried to get out from under its weight. Fury consumed every part of him, setting his skin ablaze. He was in motion before the Nybbas' sickly yellow eyes saw him. He flew at the creature, slamming it into the stone wall, burying them both in rubble.

The Nybbas hissed, fighting against his grip. He wrapped his hands around the Shediem's head and twisted. Thick black fluid sprayed him, cold and oily. He dropped the detached head, letting it roll out of his hands to the floor, its body dropping in front of him.

A noise came from behind him and he spun. His gaze locked onto Emma whose eyes pulsed with green light. Rage contorted her features, her face devoid of humanity. She wasn't in control. Levaroth pushed aside his own beast, the heat in his veins cooling. He stepped toward her.

"Are you all right?"

Her shirt and bra were shredded, producing glimpses of delicate skin that filled him with a different kind of heat.

"No thanks to you," she spat. Levaroth raised a single brow.

"I just saved you from torture that would have scarred you forever."

"I was only left in a cage with a disgusting, flesh-eating creature because of you!"

Levaroth leveled her with a stare, trying to keep his eyes from leaving her face. His body was already responding to his desire for her, but he pushed the urge away. He appeared in front of her before she could blink, touching just her shoulder, and only long enough to deposit her back into her room. He didn't stay, not trusting himself to not act on his carnal urges. Instead he appeared outside the throne room, waving Geryon away, who charged after him.

Asmodeus was back in his true form, and from the steady stream of smoke curling from his nostrils, Levaroth knew he was not in a good mood. He sank to one knee, bowing his head.

"What is it, Levaroth?" the prince rumbled.

"A Nybbas attacked your daughter. I took the liberty of placing her back in her room until I could consult you on where you want to put her. Somewhere she is not in danger and cannot be a danger."

Asmodeus assessed him for a moment then he said, "Let her stay in her room. I will have guards posted on constant watch outside."

Levaroth inclined his head again, trying to keep his satisfaction from reflecting on his face.

"I will put a team together, Master."

"That will not be necessary," the prince replied. Levaroth's eyes flicked up. "You will take first watch. I want you to get her something suitable to wear for the party tonight."

Levaroth blinked. "Master?"

The prince huffed in irritation, a plume of smoke shooting from his nose. "We received word that the Giborim are assembling their forces in preparation for an attack. My fellow brothers have joined us along with the other generals to discuss our next steps. I will need my daughter to look suitable for the occasion so I may present her as my secret weapon, and deal with my brother's disloyalty. Our king is coming."

Levaroth remained unmoving for several moments before he wordlessly nodded, sinking into another low bow before stalking out of the throne room.

———————

He appeared back in the small room. Emma leapt off the bed, ready to fight, but he held his hands up.

"I come in peace."

She folded her arms across her chest, which was now hidden again in a threadbare servant gown and scowled.

"What do you want?" she asked. Levaroth narrowed his eyes at her. She still clearly hadn't accepted his rescue as an apology.

"We need to get you something suitable to wear for your father's party tonight." He ground out the word *suitable*, knowing what Asmodeus would like to present his daughter in. As if realizing what that meant, her face turned a sickly shade of green.

313

"What party?" she asked.

"The other princes have left their territories along with the other two generals. As is customary, a party will be held to celebrate their arrival. Word has spread and they will all be eager to meet you."

Emma's arms fell to her sides, her face going slack.

Levaroth took a step forward. She backed away until her legs hit the bed. He moved until he was directly in front of her, her large eyes fearful.

When he spoke, his voice was thick and gravelly. "I need you to be on your best behavior tonight. If anyone assumes you aren't worth keeping, you might be left alive long enough to become a plaything. Then, when you're no longer entertaining, they will kill you and your mother, do you understand?"

Emma hesitated, her expression hardening, then she nodded. His hand brushed her cheek gently before he could stop himself and she stilled. Her breath hitched and it fueled his burning desire. She gazed back at him, for a moment without contempt. He leaned forward, his lips eager for hers. Then she spun under his arm, putting space between their bodies. She didn't look at him as he let his hand drop.

"Let's go," he said. Then he grabbed her arm and they were gone.

EMMA

A servant girl took her measurements. Her hands shook, a bead of sweat appearing on her creased forehead as she shot frequent, nervous glances at the large, muscled general who stood, arms crossed, watching them.

"Don't you have something else you can be doing?" Emma snapped at him. His eyes narrowed to slits.

"No."

"The world hasn't run out of widows and orphans for you to murder, has it?"

He rose a single arched brow, his mouth slanted in a frown. "I'm doing my job, and right now my job is to protect you."

She felt a sharp jab against her thigh from the servant, who was now trembling with fear.

"Go protect me outside, you're scaring this poor girl." The servant's head snapped up, her eyes wide, her mouth opening in protest, but with a huff, Levaroth disappeared. The girl cast her a grateful glance, her shoulders relaxing. Emma watched her work, trying to keep from staring at the red scars that marred her skin. Older, silvery ones slashed one side of her face, causing her eyelid to droop. She pinned a single, braided cord of brown, leather-looking material across Emma's abdomen.

"There's going to be more material there, right?" Emma asked, gesturing to her entire torso. The girl blinked in confusion.

"I'm just making what the prince ordered."

"Row—um, Levaroth?" Emma called.

The general materialized in front of them, a smirk playing on his lips.

"Is she making me a dress?" Emma asked.

Levaroth snorted. "No."

Emma's eyes widened. She looked down at the girl for help. Levaroth's presence had her backing away, bent at the waist as if awaiting punishment.

"I'll wear a dress. Can you just make me a dress?" Emma asked the girl.

Her brown eyes lifted to Emma's before glancing toward Levaroth. He exhaled a long breath, then scrubbed a hand down his face.

"Add a panel that wraps around like a skirt. But keep it short." His eyes dragged down Emma slowly. Her cheeks heated.

"Not too short," Emma said. Levaroth gave her a warning look, but she didn't care. The servant girl gave a small, jerky nod.

Once he was gone, she loosed a shaky breath and Emma chewed the inside of her lip nervously as the girl worked.

"What's your name?" Emma asked.

The girl's eyes widened, and she glanced at the door as if a horde of Shediem were about to burst in and punish them.

"What?"

"We're not allowed to have names here," the girl whispered as she stitched two flaps of material together, never taking her eyes off her work.

"What do they call you, then?"

She gave a small shrug. "Servant girl."

"Can you tell me why you're here?" Emma asked.

Again, the girl shook her head. She couldn't help but think of Haddie. Where was she now? Emma's stomach clenched as she recalled the attack of the Nybbas. Levaroth wouldn't likely be there to rescue Haddie if she was faced with something similar.

"All done?" Levaroth asked, making them both start.

The cold weight between her lungs that usually alerted her to his presence was constant in this place. The girl nodded.

"I'll collect the finished product this evening."

The girl stood in complete silence, her head lowered as she gave another nod.

"Thank you," Emma said to the girl. Her brown eyes were barely visible through her lashes, but Emma thought she could see a hint of a smile on her lips as Levaroth brought her back to her room.

"Why wouldn't that girl look at you?" she asked him.

Surprise shone on his face. "She's a human."

"So?" Emma folded her arms over her chest.

Levaroth assessed Emma's stance, noting the change in tone. "They know to keep their heads down. The punishment for disobedience is often far worse for them than death."

Rotting stench filled her nose as her mind went back to the dungeon. All she saw was darkness, and all she felt was water, cold as ice. It burned her throat and her lungs, drowning her. When its sandpaper-like tongue had run up her chest, she realized she wasn't actually drowning. She didn't want to think about how much worse the situation would have been, had Levaroth not intervened. She swallowed hard as the memory subsided, angry tears stinging her eyes.

As if Levaroth seemed to be recalling the same scenario, a muscle flexed in his jaw, his golden eyes burning with anger.

She thought again of Blaze's sister and what she must be suffering.

"Where is Haddie?"

"Who?" he asked.

"My servant."

He ground his teeth audibly. "The Giborim?"

Emma's blood froze solid in her veins.

"I'm not sure," Levaroth answered, looking away from her now.

"I swear, if anyone tries to put some creepy demon baby in

her I'll—"

In his usual fashion, he was gone without a word.

Emma wrapped her arms around herself and sat on the edge of the bed. A swirling pit of hopelessness reached up to pull her under. *What can I do now? Haddie is being tortured somewhere. They know what she is and have probably already impregnated her with some creepy demon baby. My mother is locked up on the other side of the castle and even if all three of us could somehow escape, where would we go? How will we ever get out of here?*

A while later, a soft knock sounded on her door, pulling her back from the edge of hysteria. She sucked in a few steadying breaths as she got to her feet. Her vision swam, and she grabbed the edge of the bed to keep herself from falling. The knock came again just before Emma pulled the door open.

A powerful rush of relief crashed into her, ripping a sob from her throat. She threw her arms around Haddie's slim frame. The girl's eyes widened to the size of tea saucers. Emma scanned her, looking for scrapes or bruises, but she looked just as she had the last time Emma saw her, if only a little gaunter in the face, her eyes more haunted.

"I need to tell you something," Haddie said, her tone serious.

Emma released her, the initial relief burning away in an instant. They stepped further into the room and shut the door.

"Levaroth was the Shediem that ordered the attack on my family."

Emma's heart twisted painfully. "How do you know?"

Haddie stared down at her hands, fiddling with a patch on her gray, worn dress. "He was there."

White-hot anger filled Emma, her fists clenched. She remembered Blaze saying they had killed all but one of the Shediem responsible. Her body shook but she couldn't speak. She wanted to find him and make him pay. *I will kill him.*

"I didn't tell you to make you hate him," Haddie continued. "He saved me from myself not too long ago. It was a kindness I had not seen demonstrated by anyone here. And he was the one who cleared me to return to my duties. But I wanted you to know because, though he is dangerously attractive, he is still the enemy."

Emma shook her head. "I know that. You're here in this horrible place because of him. He deserves to die a thousand painful deaths."

Haddie gave a sad smile. "I'm here because one of the Shediem had a thing for children. After it brought me here, I never saw it again."

Blaze's handiwork, no doubt. "I'm sorry."

Haddie's brows rose. "Why?"

"I'm sorry we got caught. I shouldn't have asked you to put yourself at risk like that. I promised to get you out of here and all I did was cause you pain."

Haddie reached out and grasped Emma's hand. "I would do it all over again to have the chance of seeing my brothers."

Her heart ached for the girl. She reminded Emma of Blaze and Axel so much in looks and personality. Haddie was strong and a warrior at heart. Emma hoped that if she were cursed to spend each day here, that she would learn to be as brave as her.

"Anyway," Haddie cleared her throat. "Big party tonight. Six princes and three generals in one place. I'll be down in the kitchen all evening. I just wanted to caution you to not try anything rash. Keep your head down. Blend in and try to be invisible. They'll all be high with pleasure and no one will blink twice about dragging someone who is unwilling into their fun."

Bile burned her throat as it rose up. "Thanks," Emma said weakly.

Haddie nodded, though her eyes looked troubled. She headed for the door, pausing when Emma asked, "What did they do to you?"

She didn't turn around, but still Emma heard her voice shake as she replied, "Nothing I haven't endured a hundred times before."

A package wrapped in blood-red paper was thrust into Emma's hands by a gruff, black-feathered Shediem with an elongated neck that stood watch outside Emma's door. It was the most interesting Shediem she had seen so far. To Emma, it looked like a cross between a centaur and an ostrich.

She took the package into her room, knowing what it would be. When she pulled out the garment, she gave an audible gasp, dropping it on the bed as if scandalized by simply touching it. She folded her arms over her chest and sat on the bed in resolute defiance until the guard clomped into her room, rumbling something in a language she had never heard before.

"You can tell Asmodeus I'm not coming," she snapped at the creature.

It narrowed its eyes at her and shoved the leathery garment at her.

Emma shook her head. "N-O. NO!" She enunciated loudly.

"What's going on in here?" a deep, rumbling voice said from the door.

Emma's heart hammered, her power zinging to life inside her. Leaping to her feet, she charged at Levaroth's shirtless form, her eyes catching on the sharp lines of his chest.

He gripped her shoulders and pushed her back. "What is your problem?" he asked.

"My problem?" Emma shouted, lunging again. "*You* are my problem!"

Levaroth sidestepped her as she crashed into the open door. She started forward again, only for Levaroth to disappear and reappear on the other side of the room. Before she could attack again, the guard that she had brushed past grabbed her by the waist and in a blur of motion, pressed her roughly into the scratchy blanket on top of the bed.

Her blood heated as she felt the creature's energy surge into her. Giddiness filled her. She felt the creature shift, and then the connection was broken. A thick blanket covered her before she could move, and then the Shediem was holding her down again.

She struggled to get her hands out from under herself, wiggling as much as she could, but even her lungs could not take in a full breath under the crushing force.

"Let's try this again," Levaroth said from above her. "What has gotten into you? I saved your little friend from being Shax-meat and this is how you say thank you?"

"She's only here because *you* attacked her family!" Emma shouted up at him, craning her neck to be able to see the anger boiling in his eyes.

"I've done a lot of things, Emma. It's all for the cause. I will not apologize for serving my prince and my king. It is what I was created to do. It's what you were born to do too, if you would only put your self-righteous opinions aside, you would see that!"

Emma stilled, her heart hammering in her ears. "I will *never* be one of you."

Levaroth gave a harsh laugh. "Those Giborim have their hooks in you so deep. If you don't at least try to see the other side of the coin, Emma, you will die here, and so will your mother."

Hot tears burned her eyes again. "I'd rather die than be like you."

His molten gaze hardened. "I am not going to let you get yourself killed," he growled, stepping closer. The weight on her back disappeared. As she inhaled, Levaroth stooped to her level, his face so close, they breathed the same air. "Put on the damn outfit, pretend to be the dutiful daughter, or so help me, Emma, I will slaughter everyone you love until you are just like me. And I'll start with that Giborim you're so obsessed with.

"Did you know they expect the females to produce offspring the second they commit to a male? They lock them up during the first ten years, so they have as many spawns as possible."

Emma shook her head as nausea gripped her. That couldn't be true. Hatred filled her, blinding her. She was sick of the games, sick of the lies. Sick of feeling like little more than a pawn. Heat shot through her, making her skin tingle. A sound of awe echoed within the room. Her eyes snapped open.

Golden orange flames danced all around her. Flickers of blue and tongues of red coated her skin. She was a living, breathing flame.

Her fire glinted in Levaroth's eyes as he took her in with a triumphant grin. A warmth unfurled in her belly even as she realized he had baited her. His consuming gaze filled with a possessive desire. With a jolt, the flames were gone, her anger evaporating along with it.

"What was that?" she breathed.

His grin spread, his sharp canines flashing dangerously in the flickering candlelight.

"A little gift from your father."

EMMA

Her head buzzed with the onslaught of racing thoughts. She had two powers. Was her fire harmful to the Shediem or the Giborim? Could it hurt humans? She glanced down at the floor. The stone looked untouched by her scorching flame, but the entire castle seemed unaffected by fire. Her eyes flicked back up to Levaroth, who was still looking at her as if she were his most prized possession.

"The longer you are here in Sheol, the more you'll change into who you were meant to be. Everyone changes, but it's slow. You can control fire now because you are a Shediem and being among your kind awakens your abilities," he explained. The gold in his eyes danced with barely contained excitement. "Now get dressed."

Then he was gone. The feathered creature grunted and left too, shutting the door behind it. She glared at the outfit she was supposed to wear, her stomach knotted so tightly that what little lunch she had been able to eat threatened to escape.

She wasn't sure how long she stood there, staring at the offensive, strappy outfit, hearing Levaroth's threat over and over in her mind, before she shimmied into it. She didn't have a mirror, but it was tight enough to be a second skin. A strip wrapped around her chest with three corded pieces that crossed over her abdomen and attached at her opposite hip. The skirt piece knotted on her hip and draped across one thigh, leaving the other exposed.

Every outfit Adrianna had convinced her to wear felt like a snowsuit in comparison. She didn't dare move for several minutes, for fear of the leather riding up, but as she tested it, the material hugged her skin. It seemed to be molded to her. She sighed as the guard entered her room without a knock or warning. He grunted at her, motioning to the staircase.

Her heart galloped as she followed the beast through the winding halls. Levaroth stood guard outside the grand archway, opposite Geryon. His chest was still bare, minus the crisscrossing straps that held weapons on his back. From the waist down, he wore what looked like battle armor. His eyes widened when he saw her, his entire expression smoldering in a way that heated her skin. Her arms wrapped around her middle.

She moved toward Levaroth as if magnetized. The sounds that reached her from the den that lay beyond made her stomach clench.

"I'll let your father know you're here," he said in a low voice. There was something in his tone that made the fear she had been trying to shove down rear its ugly head again. But she couldn't dismiss it now. Her skin tingled, the cold weight in her chest suffocating.

"Emma."

Her head snapped up, her eyes sucked into his mesmerizing gaze.

He looked like he wanted to haul her away from party. "Don't draw attention to yourself."

She gave a stiff nod. Then he spun on his heel and entered the raucous chamber. After a moment, she looked to her side, seeing the black, empty eyes of her father's servant on her. It was hard to know what it was thinking, but Emma thought it looked hungry. She swallowed the bile that had crept up in her throat and relief flooded her when Levaroth returned several minutes later, slipping through the gauzy material that blocked her view to the rest of the party.

She knew from the shadows that she was about to step into a lion's den. A gazelle parading through a valley of hungry carnivores.

"I'm going to try to slip you in, unseen," Levaroth murmured against her hair, braided temple to temple in an elegant crown by Haddie.

Levaroth pulled her to his side. Her skin burned everywhere it was pressed against him. She kept the urge to feed on his power at bay.

He didn't falter as he pulled back the thin barrier between her and her worst nightmare. Skin. Everywhere. Her entire body felt like it was engulfed in flames again, but after glancing down several times, she assured herself she wasn't on fire. Wild, pulsing music couldn't fully drown the sounds of the people littering the floor in their sexual frenzies. The stifling air made her dizzy.

She didn't know where to look, but her attention snagged on five other thrones that joined the one crafted of bones. Three of them were filled with dazzling, shirtless men. Women with absolutely no clothing danced around them. One of the unnaturally beautiful men, whose mouth trailed down a young, dark-skinned girl, looked up.

Pale skin. Hair so pale it looked almost white. And eyes like sparkling rubies. Her breath caught in her throat. His lips spread in a wide smile that somehow managed to look both seductive and terrifying. Without looking away from Emma, he lowered his head back to the female's body. Levaroth's grip on Emma's shoulder grew painfully tight and she looked away, deciding to keep her eyes on the floor in front of them as they walked along the flame-coated wall instead.

"Wonderful."

Emma almost didn't hear Levaroth's voice above the music. She glanced up at him. A muscle ticked in his jaw, and his eyes looked capable of setting the whole place on fire.

"What?" she asked.

"You've been in the room for less than five minutes and you've already drawn the attention of Amon." Emma's gaze momentarily flicked back to the man, whose face was mercifully hidden from view.

"Who are the other two?" She took in the bronze-skinned man with long black hair that draped over his shoulders. He sat on the end closest to them in a throne made of gold, glittering with large jewels. As her eyes skimmed the line, she saw that all of the thrones were as varied as their rulers.

"Belphegor sits on the end." The prince sipped a clear fluid from his glass. Only as he pulled it from his lips, did she notice the whitish smoke rising from the contents in a perfectly circular puff. "Levian is the one next to Amon."

Emma could see glimpses of the smiling prince through the crowd of females. His eyes were what drew her attention. Not as red as blood like her father's, nor the luminescent red of rubies like Amon's, but the subtle red of mahogany. They weren't quite as unpleasant to look at as the rest.

"Beelez is there in the crowd." Levaroth pointed to a particularly large group of people.

A flash of golden hair and muscular biceps was all she could make out through the tangle of limbs. She averted her eyes, her face hot.

Levaroth spoke again, "My Prince."

Emma looked up, startled. In less than a second, she wished she hadn't. Her father's blood-red eyes slid over her with deliberate leisureliness. He wore a black jacket threaded with gold and silver whorls, a goblet in hand. A man stood beside him, with eyes like velvet red roses, so dark they were almost black, his pupils almost indistinguishable. They took took her in, but with an edge of disdain.

Emma gave a minute tip of her head, the only show of compliance he would get beyond her ridiculous outfit. Asmodeus responded with a chuckle.

"My apologies, Mammon, for my daughter's behavior. She

is a work in progress, but I have just learned that she is a flame-wielder like myself." *Crap*.

If the man was surprised by that information, he didn't show it. "She is untrained and doesn't appear loyal in any way. How will she help us?"

A smile that hinted of knowledge only he possessed spread across Asmodeus's face. "Patience, brother."

A chill fought its way up her spine when his eyes locked on her. Death and bloodshed were a promise.

"Enjoy the festivities, Levaroth." It was an order. With a stiff bow, Levaroth began weaving his way into the sea of sweaty bodies. Her heart rate kicked back up now that she was unguarded.

She stood rooted to the spot as the two princes walked back up to the raised platform that held the row of thrones, speaking in low voices. Asmodeus sat in his morbid chair, as Mammon positioned himself beside him in a throne that glittered and shone like diamond.

Emma shuffled as close to the heatless flames as she could, hoping they would consume her.

A servant girl with warm, golden-colored skin and dark eyes that reminded her of Adrianna approached her, carrying a silver tray of cups with assorted colored liquids inside. Some smoked, some fizzed, while others seemed to be making a high-pitched whine. Emma scrunched her nose at the tray.

"Any water?" she asked. Her mouth felt glued shut from the arid atmosphere.

The girl shook her head, then glanced around before whispering, "All of these are laced with drugs that make everyone act like…" She gestured to the orgies. Emma nodded with a grateful smile.

"Thanks for the warning."

The girl's lips twitched in an attempt at a smile and Emma's heart constricted. How long had it been since that girl had smiled?

"If you want water, I can try to sneak some from the kitchen."

Emma smiled brightly, then it dimmed, remembering the danger she had put Haddie in for asking for help. "I'll be okay."

The girl dipped her head before moving on. From across the room, a pair of bright golden eyes found hers and her heart lurched. A particularly tall and well-endowed female was running her hands along Levaroth's firm, chiseled chest. He removed the woman's hands, though she just giggled, bringing her leg up around his hip and grinding into his pelvis. She looked as if she was about to climb him like a tree. A dangerous light flashed in his gaze as he lifted the girl up and placed her several feet away like she weighed nothing. The female whirled and stalked away, pouting.

Emma could see a muscle in his jaw flex. Then her view of him was replaced with pale blond hair and ruby red eyes. She started, making the raw, perfectly sculpted man before her chuckle.

"Hello, little angelic flower." His breath smelled of oranges and leather. He exuded sexuality in a way that made her blood heat, sending sensation in places that made her shift uncomfortably.

"Don't be frightened." His hand brushed her cheek, and she couldn't help but take a step back. The hunger in his gaze set off both her most basic instinct to fight and awoke the frightening part of her that wanted to move closer; to taste the danger. The prince leaned down, his mouth brushing softly against the delicate skin beneath her ear. She felt paralyzed by his carnal lust. Vaguely her mind called to her power, but nothing happened. Her brows drew together in confusion.

"Please go," Emma said, hating how weak her voice sounded. Amon grinned.

"I don't think so, little flower." He inhaled her scent deeply, drinking it in. His eyelids fluttered closed for a moment, and he moaned like an addict receiving a high. "I could smell your purity from the other side of the room."

Her breath came faster as panic settled in, and the prince's eyes glittered with excitement, his pupils blown wide. He prowled closer, and she stumbled back. The flames parted around her as her back hit the stone wall. His arms came up on either side of her, caging her in.

"Prince Amon." Levaroth's voice was low and menacing. The prince turned enough for Emma to see his eyes brimming with wrath, his fists clenched at his sides.

"You're welcome to her when I'm finished," Amon drawled with a wicked smile. "Although I plan to take my time." Fire and ice mixed in her veins at his words. His smile exposed his perfectly white teeth, his canines elongated.

"I just thought you might like to know that her skin will kill you."

"There are ways around that." He looked at Emma as he spoke. "And I was just touching her. She did not try to harm me."

It wasn't for lack of trying, Emma thought bitterly. Eager hands slipped to her thighs, pulling the fabric up, and true fear consumed her.

As his fingertips skated across her skin, a jolt of energy flooded her. The power was uncontrollably strong, sexual and dominant. The prince's eyes went wide with shock, his twisted grin fading. Emma jerked away from the sensation. It coursed through her, invading her with its wrongness. Like a poison, it attacked everything in its path, igniting her veins. A scream ripped from her throat and she dropped to her knees.

Levaroth was there beside her in an instant, taking her head in his hands. She whimpered, unable to fathom taking his energy too.

"Push it into me, Emma," he commanded, though his tone was not cruel. She couldn't speak to tell him she didn't know how.

"No!" Amon snarled, wrenching her up by her wrist. He dragged her through the crowds of undulating bodies toward the row of thrones. She watched the people in fascination and felt her body pulling toward them. Amon gave a cruel laugh before whispering against her ear, "If I didn't want you for myself, I'd let you go to them, Flower."

She wanted to. *No, needed to.* They looked so free, their faces awash with pure ecstasy. Her leather outfit felt too tight, too hot. Her free hand pulled at the straps, trying to rid herself of it.

"Not yet," Amon admonished, though his voice had become guttural. The sound tugged her closer to him. He spun her on the stone platform, in front of the thrones, facing the rolling wave of moving creatures and people. She smiled brightly at them as some of them looked up toward her.

"Now, dance little flower," Amon said. The wild pulsing beat was all around her, charging through her. *Yes, dance.* She wanted to dance. Her body began to move, and more eyes lifted to watch. She felt their hungry gazes like hot lasers on her skin. Again, she wanted to remove the leather that chafed. She wanted to be as free as they were.

Before she could slip the band off her chest, mesmerizing golden eyes were before her. Levaroth gripped her wrists, pulling them up over her head. She giggled, brushing her body against his. The friction made her gasp. His jaw clenched so tightly, she thought she heard his teeth grind together. *Why isn't he smiling,* she wondered? She frowned up at him.

"Dance with me," she purred.

A low growl rumbled in his chest. "Emma, it's Amon's power, you have to fight it."

Amon was there then, pulling Levaroth back. "This is her punishment, *General.* Next time she will not be so quick to try to harm me."

Levaroth bared his teeth, making Emma giggle again. "You guys are wearing too much clothing." Her hands reached for Levaroth's belt, but he moved away, shooting a glare at Amon.

"Run along, pet, I think it's time to pluck this little angelic flower." His knuckles brushed her chin, sending ripples of pleasure through her too-warm body.

"Amon," a deep voice said from behind Emma. She spun, to

see her father's eyes brimming with brutality.

"Ah, brother," Amon said with a lightness that didn't match the nervous twitch in his temple. "Seems your spawn is able to enjoy herself after all."

An icy chill raced up Emma's arms and spread down her spine. *More,* her blood sang. She stared at Amon's hands clenched at his sides, just out of reach.

The music blaring through the room no longer went any further than her ears as her head began to pound. Her body no longer moved, and the heat in her core cooled. Amon's intoxicating sexual energy was draining.

More. More. More. Leaning closer to the source that would feed her—make her powerful—she took an involuntary step forward. All eyes snapped to her. Her body shook with need. She wrapped her arms around herself, fixing her stare on her bare feet. Shame swam through her. What was wrong with her?

"My *spawn* is not your toy," Asmodeus said so fiercely that the entire room fell silent.

Hundreds of lust-drunk gazes swung up to settle on them. Even Emma felt a jolt of surprise at the clear protectiveness in his voice. When she glanced back up, trusting herself enough not to lunge for any of the powerful Shediem near her, she caught Amon's swirling red gaze.

Still he devoured her with his eyes as he said, "She deserves to be punished."

She didn't want to know what his form of punishment entailed. Yet the darkest part of her—the part that still hungered for his power—sent a series of images into her mind that made her knees knock together.

Asmodeus studied the prince carefully, then turned his lethal gaze on Emma. "Indeed," he replied.

Emma's body shook, not just with terror, but also cold, despite the sticky heat in the room. Amon's power was completely gone, leaving her with burning humiliation. She wished to disappear into nothing. But judging from the look on her father's face, she didn't think he was going to let her get away any time soon.

Asmodeus turned to the prince still oozing with lust. "Amon, did I tell you I had a group of particularly delicate delights brought in just for your more...refined palate?"

Nausea filled Emma as she decoded Asmodeus' meaning. Slowly, Amon's gaze released Emma, but not before it showed a promise so vile that it made her power hum threateningly. Asmodeus steered the cruel prince away, allowing her to release a breath of relief as her legs wobbled, threatening to collapse beneath her. The music filled the room again and Levaroth's rigid posture relaxed.

"Try to not draw any more attention to yourself," he growled without looking at her, then he disappeared again.

She kept to the shadows, avoiding everyone's gaze and pretending to be invisible even when several people tried to drag her into the clusters. After another hour of shivering, Asmodeus reappeared on his throne.

He beckoned her to his side on the raised platform and her stomach dropped. Her steps were unhurried, fear twisting her insides with what his punishment would be. Would he force her to join the crowd? Offer her to Amon or one of the other princes? Would she be able to fight off everyone who stood between her and the door if it came to it?

When she was close enough, he whispered, "Amon's display has delayed your true punishment, and also my brother's. But I have something else that I think will motivate you. Look." Emma followed his line of sight, her heart stopping cold. "If you do not bow to me, I will make her beg me for death."

The bound and chained figure who knelt on the stone floor held her chin high, defiance burning in her eyes. The sight of the bruises on her mother knocked the air from her lungs. Her mother's beautiful hair was knotted and tangled as if she had put up a significant fight. A fresh gash sliced one of her cheeks, but she looked unaffected. Fierce.

Her eyes were locked on Emma's as if to say *fight*. A strip of leather covered her mouth and a metal band like a collar wrapped around her slim neck. Geryon stood behind her, holding the chain.

Emma wanted to scream at the top of her lungs and slaughter every single person in the room.

As if Asmodeus sensed her rage, he said, "If you oppose me, I will feed her to my brothers."

The threat was the one prince in particular—Amon. She wouldn't let him touch her. She would give herself to him if only to keep him away from her mother. Then she would kill him.

"I will not oppose you," Emma said through gritted teeth.

"I'm pleased to hear it." Then he raised his hands, and silence descended over the room. Four of the five remaining princes walked to their respective thrones and sat, looking out on the untamed lust with pride.

"My daughter will serve Sheol. The Giborim will fall. Earth will be ours."

LEVAROTH

L evaroth rapped his knuckles softly on the wooden door
separating him from Emma. He could hear her sniffle, then
her gentle footsteps on the floor before the door opened a
crack. Her eyes were red-rimmed, her lips pursed.

"What do you want?"

Need overtook his rationale as he pushed the door open
further, filling the entryway. She stepped back but didn't attack
him like she had earlier. She was back in the drab servant's
clothing, much to his disappointment. When she had taken
Amon's energy and began dancing, it took all he had not to haul
her off against her will.

Especially to get her away from Amon, who would have
turned her into something inhuman. Unrecognizable. How he
had fought not to rip the prince limb from limb. Just the way he
looked at her made his beast roar with unstoppable rage.

"I wanted to make sure you're okay," he replied.

Her arms folded defensively over her chest. "Peachy. Now
get out."

Ah, that sass. He fought back a grin. "No, you're not." He
stepped toward her. "I know you saw your mother."

She faltered, stricken. "Yes, I did." Her soft response was like
a magnetic force pulling him in. Her head tilted back to look
up at him, exposing her slim neck, her pulse visibly quickening.

"And she is being tortured…because of you." Her tone went cold and Levaroth let out a sigh. *That again.*

"Technically she's being tortured because you tried to escape," he pointed out, his eyes still watching the steady twitch beneath her skin.

"Wow." Her voice cracked. Her eyes filled with hatred all over again and he knew he needed to act.

"Give me a chance, Emma. If you show your father that you truly mean to serve him, your mother will be sent home. This can end." He took another step closer. She stepped back. Desperation began to trickle in.

"I will find a way home, and I will take her with me. Haddie too, and we will find a way to destroy all of you, so you can never hurt anyone ever again." A solitary tear escaped, and she angrily swiped it away.

"Stop, Emma," Levaroth warned in a low voice. "Before you get you and your mother killed. I'm begging you. I couldn't—" he broke off and Emma's expression changed, her eyes widening. *I'm losing her.*

He appeared in front of her, wrapped his arms around her and lifted her body up against his. He brought his mouth down onto hers with hot, desperate need. And for one achingly glorious moment, her body responded in kind. Then her power shot through her body, robbing him of strength, power and thought.

He thrust her down onto the bed with an angry growl. The beast within roared into action, and before he could control himself, his hands grasped the fabric and tore the top of her dress open. His eyes greedily drank in the sight of the brand beneath her collarbone. *His brand.*

"You belong to me!" he roared. "Forget the life you knew, it doesn't exist anymore!"

She didn't move, didn't scream. Her eyes welled with tears.

His mouth came down on hers again, and she gasped softly. He trailed his mouth along her jaw and down her neck, pleading with her to see reason. Her heart pounded loud enough for him to hear, and though he couldn't sense her emotions, pleasure shone plainly on her face. With every kiss he placed on her blazing skin he whispered, "I know you want me too. Let me worship you. Let me have you."

Then her power was active again, acting as a vacuum where his lips touched her, but he didn't care. He was high on his desire for her. His lips became swollen, his movements slower as his breathing turned ragged. "Please, Emma," he begged. She was killing him, and he would let her.

"I hate you," she choked.

His head was heavy as he lifted it to look at her. Tears slipped down her cheeks, her eyes flooded with anger and sorrow.

He gathered his strength to speak. "Why?"

"My mother is here, in this prison. You let one of your cronies take an eight-year-old girl from her family and from just the few days I've been here, I've seen dozens of other human girls here against their will."

Levaroth's gaze hardened. "I didn't do that. I'm not to blame when their parents or their guardians sell them for as little as a single hit of heroin, or for money, or promotions, or because they simply despise them."

Shock registered on her face as if he had slapped her. "It doesn't matter, because you're one of them. Haddie has two brothers who love and miss her, and you took her from them!"

"*I* didn't abduct her, Emma!" he shouted back, getting to his feet. His muscles quaked in protest but already his strength was returning.

"But you've killed people!"

Levaroth huffed in agitation. "What does that matter?"

"It's wrong!"

"It's my job," he snarled. "It's yours too. You're just as capable of taking a life as I am."

"And that is the difference," she spat, drawing herself up with the fabric of her dress clutched together. "I would *never* kill."

He stooped so their faces were inches apart. "Whether you

choose to admit it or not, the blood that flows in your veins is from the Prince of Wrath! Death and destruction are what makes you a deadly, fearsome asset. Just because you possess a drop of Giborim blood doesn't mean you were made for them. You were made for us. For this!" His hands gestured to the room, but his meaning was deeper. *This castle. This life. Me.*

"I will never be a monster like you." Her body was tense with simmering rage.

"Yes, you will," he growled. "When everything and everyone you care for is dead, you will become just. Like. Me."

EMMA

Emma awoke to the sound of sniffling. She sat up, her mind foggy.

"Haddie?"

A slender figure froze at the foot of her bed. Emma blinked, clearing her vision. The servant girl who turned to face her was not Haddie. She was shorter and had dark skin. She sniffled again.

"I was just bringing your breakfast, Miss." She pointed to the tray behind her.

"Oh," Emma replied. "Thank you." Dread formed a lump in her throat. The servant girl nodded then started for the door.

"Sorry," Emma said. The girl paused, then turned. "Where is Hadessa?"

A sob escaped her before she could clamp a hand over her mouth. Emma's blood turned to ice inside her veins. The girl shook her head, unable to say any more before running out the door. Emma threw back the blankets and rushed to the door, but when she pulled it open, she collided with the black, feathery chest of the guard. He glared down at her as if she were an annoying insect he'd like to crush.

"Get dressed and come with me," he growled. *So he did speak English.*

Her heart pounded like a drum against her ribcage as she followed the guard, but he didn't lead her to the throne room. He led her out an open archway. The rust-colored sky felt as ominous as the courtyard filled with thousands of faces; mostly human. The rest were Shediem of so many varieties it made her power prickle with anticipation. Her lungs were tight, and cold filled her chest, making each breath harder than the last.

Thousands of pairs of eyes watched her pass. The human faces either looked at her with loathing or were weeping. The demons however…their expressions were even more varied. She stared straight ahead as she passed the six princes sitting on their thrones. Even from the corner of her eye, she could see her father's blood-red stare lit with triumphant satisfaction. Beside him stood Levaroth, arms folded across his chest, his gaze following her with hard determination. The last words he spoke to her echoed in her mind.

The sea parted and above the crowd was a line of kneeling figures, all with their hands tied behind their backs. Among the line of tear-stained faces were her mother and Haddie. Emma's heart felt electrified into a frenzy of panic.

The guard, sensing Emma's reaction, gripped her forearms. She spun out of his hold, sprinting toward the platform.

"Mom!" she screamed.

Her mother's face snapped up, revealing purpling bruises and swelling. Rage roared to life and without thought or fear, she was moving. Chaos erupted around her. She was going to get to the stage, and she was going to murder every Shediem in her path. Her hands clutched demon after demon. Energy slammed through her like a bolt of lightning. Her vision blurred. Their ashes coated her, blinded her. Lingering powers stirred in her mind. *Use us. We bow to you.*

Suffocation, illusions, shapeshifting; she wielded them better than any blade. Her foes dropped one by one. A booming voice shook the ground, but she didn't stop. She could see the dais now. She could see each face staring back at her with wide eyes.

Then cold metal bit her wrists, yanking her to a stop. Her breath came in pants but not from exertion. Elation, determination. *Death*. The craving made her skin burn. *More*, it hissed.

She fought against whatever held her in place, screaming in frustration. The groan of metal reached her ears. Her eyes flicked to the manacles that bound her wrists. The chains looked like two weeds that had sprouted out of the ground. Emma wrapped her fingers around the chains and pulled. They didn't budge. She roared, her throat aching as she flung her entire body as far as she could. She felt like a caged animal.

A single clap came from behind her. Then another, and another. She spun with a snarl. Asmodeus grinned at her with twisted glee as the princes applauded. But Levaroth did not move.

She could feel herself breaking through. The power burned away in her veins. She suppressed a shiver. Cold emptiness seeped from her skin into her bones. But the air outside was warm enough that she could smell sweat.

"Quite the show," the prince remarked.

"Why are you doing this? I agreed to join you."

Asmodeus took another step closer to her. "You say with your words that you comply." His voice lowered, the sound cutting into her as sharply as a blade. "Yet you still think you can escape. Your words are not enough." He brought his face so close to hers, she staggered back a step. His blood red eyes were cold and filled with hate. "I *will* have your unfailing obedience." Then his smile grew. "You'll soon forget about them."

His gaze moved to the stage behind her. She whirled around to see Geryon standing on the stage, a massive axe raised above his head. Before Emma could scream, or even take a breath, the axe came down, a faint whistle through the air. The weapon met little resistance. A young girl's head rolled away from her body. Emma's stomach rebelled at the sight; blood everywhere.

Screaming filled her ears and somewhere in the cacophony, hers was hoarse and raspy. Geryon sidled down to the next in line. To her mother. Words spilled from Emma's mouth in a desperate cry.

"Stop! Kill me instead! I'll do anything, just stop!"

Geryon's weapon froze mid-swing.

Asmodeus' voice was silky with delight. "Anything?"

Emma turned to face him. She would give him what he really wanted. "You can punish me instead. I will join your army, I will serve you and be loyal to you if you swear to not harm my mother or any of the servants." Her gaze slid involuntarily to the thrones. To Levaroth. His eyes didn't meet hers. His expression was unchanged. His words rattled around in her brain again. *When everything and everyone you care for is dead, you will become just. Like. Me.* This was his doing.

The air shifted as the prince grinned at her as if he had just won the war. "I accept your terms." Then his gaze swept up to Geryon. "For each slave that is left alive, she is to receive two lashings."

Emma's eyes closed as she heard her mother's strangled cry. Bile rose up in her throat as her heart pounded wildly. The ground beneath her feet shot up and carried her forward, the chains keeping her arms firmly by her sides. It flung her roughly onto the splintered wood, her knees taking the brunt of the force. She bit down on the inside of her lip to keep from making a sound.

Tension filled the air and she struggled to breathe. Her mother's body shook with sobs. Both she and Haddie sent looks that made Emma's heart crack. From the side, she could see Levaroth staring intently at her. His body was rigid as he glared at Geryon who now held a long, thick black cord in his hand. It pooled onto the ground like a snake curled, and ready to strike. She closed her eyes; she didn't want to see her mother's reaction.

The sound of fabric ripping and the air brushing her back made her look over her shoulder. If a boar were capable of a smirk, then Geryon modeled it perfectly. Hot tears burned her eyes as the shredded dress slid off her shoulders. A *crack* sounded against the wood and it reverberated all the way to her teeth. She squeezed her eyes shut again.

She inhaled a deep breath, trying to prepare herself. *At least Mom is safe. Crack.* Pain sliced through her back and she ground her teeth together to keep her scream locked inside. Cheers and shouts rang through the courtyard. *Crack.* Another explosion of white-hot agony hit her. *Haddie might get to see her brothers. Crack.* She gasped, but her lungs wouldn't fill. She choked, falling forward onto her hands. Then it started again. *I will save these slaves. Crack. Crack. Crack.* She lost count of how many times the whip split her flesh. Sounds faded, the bite lessened as she felt herself slipping. When it stopped, she was wheezing, and her arms shook with the effort of keeping herself upright.

She didn't move. The strength it took to open her eyes and see her mother and Haddie along with the rest of the servants being cut free was all she had left. Darkness edged her vision. Her mother's anguish-filled face slipped away, and she fell into the blackness below.

EMMA

S tinging. Acrid smell. Firm hands. Gentle murmurs. Blissful
sleep.

*Her mother's screams filled her ears. She watched from
the crowd, unable to move. Her father's burning red eyes met hers
as the whip stopped above his head. Flecks of liquid the same color
as his eyes dotted his face. Splashes coated his crisp, black suit. Then
he swung again, and her mother cried out. Emma's skin burned;
her power alive. If only she could make it to the stage. The other five
princes watched her with amusement as if she were a circus animal.
Levaroth flashed her a cold grin.*

"Please! Let her go!" Emma pleaded.

*When she looked back at the stage, it was Haddie who knelt
before the prince. A flash of black caused Emma to look to her left,
then her right. Blaze and Axel stood on either side of her, screaming
at her to move, but the manacles tightened. Chains sprung out of the
ground and pulled her roughly to her knees.*

"I'm trying!" *she screamed to Blaze. His face twisted with grief.
He looked back up to the stage. As his gaze returned, his features
turned cold and lethal.*

"I will kill you, Emma. You let her die. You are the enemy."

Fire shot beneath her skin, it climbed up her throat and out
her mouth. Tongues of flame licked her back even as Emma
arched away. Then the fire died, and the pain eased. *Is it over yet?
Can I just die now? Please let me die.*

343

A soothing peace washed over her, and she let it drown her. Then there was nothing.

An angelic, melodious voice hummed a tune that Emma didn't recognize. Emma strained to open her eyelids, peering through slits at Haddie. Her eyes were closed, her features relaxed. Haddie's young face was otherworldly beautiful, her golden hair tumbled over her shoulder, looking radiant. She swayed, humming her soothing tune and Emma felt a gentle tug on her hair.

"Haddie?" Emma croaked.

"I'm here."

Her eyelids opened further. Haddie's hand continued its rhythmic movements and Emma glimpsed the brush in her hand.

"Thank you," Emma rasped.

Haddie laughed. "I'm the one who should be thanking you." Emma didn't reply. "How do you feel, by the way?"

Panic stabbed through her as she realized she didn't feel any pain. "I don't feel anything."

"That would be the tincture I put on your spine."

Emma blinked rapidly. "What?"

Haddie gave her a small smile. "A Spellcaster snuck me a numbing tincture. You have accelerated healing, so you probably didn't need all of it, but I wanted to make sure you weren't in any pain. I don't think even I could have healed as quickly as you have."

Emma's voice was filled with gratitude. "Thank you."

Haddie laid the brush aside with a slow sigh. "I know why you did it...but Emma..."

Emma swallowed hard. She had sworn her loyalty. She chose a side and it wasn't the side she wanted to be on. "I know."

Tears welled up in her eyes. "There has to be a way—"

"No," Emma interrupted. "Please don't put yourself in any more danger. I will find a way out of this on my own. I won't fight for them. I can't."

Haddie nodded in understanding.

A knock sounded at the door, causing them both to start. Levaroth stepped into the room, holding what looked like a dress, his gaze sweeping over her from head to toe.

"Feeling better?" he asked.

Emma ignored him. Instead she looked back to Haddie. "Is my mom okay?"

She nodded and Emma let out a breath of relief. Haddie eyed Levaroth for a moment before looking at Emma, a question in her gaze.

"You're dismissed," Levaroth snapped at Haddie.

"She is staying."

Levaroth narrowed his eyes at Emma. "She can't come with you."

"And where am I going?" Emma asked coolly.

"To your induction."

Emma's throat tightened. "Now?"

Levaroth nodded. "Now that you're awake, you have to be inducted."

Emma's brows creased. "How long have I been out?"

Haddie piped up, "Two days."

Emma's mouth felt dry. "Oh."

"Surely she can have something to eat first," Haddie said.

He shook his head. "Now. And put this on." He tossed a purple gown onto the bed.

Emma trailed behind Levaroth into the throne room, which seemed smaller with its large occupants. Stifling dark energy slammed into her, nearly knocking the strength from her trembling legs. Five beasts that no longer looked like striking, beautiful men sat in their thrones watching her draw closer. The sixth, who could only be her father with his eyes of blood, stood, holding a glittering golden box. Shining rubies, diamonds, emeralds and sapphires shone between his clawed fingers, his features lit with satisfaction.

There was nothing left of the cruel, stunning man in the beast's place. A magnificent nightmare. He was enormous, with skin alight like magma coursing between stones. Black symbols covered his arms and neck like Levaroth. Horns protruded from his skull like two black curved and twisted daggers. Plumes of smoke curled from his nostrils as if he could breathe fire. His powerful, brutal form made her think he probably did. He was flame incarnate.

Too soon she was standing before him, and when Levaroth lowered himself in a bow, Emma followed suit, ignoring every muscle that stiffened in protest. And yet…the action felt like a sultry caress of confirmation in the back of her mind. This was her destiny. She rose before the prince could command her to do so. Packing every ounce of defiance into her expression for her father to see. Levaroth rose too, then stood to the side.

Asmodeus's eyes glinted with amusement. Amongst the endless hatred she felt for him, a small vein of awe pierced it. He looked like the creator of war. Bare-chested with glinting armor adorning him from the waist down. Knives and swords hung from his back and belt.

"My brothers," his voice was like thunder, "Today marks the dawning of Shediem rule." Figures appeared against the back wall, at least fifty of them, all concealed beneath heavy dark cloaks embroidered with gold and ruby threads, marking them as Asmodeus' servants.

All but one of the seated beasts seemed unaffected by their presence. Emma's heart beat faster as they closed in.

"Today," Asmodeus boomed. "A traitor will be rooted from our numbers. A necessary purge so New Sheol will begin strong!"

The room exploded in colored light, so bright she shielded her eyes against the onslaught. A beast's roar began, then was cut off. Emma lowered her arm and saw the cloaked figures holding a prince frozen, suspended several feet in the air. With magic, she realized with awe and terror.

None of the other princes moved, though several looked on with rigid stares. The prince her father had introduced her to smiled at the beast that silently twitched as if fighting against the brilliant bolts of color.

"The only one amongst us that can end our brother's pathetic existence, is the girl you see before you. My daughter."

Emma's heart stumbled its frantic rhythm. She opened her mouth to protest, but her father simply beckoned her forward. Images of her mother's beaten but unbroken face flashed in her mind.

Her entire body quaked as she took a step forward. Then another. And another, until she was standing before the blinding light. The prince inside glared down at her. In comparison to his magnificent height and pearlescent skin, she indeed felt like a speck of dirt marring his perfection.

Another presence entered the room, soundless and without any brilliant flash of light. The raw power flowing from him was too dark, too terrible. It knocked through Emma so completely that her knees buckled, slamming to the cold stone floor.

Within a slowly creeping cloud of shadows, inky black tendrils coiled around the figure, like living creatures embracing their master. Only a pair of bright silver eyes cut through the darkness. And they were locked on Emma.

Every being fell to their knees, except the prince held frozen, though terror flashed in his red eyes. Even Asmodeus bowed to the newcomer. The king. Emma knew it in every part of her being. Though terror threatened to strangle her, she forced herself to her feet, refusing to appear as though she too bowed to this most wicked being.

Nakosh, King of Sheol had come.

But why?

"King of Death," the room echoed as one.

The swirling black mist that shrouded him receded just slightly to reveal his full, sensual lips curled to one side in a smirk both cruel and lovely. He was so beautiful the sight of him made

Emma's chest ache. The inky blackness circled his head with jagged spikes, creating the illusion of a crown atop long, straight black hair. The form he let her see was just a human skin. But if the princes looked like fearsome giants in their true forms, what did this powerful, terrifying being truly look like? Emma knew she didn't want to find out.

"Please, continue," the hauntingly beautiful king said with a rich voice. The King of Death. Chills raked up Emma's body as the shadows seeped into the room, reaching for her. "I came to witness the girl's magnificent power. A slayer of my wicked creatures, and a flame wielder. Such intrigue."

Emma stood frozen, unable to look away from the ethereal being. He spoke of her to a room of monsters capable of killing her before she had time to blink an eye. And yet he sounded... fascinated with what she was.

"Belphegor," Asmodeus said, rising to his feet with the rest of the chamber. "You have been sentenced to death for conspiring against your king and amassing an army to take New Sheol for your own." His blood red eyes slid to Emma. "May your eternal silence be an example to all those that would rise against King Nakosh."

The shadows smiled again, as Emma raised a tentative hand toward the shimmering, pulsing beams of light.

"And may the girl who steals your soul be worthy of the crown she will bear," Nakosh whispered. She shivered at his words. Words she knew were meant just for her. Her head whipped around to Nakosh. His molten silver eyes flickered with amusement.

But his words ripped through her over and over. *That's what I do? Steal the Shediem's souls? How can they even have souls?* And what crown was she to bear? She would never accept a throne in Sheol. She planned to tear them all down, starting with her father's twisted throne of bones.

"Touch him," Asmodeus growled.

She swallowed hard, casting a final glance at the mysterious king clothed in darkness. Her heart beat so hard she feared it would rip itself right out of her chest. Her hand met the shimmering scales of the prince.

Unlike Amon's sexual power, Belphegor's energy was made of greed. It filled her so completely, pouring fire through her veins, scorching her muscles and bones, but all she could think was *more*. She drank of his power, craving the luminescent scales of pearls, of his golden throne adorned with jewels. Of his crown.

Give it all to me.

Black mist was curling around her vision, even as the light drew away from the prince's form. His body no longer shone, his eyes shrivelled into his skull. His horns were the first to become ash on the stone floor. He shrunk, until he was a hallowed husk—a truly undignified way to die—but all Emma cared about was that his well of power dried up.

She *was* power. Mighty enough to kill them all now. She spun, feeling her lips pull back as she bared her teeth. Were her canines longer?

Like in times before, a strange new ability sat within her, stroking the insides of her mind. It was hers. A wicked grin pulled at her lips. Forms swam and swayed as they drew closer.

Then there was blinding light that felt like ice ripping her flesh. She couldn't scream, couldn't move. Couldn't fight.

Her body folded over, her knees on the floor again, her forehead resting on the stone. It was warm compared to the ice surrounding her. Why couldn't she fight? She was power itself. *They should bow to me*, she thought.

Someone tugged at the fabric of her dress while she was helpless to fight them off. Her laces were being undone, she realised, but whoever took the care to untie the gown, was also careful not to touch her back.

"Do you, Emma Duvall, swear fealty to me, to the six princes of Sheol and above all, loyalty to your King, Nakosh?"

No. The raging power inside her roared in protest.

An image flashed unbidden in her mind. A lovely, delicate

face battered and tear-stained. A pang of emotion stabbed in her chest as clarity broke through. Her mother. She had to save her mother.

Bile rose up in her throat as the words came from her mouth. "I swear."

Without warning, something cold, no bigger than a coin was pressed into her right shoulder. Her breath hitched as pain pierced her skin.

The pain grew to a searing agony that burned through her shoulder blade and down her spine. The scent of burning flesh made her eyes water. The pain shot deeper, spreading like a poison, penetrating her bones. The area grew cold again, like ice shredding muscle and tissue. Every cell was invaded, filling her body so fast, Emma thought her skin would split. She didn't know she was screaming until the blinding pain began to ease. All that was left was a raw ache in her throat. And cold. Her veins were filled with ice.

A pair of boots stepped into view and then a pair of hands grabbed her, yanking her to her feet. On unsteady legs, Emma turned toward her father. The gold box was open in his hand; empty. Her arms reached back to her shoulder, feeling raised, tender skin. She bit down on her bottom lip, hard, to keep it from quivering.

"You now have the Mark of Fallen Flame. You will go where I, or your King send you and come when either of us summon you. You are forbidden from speaking that which we forbid you to speak and whatever you are commanded to do, you must do."

The air was punched from her lungs. What had just happened? The mark would now control her? Her mouth opened but no words came out.

Asmodeus smiled broadly, and in the corner, somewhere beneath the curtain of darkness, the King smiled too. Whatever he knew somehow terrified her more than the mark that could make her dance like the puppet she was.

"Now bow."

Her back bent without her consent. She fought against it, her body jerking and straining, but she couldn't right herself. Asmodeus crouched in front of her, his crimson gaze level with hers.

His breath tickled her face as he whispered, "This is what defeat looks like, daughter. You are mine and nothing you do will break my hold on you. And you know what I'm going to make you do?"

Emma grunted in pain as she strained every muscle to attack. Her muscles screamed in protest. Again, and again, she commanded her body to move but beyond the tremors, it would not obey.

"I'm going to send you back to your beloved Giborim, where you will collect information about their every move. And when my army of powerful hybrids are matured, I will force you to slit the Giborim's throats."

His words drove a dagger into her heart. Worse than the lashings or her new branding, was the thought that she may have to betray the Giborim. That she might have watch as a stranger in her own body as she tried to harm Blaze. Her stomach clenched so hard she nearly retched at the prince's feet. The realization that she had played into his hands was a thousand times worse than death.

"Now, go back to Seattle and play nice with the Giborim."

LAURA

The handsome, terrifying prince backhanded her. Stars bloomed in her vision. Warmth trickled from her split lip. It was all too easy to slip inside the place in her mind that was reserved for when her father would beat her. She was no stranger to pain. This monster would not have the satisfaction of hearing her scream.

He grabbed a fistful of her matted, bloodied hair. It had once been beautiful. His face drew close to hers and for a moment she imagined the bitter smell of alcohol. But when he grinned, his teeth were all perfectly white, his canines slightly elongated, adding to the image this monster chose for himself. His eyes swirled with all the blood he'd shed. Hers was only a drop in the infinite sea of death he dealt.

"We're going to have lots of fun catching up, don't you think?"

She didn't answer. He hit her again.

"Scream!" Flames danced over every inch of his perfect skin, his control slipping. "I own your daughter. I own you. She will kill whoever I tell her to. With just the snap of my fingers, I could make her torch her entire planet.

"The King is pleased with her. He watched as she drained my brother of his power. She is just as powerful as he was now. And she is my puppet, just as you are my dear."

Laura spat in his face. The flames dissipated. He smirked as he wiped his face.

"You can vow silence all you want, my precious," he dragged a cold, slender finger down her cheek, along the sharp ridge of her jawline. Blood stained his finger red. His gaze never left hers as he licked it clean. "Pain is not the only way to make a person scream. And by the time my kingdom is established on your human-infested planet, you will sing whatever tune I command."

Fear and disgust coiled together inside her, rising up to choke her. *Sergei!* Her mind screamed for him, even though she knew he could not hear. Her friend. Her protector. What would be left of her in a week, a month? Would she ever see the man who kept her sane all these years? Who comforted her when fear had overwhelmed her, consumed her? She loved him. And she would die within these stone walls far from his love and protection. She was resigned to that. Because she would sooner die than let this monster wrong her a second time.

"Are you ready, Nadia?" the prince purred. He cupped her face tenderly in his cruel hands. "Let's have some fun."

EMMA

Fresh air filled her lungs. Large, fluffy flakes of snow fell from the gray sky. The afternoon was quiet. Peaceful. Things looked new and yet, like they had hardly changed at all, but Emma knew they had. Because she had.

She had killed a prince. His power still lingered in her—for how long, she didn't know—making her feel strong enough to split the earth. The gown she still wore, rustled loudly against the blanket of white, and she grimaced. With a thought, the gown changed, her beloved skinny jeans hugging her thighs, a warm sweater wrapping her torso beneath a large winter coat. No amount of layers would keep away the cold that inhabited her.

The grounds were empty. Even the two guards that stood watch of the gate were gone. Likely to sip a hot beverage and thaw their extremities from the chill. She approached the gate wearily.

Her fingertips brushed the iron gate before her. Like an electric zap, the contact bit at her skin, making her suck in a sharp breath. The shrill shriek of the siren jarred her. Instantly, as many as thirty soldiers poured out, looking ready to fight. Her eyes searched the faces that had all began to fall with confusion. A dark-haired, broad-shouldered male who was every inch a fearsome warrior shouldered his way to the front.

When their eyes met, he stopped dead. Emma's heart leapt up in her throat. His stormy gray eyes searched her. A familiar curl of warmth unfurled inside her. But still the cold lingered in her veins. It was part of her now. Even the wards recognized her as the enemy.

"Open the gate!" Blaze shouted. A few of the Giborim exchanged uneasy looks. But after a long moment, the gate swung in. Neither moved at first. Then, all Emma could hear was the crunch of his boots as they sank into the snow and ice that coated the ground. The frigid air had frozen her to the spot and all she could do was watch each step that drew him closer. But he didn't stop. He pulled her to him gently, his arms wrapping around her. Her body remained stiff in his embrace for several moments. The heat pouring off him thawed her resolve and she melted into his warmth. His grip tightened.

His touch was a comfort, a safety. She choked out a sob against him. Something rumbled in his chest in response.

"Let's get you inside."

Crossing the threshold, into the warded grounds sent a spike of pain down her spine, but she ignored it, her jaw clenched. It didn't push her out, but her limbs grew heavy, like trudging through deep water.

Emma let herself be guided through the snowy grounds. She refused to look at the passing faces. For now, she was safe. But the mark on her back, though concealed from the suspicious faces that sensed the change in her, felt like a neon sign for everyone to see that read: fake. Enemy.

Silently, she vowed to those around her, and especially to the one who welcomed her in without a second thought: *I will find a way around the Mark. I will burn all of Sheol, and I will paint the earth in the ashes of anyone that tries to stop me. I am a weapon of fire and ash, I belong to no one.*

Acknowledgments

Years of my life were poured into this idea, this concept that I just had to write. There were many, many days of solitude so I could just get it done. I wasn't forthcoming about it until it began to take shape, but once I did, the response was overwhelming and I have so many people to thank, so hopefully I don't forget anyone.

Thank you most of all, my wonderful, patient husband, for the constant encouragement; for the desk and dedicated writing space that made me feel like I could truly write this story, and for giving up weekends and evenings to watch our son so I could write.

Thank you to my mum and dad for cheering me on and showing all the enthusiasm I needed to keep going, even when I fell into my pits of despair. (Because there were oh, so many!)

A huge collective thank-you to my beta readers, and a special shout-out to my critique partner, Amy, you are a Rockstar! You were all so gracious to read my ugly drafts, my horrific drafts, and my not-so-great drafts. Seriously. Amazing.

To my cover artist and formatting genius, Dean Packwood, you are a god of epic proportions. Seriously, the fact that you didn't just wring my neck when I changed the concept for the millionth time shows your patience.

Thank you to all my friends and family for the enthusiasm and support.

And to Noah, when you're old enough to read this, I want you to know how thankful I am that you were such a good sport. Shaun the Sheep may have been your constant companion over the last year, but your sweet little face is what kept me going. This is for you.

About the Author

Brittany is an American by birth but a Kiwi at heart, living in the wondrous New Zealand with her husband and their son. Writing has been a passion since she was very young. In middle school, she had articles published in the local newspaper, and the school paper in high school. She attended the Institute of Children's Literature with the hope of one day creating stories for the world.

Printed in Australia
AUHW010908030120
321947AU00002B/2

9 780473 471453